Bathed in the  looked eery and surreal, the green ...

appearance. Carson edged forward another step, flicked ... the shop. Everything else looked fine. Clean, neat and well ordered, a place for everything and everything in its place.

Except Carl.

Carson cleared his throat loudly, tried again. "Hey, uh... Carl! Dude... you okay, bro?"

Carl's hand twitched.

Carson's twitched too. He stopped talking, eyes glued. The figure started to sway, gently, side to side. Carson thought he detected a low, barely audible moan. He also noticed something dark at the figure's feet. Dark and wet.

Carson eased forward another step, palms starting to sweat. "You okay, dude? You don't look so good. I mean, we just met, so I don't know, maybe this is a regular thing for you..." Carson froze.

It was blood.

The pool at the clerk's feet shone bright and red in the reflected neon. And there was too much too close for it to be anyone else's or for the clerk's condition to be anything but unpleasant. As the realization hit him like a punch in the gut, the figure's head slowly began to swivel. A low, animal groan leaked out from between cracked lips.

"Nnnnnnn..."

He sounded hungry.

Carson's blood went cold. "Oh, crabapples..."

SUNDANCE RULES - AND SO DO YOU!

Chris Weedin

OTHER BOOKS BY CHRIS WEEDIN:

Graveyard Shift: The Adventures of Carson Dudley
Book 1 - *Midnight Snack*

Horror Rules, the Simply Horrible Roleplaying Game
Horror Rules Rulebook
Horror Worlds
Ghostowns & Gunsmoke
Script Crypt Vol 1: Psychos and Sickos
Script Crypt Vol 2: Four Damned Scripts
Script Crypt Vol 3: The Better to Eat You With
Script Crypt Vol 4: Very Bad Places

THE REVIEWS ARE IN FOR GRAVEYARD SHIFT!

Graveyard Shift

The Adventures of Carson Dudley

Book Two
ANOTHER ROTTEN NIGHT

Chris Weedin

A Horror-Comedy Novel
Inspired by
Horror Rules, the Simply Horrible Roleplaying Game

A Crucifiction Games Book

Crucifiction Games
NO PAIN, NO GAME

To Rob
Who has forgotten more about zombies than I will ever know. When the Zompocalypse hits, I choose you.

CHAPTER ONE

Bad Dreams

Carson sat bolt upright in bed, heart hammering, brain thick with sleep. There was a repeat of the knock on the door, knuckles on wood, and he was dimly aware that it was the knocking that had awakened him. He struggled to throw off his sheets and the stubborn clutches of a vague and disturbing nightmare, both of which he had been wrestling with in a deep but troubled sleep. "Coming! I'm comin'..." he mumbled and shouted, too foggy to wonder who could be knocking at his door at three in the morning or to consider whether or not he was wearing pants.

Carson staggered across the floor toward the front door, misjudged the distance in the dark, crashed into it face first. He winced, clutched his head. "Whozzit?!"

There was a slight pause.

Then a voice, soft but clear: "It's me. Don't you remember?"

Carson processed for a moment. "Whozzit?!"

Another pause. "We don't have time for this. It's important. I want.... I want you to come with me. Now. Someone... needs you."

Carson blinked bleary eyes. It was dark, his head hurt, and he wanted to curl up in his warm soft bed, pull his Batman sheets up around his neck and drift off into the blissful, empty world of dreamless sleep. He tilted forward, eased the undented side of his forehead gently against the smooth, cool wood.

"Carson?" It was a woman. "Are you there?" She sounded scared. Worried. Desperate. "It's about... about what happened. Before."

He should care. He really, really should. If only he wasn't so...

"It's the Curio Shop."

He was wide awake. "Curio Shop? Did you say..."

"Yes."

He lifted his eye, still bleary but now wide open, to the peephole, blinking, struggling to focus. On the doorstep of the basement landing, wedged between ivy-crawled concrete walls, stood a slender brunette, young, moon-faced. Pretty, even through the fish bowl. She looked back over her shoulder, seemed to shiver.

Pretty and worried.

When she looked back, it was as if she could meet his gaze, even through the thick one-way glass of the pinhole. Her eyes matched her expression, worried... and something else. There was movement in them, something deep, desperate, almost hungry. For a moment, they held him, looked right through the glass, right into him, held him like a squirrel in its underwear in the path of an onrushing SUV.

Carson threw the deadbolt. "Jus' a sec... pants..."

They were in the street before he realized it, out of the darkness of his basement apartment at Granny Dudley's and into the darkness of the midnight streets of Las Calamas, Belfry District. Dark to dark. Hurrying. The brunette hugged herself through a long navy pea coat, buttoned tight against the night. She was pale and drawn. And paranoid. She checked every shadow and cranny, firing furtive glances at rooftops and manhole covers, looking places one usually didn't look for purse-snatchers. Carson's head was still fuzzy. He didn't remember leaving, how they'd gotten so far, if he was wearing pants... was he wearing pants?

Jeans.

He sighed with relief, ran his hands along the familiar faded denim, his favorite pair, same ones he'd worn to the House of Beef months ago, when they'd fought Vanessa. He shivered, skin going goosey as an image of her ravaged face swam before his eyes. His right hand flexed, missing the grip of his Louisville Slugger, and he immediately regretted not snatching it up on the way out. Since the House of Beef, he always kept it in the bucket by the front door, along with his lightsaber umbrella. Never could be too careful. He'd learned that the hard way.

Funny. A very, very tiny part of his thinking apparatus seemed to be screaming that at him now, like Whoville was on the road to another major shakeup, and he was the only one who could stop it.

Think. Think think think.

Questions. Questions would help.

"Why, uh... what's... you said someone..."

Carson struggled to put words together in a way that made sense. He shook his head to clear it, screwed his eyes into focus on the woman. She turned to him, the corners of her expressive mouth turned down into the slightest frown. It cut through him and left him with an inexplicable sense that she knew more than he did and that what she knew, he was fairly certain he didn't want to know, but that he would find out soon whether he wanted to or not. It was that kind of frown. He also felt... struggled... somehow... that he knew her. Recognized her. Or should. He blinked, rubbed his face, wrestling with the inert mass of his brain, tugged at his chin beard like the pull on a lamp, hoping to pop the light bulb into life.

Nothing came. Still... he should know that face...

"Yes. Someone needs you. Now hurry... it's just ahead. There..."

Suddenly, through the fog ahead... *fog?* He blinked again. He hadn't noticed it. But there, through the swirling, soupy gray, the comforting green-and-yellow neon of the 24/7 sign shone like a beacon. His hopes rose.

The 24/7.

The mini-mart.

Home.

"Oh, baby! The store. Sweet! But why'd you...?"

"No. Not there. *There*..."

He followed the line of her pale finger, pointing across the street to a grim, shadowy, blockish structure that huddled in the night. It swallowed light like the fog. Carson's fleeting grin cracked, fell apart.

The Curio Shop.

Nervous juice squirted through his stomach.

"Come on," the girl breathed. "There's no time to waste." She ducked across the street, and far too quickly, they were there. She paused before the door, checked over her shoulder, hands stuffed anxiously in her pockets. Overhead, the weathered antique sign, barely legible in the dark, brooded down over them like a guillotine blade. Innocent and harmless at rest, it dared all comers to step beneath it.

Carson hesitated. Had they crossed the street? He glanced back,

 3

unsure of the last few moments. The 24/7 sign had vanished, swallowed in the mist. Not even a faint glow pierced the gray. Gone as if it had never existed.

"Carson?"

"Uh, yeah. I'm... I'm here."

He shivered, stared up at the sign above them, at the old fashioned paneled door. He'd been here before. Lots. How many times? Dozens. Standing right here, staring into the dirty windows at the musty, cramped store, its shelves packed with shrunken heads, skull candles, gargoyles and other odd bits of cheap supernatural brick-a-brac. He couldn't keep away. It drew him. Mesmerized him. Even now, his breath caught a little as he stared into its darkened corners, imagination tugging at the looser threads of his sanity as he let it run a little with the possibilities.

"But we can't get in," he grumbled. "There's never anyone..."

A creak of rusty hinges, a whiff of mustiness and a hint of something else... spicy, faintly earthy. A shiver of something colder than the fog slid from the black maw over his skin.

The door was open.

Carson's jaw gaped.

The girl's face was a ghost in the night. "Follow me. Stay close." She ducked inside. He hesitated. Just a moment. On the threshold, hands clammy. It was like facing the first step out of an airplane, or into the doctor's office the day he calls and says, *There's something on this x-ray we need to discuss.*

Carson sucked in a deep breath of cool night air. It tasted like mystery. He plunged in.

And rapped his head smartly against the door frame.

"Watch yourself," the girl murmured. "It's low."

Carson rubbed his new sore spot briskly. "Yeah. Ouch." Then he took a step, and the pain vanished in a wash of adrenaline. A thrill shot up his spine.

He was in.

After all those months of staring, wondering, waiting... the Who's were screaming at him again, but he bottled them and stuffed the lid on tight. He was in now. It was answer time.

They were moving quickly through the shelves, shadows and shapes blurred in the dark. As they moved deeper, Carson's skin tingled, the hairs on his neck standing up. There was something, just at the edge of perception, an oppressive sense of something *wrong*.

Something very much like... evil? He could almost taste it, bitter and sharp.

Something brushed his skin, sent shivers up his arm. He heard whispers, turned sharply. Nothing there. He turned back and came face to face with a face. Hooded, haughty, poised over a struggling blonde in a gauzy robe strapped to an altar, long steel sliver of knife poised to strike at her pulsing heart. The image swam before his eyes, he gasped and jerked back... then caught himself. It was a portrait. Nearly life size, surrounded in a gold filigree frame. For some reason, it took his breath away. The eyes under the cowl held him. They were pits of night, pinholes in the abyss. Black and cold as death. And they weren't looking at the victim on the altar. They were looking at him.

"Over here... quickly!"

Somehow he had lost the girl... had wandered off in the little store. Only now that he was inside, in the dark, it no longer seemed little. She beckoned from the far side, a wisp of pale skin like a sliver of moon peeking through a black curtain. He tore his attention from the eyes with difficulty and moved toward her whisper.

They were in another room, trotting fast, breath rasping over nerves and adrenaline. More smudgy shapes lurked in the darkness around them, crowding close and looming large. Carson's head spun, and he felt like he was under water, struggling to see, to hear, to find which way was up. It was as if he was working his way down the gullet of a large and hungry shark. Or something worse.

"Not much further now," the girl muttered. She caught the wild look in his eye. "The shop is bigger than it looks. It's because..." the rest of her words became garbled and he missed them.

"What... what did you...?" He struggled to focus, but a whiff of something repulsive drifted through the dark, snatched his attention. "Ugh!" He wrinkled his nose. "Stinks..."

She smiled wryly. "Everyone says that the first time."

They moved on, the girl just a head of him, silence falling like a cloak. Another room. Another.

A door slammed. He started, whirled, and realized they had stopped. And the girl was there - *behind* him now. She stood in the sudden silence, a slip of a thing in the dark, framed by the black, peeling wood of an ominous looking door. He took an unconscious step backward, glanced nervously over his shoulder at the way they'd been going and tried to wrap his brain around how he had gotten from following her to in front of her. But there were no answers in that direction either. Just a plain wall, set with aged, cracked stone, dank and crawling with lichen.

Dead end.

"There. That's better."

Carson turned, confusion making his face as blank as the wall. "I don't..."

"No." Her voice had an edge to it. "You don't."

Something had changed. The young woman looked smug now, hands resting loosely on hips, smiling an unpleasant smile. She pushed a cold gaze around the small, dank chamber. "I like this better than your place. It's more private. Don't you think?"

Carson sucked air, steadied himself. He could see his breath, a puff of white. He shivered, but not from the sudden cold. Something was wrong. Very wrong. He cleared his throat. "You said... er... you said someone needed me..."

"I lied." Her mouth was cruel, the moon shape of her face changing from full to sickle as she slid a sidelong glance at him from the shadows. She took a step and another, stalking, keeping parallel to him, casual but calculating. Lean, pale fingers slipped the buttons on her pea coat.

One. By one. By one.

Her eyes never left him.

She tsk-ed, her bottom lip forming into a petulant pout. She shook her head. "You've been a bad boy, Carson." Dark eyes bored through him, unblinking. They were stirring again with the strange movement he had seen through the peephole. Only now it was different. Meaner. Hungrier.

Just about the time Carson was thinking he might want to make a break for the door, she switch-stepped, and swung gracefully back in front of it like a lioness stalking prey, making sure she was always between him and the exit.

When she was in front of it again, she stopped. Black eyes pierced him. "You've done bad things."

With a sultry shrug the coat slipped off her shoulders and hit the floor. Carson's jaw followed. Underneath she was decked head to toe in leather buckles, straps and milky white skin. She grinned, hands flexing like claws, and tossed her long brown hair back over shapely shoulders. Carson's blood went cold. The whole scene was starting to feel familiar. Dangerously familiar. His shiver was back, and it brought friends.

 6

"You took someone from me," she drawled, enjoying the tangible sense of panic, relishing Carson's fear and the trickle of nervous sweat that ran down out of his tousled hair across his cheek. "Someone very, *very* important."

Carson edged away, checking for exits, feeling his stomach lurch. There was nothing. "I took... so... leather... what now...?"

Then it hit him.

"Wait..."

He did know this girl. Or her face at least. He'd stared at it every day for a week. It had hung in the mini-mart window on a missing poster just below the words *Have You Seen This Woman?* His heart gave a jump, skipped two beats.

The girl leered. A booted heel clicked. She took a step, not sideways now, but directly at him. The lioness had found her prey. She was moving in.

Carson retreated, was stopped immediately by the wall. He felt it against his back, as cold and hard as her eyes.

"You..." he stammered. "Vanessa... you're one of...!"

"Yes..." A step.

"And I..."

"Yes!" Another step. A pair of gleaming fangs slid out, like needle tipped exclamation points.

Carson's breath locked in his chest. His arms were frozen, unresponsive, dead. "You... you were...!"

"*Yes!*"

"And now you're gonna...?"

She threw back her head, tore the air with a fiendish cackle. It was a tune he had heard before - but from a different set of pipes - and it still turned his legs to jell-o. When the girl looked back, her eyes were lit with the hot red glare of hell, her face a Halloween mask of pure mean stretched over hate.

"*Yes...* Carson Dudley... *YES!!!*"

"Crap."

She leaped.

And then someone else was there, a blur from the shadows, a lean figure tackling Carson a split-second before the vampiress struck, driving him through a second door he hadn't remembered seeing. Then, they were bouncing and rolling down cracked wooden stairs in a flurry of limbs and hard edges and Carson was too busy and stunned and terrified to care.

 7

They rolled to a stop on a cold hard floor. Carson wrenched free of the tangle, crab-crawled like a lobster in a pot to a stone wall and huddled there, breathing hard, fighting to see where he was, who had saved him, what freakish thing was going to happen next. His eyes focused on the gaunt scarecrow just picking himself up off the floor.

The man made a weary salute. "Hey there, soljer..."

It was Pete.

Carson's brain froze. "Durrr..."

The old hobo grinned at him, cast a wary eye up the staircase at a rusty iron door and listened. An angry muffled hiss, like a tigress trapped in a teakettle, filtered down to them, followed by a vicious *thud!* that made the door shudder. Carson jumped and wedged himself further into the corner.

"That'll hold 'er... fer a sec." Pete wiped his brow with dirty fingers and tugged a battered ball cap down over sparse gray hair. He glanced up the stairs, shook his head. "Close one."

Carson found his voice. "Pete...?! You... you're dead!"

"Yeah." The old hobo sauntered over, hunkered down beside him. "But it hasn't hurt muh appetite much." He grinned. "Got anythin' ta eat?"

Carson patted his pockets mechanically, fingers numb. "Uhh..."

The hobo's face fell. "Nuthin', eh?"

"Sorry... I was in bed, Pete. Don't usually carry a Twinkie with me in the rack..." He rubbed his eyes, stared, as if he expected the old hobo to suddenly vanish. "But you... how... how did...?" The question was chopped off as a sudden stink washed over him, garbage in the sun or week-old roadkill. It was like the smell above, only worse. He coughed, eyes watering. "Ugh! It stinks...!" He clutched his nose.

Pete smiled wryly. "Everyone sez that the firs' time."

"What *is* that?! Is that... is that... you? I never... I never noticed..."

"Not me, soljer. Not no more. Not since." The genial grin slid off Pete's face. "This... this is somethin' worse." Carson noticed for the first time that the old hobo's eyes were blue. Cool, icy blue. The red, rummy haze they'd hidden behind all those long years was gone. Carson stared, mesmerized.

Pete glanced about at their unsavory environs. The droopy grizzle of his cheeks pulled down into a frown. "There's more shadows in this town 'n there should be," he muttered. "And smells."

A sudden, loud *bang!* snapped their heads toward the top of the stairs.   Vicious curses floated down, muffled but sincere and invigorating. Carson struggled to rise, feeling claustrophobic and like he needed to sprint somewhere. Pete extended a hand, long and bony in a stained fingerless glove. Carson took it, felt himself pulled to his feet.

"We ain't got much time, pardner."

"Time?! Time for what?" The room was spinning.

"Yer on the front lines now, soljer. Yer uh... howda they say it? Aw, yeah - yer 'the man.' An as such, they'ze some things you need to know. 'S my job ta fill ya in. This here..." Pete waved a hand about them. "Is a sitrep."

Carson was in the center of the room, somehow. The floor was bare boards now, creaking under their weight, and the room swung crazily under the light of a naked bulb that had suddenly appeared. He felt dizzy again.

"Er... things...?"

"How many rooms did ya come through, kid?"

"Rooms?"

Shadows swung and danced, making Pete's craggy, weathered face a charcoal sketch. "'S important."

"Uh... six. I think. No... seven. Seven?" He wasn't sure. It was a guess.

Cracked lips formed a grin. Pete nodded in satisfaction. "Good. S'good, soljer. Yer learnin'. The eye don't lie, jes' like I toldja. Yer gettin' a good sense. And you'll need it." He rolled his head about the room, a wily old wolf on the lookout for hunters. Carson's eyes were drawn to his turkey neck, weathered, tanned and bunched with wrinkled folds. A thin strip of fish belly white showed where the familiar stained red bandana had once hung - and now was gone. The bandana was Carson's now. He reached unconsciously for it, found it missing from his own neck. It sat, he knew, stuffed in the recesses of the drawer of his night stand, its home for several months. Packed up. Put away.

Forgotten, like the old hobo.

He regretted it with a sudden pang.

Pete's neck was also free from that ghastly wound, the one that had ended his life. Carson knew it should be there but wasn't. His brain struggled to process.

"Pete... I... you... bandana... cement mixer..."

"Yeh, I know, soljer. I'd sing *Crazy Train* fer ya, but we ain't got tha time." A thunderous *crash!* sounded above, jarring the room, and was followed immediately by another. There was a screech of metal and the savage scream that followed sounded a little less like it was trapped behind a sturdy door and a lot more like it was going to be joining them soon in the basement. "So... this here's one o' them 'need to know only' situations. And son, trust me... ya need to know. So listen up, and listen quick. Can ya do that, soljer?" His cool blue eyes locked on like tractor beams.

Carson nodded, his mind a whirl. He met Pete's gaze, felt it pull him back. Ground him. He swallowed, steadied himself. He nodded again, this time with conviction. "Yeah. Sure, Pete. I'm in the basement of a nightmare freakhouse with a whacked out vampire chick looking to do me dirty six ways from Sunday. You may be dead, but right now you're the only friend I've got. What the hell. Hit me."

"Good Joe," Pete nodded, pleased. "Alrighty, then, first things first." The blue eyes again, like halogen headlights, blazed suddenly, lit with an earnestness and intensity that Carson had not imagined possible. He couldn't look away, couldn't speak.

This was something big.

He braced himself, clamped down on his scattered thoughts, listened hard.

"No one gargles at midnight."

Carson blinked. "Er..." He blinked again. "I don't..."

"Nope. Ya don't. But ya will. Thet's where it starts, soljer. You'll see."

A rending screech of claws on metal tore through air and nerves, and it took Carson's tortured ears a second to figure out that there was a scream mixed in, filled with the passionate desire to tear something limb from limb. Something like him.

"Wish like fungus she'd cut thet out... s'hard ta think... 'bout as useful as a cardboard crapper..." Cracked lips pursed in thought. "Alrighty," Pete's gnarled hands settled on Carson's shoulders, their grip surprisingly strong. "Here goes..." He fixed him again with penetrating blue eyes.

"The first is done. History. The second is here, we covered that. Next, now lessee... next comes... death." A shadow passed over the deep crags of Pete's face - it wasn't from the swinging bulb, but something inside. Something troubling. Then it passed, and he was pressing on. "And death, and life, no interruptions. Then a long journey to a very dark place. You'll have a choice ta make there, about the light. That could end it all, right there. After that - the wild one. And the little one. She'll be in trouble, big. Tell Dex ta be strong. And look outside." His gaze drifted, as if he were listening to something, then locked back. "Now, jes a coupla more, yer close, soljer. Here's the next; there's *five*. Don't ferget. *Five*. And last... the end. They'll all come back, I reckon, or purt near. And one o' the lights'll leave. Fer ever, this time. No foolin'. Has ta be that way, wish it weren't, but there it is. But when it's over, it's over. If you want."

Hands clenched his shoulders in a final encouraging squeeze, then slipped away, along with Pete's intensity. He looked suddenly worn out, so old and weathered that Carson could almost see through him. Like the old Pete.

"Thet's it. Thet's all. The rest is up ta you." With a final sad smile, the old hobo turned to leave.

Carson could see nowhere he might go but felt a sudden stab of loss and anguish nonetheless. He reached out. "Pete... don't...!"

"I wish I could tell ya more. I really do."

"But... but..." Carson's feet were frozen, legs tingling and prickly as if long asleep. He couldn't move, was finding it hard to think again. A fearsome blow from above shuddered the door and drove a dent clean through it. "What... what about her?!"

Pete glanced up the stairs, then back at Carson. "I wouldn't fret much about her. *That's* the one ya need ta worry about." He jerked a thumb at the far corner where a tall, shadowy slash of darkness lurked, a hole ripped in the black fabric of the room. Even as Carson looked, he felt his breath leave him, his knees buckle, slammed by an overwhelming wave of malice and dread.

It was watching.

Waiting.

More deadly and treacherous than a dozen like the girl at the top of the stairs. Carson knew it, instinctively, absolutely; just as he knew that they would meet someday. Somehow. Somewhere. But not today.

"Don't worry, son," Pete turned up his collar, tugged down his cap. "Y'got friends. Don't ferget 'em, even when things are at their worst. That's when you'll need 'em the most." He turned toward the blank wall, then paused one last time. "Oh, one more thing, soljer..." He fixed Carson with his eyes, a wise old barn owl with ragged feathers. Above, the thunderous assault on the door intensified, now relentless, deafening, unceasing, blow after fearsome blow. Dust and debris filled the air, danced in the crazy yellow light, obscured Pete's form. He seemed to shimmer. His voice dropped to a hoarse whisper but was somehow still audible. "Somethin' *real* important. Real important..."

Carson licked his lips, cast an anxious glance up the stairs. She was coming. They had only seconds.

"Yeah? What?!"

A beat. A frown. Again, it was as if Pete was listening.

"I can't tell ya."

"Don't do this to me, Pete!"

"When it happens, you'll know."

"Pete... that *sucks*! Give me something!"

"I can tell ya this - it ain't as bad as ya think." The unreal clamor reached a fever pitch, battering and buffeting them. It sounded like the whole place was coming down.

BAM... BANG... CRASH... SLAM...!!!

Then, with a suddenness that took Carson's air away, it stopped. It was the moment, the pause, the breath between the gasp and the breaking of the bone.

Pete locked eyes with Carson. "Jus' head toward the light."

He winked.

Then a thick rivulet of blood started down his neck and all the color drained from his face. Pete sighed. "Here we go again..."

The door exploded, flung down the stairs, smashed off the far wall. In its wake, swept a billow of seething black mist, born on savage, unholy winds. A howling scream filled Carson's mind and soul with knives. From the heart of the storm, lunged a nightmare in leather, a face of fangs, terrifying beauty and a lashing red tongue, claws outstretched, jaws wide, rushing, reaching...

Carson sat bolt upright in bed, heart hammering, brain thick with sleep. There was a repeat of the knock on the door, knuckles on wood, and he was dimly aware that it was the knocking that had awakened him. He struggled to throw off his sheets and the stubborn clutches of a vague and disturbing nightmare, both of which he had been wrestling with in a deep but troubled sleep. "Coming! I'm comin'..." he mumbled and shouted, too foggy to wonder who could be knocking at his door at three in the morning or to consider whether or not he was wearing pants.

Carson staggered across the floor toward the front door, misjudged the distance in the dark, crashed into it face first. He winced, clutched his head. "Whozzit?!"

There was a slight pause.

Then a voice, soft but clear: "It's me. Don't you remember?"

Carson processed for a moment. "Oh, snap..."

CHAPTER TWO
Pain Points

"Carson...? Mr. Dudley...?! Mr. Dudley!"

Carson's head jerked up, a sheet of paper drool-pasted to the side of his face. "Hmmm?"

"I said, do you have any questions?"

"Um... nope. No. No sir, Mr. Kinkade. Uh... I'm good."

"Then you understand the new closing procedures?"

Carson glanced around quickly for the page he'd been reading, found it stuck to his cheek, snatched it away. It left a smudge of ink, a guilty black brand. He smoothed the moist, crumpled page, neatly smearing much of the text. It was now practically illegible. He winced. Casually, or so he hoped, he slid his hand over it, concealing the evidence. "Er... yup. Got 'em cold." He stifled a yawn.

"Very well." Kinkade sounded less than convinced, but as usual his corporate monotone was hard to read. "There will be a skills parade soon to assess your level of understanding. Be ready. And since we're on the subject..." Kinkade launched into a short speech about the importance of rules and paying attention. He didn't mention Carson's name specifically. He didn't have to. Carson ducked his head into the crook of his arm, stifled another great yawn as the man droned on. He glanced around discretely, looking for some indication as to how long he'd been dozing.

The store, however, still looked unfamiliar, making it hard to tell. All his usual landmarks had been swept aside in the wave of changes the new boss had made in recent weeks. It was like coming back from vacation and finding the housesitter had rearranged all the furniture and put up flashy new signs about the deal of the week and made all sorts of rules about where you could put the Doritos and any personal items you happened to bring in. Everything had changed. He hated those changes.

"What do you think, Mr. Dudley?"

Crap. Zoning again.

"Er... yes. Definitely."

Kinkade quirked one of his severe black brows.

Wrong answer.

"Really?" The exec frowned slightly, making Carson feel like he'd just told Mr. Spock that logic was dumb. The sleeves of Kinkade's pressed and polished suit whispered as he scribbled notes on a tablet computer. The unit was like an extension of the man's body, as cold and impersonal as Kinkade himself - an accessory for the cyborg. Carson felt his heart sink; his eyes locked on the unforgiving, unforgetting tablet. He hated that tablet.

With a final decisive tap, Kinkade lifted his gaze. "Frankly, Mr. Dudley, I fail to see the logic in that answer. These are the closing till procedures. Critical product knowledge. They seem to be a pain point for you. Please review Section Seven of the Operations and Procedures Manual." Kinkade thought for a moment. "And Section Eight."

"You know," drawled a voice. "It may be a good idea to review four also. Some good stuff in there." The voice had a slight rasp to it, like a metal file over vocal chords. Carson winced. He hated that voice.

"Yes. Quite right. Section Four as well. Thank you, Mr. Plugg."

Carson forced a smile. "Yeah. Thanks, Stan."

Stanley kicked back on his stool, hands tucked behind his head. "Don't mention it." Stanley had a few years on Carson and more than a few pounds, and he didn't wear either very well. His thick features were haggard even behind the smug smile currently tainting his lips, and he smelled faintly of cheap cigarettes and strongly of cheap cologne. A mass of curly, oily rocker hair glinted under fluorescent bulbs, a curtain for small dark eyes. The hair was a perfect match for his customary death metal T-shirts and vinyl pants, as well as a host of unsavory tattoos that any mother in her right mind would fight to the death to prevent, regardless of her child's age; these days, though, Stanley covered it all up with a kiss-up attitude and the respectable tan fabric of an official 24/7 work shirt. It was the same one Carson wore - itchy, hot and smelling of polyester and corporate sellout. He hated that shirt.

Kinkade tapped his tablet. "I'm scheduling a knowledge transfer session on the subject as well. A deep dive into the Omni-Biz 7520 Transaction Processing System." He thought, tapped. "Perhaps a CWBS."

"Er..." Carson pursed his lips. "CWBS?"

"Collaborative White Board Session. Standard TLA."

"TLA?"

Kinkade stopped tapping, looked up. He blinked. "Three Letter Acronym."

"You've got an acronym for your acronyms?" Carson knew he shouldn't have said it, but the question just slipped out.

Kinkade looked back at his tablet, tapped again. "I'll add Section One. You'll find it an excellent refresher on Seven Corporation's business terminology."

Inside, Carson died a little. Outside, he somehow managed to maintain an appreciative smile. It was broken up seconds later by yet another tremendous yawn. When he recovered, he found Kinkade staring at him again.

"Late night?" Kinkade asked, his eyes magnified to slightly unnerving size behind his Coke-bottle glasses. The glasses were typical of Kinkade: black, square and thick, not in a chic retro designer kind of way, but in a stereotypical 1950's TV dad kind of way. The rest of Kinkade was similar, Carson thought, but not in the wholesome, happy, 1950's TV dad kind of way. With his blank expressions, severe brown suits and boardroom haircut, Kinkade was more like the dad of that jerky kid who lived next door - the one who was never allowed to play baseball or wear short pants or take a pocket knife on the Boy Scout trip or do anything else fun. He was the one who made you run up and hug your own father whenever you saw him, because anything would be better than to be saddled with that poor kid's dad.

And now Carson was saddled with him.

Kinkade touched the severe knot on the severe tie under his severe

 15

collar and regarded Carson severely. Apparently, the question hadn't been rhetorical. He was waiting for an answer.

Carson forced his smile to stay, even though he knew it was plastic. "Actually, no. Early morning." Another yawn came on, but he killed it with ruthless, superhuman effort and what he was sure was an unsettling grimace. "Not... you know, anything crazy, just a bad... bad dream kinda... not like a nightmare or anything, I'm way too... y'know... old for... just one of those that..." He hiccuped loudly. It hurt. Swallowing the yawn had produced unforeseen consequences. He clutched his chest and gave up, letting the miserable, rambling thread of his explanation die a quiet death.

Kinkade stared at him. After a moment he blinked. "I see." He scribbled on the tablet. Carson rolled his eyes, groaned inwardly. He hiccuped again, loudly. Again, it hurt. He hated hiccups.

"Next order of business." Kinkade mercifully moved on, apparently left with nowhere to go but up. "Mr. Plugg - excellent work on the walk-in freezer. Your new arrangement of the fryables should provide a significant increase in freezer-to-floor. I don't know why anyone would have staged the Taquitos where they were." Kinkade shifted his gaze pointedly to Carson.

Carson briefly considered telling him why he'd done it: to hide the blood-drained corpse of a rancid hobo who had been viciously killed in a vampire attack. Instead, he just shrugged and smiled good-naturedly.

Stanley showed his yellow teeth in a grin. "Ditto, Mr. Kinkade. What's this guy thinkin', hunh?!" He punched Carson playfully on the arm. "But hey, let's give him a break. He's been havin' bad dreams. Me?..." he shrugged humbly. "I'm just glad to help."

"Indeed. You show humility as well as initiative. *That's* the kind of person Seven Corporation is looking for. Now then...on to other matters." Kinkade set his tablet down, turned to face the front windows, hands clasped behind his back like an uptight British sea captain preparing to address the crew. Late afternoon sun streamed through the panes, limning him in what some might describe as a rosy aura, but what to Carson looked like the red flush of brimstone.

Kinkade rounded, stared at them. He opened his mouth. A single, solitary word dropped out: "Fujikacorp." He began pacing in neat, measured strides. "As you undoubtedly know, Fujikacorp is the parent corporation of the Super Maxi-Pad convenience store franchise. They have held a top market share of this arena in Asia for years. Now, they intend to move into the United States. And they intend to start in

California. Specifically, Las Calamas. Here. This, gentlemen, is a declaration of war." He stopped, faced them, expressionless. "Make no mistake - they intend to crush us."

A moment passed. Then the pacing resumed. If Kinkade was upset by his ominous pronouncement, he gave no indication. "And they are well positioned to do so. Tough, aggressive, experienced, well managed and willing to take hits in order to get a wedge into the competition. Pay no heed to their initial naming blunder. It was a fluke. A minor setback at best. It won't happen again. Fujikacorp will come back from this stronger than ever, and even hungrier for a victory. Ichiro will see to that."

"Yeah, he's pretty good," Carson nodded, finally happy to be able to contribute. "I've seen him play. Big fan. I don't get it, though - does Fujikacorp own the Mariners now?"

Kinkade blinked at him. "What are you talking about?"

"Er... you said Ichiro..."

"Not *that* Ichiro," Stanley pitched in, not even trying to hide a gloating grin. "Mr. Kinkade was talking about Ichiro *Fujika*."

"Um. Right." Carson squinted at him, still struggling. "Er... I don't..."

"The CEO of Fujikacorp. Super-Maxi Pad's *boss*."

Kinkade nodded once, as if any additional nods would be wasteful. "Precisely. I see someone has done his homework." Another glance at Carson. "And it's good that you have. Ichiro Fujika is a dangerous foe, as shrewd as they come. Cold, calculating, ruthless... a genius in the field of convenience store management The youngest CEO in Japanese history, he is a student of all modern tactics, both business and otherwise. Sources claim he reads a chapter of the *Art of War* every morning, even before the financials. They call him the Shogun."

"Oh. Right." Carson tried to sound indifferent. "*That* Ichiro." He hiccuped loudly.

Kinkade pressed on with his monotone address. "Fujika arrived in the country several weeks ago. Since that time, his company has filed no less than thirteen writs, injunctions and fair business practice disclosure notices aimed directly at us. This is just the first salvo. The storm is coming, gentlemen. And soon."

He paused, shifted his gaze to the front windows as if he expected a column of Japanese businessmen to march up to the mini-mart and lay siege to it at any moment. When nothing materialized, he turned once more to his employees.

"Which brings me," Kinkade told them, "to our final order of business: the night manager position." An expectant hush fell. Both Stanley and Carson sat up a little straighter. This was the part they'd been waiting for.

"As you know, " Kinkade said, "the decision has come down to the two of you." He stood motionless now in the center of the store as if the topic was far too important for him to pace or even blink. "I have been observing you closely and will continue to do so over the course of the next few weeks. In addition to your standard duties, I have also prepared a series of productivity milestones that will help me to determine the most worthy candidate. I cannot stress, gentlemen, how much is riding on this decision. Whoever is selected will shoulder much of the burden of defending this store against the Super Maxi-Pad incursion. As Strategic Planning and Operations Manager, Western Region, and Acting Store Manager of 24/7 Franchise Unit #417, it is my responsibility to make sure that the right man is there to do the job."

He fixed them with an expression that Carson took to be one of grave sincerity, but since it looked exactly like all of his other expressions, he was left to guess. "Give this next few weeks everything you've got, men. I expect nothing less. And neither does Seven Corporation. Questions?"

Except for another hiccup, the room was silent.

"Good. Expect my decision by the end of the month."

And with that, the meeting was over. Kinkade scooped up his tablet, turned on his heel and headed for the door without another word.

Stanley lurched quickly to his feet and started after him, pausing just long enough to clap Carson on the shoulder. "Keep havin' them scary dreams, Widdle Cawson," he murmured. "You're makin' this too easy. And hey... don't forget Section Four." He cackled in Carson's face, treating him to a wash of stale cigarettes and some kind of fried food, most likely something with cheese. Still chuckling, Stanley hurried off in pursuit of their boss. "Excuse me, Mr. Kinkade? I wondered if I could talk to you about our grease policy. You see, I had a few ideas..." his voice faded away as he and Kinkade disappeared out the front door, already deep in conversation. The electronic chime warbled in a weak, sick way, and Carson was suddenly keenly sympathetic. He let his head slowly dip forward, thump onto the counter.

He hiccuped

The cool of the glass was nice. He felt it soak up into his red face, sooth away some of the humiliation of the last hour. Meetings like this had been the norm since Strategic Planning and Operations Manager, Western Region, and Acting Store Manager of 24/7 franchise unit #417 Ross Kinkade had arrived over a month ago. He was brimming with corporate buzzwords, big operational changes and about as much personality as a boiled brick. Even so, the extra work, extra studying and Stanley's blatant brown-nosing had been tolerable... right up until today. Last night's dream had done a number on him alright, made him look the perfect fool. There was blood in the water and Stanley had been quick to strike.

Carson groaned at the thought of his rival, rolled his face to sooth the other side of it and caught sight of the new cash register. The Omni-Biz 7520 Transaction Processing System. Bane of his existence He groaned again. Here was something, if possible, even worse than Stanley. Here was the embodiment of nonsensical change and the evil of corporate America, a great, hulking, self-important brute of a thing, loaded with buttons, drawers, LED's, touch screens and more circuitry than the operations panel of a nuclear sub. It was nothing like the good, old-fashioned, everyday till that Carson knew by heart. He could have operated that one in a total blackout. And had. Twice.

The Omni-Biz was the symbol of everything life had become at the 24/7 of late: overwhelming, complicated, bureaucratic, technical, money-hungry and about as much fun as a kick in the crotch. He hated that cash register.

Carson sighed, rolled his face back the other way to block out the sight. "At least I've still got you, eh girl?" He patted the counter affectionately. "They can't take you away from me." As he stroked the glass, something brushed his fingers. He glanced up, spotted the thick, self-important bulk of the 24/7 Operations and Procedures Manual. He sighed again as he remembered Kinkade's little homework assignment. Groping for the book, he reluctantly dragged it close, eyed it with distaste.

"You suck," he told it.

It didn't make him feel any better.

Carson was about to open it but, after a second thought, spun it round and laid his head down on it instead. For an operations manual, it made a decent cushion. "Jus' a quick rest," he murmured, exhaustion sweeping over him. "Then up and at 'em... Fujikacorp... storm is comin'... gotta be ready..." His eyes slipped closed and his breathing slowed, became steady. Outside the blazing summer sunshine faded to orange, then pink, then deep purple.

"You know, pillows make better pillows."

Carson jerked awake. His eyes focused on a pretty blonde in a red stocking cap. She stood across the counter, hands on slim hips, the worn lines of her face making her look older than she really was. They could not, however, disguise her amusement.

Carson laid his head back on the book. "And Ichiro makes a better Shogun than a batter."

"There's a rule that says you don't have to start making sense until a full minute after you wake up. I'll start my watch."

"Who says I'm awake?"

"My bad. Shall I tell these nice folks to come back, then?"

Carson's head snapped up. Behind the blonde, a line of shoppers had queued up. It was obvious from their expressions that they did not share her amusement.

"Son of a...! Welcome to the 24/7... a restful place to shop. Find everything okay?" Carson set to work ringing up sales. Kiki drifted into the aisles, drifted back minutes later as the last customer left.

Carson hit his worn leather stool, duct tape squeaking on jeans. He slumped against the counter, ran a hand through his casual brown hair. "Sheesh. What a day. How long was I on display?"

Kiki slipped out of her patched canvas backpack and joined him in his slump, a slip of a thing in a white tank top and faded khaki cargo pants. Faded, Carson noticed, like her expression. She looked as tired as he did. If not more.

She smiled. "Not long. I think your job is safe."

"Think again. That's not my first nap of the day."

Kiki winced. "No?"

"No. The sandman already came to see me during night manager 101."

"Kinkade?"

"Kinkade."

"Ouch. At least Stanley wasn't..."

"Yeah. He was."

"Make that 'ouch' a 'wowza'."

"I need a Freezie." Carson reached for a cup, jammed it under the spout and turned loose thick, icy curls. "You want?"

Kiki shook her head. "Just stopped by to say, 'hi'. Can't stay long." She glanced at the Operations and Procedures Manual, now also smeared with drool. "So what is that?"

"My pain point."

"Beg your pardon?"

"Pain point. It's the way corporate types say, 'something you need to work on.'"

"Then why don't they just say 'something you need to work on'?"

"Because then they wouldn't sound like they knew more than you," Carson tapped his noggin knowingly. "Got me?"

"Not really."

"Then welcome to the club. That's *exactly* how I feel around Kinkade. Half the time I don't even know what the heck he's talking about. That dude is the buzzword king. For example, instead of 'task' or even 'job', he says 'productivity milestone'. How lame is that?"

"About an eight, I'd say."

"I swear, sometimes I think he just makes up words right on the spot. I mean, check it out: any solutioneer worth his salt could bottomize the blame width of the squality gap, as long as he qualidated it, checked his magication and didn't poof the box."

"Impressive."

"And all made up. Every one. I just whipped 'em right out. Bet you couldn't even tell."

"I was a little curious about 'squality gap'."

"Well," Carson slapped the counter. "Forget him. Right now, I need the kind of headache that comes from a cup, not a corporation." He jammed a straw into his Freezie and took a long, needy pull. A morphine grin spread slowly across his features.

"Better?"

"Jus' a sec..." Carson mumbled, pressing a palm to his forehead and wincing at the sudden rush of pain. "Oh yeah. Yeah. Baby. Ow. Better." He eased back onto his stool, relaxing as the sugar and cold worked away at his stress. "So, where ya been lately? What's it... four, five days since you dropped by? School must be slapping your backside, woman."

"Just... just busy, you know." Kiki flicked a look at her battered watch, as if to underscore the notion. She was trying to look casual but Carson could sense that she was fidgeting as if she had somewhere to be. "So..." she quickly changed the subject. "What's new?" Her eyes roved about the store, noting details, scanning changes, categorizing as she always did.

"What's new? That's easy: everything." He rolled his eyes. "New and wacky and right on the edge of downright freakin' annoying. I tell you, between the redecorating, the crazy swing shifts, all the training meetings and cramming for the corporate playbook, I'm beginning to feel a little punch drunk."

"Well, at least you look slick, Slick." Kiki indicated his uniform. "If you're planning on going bowling later, that is."

Carson glanced down at his shirt self-consciously. A garish red name tag stared back, declaring to the world *HELLO! My name is Carson Dudley!* He grimaced. "Yeah. I'm lovin' the shirt. Lovin' the whole darn ride. This corporate la-la is about as far from Jack's way of doing things as Billy Ray Cyrus is from his next hit single. Check this out..." Carson spun the operations manual to face her, pointing out a line of text. "*Eternus Vigilo.* It's the Seven Corporation motto. Got bored the other day so I Googled it - translates to 'Always Watching'. How's that for a confidence builder?"

"Nice. Almost as bad as that Super Maxi-Pad slogan - the mistranslation... how did that go...?"

"'Here Comes the Flow of the Month'. Don't get too attached though - rumor has it they're working up a new one."

"Engrish at its finest."

Carson grunted. "Makes about as much sense as ours. 'Always Watching'?! What kind of motto is that?! It makes me want to work hard and jump off a bridge at the same time." He waved off an irritating fly.

"Have you made up your mind which one you'll chose?"

"I'm working on it."

"So I've gotta ask... if it's such hell, why are you doing it?"

"That's easy." Carson folded his arms. A determined look settled onto his face. "For Jack. He built this store from the ground up. It's his legacy. I can't let it fall into *Stanley's* grimy little mudpaws." He shuddered. "No way. Not my beautiful gal. It'd be like letting Cousin Eddy take your sister to the prom. Plus, I don't know... after Vanessa..." he searched for words. Finding none that fit, he settled for another pull on the Freezie. "S'good... s'real good..." He sucked again, winced as his head swelled with delicious icy fire. "Ow... I needed to do something. Ooh, hurt so good... stretch my wings, seize the day; you know... *something*. You kill a vampire, it's a little hard to go back to Cheetos and Wii in Granny's basement."

"Well, well, well." Kiki's amused smile took on a hint of approval. "Self improvement? You?" She touched her cap. "On behalf of myself and all the other starving students at Las Calamas Community College,

I salute you."

"Give 'em my thanks.   Anyway," he took another pull of the Freezie, "everything was going pretty well until last night..."

Kiki caught the faint haunted look in his eye. "Last night...?   What happened - everything okay?"

"Yeah.   Er... no.   I mean... kinda.   It was just this... crazy dream I had."   Memories of it surfaced unbidden, bringing a host of feelings and sensations, all unpleasant.   The aftershocks rippled across his face.

Kiki perked up, tired eyes searching his, mildly concerned. "Dream, eh?   Sounds more like a nightmare."

"You could call it that.   Couldn't sleep a wink afterward, threw me right into a tailspin.   It's still rattling around up here..." he tapped his head, sighed.   "I dunno... guess I just let it get to me.   Really screwed up with Kinkade today.   Must've looked like grade A noob sauce."

"Hey, don't sweat it.   You'll bounce back.   Don't take this the wrong way, but I think - and I mean this - that you were *made* to work in a mini-mart."

"And *that's* what plucks my chicken!"   Carson threw up his arms in frustration.   "I could do this job in my sleep!"   He shot her a warning look.   "Not a word..."

Kiki made a zipping motion across her lips.

"...and all it takes is one freaky nightmare to make me look like I just fell off the trainee truck."   He sighed again, shook his head. "Stanley took the bit there, that's for sure.   He's had it out for me ever since Jack recommended *me* instead of *him* for the night manager spot. Not that it made any difference.   Man, now he's got a chance to make life the suck.   He's gonna work this one like the KGB."

"You'll tear him a new one.   Promise."   Kiki held his eyes.   Her look was so full of confidence that it gave him a little of his own.

He forced a crooked smile.   "Thanks."

"No charge.   So," Kiki broke the mood, "tell me about this whopper from last night.   If it really did *that* big a number on you, I expect it to have at least three talking animals and a lot of pudding."

"What the lady wants, the lady gets..."   Carson spilled the entire dream as he worked on his Freezie.   Strangely, rather than fading, the details of it only seemed to have grown more vivid.   "And when I woke up," he finished, "There she was again... knock-knock-knocking on my door."   He shivered slightly with the memory, stirred the dregs of his Freezie.

"Hold up..."   Kiki pursed her lips, studied him.   "Did you just say...

when you woke up from this little horror show... there was *actually* someone at your door?"

"Not just someone. *Her.* Same girl. The one from my dream."

"Um..."

"I kid you not. It was her. Scout's honor." He held up some fingers, struggled to get the right ones. "Man, I could never do that... okay, Vulcan's honor." He made a "v" with his fingers.

"Congratulations. You just earned your nerd patch. So how do you know? That it was her, I mean."

"When I saw her through the peephole I almost peed myself. Good enough?"

"The judges will accept that." Kiki studied him again, thought for a minute. "Did she say anything?"

"Did she ever. Same *exact* thing as in the dream: 'It's me, don't you remember, someone needs you,' yadda, yadda, yadda, good-bye sleep."

"You don't usually expect that kind of behavior from a figment of your imagination. What did you do after that?"

"What any self-respecting suburban basement dweller would do: I grabbed my baseball bat and told her to split, ASAP, or I was gonna call the cops."

"And did she?"

"Yup. She must've gotten the message that I didn't feel much like talking. I guess I was shouting pretty loud - woke Granny up and everything, busted a lamp waving my bat around. I went a little... well, not quite Sheen... more Busey, really. But you get the idea."

Kiki tugged a blonde lock from under her cap, chewed it thoughtfully. Her brain was working, processing. It was a puzzle, and that she could never resist. "This girl - you said you knew her?"

"*Recognized* her. She was a customer, around the time we tangled with Vanessa."

"What's her name?"

Carson shrugged. "Heck if I know. Saw her last name on the credit card. Some bird, I think... Hawk, Crow, Albatross, something. I sold her Tic Tacs," he added as an afterthought.

"You can pull out that factoid, but you can't think of her *name*?!"

"Hey, I remember snacks, not people. What can I say? I'm good at my job."

"Alright, then. Let's see if I'm good at mine." Kiki spread her hands on the counter, ready to pronounce her findings. "Here's how I

 24

see it. You've been stressed - working hard, putting up with corporate, lots of extra hours - plus you're still a little shaky from the vampire thing. Mix in some regret about the passing of a dear friend - which was not your fault, by the way - shake well and *voila*... serve it all up in the form of one messy, freaky subconscious sucker punch. Nasty, yes. Weird, certainly. But just a dream." She sat back.

Carson frowned, dropped his empty cup in the trash and slouched against the food warmer. "Yeah," he mumbled. "That makes sense. I guess. Except..." His face was unreadable.

"Except you don't like sense?"

"It just felt..." he struggled for the right word. "Solid."

"Solid. As in *real*? Carson, it was a *dream*. I admit, you were on target with the whole 'vampire' thing awhile back, but this is different. Way different."

"You're telling me," he agreed heartily. "And I'd even buy your Doctor Phil right up until the very end - the girl. What about Tic Tac? She just *happens* to show up at my door at *exactly* the moment I'm waking up, saying *exactly* the same thing as in my dream?"

"Stranger things have happened."

"Name one."

"Lady Gaga."

Carson opened his mouth, shut it. "Can't argue that one."

"And anyway, maybe her car just broke down, maybe she was lost, maybe *she* needed help. You might have just asked her and found out, but I'm guessing you missed your chance when you chased her off with a baseball bat."

Carson reached for his Freezie, forgot that he'd finished it, collapsed back onto his stool in frustration. "Yeah. You're right." He threw up his hands. "Curse your Vulcan logic. You're right. Still," he pouted. "It felt solid."

Kiki watched him for a moment. "So... *was* it solid... or not?" She was pushing him.

"I don't know! I think..." Carson floundered. "I was... there's just some... well, for one thing, look..." he pointed to a thumb-sized plum on his forehead. It looked dark and tender, just turning yellow around the edges. "What about this?! In the dream, I hit my head on the doorframe going into the Curio Shop."

"In real life you hit it on your door."

Carson blinked. "My head hurts."

"Take an aspirin. Then forget about your dream." Kiki glanced for

25

the umpteenth time at her watch. She'd continued to check it surreptitiously during their talk, but this time, when she noted the hour, Carson could see her face tighten.

"My slow descent into madness boring you or do you have a hot date?"

"Hm? Oh, no... just a... just a thing. Look, Carson," she said brusquely, rising to her feet. "When's the last time you took a break?"

"Five days ago. I stepped outside for a few minutes. Watched a dog do his business across the street."

"That's hardly a week in Hawaii."

"I wouldn't know."

"That's my point. You're too laid back for this kind of pressure and it's getting to you. Give yourself time to unwind. Get out of the store and do something. Something fun."

"I guess I could see if that dog is still there..."

"I mean it, Carson - take a break. Go play some vids, take in a movie, or... hey, when's the last time you hit a volleyball?"

Carson propped his sneakers on the counter, thinking. A young couple entered, and he waved absently, lost in thought. "Awhile. Weeks, I guess." He paused a moment. Then, decisively: "Too long!" The stool came down with a thump. He was on his feet. "Weather's been awesome, too. Summer won't last forever. Heck, why not - I've got Wednesday off; I'll hit Stoker Beach before work and blow off some steam."

"That's the spirit. And just to make sure you show..." Kiki hesitated, weighing some internal matter. "I'll meet you there."

"You? On a beach? You realize what happens during the day, right? Sun, people, noise..."

"I'm familiar with the concept. Actually, I think it might do me some good, too. I could use a little R&R myself."

With the suddenness of a slap, Carson realized she meant it. He'd been so preoccupied with his own worries that he hadn't noticed how wan and weary her face truly was. She always carried more lines than were good for her, but it suddenly struck him that she seemed scraped a little thinner than usual.

"Okay," he nodded. "Deal." The fly from earlier returned, and he waved it off again. "And thanks for getting me off the pity potty. The reward is one jumbo beef jerky stick, courtesy of L'il Pepe - don't worry, it's not the jalapeño kind. Health department took those away." He slid a shrink-wrapped meat stick into her backpack as she slipped

26

into it. "And keep your money in your pocket, woman. You earned it."

It was a risk. Kiki usually turned sour at the slightest mention of charity. This time, however, she was too tired - and hungry - to fight. "You sold me. Wednesday noon, then. Stoker Beach."

"I'll be wearing the striped full body one-piece. You can't miss me. And hey!" His head snapped up, eyes lighting. "It's Gang Night! Sweet! After that we can meet up with Dex and Becky!"

"Gang Night... already?" Kiki touched her stocking cap. "Time flies." As if reminded, she glanced yet again at her watch. She sighed, lowered her arm as if the implement was suddenly too heavy for her to bear. All cheer fled from her face, chased off by an even older acquaintance - weariness. "I've gotta go. You take care - and don't worry so much. It was just a nightmare."

Carson nodded his good-bye, turned to help the young couple as they approached the counter. He kept busy for the next half-hour, dealing with a late afternoon rush of nine-to-fivers and neighborhood kids stocking up on calories for another night of summer revelry. There was a short lull after that, which ended with the arrival of a looming shadow across the front door.

A mountain of a man lumbered through after it, his great shaggy head a mass of dreadlocks. Light winked off the cheap gold-plated badge pinned to the chest of his blue polyester uniform, making it look more important than it really was. "S'up, Dud?!" His booming greeting shook the shelves, brimming with uncharacteristic good humor. "Gold Shield is in the house!"

Carson feigned a look of relief, set down the mop he'd been pushing around. "Why, if it isn't Officer Dexter Jackson - and not a moment too soon! I think I saw a defenseless Ho-Ho over on aisle three."

"Uh-uh..." Dex wagged a thick finger. "I ain't that easy no more. Lookie here..." he spread tree trunk arms and turned himself sideways. "Notice anything different?"

Carson examined him. "New badge? New gun? New gun-badge?"

"I lost another pound, man!" Dex sucked in his gut, expanding a chest that was already the size of a Volkswagen and threatening to burst the brass buttons on his shirt.

Carson resisted the urge to duck. "Right on! You loose any more weight, I'm gonna have to start calling you 'Tiny.'"

"Try callin' *this* Tiny..." Dex flexed, bunched the muscles in his

27

arm. While powerful, Dex's body had always lacked definition. Now, however, Carson could see the beginnings of a very dangerous and monstrous bicep beginning to take shape.

He whistled. "Arnold Schwarzenegger called. He wants his guns back."

"And that's my weak arm."

"I'll let the Ho-Ho's know they have nothing to worry about."

"Damn straight. Only thing I been poundin' lately is free weights."

"They'll be so relieved." Carson took up the mop again. "So, I'm proud and all, but I gotta ask - you hit a plateau or something? Last month it was ten pounds, a week ago five, now it's just one. If those Ho-Ho's find out you've been cheating on 'em..."

Dex shrugged, looking suddenly evasive. "Naw, man. 'S nothin' like that. Just... y'know, work. Stress n' whatnot. Job is kickin' my *&*^$ lately. Been havin' a hard time finding the mojo to workout."

"Things still looking a little bleak in the loss prevention field?"

"You could say that." Dex tapped his leg for a moment, his earlier good cheer fading. "You could even say they &^%$! suck." He wandered to the front counter, grabbed up a tattoo magazine and starting leafing idly through it. "We lost three more gigs this week. Rodney let another badge go. Says if things don't turn around... well, let's just hope they turn around." He thumbed through a few more pages, shook his head at the pictures. "Man... some day they're gonna run out of things to pierce."

"Here's hoping. On both counts."

Dex slipped the magazine back in the rack, selected another. This one read *Cocked and Locked!* in massive letters spelled out in bullets. "Anyway... I still got the 24/7. I thank my lucky charms for this little lady. Without her, ol' Dex would be out of a job." He settled his bulk affectionately against the counter. "Anyway... just life." Flipping another few pages, he let his mood blow over. "No Ross tonight?"

"Oh... so it's 'Ross' now? There's a bad idea. You want to keep seeing this little lady, I'd make sure to call her daddy, *Mister* Kinkade."

"Aw, don't be a Nancy. Take it from me - bosses are all the same; they like a little back talk from the hourlies now and then. Makes 'em feel like one of the guys or somethin'."

"I don't know about this one, Dex. I'm pretty sure 'being one of the guys' is pretty far down on his list."

Dex caught the grim expression on his friend's face. "Ol' Ross is really gettin' to you, hunh? I can see that." Dex grinned. "He's got

 28

himself a big ol' stick shoved up there, don't he. Never cracks a smile, never laughs, always staring at folk with them big ol' blank eyes... looks like the walking dead if you ask me. Hell, I half expect him to come for my brain any second. Creepy. Hey..." Dex was struck by sudden inspiration. "Y'know what he needs?! A good nickname! Take all the spooky out of him. We used to do that with the sarges back in the Army." Dex eyed the ceiling tiles, thinking. "Kinkade..." He let the name roll around his brain. "How 'bout... 'Kinky'?" His grin spread, a swath of white teeth like a new picket fence. It made him look scary. "Yeah, that'll stick. Kinky. Good ol' Kinky."

"Great. That's not gonna get lodged in my brain at all."

"It'll help. Trust me. Ol' Dex is never wrong."

"Thanks, Doc. Now, if you can just do something to make Stanley tolerable."

Dex's smile faltered. "Stanley." He said the name with real feeling. "That guy's just a douchebag." Dex turned back to the magazine. "Most of the remedies I can cook up for that clown start in here." He stopped on a full color fold-out and whistled. "Now here's a beaut. The new Sig. You could make some holes with this. Hey, speakin' of holes," he looked hopefully at Carson. "You wanna go shootin' this week?"

"Sounds destructive. And fun. But, I'll have to take a rain check. I've gotta put in some more OT for this night manager thing, and at this point, me spending time with a loaded gun is just a bad idea."

"Too bad. You put up some good papers last time. Plus... I got a great technique I think you could use. Vis-u-al-i-zation."

"Helps with accuracy?"

"Nope. Aggression. I just put up a blank piece of paper and picture something on it I'd like to shoot at: *Star Wars Episode 2* for example. Or anything with the word 'diet' in it. Or France."

"Sister Becky?!"

Dex shrugged. "Sure. Maybe a coupla times..."

"No, really..." Carson dumped his mop and strolled toward the front. "I think that's Sister Becky!" He shoved open the door and squinted against the blast of heat and the fading sun.

At the edge of the parking lot, a lean, rigid figure clothed entirely in black was arranging a line of children. They had just debarked from a school bus with *St. Timothy's Sacred Heart* emblazoned on the side in scrollwork letters. Below it, festooned with cartoon wings and halos, were the words *Little Angels' Clubhouse*.

Carson stood grinning. It was Sister Becky alright.

From across the lot, her rich Irish brogue reached him easily. "There now, Jacob, into line," she clipped. "Back in place, Becca; no, I do not particularly wish to know what Jack said and I am quite certain you do not either. 'A fool's words are a dish enjoyed only by himself', as the saying goes, and you would do well to abide by it." Sister Becky marshaled the children with all the efficiency of a master drill sergeant. In moments, the milling, giggling throng was lined up for inspection and ready to move out.

"Now then, we shall enter the store single file on my mark. You each have your companion. Make certain to keep them close. When I served in the... the... spiritual assistance branch, it was a grave matter to watch one another's flanks. Cherish this responsibility - I know I did." She turned to enter, spotted Carson. "Oh, dear me, good evening, Mr. Dudley! I failed to see you there. Children, this is Mr. Dudley. Say hello."

The children chorused a polite greeting. Carson grinned and lifted a hand. The sight of Sister Becky playing mother goose to this chattering, nose-picking, wide-eyed flock struck him as both tremendously bizarre and highly entertaining.

"Yes yes, you're all dears," Sister Becky cut them off curtly. "Now then - you shall have precisely ten minutes to make your selections. After that, we shall board the bus and take our leave. Anyone left behind will be precisely that. Billy, I should be especially watchful if I were you. Remember the incident at the aquarium There will not be a helpful dolphin to assist you *this* time. Tut tut, then, off we go..." Sister Becky struck out for the mini-mart, head high, kids trailing in a ragged procession.

Carson held the door as they passed, shaking his head in wonder. He had seen Sister Becky stand toe-to-toe with an elder vampire. Now, she ran a daycare. He wasn't sure which one seemed more unreal. She posted beside him, busy counting heads.

"Little Angels' Clubhouse?" Carson leaned in, flashed her his crooked grin.

Sister Becky seemed to wither at the name. She rolled her eyes. "A ghastly appellation, Mr. Dudley, I agree. And most certainly *not* one of my choosing." She sighed. "As was this appointment." She shook her head ruefully, still counting heads. When she was satisfied that all were present and accounted for, she followed them in, Carson sauntering along behind. The children erupted into delighted chaos and stormed the aisles, talking excitedly and pointing and gawking at everything. They broke and swerved around Dex, who stood rooted in place like a boulder in a flood of SpongeBob shirts and Hello Kitty backpacks.

The guard's face darkened, looming over the children like an ugly, threatening rain cloud. The change was sudden and startling - even for Dex. "I'll be outside, Dud," he rumbled over the noise. "For awhile." Head down, he bulled his way to the front and out.

Carson frowned as he watched the guard disappear. "Wonder what got into him? He didn't even take a shot at you."

"That is just as well, Mr. Dudley. I am afraid I have neither the time nor the energy to exchange the customary pleasantries with Mr. Jackson tonight. As you heard, we are on a tight schedule. The coach driver graciously agreed to my request - after I impressed upon him the urgency of it - and agreed to this slight detour. We still, however, have a schedule to keep. So..." She snapped a hand out expectantly, her bony, steely fingers open and waiting. "May I have it?"

"May you... er..."

"You did write it, did you not? As I requested?"

"Smackers! The nightmare. Yeah!" With a jolt, Carson remembered his early morning call to Sister Becky. After things had calmed down in the wake of his dream, he had found himself with a sudden, gnawing need to talk to someone - anyone. Why, he wasn't particularly sure. Maybe he'd just needed to hear a familiar voice, or maybe Kiki was right, and he was feeling guilty over Pete's death. Whatever the case, he'd called Sister Becky. And her advice had been unexpected - while she wouldn't hear the details of his dream, she had insisted, rather mysteriously, that he write it all down and give it to her. Carson had obliged, grudgingly, but found some comfort in the process. Just getting it on paper had helped. In the end, he was glad for it.

"Just a sec," Carson ducked behind the counter and rummaged for the page. "It's right here..." A moment later he produced a single folded sheet of paper, passed it to her. "Did it right after we hung up. Though, I still don't know why you didn't just let me *tell* you about it..."

"Dreams are peculiar things, Mr. Dudley. Enigmatic. It is best to put them to paper straightaway if there is anything to be learned from them. It helps the mind to sort them through, for one, and for another..." she swept the chaotic, child tossed store with a weary frown, "I simply haven't the time to listen."

"Yeah," he suddenly felt guilty for involving her. It was obvious,

31

she had plenty to occupy her already. "Look, I'm sorry. Maybe I shouldn't have..."

"Nonsense, dear." The weary frown was replaced by a weary smile. "You did the proper thing. I only wish I'd had time to hear you out when you rang this morning. Unfortunately, we had a bit of a situation brewing, and I simply could not separate myself from it. Which reminds me..." she reached discretely under her habit and drew out a plastic bag. "Dispose of this, will you? There's a good lad." She craned her neck, checking little pink faces to make sure one in particular was nowhere near.

Carson took the bag, peered inside. He immediately regretted it. A fleshy lump that vaguely resembled a cross between a large toad and a pound of undercooked hamburger stared back at him. "Jehoshaphat! What the...?!"

"Mind your volume, if you please, Mr. Dudley," Sister Becky cautioned. "There was an unfortunate incident with the microwave this afternoon, and poor Hannah has been inconsolable ever since. I was compelled to bring these tragic remains along since their owner believed, against all good reason and God's natural order, that they might somehow spontaneously revive. This is my first opportunity to rid myself of them, and I should be loath to spoil it."

Carson made a face. "Yuck." He carried the bag at arm's length to the nearest garbage can. "Well, look on the bright side: you may not be scrapping with the dead any more, but you still get to spend time with them."

Sister Becky trailed slowly behind. "Yes, well, I had hoped to be doing considerably more of the former." She kept her voice low, making certain none of the children were within earshot. "Our recent encounter more than whetted my appetite for my former pursuits. As you know, I presented a full report to my superiors and requested reinstatement. It was my prayer - my fervent prayer - that I would be removed from my librarian's duties and returned to the field of battle. Unfortunately," she frowned. "I ended up in a daycare."

"Tough break."

"Indeed. And I owe it almost exclusively to Father Black," she said the name with vigorous distaste. "I do believe the man is trying to do more than merely dissuade me - I believe he is attempting to crush my very spirit. Bouncing me from one fool's errand to another... not that our children aren't a precious gift from God and don't deserve the very best care, of course." She flashed a pious smile. It faded. "I simply believe this is not the ideal fit for a person of my... talents."

"I've seen your talents. I'd have to agree."

"That is truly kind, dear lad, and a sentiment much appreciated. If only Father Black could have seen what you have," she shook her head ruefully. "I should be back in my chosen profession in a blink and not squandering my God-given gifts in this misery. Although I must say," she added as an afterthought, "I find that a lifetime battling the forces of hell has prepared me fairly well to deal with children K-8." She sighed with resignation. "But, alas, the die is cast. There is simply nothing to be done but endure." Carson expected one of her colorful colloquialisms at this point, but for once, nothing came. Instead, she merely stood in silence, looking dogged and stoic.

Her gaze drifted to a nearby pair of children, who were gleefully stabbing their fingers into a sponge-cake and watching the dents rise. "Even so," she murmured, and her expression was suddenly gentle, almost wistful. "There are moments I almost rather enjoy."

From somewhere deep within the voluminous folds of Sister Becky's habit, a muffled tune interrupted her ponderings. She made a noise of pure exasperation, face pinching like the pucker on a withered apple. "But most of it I find *truly* detestable." She groped clumsily through her garment, fished out a squalling cell phone that was several models old. She held it with almost as much distaste as Carson had the sack of exploded toad.

"That music... is that..." Carson listened, struggling to place the ring tone as Sister Becky struggled to make it stop. "Is that... *Taps*?"

The old nun wrinkled her nose peevishly. "I am afraid so. Both the device and its baleful tune were left to me by Sister Mumpus, my predecessor and the former directress of the..." she shuddered slightly as she said the words, *"Little Angels' Clubhouse.* It was her final act, just before she went on extended leave for her nervous condition. It was also the only time I have ever seen her smile. A cruel expression, it was. Aha!" She snapped the phone open, brandished it victoriously, then held the wrong end to her ear. "Good evening, caller, this is..." she stopped, reversed it, tried again. "Good evening, caller, this is Sister Becky Bischoff on the line..." The voice on the other end cut her off. It was insistent and upset. Sister Becky listened intently. "I see. Yes. No, I do not know how far something has to be up a child's nose before it warrants a trip to the emergency room. No. Yes. Very well. I shall be there straightaway."

Sister Becky snapped the phone shut, ground her teeth fiercely, then did her best to adopt a beatific smile. It failed on all fronts. "Well. I had best be off. Duty, it seems, beckons once more. Your time is up, children!" She called into the store, clapped her hands sharply. "Kindly present your purchases to Mr. Dudley, and we shall be on our way. Single file, now, mind your manners!"

As the children mobbed the front counter, Sister Becky took a moment to reach across and pat Carson's hand. She offered her best motherly smile, weary though it was. "And do not fret, dear boy. I shall give your dream account a thorough perusal... just as soon as I find a moment to myself." Then she was off, a blur of fussiness and organization.

Watching her, Carson had a hard time imagining exactly when that might be. It occurred to him, as he began ringing up the ecstatic children, that he wasn't the only one with pain points. Maybe, he thought with a wan smile, having the corporate blues wasn't the worst thing that could happen.

He was absolutely, completely correct.

CHAPTER THREE

Mercury Rising

The white ball hung suspended in the air, hovering for a brief moment, eclipsing the blazing orb of the sun. Behind it spread a blanket of the bluest sky, unmarred by a single cloud. A seagull wheeled in the distance, serene and peaceful, over an endless expanse of ocean. The water was almost as blue as the sky, bedazzling and breathtaking under the sparkling sun, dancing with light as if a bucket full of diamonds had been tossed across it. On the horizon, a sailboat tacked majestically.

A moment the ball hung, frozen in time and space.

Then it was spanked viciously from the sky with an overhand slam and driven through the air like a missile. Carson hurled himself forward, fingers stretching desperately... and missed by inches, burying his head in the sand. Thankfully, it helped to drown out the cheers and victory cries that were meant for someone else.

Carson picked himself up dejectedly, spitting sand. He glanced back up the beach at the blob of red that had distracted him just before the spike. It was a folded towel, not a stocking cap. For the hundredth time.

"What gives, dude?!" From the other side of the net, a tanned hunk trotted up, grinning ear to ear. "I've seen you rock tougher hits than that. You been off your game all day!"

"Sorry, Vince," Carson brushed sand moodily from his sweat-soaked board shorts. "Guess my head's not in it. What time do you have?"

Vince checked his watch. "Almost two o'clock... five minutes later than last time you asked. So..." Vince scooped up the ball and tossed it to Carson. "Rematch?"

"Pass." Carson tossed it back. "But thanks..." he gave the beach one last look, end to end. No red in sight. "It beats watching a dog take a dump."

Vince looked perplexed. "What's that mean?"

"It means I'm going shooting. Catch ya later." Carson turned on his heel. He reached his duffel and dug out his phone, jabbed buttons. "Dex? Yeah, it's me. That offer still open?"

"Sure, bro," Dex's voice came back, tiny through the speaker but still large. "I'm always up to shred some targets." He paused, catching the note in Carson's voice. "Shall I bring blank paper?"

"No... but bring lots of ammo."

****

Carson was in a *Kung Fu* tank top and a prickly mood by the time Dex pulled up at the curb forty-five minutes later. He tossed his bag into the back seat of the white two-door rice burner and slumped into the passenger seat, slamming the Gold Shield emblem behind him harder than he'd wished. He'd had time to simmer in the blazing sun and was hotter even now than before. Too many late nights and not enough early afternoons had taken the glow off his sun tan, and he was feeling red. In more ways than one.

The car wasn't moving. Dex stared at him, dark brown eyes probing. He rode with the seat ratcheted back to the maximum, which made him look like a teenager cruising the ave but was necessary to avoid permanent neck injury. The car was far too small, ridiculously small, and it suddenly irked Carson. It was like Cinderella's stepsisters had decided to go one better, and instead of just jamming their foot into the glass slipper, they had stuffed an immense black man into it.

"So..." Dex broke the silence. "I'm guessin' I'm not your first choice."

"I've got sand in my shorts. Can it wait?"

"Anything else rubbing you wrong?"

"Your car's too small."

"Saves on gas. Long as I'm drivin' it, fill ups'r on the company."

"Yeah, well... it's too small."

Dex's gaze held him for a moment longer, the brown pools measuring, pondering, deciding whether or not to rise to the insult or let it pass. He let it pass.

Shifting into gear, Dex scooted the car out into the busy boardwalk traffic, narrowly dodging a gaggle of tourists who happily gave him the finger. Dex ignored them too, driving as he always did with one meaty wrist hanging effortlessly on top of the steering wheel. Compared to his giant frame, the little car looked like a toy, and that was precisely how he treated it. He took the next corner too sharp and almost clipped a Japanese tourist snapping pictures by the curb. The fellow leapt aside with remarkable agility and the same look of shock and surprise that Carson had worn the first time he rode with Dex. They arrowed off down a broad, straight boulevard running parallel to the boardwalk.

The car was silent. Dex was dressed in cargo shorts and a button down short sleeve shirt, currently unbuttoned, over a straining wife beater. His feet, still in heavy work boots, worked the pedals with an almost careless disdain, one moving only a fraction to cover both brake and gas. Occasionally, Dex would cut someone off or drive up a car's exhaust or threaten to clip the toes of a pedestrian who was too slow in a crosswalk, and there would be a muffled burst of profanity - again, which Dex ignored - but, otherwise, it was quiet.

Usually, Dex's driving made Carson feel edgy and like he should shut his eyes, but today it struck a chord. Today, he found that he almost enjoyed it. He relaxed a notch. "Kiki was supposed to meet me. She stood me up."

Dex grunted. "She could probably smell you. You stink, bro. A whole ocean out there and you couldn't even take a sec to rinse the man smell off?"

Carson felt the corners of his mouth tug upward. He lifted one arm lazily, angled it so that the car's fan blasted his body odor directly into Dex's face. "Sorry. The ocean was out of order. Man, it's hot." He leaned a bit, making sure his moist armpit brushed Dex's cheek.

Dex slapped his arm down, rocking the car dangerously. "Get that outta my face, fool! I *will* use the pepper spray!"

 37

Carson's smile bloomed. He laughed. Even though Dex wasn't running the AC, it suddenly didn't feel as hot.

Dex brought the car back under control. "Any stops?"

"Just Granny's. I need to pick up the King."

The big man nodded. "So... she stood you up?"

"Yeah, she was a no show. No big. Probably studying for a mid term or something. Rush job at Lucky Earl's, maybe."

"You didn't call her?"

"No cell phone."

Dex made a left hand turn that nearly pushed Carson's face through the window. "No cell phone?! That girl? She has tech comin' out her *&^%$, and she don't carry a cell?"

Carson shook his head. "Guess she likes it that way. You know Kiki." In all honesty, it had never occurred to him as strange. Having a cell phone was connection, and connection was one thing Kiki never seemed to desire. In general, she liked people about as much as a summer hemorrhoid and needed them even less.

Dex accelerated through a close yellow and then an obvious red. More cursing erupted behind him, joined by a loud honk. Again, he ignored them. "Makes about as much sense as gettin' out in the hot sun and dancing around punchin' that little ball. You gonna die of heat stroke out there. Or get yourself a melanoma."

"Don't knock it, Tiny. You keep lifting Volkswagen's and ignoring cardio, you're gonna be the best looking guy on the slab. Maybe you should come play a few sets. It'd do you some good."

"You don't wanna see this in a Speedo."

"I thought you were losing weight?"

Silence.

"C'mon, it was... what... a pound last week?"

Dex kept his eyes on the road and minded his driving, which was a sure sign that something was wrong.

Carson shrugged. "Hey, no worries. Even the Biggest Losers have bad weeks. I remember one time this guy snuck in a whole ham..."

"Don't wanna talk about it."

"Fine. I'm just saying. A little exercise."

"What is it with my weight all the time?!" Dex's hand was a fist on the wheel. "Damn! You're as bad as my ex."

It was getting hot again. Carson felt the prickle but pushed it back down. This was Dex, he reminded himself - not Kiki. "Your ex..." he mused. "Now I'm just confused - are you insulting the way I dress or

 38

my cooking?"

Dex didn't smile, but Carson could see some of the tension drain from his shoulders. "Both. And while we're at it, your aim too. You shoot like a girl."

"Ha! You forgetting the last time we played *Gun Battler 3?* This girl shot circles around you, Big Man."

"That's just a *&*^$@ video game - it don't count. Don't know how I let you talk me into that crap... ain't even real. Real life is totally different."

"Yes. Yes it is. For example driving. Driving is an excellent example of things you can do very recklessly in video games that have very serious consequences in real life." Carson braced himself against the door as Dex negotiated a particularly sharp right that jammed the gear shift into his thigh and almost put him in the guard's lap.

"You want real?" Dex waved a fist in his face that was the approximate size and density of a twelve pound bowling ball. "I'll give you real. Right upside the head."

Carson snorted, rolled his eyes. "That's your comeback? That you could beat me up?"

"Damn straight."

Carson opened his mouth to retaliate, but the flat dead look in Dex's eyes gave him pause. "You *are* saying you could beat me up."

"Not tryin' to start nothin'. I'm just sayin'. I'd murder you."

The heat was back. Worse than ever. Carson hesitated, caught on a wave of it, momentarily uncertain as to whether the guard had actually been ribbing him or... he shook himself, shrugged off the feeling. That was the trouble with hot - it always made things worse than they seemed. "Maybe... but you'd have to catch me first." He showed his crooked grin. "Which brings us back to cardio..."

Dex tapped the brakes, throwing Carson's head sharply forward into the dashboard. "We're here." White teeth grinned.

****

The shooting was good. Showered and changed, Carson was feeling cooler by the time they arrived at the 24/7. There was nothing, he ruminated, like blowing the hell out of a couple dozen paper targets to take the edge off your day. He hummed a snippet of the latest top ten hit as he rotated taco sticks in the warmer, reflecting on the therapeutic benefits of high caliber firearms. It hadn't been his best showing ever, but he was improving. He even came close to Dex once - when the guard had been shooting left handed with his eyes closed. Not stellar, but it was progress.

Progress.

Carson chuckled at himself. He had never been overly ambitious, but recently he had felt a strange restlessness when he wasn't *doing*. It had been Vanessa, of course, just like he'd told Kiki. After their battle, he found himself looking for something more than just the same-old, same-old. More than just zoning in front of the TV and waiting for the next superhero movie. The feeling waxed and waned but was strongest when he was idle. It was an itch best scratched by learning, growing, improving. By progress. It still felt strange and new, but it was one of the best things to come out of the encounter.

And then there was Gang Night.

Carson moved on to the wieners, pondering the event that had lately become such a huge part of his life. Ever since they had put down Vanessa, the group of four had been meeting on a weekly basis: every Wednesday at the 24/7. He, Kiki, Dex and Sister Becky would gather, swap stories, scarf junk food and talk... about vampires, the weather and everything in between. Carson had put the whole thing together. He didn't know why, but it fit - just needed to be done. There was no plan, no purpose, just the four of them hanging out. Like family. He paused with the revelation, holding a sweating polish dog in mid turn, and smiled.

But every family had its problems.

The smile flattened. Gang Night had started fine, but things had been slipping lately. They had missed two of the last four, either because of Kinkade or a half-dozen other excuses from the gang. No shows. Just like Kiki today. Carson shook his head. People were busy, sure... but family came first. Granny always said that. And it was time he remembered it. Time they all did. He resolved to make Gang Night important again - whether they liked it or not.

A flush sounded from the restroom, the door squeaked and Officer Jackson strolled out. "Nobody here yet?"

"Just us. If you're gonna sing, now's the time."

Dex sent a weak smile his way, browsing shelves as he came. By habit, he snatched up a bag of marshmallow fudge cookies, hesitated, put it back. Reluctantly, he chose a box of plain animal crackers instead and walked them to the counter. Dex flashed the box at Carson, looking the other way as if the circus animals were a controlled substance. "On my tab."

"Forget it. I gotcha covered. It's Gang Night."

Dex grunted his thanks. He ripped the top off the box and swallowed the contents in a single mouthful, like a handful of aspirin.

Carson watched him crunch. He glanced nonchalantly over Dex's shoulder. "Those Ho-Ho's are starting to look nervous again."

"They're safe," Jackson mumbled around the remains of three lions, a hippo and several giraffes. But the look of longing he cast in the Ho-Ho's direction was far from convincing.

"What's up, Doc? I thought you gave up the sweet stuff?"

"I did. I am. No problem. This is jus'... these are crackers, man, lookie here, on the box..."

"Dex... I'm a cracker. Those are cookies."

"I know, I know..." Dex mumbled, guilty. "S'just this rotten diet..."

Carson was about to comment when a whiff of odor brushed his nostrils. He sniffed, immediately regretted it. His eyes watered, and the breath caught in his throat as an almost visible stink wafted over him from the direction of the bathroom. "Whoa! Speaking of rotten!" He batted at the invisible foe. "Is that you, or did we just get attacked by Colon the Bowel-barian?!"

"Sorry. Sorry for droppin' ordinance. S'just... work, y'know. Stress and stuff." Dex shifted, eyes roving. "Sorta fell off the wagon. Had a coupla chili dogs last night. Just to get me by."

Defending his nose with a sleeve, Carson hastened across the store and flung the restroom door shut with his foot. "Yeah, well... don't let it happen again, or we're gonna have to repaint."

Dex smiled sheepishly. "Do I get to pick the color?"

Before Carson could answer, the front door swept open, and a dark figure loomed, accompanied by a swelling symphony of imposing electronic noise. The music - stirring, sinister and hauntingly familiar - was emanating from somewhere deep inside black robes.

Carson propped an elbow on the counter, listening. "Is that...?"

"Yeah," Dex nodded. "It is. The *Imperial March.*"

Carson hummed along. "Dun dun dun, dun dun-dun, dun dun-dunnn... yep, that's it. Good ears. *Empire Strikes Back*?"

Dex nodded again. "That's the one. Didn't know you was a *Star Wars* buff, Old Goat."

"Ah." Sister Becky marched into the mini-mart with a sniff. "I see this dolorous tune is known to you."

"Me and all the other Rebels," Carson confirmed. "That's Darth

41

Vader's theme song."

"I like it." Dex folded massive arms, nodding his approval. "Black robes, scary face - you got a whole Dark Side thing going on there. It suits you. Sith-ter Becky Bischoff."

Carson ignored him. "Your phone again?"

Sister Becky nodded curtly. The intense summer heat seemed to have baked a sour expression into her wrinkled face. "That would be my David... the little miscreant. He has a king's name, but the disposition of a Philistine. He offered to change the tune several days ago and, like a fool, I agreed. I have been drawing smirks and snickers from thence onward. Well. We shall see what develops when the Philistine and I next meet. 'Laughter and weeping may both make music, depending on whose ears they fall'."

From the look on her face, Carson was certain of who would be weeping and who would be laughing. The ring started again. Again, Sister Becky made no move to answer.

Dex quirked his eyebrows. "Hey, Darth Becky - you gonna answer that? Could be the Emperor."

"Absolutely not," Sister Becky stated flatly. "As baleful as it is, I find that when I answer this device, it is generally even more unsettling."

Carson chuckled. "Fair enough. I... whoa! What's that smell?" His eyes went involuntarily to the restroom, back. "I mean, that *other* smell..."

"That, Mr. Dudley, is vomit."

"Er... yours?"

"No, fortunately." Sister Becky considered briefly. "Or perhaps unfortunately, depending on your take. At any rate, it was formerly the property of a young lad in afternoon latchkey - Thomas. A hot dog and some potato salad, I believe." She glanced down at a stained patch of her habit. "Perhaps some creamed corn, though it is difficult to tell. He made his donation shortly before pick-up, and I did not have the time to properly tidy up. Nor the patience, I must admit. It was day's end, and I was *quite* ready to take my leave. Now that I am here, however, I shall gladly avail myself of your lavatory..."

She turned toward the restroom, but Carson stopped her. "Trust me - that won't be an improvement." Carson shook a tub of meat sticks at her. "Why not settle for a good sit and a piece of jerky? Looks like you could use both."

She reached gratefully for the tub. "With pleasure, Mr. Dudley.

 42

With pleasure."

As she tucked into her snack, the three chatted about life, work and the heat, which was currently setting records in Las Calamas. It was pleasant, even with the occasional barbs Dex and Becky flung at each other. For awhile, it felt like old times.

Whenever he was on the verge of relaxing, however, Carson's eyes strayed to the door. He was growing increasingly anxious for Kiki to arrive and for Kinkade not to. He wasn't sure how things would go when Kiki showed up, but he was fairly certain what would happen if the boss did. There were policies about what Kinkade referred to as "fraternization", and Carson was currently breaking several of them. With Jack, it had just been part of his job to socialize, mingle with the locals, develop relationships with the neighborhood folk. It had been "good business". But with corporate, it was "none of his business".

Carson served a few customers as they trickled in, then abandoned the counter and started straightening shelves. It was his favorite nervous pastime. And by now, the others knew it.

Sister Becky watched him a moment, having just finished a tale about a particularly onerous encounter with an escaped hamster named Gerold that had recently terrorized the *Little Angels' Clubhouse.* "Mr. Dudley, are you with us?"

"Hmm...? Yeah. Yes, yup. Totally. Hundred percent. Gerold. Cute little guy. Three strikes for biting, and still they want to hold him. Kids. Gotta love 'em! It's just... Kiki. She's late, you know. After recent events, I pay a little more attention to tardies."

"Tut tut, Mr. Dudley. Ms. Masterson is both self-reliant and resourceful. I am certain she will... ah, here she is now." Sister Becky treated herself to a gentle "you worry too much" smile and tilted her head toward the front entrance, which was just beginning its sickly warble.

Kiki shuffled through, stifling a yawn. "Hey, gang," she lifted a hand. "I miss all the jalapeño poppers?" She looked like a wilted sunflower in a tank top and backpack.

"I saved the greasiest one for you." Carson smiled, releasing the tension he'd been using to bruise the bread products. Kiki eased onto a stool and he served her up a plate of fried foods. Relief battled pride for position in his mood, and he let them go at it for a moment, watching her greet the others. She looked tired. Hot and tired. She had even removed her trademark red stocking cap, blonde hair hanging limp and damp against her neck.

With effort, Carson shoved pride into the backseat. He was sure Kiki had her reasons for ditching earlier, and he resolved not to make it an issue. "You're cooked. Looks like you could use a nice cold Freezie." He poured her one, slid her the cup. "Special flavor this month - white. Very nice."

"Thanks. So how are things?" She turned her cool blue eyes on him, although after the heat, they didn't seem as cool.

Let it go, Carson reminded himself. *Don't make it an issue.* He shrugged, polished a non-existent spot on the counter. *Or at least, not a big one.* "Fine. Super. Life's a beach."

"Good. Good." She picked at her meal with a plastic fork.

"In fact, you might say that I've had a *ball* lately."

"Uh-huh."

"A real ball. A *volley* of fun."

"Got it. Fun."

"I've *netted* myself some real entertainment. With other people. In the sand." He stared at her, eyes full of meaning.

Kiki looked at him, eyes blank. She was like a doll on a dime store shelf - cute, plastic and completely devoid of understanding. "I don't..."

"In fact, you might say that I went to the beach to meet you for a game of volleyball, and you didn't show up."

It took a second. Then... "Oh, Carson...!"

"Yeah. Face palm."

"*Double* face palm! Oh, Carson, I am *so* sorry!" She was, and in that moment, he knew it. "I... I was... I just... I totally forgot!"

"That's a relief. I'd hate to think you did it on purpose."

She bowed her head, peeked up but couldn't look him in the eyes. There was anguish in her face. "It's just... I was... busy. Can you... can you forgive me?"

Carson leaned back with folded arms, regarded her, considering. "I can. But now..." he gave her an ominous wink. "You owe me."

"Deal. And definitely. Rain check!" She smiled, small and tentative, in a way that meant his forgiveness wasn't the issue. She wasn't about to forgive herself. "I'll make it up to you. Promise."

"Make it up to me by eating something. You're just picking at that food. How's it supposed to harden your arteries if you leave it on the plate?"

Kiki obediently popped a morsel into her mouth.

Carson watched her chew. "Good. And no funny business with the napkin-swipe or the fake swallow. My sis and I tried 'em all when Dad was teaching us to like seafood - he could spot every one and so can I. Came close sometimes, though," he mused. "The waiters down at the Fish n' Ships used to place bets."

Dex chortled. "Fish n' Ships... that the place down on the waterfront? Got them f..." He felt Sister Becky's eyes on him, grudgingly reconsidered his choice of words. "...funky outfits?"

"That's the one. If you're not afraid of clowns beforehand, you will be after."

Kiki reached for another bite. "Funky outfits? What's wrong with them?"

"What's wrong with them?" Carson piled a handful of mozzarella sticks on her plate. "To answer that question, you'd first have to answer this one: what's wrong with a grown man wearing an eyepatch and a doo-rag and limping around saying, 'Arrr, mateys, welcome ta the Fish n' Ships! Will ye be needin' a booster seat fer the wee squab?!'"

Dex guffawed, slapped his thigh. "That's the bit! Damn! I've done some things for a dollar, but I ain't never hit bottom like that."

"Most of them are happy for the costume," Carson shook his head. "It's harder for people to recognize 'em that way. Still, the squid is cool."

"Squid, Mr. Dudley?" Sister Becky asked. She seemed, at last, to be relaxing.

"Yup. A big one, too. They got it stuffed inside a jumbo fish tank right in the middle of the restaurant. Loved that thing when I was a kid. After Dad read me *20,000 Leagues Under the Sea,* I couldn't get enough of it. I used to beg him to go there just to see the thing... after we learned to keep the food down." Carson slouched against the nacho cheese tub, his eyes lost in the past. "Must be 30 feet long. Wish I could have seen it in the wild."

Dex scoffed. "In the wild?! You're kiddin', right? That thing's just a sorry chunk of Styrofoam. No way it's real."

"I gotta go with Dex on this one," Kiki agreed. "I say fake."

Carson shrugged. "People said the same thing about Ricardo Montalban's chest in the *Wrath of Khan.* And that was real."

"Say what?!" Dex's eyes flew wide. "No way that tanning bed Nancy had pecs like that. He was wearing some kinda fakey chest or somethin'... watchacallit... prosthetic? No old dude is that buff!"

Carson rolled his eyes to Kiki. "Care to settle an argument?"

"Already on it." Kiki had her laptop out and open, face washed in the glow of LCD backlight and forbidden knowledge. She whipped her

45

hands across the keys, expertly flipping pages and jumping screens, on the hunt, weariness and guilt forgotten. "Let's see... yikes, whatever you do, never type 'celebrity prosthetic chest' into Google images. Let's try it this way..." fingers blurred. The screen flickered, pictures, text, colors. "Here we go." She slowed, leaned in intently, scanning. "And the winner is..." Kiki paused dramatically, then whirled the laptop to display a page of information. "...the mini-mart clerk from Las Calamas! Those pecs are real."

"What the...?!" Dex crowded the counter. "No way! Bony old..." his voice dropped into muttered profanities.

Sister Becky peered over his shoulder approvingly, for once oblivious to his tirade. "Yes. As I expected. I shall never forget the way Mr. Montalban cut a figure in his whites on *Fantasy Island*. He was the very image of a man. Before I joined the Order, I confess to many a daydream of myself in his arms."

Dex shot her a disgusted look. "I got images in my head now, old woman. Images I got to live with."

She tsked him. "Now, Mr. Jackson, they were always quite respectable, I assure you. However..."

"I promise to give up swearing for a month if you stop talkin' right now."

"If I thought for even a moment that you were capable of such self control, Mr. Jackson, I should leap at the opportunity. However, out of modesty, I shall keep my history with Mr. Montalban to myself."

Carson smiled at their banter. It was starting to feel like old times again.

"And speaking of dreams, Mr. Dudley," Sister Becky disengaged from the brewing sparring match and fixed Carson with a meaningful gaze. "This seems an opportune time to share my reflections concerning yours."

Carson scrunched his brows. "My... whoa, yeah... the nightmare." With the chaos of the past few days, he had all but forgotten.

"Yes. Quite." Sister Becky fixed him with eyes like emerald pinpoints. "Or shall I say... your *vision*." The *Imperial March* sounded again, suddenly, making an ominous underscore to her remark. Kiki started, stared about for the source of the noise, but no one offered an explanation. Sister Becky, as usual, made no move to answer.

Carson frowned. "Vision?"

"Yes, Mr. Dudley. Vision. Or 'prophetic dream', if you prefer; but whichever way you take your tea, it still gets served in a cup, as the saying goes. This was communication from beyond."

"You're telling me Stinky Pete is now my Ben Kenobi? That's a little hard to swallow."

"Perhaps in this day and age, Mr. Dudley. But in less jaded times, when our hearts and minds were more in tune with the Creator and less befuddled with Music Television, such things were accepted without question. Take Joel 2:28, for instance: 'Your old men will dream dreams, your young men have visions.' I have read and re-read your narrative, prayed and consulted Scripture. My conclusion is simple and inescapable: yours was no ordinary dream. It was a message."

Dex scoffed. "A message?! From who?"

"Whom," the nun corrected absently. "From God. Who else?"

Dex rolled his eyes. "From God?! If the Almighty wanted to give junior here a message, why didn't He just appear on a mini taco and tell him in person?"

"An excellent question, Mr. Jackson. Tell me - if you were to send a message to an infant, how would you do it?"

"I'd start by pretending I was talkin' to you."

"Very well. And how would you deliver your message?"

"For one thing, I'd wait until you stopped flappin' your gums - assuming that would happen at some point. Then I'd lean in reaaaaaal close, right up in your face, so's to make sure you wouldn't miss a word." He demonstrated, leering.

"Excellent." Sister Becky held her ground. "And would I, with my far inferior mental capacity, be certain to understand every word you spoke?"

"Hell no! You'd be lucky to come away with the general idea. If that."

"Your words, then... you are indicating that they would be difficult for me to comprehend?"

"Definitely." The leer widened.

"You might employ some other method then...?"

"Pictures. Big bright ones. Probably drawn in crayon."

"Thank you, Mr. Jackson." She inclined her head politely as if conferring with a much larger, much angrier nun over a point of theological debate. "I concur."

Dex looked suddenly confused. Then he looked angry.

"What the... wait a sec! What you drivin' at, Darth?!"

"You have just precisely described Mr. Dudley's prophetic dream: a message delivered to a lesser being in a resting state, presented in a

47

simple visual format in which you hope the general meaning is grasped, but in which you offer few concrete details. You asked why our Lord, if he had a message to deliver to Carson, did not simply tell him. My answer to you is this: He did."

Dex opened his mouth, found nothing to fill it, closed it.

"Okay, okay," Carson rapped the counter with his knuckles, piqued that Dex had hijacked the conversation and still itching for answers. "The Big Guy's got His own way of doing things, I get it - mysterious ways and all that. Here's what I *don't* get: if it *was* a message... what the frack did it mean?"

Sister Becky folded her hands sagely in her sleeves. "My dear boy..." She fixed him with her most knowing gaze, beamed a gentle, pious smile at him. "I have absolutely no idea." The *Imperial March* sounded yet again, negating both her smile and her calm. She sighed.

"Okay..." Kiki gave up her battle with curiosity. "If no one's gonna tell me, I'll ask... why do I feel like I'm on the Death Star?"

Sister Becky sighed again. "I am afraid the fault is mine, dear child. It is this *infernal* device..." Sister Becky fished through her robes, came up with the cell. "And I fear I have ignored it long enough. Do excuse me, won't you?" She answered the phone, turning her face away discretely. "Yes? Yes... of course. Certainly your worship... I shall. Yes... yes, I understand." She snapped the phone and the conversation shut. She was no longer relaxed. "Well. That was Father Black. Again. A parent complaint of some kind that he wishes to discuss. I had best not keep him waiting."

"A sec before you go?" Kiki reached for the phone. "Let me take one monkey off your back at least."

"Ah! Dear glorious, precious child," Becky looked as if she might weep. "You are indeed a blessing from the Heavenly Realms!"

Kiki took the phone in tech hungry fingers, handling it like an old pro. "My pleasure. What's your data plan like?"

Sister Becky looked slightly bemused. "I have data?"

"Never mind. Just gimme a minute."

As Kiki bent over the phone, already absorbed in buttons and menus, Carson tried to grasp at the threads of his rapidly unraveling evening. Gang Night was disintegrating again, and his nightmare - vision, prophetic dream, whatever - had come storming back, making it hard to think. Images, impressions and emotions swirled in his brain, temporarily suppressed but now springing vividly to life. It was like wreckage buried at the bottom of a lagoon, stirred up by a passing tsunami. He felt himself getting caught up with it.

"Hold up, Sister B... just hang on a cotton pickin' minute! Message... prophecy... I don't get it! It just doesn't make sense! Why would God... why would anyone... send me a *vision*?!"

A voice cut in, dry and flat. "Did you say... 'vision?'"

Carson started, whirled.

It was Kinkade.

He hadn't seen the man enter, didn't know where he had come from, but there he was, tablet and all, close enough to touch. It was creepy.

"Kinky! Er... Kinkade... *Mister* Kinkade! I... uh... didn't see you there. Er... hey," he finished lamely.

Kinkade blinked. "There's no such thing."

"Say what?"

"Visions. There is no such thing."

"Er... alright..."

Sister Becky opened her mouth, but Carson waved her off discretely. There would be enough collateral damage already without a full blown theological engagement.

"There are, however," Kinkade pressed on, "Such things as policies. And Seven Corporation has strict ones about fraternizing on company time."

"Yes. Yes they do - *we* do, that is, me being part of Seven Corporation - and rightly so. Fraternizing is very unproductive." Carson edged in front of the small smorgasbord he had laid out on the counter. He was fairly certain there were policies against that as well. "They were... uh... just leaving." He shot apologetic glances at his friends, who had already caught on to the awkwardness of the moment, as if someone's dad had walked in on a steamy truth or dare session.

They mumbled hasty good-byes and made to leave. In the process, Sister Becky gathered the remains of her small meal, and as she did so, glanced absently at Kinkade. She paused. Her eyes narrowed. Wrinkled brows knit in concentration for a moment. Then, they relaxed, and she seemed to make a sort of faint, internal shrug. A moment later, she followed Kiki out the door.

Kinkade turned his TV dad glasses on Dex. "You're on duty." It wasn't a question.

"Sure am... Pops." Dex smiled good-naturedly, hitched up his jangling, overburdened equipment belt and headed for the door. He winked at Carson as he passed. Peering sidelong at Kinkade, Carson couldn't be sure of what was going on behind the pale, bookish features,

 49

but he was dead sure it wasn't the thrill of being "one of the guys". Carson realized with a sudden sinking feeling that Gang Night had just become the latest in a growing string of Seven Corporation fatalities.

"And in the future, Mr. Dudley," Kinkade looked up from another series of taps and swipes. He wore a look similar to all of his other bland, corporate expressions, with one exception: the frown. That was new; Carson noted. It wasn't a good sign. "I will thank you to refer to me as *Mister* Kinkade."

"Evening, Ross!" The door warbled again as Stanley sauntered in.

"Good evening, Stanley," Kinkade checked his watch. "You're early. As usual. Excellent. *That's* the kind of person Seven Corporation is looking for."

"Hey, C-man," Stanley flashed Carson the rocker salute. "How's it hangin'? Another scorcher out there. Man, these things breathe like a dream though, don't they?" He patted his 24/7 uniform shirt, winked. With a wince, Carson realized he had forgotten to wear his own in the rush of beach volleyball and target practice. He suddenly felt naked.

Kinkade glanced at Stanley, who was still flaunting his own shirt like a peacock's plumage. The exec's eyes narrowed. Realization dawned. His eyes flicked back to Carson, gave him the once over. "You're out of uniform."

"Yes. Yes I am." Carson could think of nothing to say that would sound convincing on the *Reason you left your last employment* line on a job application, so he let it go at that.

Kinkade stared at him for a moment, then bent and scribbled on his tablet. "I see."

"So," Stanley was ebullient. "We ready to get started?"

"Of course." Kinkade prepared his tablet with another swoosh and two taps. "Since we're all here, I see no need to wait."

"Um..." Carson scratched his chin beard, trying to piece together why he was the only one who seemed not to know why everyone was there and what they were about to begin doing. "Sure. What, exactly?"

Kinkade blinked at him. "The skills parade. Closing till procedure. You were told it was coming. Surely you saw the notice?"

"Notice... yeah... uh..." More scratching. Carson had looked at the employee bulletin board every day for the past week. He racked his brain. There had been no notice.

Stanley strolled to the board, tapped an important looking piece of paper with the word NOTICE at the top in giant red letters. "I'm surprised you didn't see it, man. Been up here for days." A shark's grin. "Not like you to miss a memo."

Carson could feel his face growing hot but bit his tongue.

Stanley.

He hadn't seen it because it hadn't been there. Stanley had seen to that, the little weasel. The smirk on Stanley's face was proof enough.

"Ah," Carson squashed his anger and forced a rueful smile. "Yup, there it is. Just like magic! Like a magic trick, wouldn't you say, Stan? The old disappearing memo trick." He chuckled, but the sentiment stopped at his eyes. "Guess I was just working too hard to notice. Work, work, work; train, train, train, that's me!"

"Then we'll start with you." Kinkade posted himself by the till. Inwardly, Carson groaned. Backfire. "With all of that practice, you must be more than ready."

He wasn't.

Carson fumbled his way through the procedure, egged on by Kinkade's incessant tablet-tapping and Stanley's ill-concealed smirks. The errant beeping of the till picked at his nerves with every missed stroke, sparking a headache. Finally, the slaughter ended, and he stepped aside, face burning. Stanley flew through the process, making the register sing like the world's smallest and boxiest concert piano.

"Perfect, Stanley. Top flight. No missed keystrokes, balance correct. You have excellent attention for detail. *That's* the kind of person Seven Corporation is looking for." Kinkade scribbled on his tablet for a moment, tapped once with satisfaction and looked at Carson. "As for you..."

"I know..." Carson cut in, with a little more pepper than he'd wanted. "Section Four."

Kinkade's little frown was back. His eyes narrowed the slightest fraction, another new addition. "Add Section Five. It covers proper forms of address between hourly employees and management." Tap tap.

"You might add Section Eleven," Stanley chimed in helpfully. "I know it really helped me."

Carson gritted his teeth and settled in as Kinkade launched into another session of knowledge transfer, glaring at Stanley and fuming at what was fast becoming open betrayal. If that's the way Stanley wanted it, then so be it. It was on. He would show that greasy, low-life, Black Sabbath reject what...

"... and so, Carson, you'll be first."

Carson snapped back to the present, silently cursing himself for

 51

silently cursing Stanley. Once again, he was zoning. And clueless. Impulsively, he jumped to his feet, taking the initiative. "I'm first, yeah! Alright! Let's do this!"

Kinkade blinked at him. "Do what?" Stanley had to hide a grin behind his hand.

"Er... the... thing..."

"I fail to see how you can begin instructing a trainee until he actually arrives."

"Yeah. Um..." Carson sat down. "Excited... that's all..." he mumbled. Inside, he groaned again. Trainee. It was the word every employee dreaded.

"As I was saying," Kinkade was saying. "This will be the next productivity milestone in the decision for night manager. You will both be evaluated on your ability to bring our new trainee up to speed on 24/7 procedures. His performance will directly reflect on yours. Remember Section Fifteen of your Operations and Procedures Manual on the qualities of effective managers - MOLD: Motivate, Organize, Lead and Delegate." Mentally, Carson added Subjugate and Emasculate. "Any questions?" Kinkade looked directly at Carson when he said it.

Silence.

"Very well. Your trainee's name is Josh Decker. His first shift starts in one hour. And Carson..." Kinkade focused on him, and he felt like he'd brought Dad's car back with a big ding on it. "Let's keep our eyes on that bulletin board, shall we?"

Carson nodded mutely and with that, mercifully, Kinkade took his leave. Stanley was in tow as usual, already jabbering about a new plan for keeping the donuts fresh. Carson's eyes turned to the bulletin board, and he stared holes through the meeting notice. Hopping the counter, he ripped it off and crumpled it angrily, letting his blood finally boil over as he thought of Stanley's treachery. With a curse and a mental commitment to start watching his own back, he snatched up the employee manual and flopped onto his stool.

Light foot traffic and simmering anger kept him from making any real progress, which was further impeded by the same annoying fly from last night. Only this time, it brought a friend. It was an hour later when Carson finally tossed the manual down and headed into the store. He set to work rearranging the chips aisle, trying to clear his head.

Carson was half-way through the Uncle Arthur's when he heard the noise. He lifted his head, a bag of chips clenched in his teeth and another in each hand.

"Eeeriiiibibibiit."

He frowned.

Setting the chips down he clambered to his feet, listening.

Nothing.

With a shrug he bent down...

"Eeeriiiibibibiit."

This time, he eased quickly out into the main aisle, then slowed, head cocked, trying to locate the source of the sound. It was bizarre to be sure, vaguely like the croak of a frog but decidedly different, as if some animal was caught in a crevice or injured somehow, unable to draw enough wind and in terrible pain. There was something about the noise that set his nerves on edge - slow, awkward, unnatural. Weird.

Carson froze, listening.

Nothing.

Whatever it was, it was gone. Perhaps it had been his mind playing tricks, or one of the multitude of new signs rubbing in the breeze from the AC. It did feel colder, he realized. Much colder than it should be. An involuntary shudder ran through him. He trotted over to the thermostat, turned it up. As he did, he passed in front of one of the big front windows, and a wisp of shadow from outside caught his eye. Another chill went up his spine, but this time it wasn't from the temperature. There had been something about the movement, something furtive, stealthy. Something almost...

Dangerous.

A second tingle of nerves trickled through his body.

Before he knew it, Carson was headed for the front door, dodging behind the counter for his bat on the way. He pushed through into the night, casting about for a sign of something, anything. Intense heat and humidity washed over him, but it was almost like a secondary sensation, as if he understood the warmth rather than felt it, like pulling on a blanket over fever chills. On the inside, he was still cold. He stood in the parking lot, breathing hard for no reason, staring about.

Not a soul in sight. Dex's car was gone. He shared patrol duty now with another store across the Belfry District and wasn't due back for - Carson checked his watch - another hour. He was alone.

Or was he?

A flicker of movement caught his eye, further down the street. He trotted quickly to the sidewalk, straining to see, knowing he shouldn't go but unable to stop himself. As if he were being drawn.

 53

A plastic cup rolled against the curb ahead, stirred by a gust of wind, and his eyes locked onto it... no, he shook his head, that wasn't it... there! Something else... at the mouth of an alley the next block down. Carson's eyes narrowed. A tatter of something... stirring in the same breeze... he peered hard, shielding his eyes against the glare of the street lamp halfway between himself and the dark maw of the alley.

There. Yes. That was it. He tilted his head and saw - or imagined he saw - *something*. Something dark, shapeless. Another shadow in the shadows. His eyes strained to pick out form, failed. It was there, he knew it, just at the very edge of his vision...

For an instant, the briefest of moments, he had it - a lean form, long arms, a slash in the darkness. Tall, angular, wrapped in a tattered garment, moving ever so slightly, swaying...

Then it was gone and he was staring at shadows, palms sweating, heart pounding; if indeed *it* had even been there...

Bang!

Carson whirled, desperately seeking the source of the noise. His eyes lit immediately on the Curio Shop. Just a block away, stark and soulless and mocking him with its emptiness, it stared back like a living thing through its dark, vacant windows. Carson breathed hard, eyes roving, probing, desperate to find what had caused...

A stack of toppled crates lay beside the fire hydrant at the side of the store. Carson forced himself to relax, slowed his breathing. Images from his nightmare, vivid and haunting, crowded his mind ,but he shoved them ruthlessly aside.

The wind, probably. Or a cat.

That was it. Just a cat...

"Hey!"

He jumped, swung with the bat, barely managed to check it before it tagged a clean-cut, nice-looking kid in the face. Carson's heart hammered painfully. "Odin's beard!" He lowered the bat, willing his grip to relax but not having much luck. The summer heat washed over him in a sudden wave as if someone had opened the door to the furnace. The cold was gone. In its wake, Carson felt drained and exhausted. "Dude...! Clear your throat or something next time! I almost got a base hit off of you!"

The newcomer stood frozen, face locked in the expression one usually wore just before nearly getting cold-cocked with a baseball bat.

Carson frowned at him. "What do you want, anyway?" Nothing. "Well?! *Hello...?!*" He snapped his fingers.

 54

"Uh... yeah." The kid started. "I'm, uh... I'm Josh. Josh Decker. I'm the, uh..."

"Oh," Carson's stomach sank. "Right. The trainee."

It wasn't his night.

In an effort to salvage what little he could of an event that would undoubtedly end up on an employee review some day very soon, Carson pried his fingers off the bat and grudgingly stuck a hand out. "Carson Dudley. Let's, uh... let's get inside," he mumbled. "Hot out here..."

Josh hesitated a moment, then shook his hand. He trailed him into the store, eyes still a bit wide. "Was that part of my training?"

"No. I thought I saw a muskrat. Can't be too careful." Carson stashed his bat and struggled to marshal both his thoughts and his temper. The day was sliding toilet-ward again, fast. Kiki's forgetfulness, the surprise meeting with Kinkade, Stanley's betrayal, the probable end of Gang Night, phantom noises and now *this*. It was the last thing he needed. He was in no mood to train anyone.

Josh cleared his throat, sensing the awkward tension. He tried a tentative smile, watching Carson cautiously from behind plain glasses. "They've got muskrats where I come from." He was a clean cut kid, with a shock of almost blonde hair like the wheat fields of some mid-Western town where the rest of his simple, honest demeanor and friendly wholesome good looks probably came from. He looked like a decent trainee, standing there in his white polo and jeans, a fresh, moldable eager trainee, and that should have made Carson happy. But it didn't. Instead, it bugged him. He shouldn't be mad, but he was.

And that was just too bad for Josh Decker.

Carson fixed him with a cold look. "What part of the Ozarks is that?"

"Er... it's Oregon, actually. I was born and raised..."

"Lovely. Lovely story. Look, muskrats may be a hot topic back home, but here at the 24/7, the only one that matters is 'work'. So... you've been behind some animals, that much is clear. How about a cash register?"

Josh hadn't. Unfortunately, Carson was still grossly unfamiliar with the Omni-Biz 7520 Transaction Processing System himself. He was thirty minutes in before he realized he was teaching Josh wrong and had to start over. Simmering anger pushed him to go faster than he should, and he found himself taking his frustrations out on the new guy. He knew he should stop but couldn't help it, a fact which only made him angrier and caused his budding headache to flourish. His face grew hot and flushed, and the feeling wouldn't fade, like he hadn't cooled down since he came back inside. After an hour, Carson remembered he'd banked the AC, but by that time, he was too angry with himself and life in general to admit it and turn it down.

By the time another hour passed, he had gone over the procedure three times, each version different than the one before. Although he knew it was his fault, he was still blaming Josh. The incessant, nagging beep of the register stabbed at his brain like an icepick, driving deep into the nasty knot of pain just behind his right eye.

Carson flicked away an innocent pincer bug that had dared to crawl across the counter. "No... no..." he gritted, pushing Josh's hands away. "Subtotal, *then* function six. They do have schools in Oregon, don't they?"

Josh laughed weakly. "Heh... yeah." He cast about forlornly, as if he was hoping to wake soon and discover that his first night of training had all been just a bad dream.

"Alright then, again. Subtotal, then function seven."

Josh fidgeted, hesitating, hand hovering over the button.

"Well?!"

"You... you said function six..."

Carson's frontal lobe pulsed with pain, and he put a hand on it. "Great Caesar's Ghost, man, it's not rocket science! Just..."

The front door made its sickly chime, and Dex sauntered in, fanning himself with a magazine. His great face was shiny and the armpits of his uniform were decorated with dark circles. "Oo-weee! It's hot as Shakira's sheets out there...!" He stopped as he caught sight of Josh. "Well, well... I thought I smelled fresh meat. You must be the new guy..."

Carson waited impatiently as they introduced themselves. Josh was polite and didn't seem intimidated by Dex's size and brashness, which only irritated Carson further.

"Say," Josh indicated the magazine Dex had been using as a fan. "Is that the new Remington?"

"Yeah." Dex flashed the cover. "First reviews are in. You shoot?"

Josh smiled, shrugged humbly. "I used to hunt a bit back home. Where I come from, that's how we unwind."

"Oh yeah?" Dex brightened at the possibility of another gun enthusiast. "Where's that?"

"O-ree-gon Territory," Carson butted in testily. "It's full of

 56

muskrats; you'd love it.   And by the way..." he snatched at the magazine, missed, grabbed at it again. "You planning to pay for this, or are you just mooching again?"

Dex frowned. "I was just flipping through it on my break. Forgot to bring it back in. Which I'm doin' now."

"That's a comfort," Carson stuffed it back in the magazine rack, badly bending the cover. "So much of your mooching ends up in your stomach, I'm glad this survived."

Dex made a fist.

Josh swallowed hard, eyes darting between them. "So, anyway..." he cleared his throat. "Man, that new Remington..."

"It's hot out there, Dud," Dex rumbled dangerously. "Maybe you need to turn the AC down. Get yourself cooled off."

"And maybe you need to start showing up on time. You already got me in trouble with that stupid 'Kinky' nickname; now I've gotta cover your tardies too?" Carson let the jab fly, then turned back to Josh, intent on ignoring where it landed. "Now... hit subtotal, then function *seven*..."

Josh stared at the register, perspiration visible on his forehead. "Uh... yeah..." He hesitated, hands hovering over the register like it was a snake that his buddy had just told him was "safe". "So... seven...?"

Carson could see Dex out of the corner of his eye. The guard hadn't moved a muscle. He looked like a giant statue of chiseled pudding, rigid and imposing but also soft and shapeless. Dex stood where he was for a moment. Just a moment. Then, abruptly, he lurched into the aisles. Carson continued to mumble incoherent instructions and mash buttons, aware that Josh was staring at him with the expression of the hopelessly lost.

A shadow fell across them. A large, angry shadow. Something thumped onto the counter. Carson winced at a nasty throb of headache, crushed a flutter of guilt and looked up into Dex's hard stare.

A box of snack cakes sat on the counter between them.

Carson shot a glance at it, up at Dex. "Giving up?"

"I eat when I'm stressed."

"So?"

"I'm stressed."

"Find something else to deal with it," Carson snapped.   He snatched up the package. "How much stress does..." he checked the nutrition info. "...400 calories remove, anyway?" He stabbed a few keys on the till, and the beeps in turn stabbed into his aching head,

 57

making him feel sick. "What's with the Little Debbies, anyway? Nutty Bars aren't your usual binge."

"They're smaller."

"Then how come you aren't, Fatso?"

For a moment, there was absolute, complete and total silence.

Carson's words hung in the air between them. There was no excusing them, no hiding them and no way to take them back.

Ever.

Carson didn't look up; he just jammed the subtotal button over and over again like he was doing something very important rather than trying to ignore the fact that he had just kicked his best friend in the testicles. Dex stood right where he was. He didn't make a sound. Didn't move a muscle. Then, abruptly, he turned with a squeak on his size fifteen boots and walked straight out the door. Carson, in the very tiny, very remote part of his brain that wasn't pulsing with pain, marveled. He had never realized that the big man could move so quietly.

"So..." he continued matter-of-factly, as if nothing had happened. "Once you press subtotal, which function key do you hit?"

But Josh didn't answer. He just stared mutely at the till, his honest, Oregonian face frozen. He shook his head the slightest fraction, either to indicate that he didn't know or that he didn't care, Carson was unsure which.

Carson didn't push him. And he could hardly blame him. That was the trouble with hot - it always made things worse than they seemed.

Except when they were already as bad as they could get.

CHAPTER FOUR

Fujikacorp

"Carson...? Mr. Dudley...?! Mr. Dudley!"

Carson's head snapped up, rousing him from his daze. He had been mulling over his argument with Dex for the last two days but was no closer to feeling any less the ass and plenty closer to losing his job because of it. He had been smack in the middle of a knowledge transfer with Kinky - *Kinkade*, he forcefully reminded himself - when this last brain drift occurred. Even Kinkade's unruffled exterior was starting to ruffle.

"Yeah... yes? Yes sir?"

"Once more - function *six* or function *seven*?"

"Six." Carson would never forget it now.

Kinkade frowned slightly. He had started doing that now, breaking the almost perfect track record of corporate non-expression he had maintained up to this point. He never did it for anyone except Carson, however. Carson didn't take that as a good sign.

"Correct." The admission escaped only grudgingly. To Carson it sounded more like *Good guess.*

The two stood behind the counter, Carson doing his best to somehow look interested in what Kinkade was saying while his conscience pounded him relentlessly over how he had treated Dex. It was a challenge.

"That's enough for now." Kinkade closed his copy of the Operations and Procedures Manual with a snap. Carson resisted the impulse to leap onto the counter and shake his rump in celebration. "You seem to finally grasp some of the fundamentals. See that you don't backslide."

Carson mumbled something obedient and conciliatory and wrestled with several new impulses to resist. He stood uncomfortably, waiting to be dismissed, but found that Kinkade was making no move to do so. The man just stood there, drilling Carson with his disapproving father look, which was coming along quite nicely. In his hand, Carson noticed, he held an official-looking envelope.

Finally, with the expression of someone who had just decided that the best way to clean a toilet was to jump in and get it done, Kinkade spoke. "I have a productivity milestone for you."

Carson waited. Milestones from Kinkade were more like millstones: burdensome, tedious and unpleasant. But this one... there was something in Kinkade's voice, something different. And for once, he wasn't tapping. Carson looked attentive and kept his mouth shut.

"Frankly," Kinkade droned, "I would rather give this responsibility to Stanley. He has displayed remarkable competence and a robust corporate attitude. But your previous employer - Jack - was most insistent. And at Seven Corporation, we greatly value our franchise owner-partners." Kinkade slid his fingers across the seam of the envelope. Carson glanced casually at it, noting the gold-foil SEVEN CORPORATION logo embossed on the return address. It looked expensive.

"This document," Kinkade pressed on, "must be delivered to Fujikacorp. By hand. The corporate headquarters building in Webber Plaza, downtown. Do you know it?" Carson started to answer, but Kinkade didn't wait. "The address is on the envelope. As I mentioned previously, Ichiro Fujika has had a team of lawyers throwing road blocks at us. They have requested certain documents. Important documents. When Jack signed them, he requested that you deliver them." Kinkade studied him a moment. "For some reason." He held out the envelope. The gold embossing glinted.

Carson took it. "Got it. Fujikacorp HQ. Very important."

 60

"Deliver it to their legal department. Twenty-fifth floor. The office number is on the envelope. Make sure you leave it with an executive or a legal aid, not just a clerk or in a drop box somewhere. This is important, Dudley. This affidavit is a critical piece of ammunition in our bid to block Fujikacorp's advances in Las Calamas. It needs to get where it's going. Today."

"No sweat. I'm on it. Oh, uh... I don't get off until nine, though..."

"You may deliver the letter after your shift. Fujikacorp never sleeps." Kinkade's steady gaze bored into Carson, and he could almost hear him thinking *unlike some people.*

"Roger that. Tonight, right after work. You can count on me."

Kinkade stood a moment longer, silent. He looked like he was half-considering snatching the envelope away and having Stanley deliver it. He blinked. "I certainly hope so." With that, he turned on his patent-leather heels and was gone.

Carson let out his breath and tossed the envelope onto the counter... then quickly thought better of it and tucked it into his shirt pocket. He couldn't - wouldn't - let Jack down. Not again. The old dude had gone to bat for him one last time, and he wasn't about to let him eat dirt for it. Thoughts of Jack reminded him of the old days and how much things had changed. He felt his mood darken and shook himself. He needed to get out, have a little fresh air, let his brain run on idle for a bit.

Carson served a few customers then glanced out into the street - traffic was light and mostly headed the other way, toward the middle income, older home residential districts that made up two thirds of Belfry. Everyone was either going home for eats or off to someplace cooler, and it would be quiet for a bit. He swung through the store toward the back door and the alley beyond, snagging his bat and a blue Freezie on the way.

The store, usually cool and refreshing on a hot August day like this, felt hot and stuffy instead... *was* hot and stuffy. The fault was entirely Carson's. His one positive contribution to the economic status of the 24/7 had been turning down the AC, a fact which Kinkade had praised but which Stanley had promptly taken the credit for. Carson hadn't bothered to argue. The way his luck was going, if he'd managed to convince Kinkade it was his idea, the unit would have exploded on the spot and destroyed the store.

And then there was the smell.

Carson came up short in the candy section. His nose wrinkled as a familiar, unpleasant odor wafted across his path. It had started a day or two ago, a stink like a dirty diaper in a radiator, popping up at odd times and places throughout the store. Always just a whiff, it never hung around long enough for Carson to identify its source. Not that he particularly *wanted* to. His current position on the pecking order put him the closest to cleaning it up, whatever it was, and that was an honor he could do without. Besides, Kinkade hadn't said boo about it, and the way Carson figured, he had enough problems already. Best to let it lie until the toilet exploded, or a sewer pipe burst and pray it happened on Stanley's shift and not his.

Swinging through the big steel back door into the alley, Carson felt the intense heat like a fist. The sun had already settled behind the Las Calamas skyline on its way for a red embrace with the Pacific, but it was far from cool. Carson stood for a moment, eyes closed, wishing he was at the beach. He imagined the whiff of salt air, the feel of the spray on his skin, the sand between his toes, the curve of a volleyball in his hand. It brought a smile to his face.

A whiff of stink crawled up his nose. The smile fell. There it was again - less persistent out here in the alley, but noticeable even with all the moldering garbage, sun-baked cheese tins and mystery stains. Carson sighed. Story of his life.

Carson flicked on the old store radio, rooted through a nearby crate for empty cans. He always kept a few on hand for stress relief, and if he ever needed them, it was now. He fished one out, tossed it up and smacked a double into the far wall. It felt good. The radio crackled.

"I hear you there, Chuck! Alright, drum roll, please... the number one reason NOT to go out in the heat wave is..."

Carson tossed another can.

SMACK!

A triple, easy.

"...You might see Mayor Klapp in her bathing suit!"

The radio played a furious burst of bells and shenanigan music, like a game show wrapping up the final round. The DJ's laughed.

"Phil, we're gonna get calls!"

"Hey, our job is to serve the public. And a PSA like that can save lives. Have you seen Mayor Klapp lately?"

The radio played a canned *moo!* followed by a loud cow bell.

"More! More cow bell!"

Carson whacked another can, this one a fat chili tub. It sang through the air, smacked off the bricks with a satisfying *pwang!* Carson grinned. If that one wasn't out of the park, it was close.

"But seriously, Chuck, it looks like we're in for another week of record highs."

"That must be the KBRZ weather guy I saw with his head stuck in the freezer then."

"We've got a freezer?! Outta my way!"

"Don't go away and don't touch that dial... we'll be right back with the hottest hits for the hottest nights, here at 105.5FM, KBRZ, the Breeze. Hey, Phil... if our call numbers were ten higher we'd be the temperature!"

The chatter faded into a tire commercial and Carson tuned out, focusing his attention on the next can. He swung, just clipping a single that skidded past the imaginary short stop.

"Oh. Hey."

The bat dipped and Carson looked back at Josh Decker, leaning out the back door. He was wearing his official, fresh out of the wrapper 24/7 uniform shirt, neatly pressed and buttoned up to the neck. Josh gave a half-hearted wave, looking uncertain. "I, uh... heard the noise. Sorry..."

"No worries," Carson smiled. "This is just pre-season, so coach won't mind you hanging out. Just make sure to return any foul balls. He gets cranky if they show up on eBay." He took a pull on his Freezie. He could never quite place the flavor, but blue always made him feel cooler.

Josh smiled back, hesitantly. "I, uh... I'm surprised to see you here. Thought you'd be off tonight."

"'Fraid not. Kinkade has me working swing today, so he and I could spend a little quality time together." Carson switched off the radio, set down his bat. "Actually, I'm surprised to see *you* here. After how I came on the other night, I figured you might be trying your hand at one of those crab fishing boats. Or maybe working as an orderly at Arkham Asylum. Something easier than putting up with me." Carson thrust out his hand. "Lets start over - Carson Dudley."

Josh took it. "Josh Decker." It was a farmboy's hand, calloused and strong, no stranger to hard work or a friendly shake. He had a good grip.

Josh smiled.

Carson smiled.

They were good.

"So what brings you to LC, Josh?" Carson lead the way into the store, catching up his things.

"Work," he answered promptly, holding the door. "Or that's what we're hoping. It sounds kind of silly, but we came up here chasing a dream."

"I hope it wasn't the 24/7, cuz I'm pretty sure there's already a couple in... where was it... Oregon?"

Josh laughed. "No, heck no! This is just temporary. I'm going to be a firefighter."

Carson stowed his goods and hopped up on the counter, sucking at his Freezie until his brain danced with blue fire. "Cool... ow... right on. Firefighter. If you like it hot, this is apparently the place to be. Anyway, it's good to have you on board... you and whoever the other half of 'we' is."

"My wife, Lauren. We moved up from Oregon last week - Eugene. Got married a couple months ago. I was a volunteer firefighter there for three years. It's all I ever wanted to do, I guess. So, we figured we'd come up here and see if I could get on somewhere full time. Big city and all, you know how it is."

"Well, that sounds great. If you need any help, let me know. I'd be happy to set something on fire for you. Y'know... a little practice."

Josh frowned slightly. "Thanks... I don't think that'll be necessary..."

"I was kidding."

Josh looked relieved. "Oh."

"You'll probably want to set the first few on your own, being new and all."

This time, Josh grinned.

They spent the next hour at the till, handling the early evening crowd and making small talk. Carson found Trainee Decker to be genuinely likable. He was soft-spoken but direct when he needed to be and plenty quick on the uptake. Anything that suggested otherwise was due to an affable small town naivete and not a lack of anything upstairs. By the time the hour was up, Carson was quite satisfied with his progress.

"Right on!" Carson clapped him on the back. "Eugene, you are on fire. Which, I believe, is more or less the direction you want to go, so grats." He still had a tiny suspicion that he'd taught Josh wrong, but for the moment, he ignored it. It felt too good just to be feeling good. "Hey, tell you what - let's celebrate. Get out there and grab yourself a treat. You've earned it."

"Take something from the store?" Josh hesitated. "You sure it's..."

"Legit? Completely." Carson pulled a notepad out of the till, brandished it. "Meet the employee tab sheet. Know it. Love it. Be it. And write down two of whatever you pick out next to my name. That's *two*, rookie - one for me, one for you. So pick something I like!"

Josh nodded, hustled obediently into the candy aisle. "Something you like? Easy..." He carefully scanned the rack. After a moment, he stopped, pulled two candy bars and tossed one to Carson.

Carson caught it. "Baby Ruth? Interesting. I'm more of a Snickers man myself, but hey, it beats Abba-Zaba..." He stopped. Suddenly, something didn't feel quite right. "Hey... why Baby Ruth?"

Josh was strolling back to the counter, carefully peeling back his own wrapper. "Stanley."

"Stanley?"

"Sure. Your weekly shipment," Josh said, as if everyone in the world had a weekly shipment of candy bars. He took a bite of his Baby Ruth, chewed and swallowed. "He was dropping the box off in your locker."

"A whole box?! In my..." Carson's voice trailed off. His face was starting to feel hot again. *Stanley.* "No kidding."

"Sorry... hope I didn't ruin it." Another bite, chew and swallow. "He said he wanted it to be a surprise."

"I'm sure he meant that."

"Sounded like he did. I told him surprises were fine, but where I come from, we do things face to face." Josh shrugged. "Must have struck a cord. He put them back after that."

"No foolin'. Well, you know, I never use that locker anyway. Probably would've gone to waste, unless there was, oh, I don't know, some kind of surprise locker inspection or something..."

"Come to think of it," Josh pondered. "I *did* see a memo about a locker inspection. But I'm sure you saw it too."

Carson glanced at the empty employee bulletin board. "I'm sure I did too."

Josh carefully wrapped up the last of his bar, stowed it away in his pocket. He paused, frowned. "I don't know if I should say anything... I mean, I just started here and all. But... there's something about that guy..."

"That sensation is known as a disturbance in the Force, padawan. You'd do well to trust it."

"Pada-what?"

"*Star Wars.* Wookies, Jedis, light sabers, you know."

"Oh, the movies. Yeah, I've heard of them."

"*Heard...*?! Oh man. Oh my. You got to the big city just in time," Carson threw a friendly arm around Josh's shoulders. "Forget about the cash register, Trainee Decker. It's time to launch ourselves on an educational journey to a time long, long ago, in a galaxy far, far away... Just FYI, though," he paused matter-of-factly. "I'm skipping midichlorians, 'cuz my Star Wars universe doesn't have room for that kind of dumb." The short screech of angry brakes cut him off.

Carson glanced out the window, caught a glimpse of a white two door rice burner lurching to a halt in the parking lot. He realized, with a sudden squish of guilt, that it was Dex. "Crabapples."

"What's wrong?"

"What's wrong? I whizzed in a man's cornflakes. Big time. A man who happens to be one of my best friends. And who also happens to be very large, carries grudges and is always armed. That's what's wrong." Carson slumped dejectedly against the stainless steel side of the Freezie machine. It was cool and gave a comforting hum. Only, he didn't feel comforted.

"There's an easy fix for that."

Carson looked at him. Josh was standing beside the register, looking much wiser and more sage than anyone with a polyester mini-mart uniform shirt buttoned up to the neck really had the right to look.

"You mean apologize, don't you?"

"I mean apologize."

"I don't know if that'll work."

"Doesn't matter."

"Why not?"

"Because it's the right thing to do."

Carson stared. "Sheriff Andy would be proud."

Josh smiled humbly. "Thanks. I..." He stopped, puzzled. "Who?"

"Never mind. I'll explain later. Watch the counter, willya? I'll be right back... I hope." Carson pushed off and headed for the door.

The heat hit him like a wall, but he ignored it, making a bee-line for the Gold Shield logo on Dex's car door. A mass of great shaggy dreadlocks was visible through the driver's side window. Carson tapped. Nothing. He waited. Slowly, after a long agonizing minute or so, there was movement. With a noisy squeak, the glass rolled down a few turns. Dex's eyes were fixed straight ahead, glaring.

Carson waited a beat. "I'm sorry. I was a jerk."

"Don't sell yourself short. You were a *&^%$."

"I'd have to look that word up, but I'm pretty sure, if I did, I'd end up agreeing with you."

Carson peered into the dark interior of the car, probing the dusky, fierce exterior of Dex's face, searching for any sign of a crack in the stony mask. There was none. "I mean it, Dex," Carson said. "I'm sorry."

Dex snapped a look at him, still fierce. "You talked a lot of smack last night."

"I did."

Dex's face turned front again. "But," he forced the word out, grudgingly. "One thing you said was true. Hard as hell to take. But true." He hesitated, big hands tight on the wheel. "I'm eatin' again, Dud. I lost it. Fell right off the wagon, face plant, smack into a pile of Ding Dongs. Told myself I wasn't gonna..." Jaws clenched in an angry grimace "You know what hurt the most?" Dex looked him dead in the eye. "You were right."

"I still suck."

"Ain't tryin' to talk you out of that." The ghost of a grin played on Dex's thick lips. Finally. Carson felt himself relax, felt some of the tension drain from his shoulders. It was the sign he'd been waiting for, praying for the last two days. Everything was going to be okay.

Dex thumped the steering wheel. A sigh escaped him, taking some of his own tension with it. "It was them damn Nutty Bars," he mumbled, eyes awash in a sea of self-loathing. "Mary S. got me started. You know, the gal from dispatch that has them horses? She said they were 'just good to take the edge off'. Hell that! They're like little brown crack bars. Suck it! Been pickin' 'em up cross town, so you wouldn't know." He shook his head with bitter resolve. "But that's over now. I'm done with 'em. Done!"

Carson noticed, during Dex's confession, that his free hand was toying with something... something that glinted in the fading sunlight. It looked like a necklace, the chain small as if it belonged to a child. There was a nameplate with faded pink lettering and butterflies that he was just unable to read.

Carson squinted at it. "What's that?"

"You said somethin' else the other night - something besides 'Fatso', which I still ain't forgivin' you for - something that got me thinkin'. You said I gotta find somethin' else."

"Guess I did. So that's...?"

"Somethin' else."

Carson's interest was piqued. "Cool. So what...?"

"Uh-uh. We ain't friends again, yet. Ask me when I don't wanna kick your *&^%$." The necklace disappeared into a pocket.

"Fair enough." Carson straightened, glanced over as a car full of twentysomethings pulled into the lot. "Look, I gotta get back. But, I'm off in an hour. Whaddaya say we grab a bite. My treat. We can head back to my place, check Netflix for some shameless, god-forsaken shoot-em-up no one's ever heard of, maybe throw down a little *Shootin' and Shoutin' 2* on the console. I'll even let you win."

"Damn straight you will. A lot."

"Sweet! It's a... ah, crap," Carson soured, suddenly remembering the envelope in his pocket. "I need to drop something off at Fujikacorp. Tonight. Kinkade's got me delivering his mail now."

"Fujikacorp? Big tower down at Webber Plaza?"

Carson nodded.

"No prob. We can swing by on the way. Always wanted to see how the other half lives..."

****

It was well past eleven when they pulled up in front of the towering glass and steel monolith that housed Fujikacorp's corporate presence in Las Calamas. One of the newest structures in the city, it was also one of the most awe-inspiring. With its clean lines, elegant form and severe but daring execution, it was like a thirty story glass and chrome spike jammed proudly into the center of Las Calamas' economic chest. Mini spotlights drew the eye to the burnished, stylishly sophisticated FUJIKACORP logo anchored to the building's front. Nearly two stories tall, it glowered haughtily down at them. It was flanked by a pair of flags that rippled sedately in the warm sea breeze, as if too important to actually flap. On one, the blazing red sun of the Japanese flag stood out, while the other held a curious, interwoven, three-pointed symbol, blue on black.

Carson and Dex sat at the curb, parked by a low wall of immaculately manicured shrubbery. Staring up at the massive letters, awed in spite of himself, Carson was certain the sign alone cost more than Granny's house. They were just outside the cathedral-style overhang that loomed over the front entrance. It was like sitting in front of some impregnable, futuristic tower of doom. On a little white pony.

Carson stuck his head out and craned his neck. The majestic

 68

structure disappeared into the night sky and a low-hanging cluster of clouds. "Makes you feel small."

Dex snorted. "When you're my size, that ain't a bad thing." He shifted the car into drive and pulled onto the slate tiles of the entryway. Easing up to the walk, he shut off the engine and they climbed out. A broad path led them past a fountain and several bonsai trees to the sweeping brass-and-glass front doors. The breeze sighed about their faces, a welcome balm from the wilting heat of the day. Dex pushed through the heavy glass doors, and they found themselves in a spacious marble foyer, tastefully decorated in Asian modern. Subdued lighting illuminated a smattering of freakishly expensive artifacts and prints that added depth, spectacle and an undeniable amount of we-can-afford-this-and-you-can't-so-we're-better-than-you feel.

Dex whistled, cast an envious glance about the place. His eyes probed for the lofty ceiling far above but couldn't find it. "Damn! How come I never get a job guardin' a shack like this?" He belched loudly, the reverberations rattling the front windows and threatening to set off the building's motion detectors.

"That, my friend," Carson clapped him on the back. "Is one of life's great mysteries."

Dex chased his previous belch with an encore and fanned them both away. He shook his head in bewildered resignation.

Carson gestured across the lobby to a massive sweep of cherry wood, polished to a high shine. "Looks like the front desk. Shall we knock?" He set out, footsteps echoing eerily on the marble floor. They reached the counter and stopped, looking for signs of life. There were none. Behind the counter, hulked a massive, elaborate stone sculpture of an ancient Japanese fortress, complete with miniature trees, soldiers and other breathtaking details. But nothing else.

"Guess they have coffee breaks in Japan, too. Let's see ourselves up, shall we? Hrm... elevators..." Carson glanced at a huge LCD map mounted on the wall. "Ah... this way." He set off but was stopped after only a short way by Dex's hand on his arm.

"Whoa, now..." The guard had halted beside a large glass display case. It dominated one section of wall. "Now, ain't that somethin'." Inside the case, bathed under a pale, ghostly luminescence, lurked a suit of black *o-yoroi* armor, aged, pitted and weathered. Undoubtedly ancient and faded with the centuries, its bold ties, leather straps and laminated bands nevertheless appeared tough and serviceable. A broad, sweeping *kabuto* helmet crowned the set, its great upward curling plates like the horns of some ferocious haughty beast. In its shadow, a fierce iron *menpo* mask glowered down at them, empty hollow eyes and twisted grimace a savage mockery of human features - demonic, challenging, fearsome. The suit lurked before them in its case, like some ugly, beautiful, great cockroach.

Dex leaned in close, taking it all in, his breathing deep and reverent. Carson did too. He had a sudden, vivid impression of the armor in motion, its owner wading through the thick of battle, savage eyes burning through the *menpo* mask, dealing death as he went, surrounded by the screams of his foes and the crackle of flames. He leaned a little closer, stared at the shiny laminated surface of the breastplate. He could pick out individual scars and dings. Sword strokes.

"That's the real deal."

"Freakin-A right it is." Dex shook his head wonderingly. "Samurai. Now, there's the original one-of-a-kind mutha trucka badass." He squinted at a brass plaque hanging inside the display case. "'A suit of armor belonging to Lord Hironagi Tomoru,'" he read. "'Also known as the Warlord of Death. Lord Hironagi served the Ashi... Ashika... Ashika-something Shogunate during the chaotic Muromachi Period c. 1560 A.D. A fierce warrior and cunning strategist, he was involved in almost every major battle of the conflict.'" Dex leaned back and folded his tree trunk arms. "And probably kicked &^%$," he added.

"The Warlord of Death," Carson echoed. "Heck, if this is what passes for motivation around here, maybe this Ichiro's a threat after all."

"Ichiro? Does Fujikacorp own the Mariners now?"

"Not *that* Ichiro. Ichiro Fujika. The boss of this little outfit. A real sweetheart, apparently. They call him the Shogun."

Dex was only partially listening. He cast a hungry eye over an array of weapons also on display beside the armor: a *naginata*, a long black horseman's bow and a set of curved samurai blades in ornate antique sheaths. He shook his head admiringly. "Man, a katana... I've always wanted me a katana."

"Yeah. Like Bruce Willis in *Pulp Fiction.* Or Tom Cruise in *The Last Samurai.* Freakin' awesome."

Dex shot him a look as if he had just pushed a small child down the stairs. "You do know your Japanese heroes are two white guys?"

Carson shrugged. "Don't blame me - blame Hollywood." He turned and strode for the elevators, now visible down a wide hallway.

Dex tore himself away, glanced back once over his shoulder as he thudded along behind. "Hollywood sucks."

Carson jabbed a button, and the car was there almost instantly, doors gliding open without a sound. They stepped inside.

"Man, whatever happened to the *Seven Samurai*?" Dex was still brooding. "Now those muthas had katanas... and they could *use* 'em."

"Yeah. Katanas. Definitely cool. But I'd rather have a lightsaber myself. Or you could have a katana that *was* a lightsaber." He pondered that for a moment. "If I had a lightsaber, it would be a katana."

"If I had a lightsaber, you'd be dead. And so would Tom Cruise. *And* Bruce Willis." Dex thought for a moment. "Well... Tom Cruise, anyway."

The door opened, and they stepped out into a long, elegant hallway, filled with shadows and soft accents from diffused lighting. Like the front desk and lobby, it, too, was completely deserted.

"Dude..." Carson mused, shaking his head. "I thought this place was humming around the clock. 'Fujikacorp never sleeps,'" he muttered severely, in a fair impression of Kinkade. "Never sleeps my ascot. Looks like a Hanson concert. Well," he peered at the number on a nearby door, getting his bearings. "Let's see if we can catch someone at home." He set off down the hallway, footsteps noiseless on a richly embroidered Asian print carpet.

"Wish Kiki was here," Dex rumbled. "She could just whip up a map on her thingie and *wham-bam!* We'd be outta here and rocking the vids."

"Yeah. Vids. Hey, speaking of Kiki," Carson's tones were hushed, unconsciously reflecting the somber, silent nature of their surroundings. It was like being in a funeral home after hours. "You notice anything... weird about her these days?"

"Whatchyou mean, 'weird'?"

"I don't know... just... weird. As in strange. Not like bi-winning or tiger blood strange, just sorta... off. I mean, she's always kept her own hours, but I don't know... lately, she seems to be... somewhere else."

Dex shrugged. "She's got school. I know that put a real kink in my bonnet back in the Army. And that was just learnin' about the best place to stick a bayonet and how to keep your parts clean in the bush. All that brainiac stuff she's doin'..." he whistled. "Gives me a headache just thinkin' about it. We there yet?"

Carson checked another number. "Close. Just a few more.

Anyway, I don't know. She's always ducking out early, coming in late, checking her watch... totally dissed me that day at the beach... I think it's something else. Something besides school."

Dex waved off his worries. "Probably just a boyfriend."

"No way," Carson stated flatly. "Impossible."

"Why not? She's cute, smart, available... that college is crawling with horny dudes. One of 'em is bound to notice her sooner or later."

"First of all, she woulda told me. And second of all... she woulda told me."

"Oh. Oh, right. Yeah. Sure." Dex tilted his head airily.

"What?"

Brown eyes rolled to face him. It was the worldly gaze of an older brother about to lay down one of the inescapable facts of life. "Listen up, bro - it's about time you..."

A strange, faint gurgling sound interrupted him. It was muffled, almost inaudible, and they would have missed it completely if not for their hushed voices.

Carson made a face. "What the Helena Montana was that?"

Dex glanced back, shrugged. "Guess they gargle in Japan too."

"Dude... no one gargles at midnight."

With the words, Carson stopped.

Dead.

They were Pete's words. Straight from his vision. And they hit him like a nine pound hammer, right between the eyes.

"What's up?" Dex had stopped too.

An involuntary shudder ran through Carson, and his head spun crazily. The weird sound came again, through a closed door just down the hall behind them. It sounded again, faded... then was gone.

"Nothing... just... uh..." Carson put a hand on the wall to steady himself. He had forgotten the dream again with the stress of the last few days, but it was back now, every bizarre detail, more real and intense and skin-tingling than ever before. For a moment, it was hard to breathe. Pete's words banged around inside his head, echoing over and over.

Thet's where it starts, soljer. You'll see...

And now, he had to. There was no other choice.

Carson considered telling Dex, decided quickly against it. He was pretty sure how the big man would welcome the return of the prophetic dream theory. "Maybe we should... check it out. Gargling means people. People means getting rid of this." He waved the envelope, still

 72

staring hard at the door, unable to take his eyes off it.

Dex rounded. "Fine with me. Sooner we find somebody, sooner we're cappin' bad guys."

Carson put his hand on the door handle, palm slick with sweat, heart hammering. He hesitated a fraction of a second, then pushed. Inside, was a small, bare room, spartanly furnished. A bare desk, a chair, a phone... and another door. Carson licked his lips. His skin tingled. That was it. He hesitated again, then stepped in.

Somehow, he knew that the answer lay in the next room. His eyes fixed on the far door, and he padded up to it, moving quietly, more out of instinct than any plan. He reached the door and stopped. The gargle came again, louder now. This time, they could also make out another sound: a long, whispering hiss, faintly metallic.

And wholly unnatural.

Dex was at his side, brow furrowed. "What the hell..." he whispered.

Carson shot him a glance, touched the handle. "Dunno. But I vote we find out."

Dex paused, eyed the door, looked back to Carson and gave a short nod. He reached behind his back and drew out a blocky, short barreled .40 caliber from a pancake holster. "Just in case." He thumbed off the safety. "Ready?"

"Steady."

"Go."

Carson turned the handle and pushed. There was the faintest squeak of hinge, the whisper of door on carpet. Then, they were looking at a ninja just finishing a long draw cut across the throat of a twitching corpse. Carson had just a second to take in a slumped figure behind a desk, a sickening river of red, a crouched black figure.

Then the assassin's hood snapped up.

A heartbeat.

And all hell broke loose.

A black arm snapped, snakelike, the motion too fast to follow. A pair of wicked iron shuriken thudded into wood, one-two, right where Carson's right eye would have been if the door hadn't hit the wall after he'd shoved it open, bounced back and bumped into his head, taking the deadly missiles in place of his face.

The figure leaped even as it threw, vaulted the desk, rolled into a spring and twisted in mid-air, slamming Dex's chest with a spinning back kick that staggered the big man and sent him stumbling back into

 73

the anteroom. Before even touching the ground, the assassin had drawn a long straight *ninjato* blade, landing in perfect stance. The sword leapt for Carson's throat without mercy or hesitation.

But, Dex had been kicked before. Even as he slammed against the far wall, his weapon was up, and he was firing, dazed and off balance but guided by instinct and training. A double tap sounded, one bullet punching through dry wall, and the other *ping-ing!* off the *ninjato* as the shots narrowly straddled their target's head.

The ninja moved like lightning. A dart of black in the shadows, it dove past Carson, rolled again and came up already thrusting, sword punching straight through Dex's shirt, an inch of belly and into the wall behind as the guard twisted desperately to the side. The blade yanked out and stabbed again.

"Boo-yah!"

A wooden chair crashed across the black back just as the ninja struck. Carson had shaken off his shock and lunged for the nearest weapon - the chair - arriving just in time. The blade swung wide, made a matching wound on Dex's other side. Blood spattered but the ninja went down.

With inhuman skill, it lashed out with a kick even as it was flung to the ground, sweeping Carson's legs from under him. They hit the floor at the same time and were up almost instantly, Carson in a mad wild scramble and the ninja in a smooth catlike bounce.

Carson's chair was up and ready when the attack came. A blinding flurry of steel flashed before him, sending woodchips flying as well as a lock of his hair. In a blind panic, he swung, smacked the *ninjato* quite by accident and sent it spinning across the room. Before it hit, an iron foot snapped into his gut, doubling him with a *whoof!* A second kick wrenched the chair loose and sent it flying, and then sparks danced in his brain as a pair of open-handed blows collided with his skull. The wall behind him stopped his fall, and he had just enough sense left to cover up as a vicious knife hand flashed out toward his throat. A second got through, half choking him, then a numbing strike sent fire through his shoulder and he lost the use of his arm.

"*DOWN!*" Dex thundered, and Carson shot his legs straight out and dropped. The booming report of the automatic erupted, staccato shots and muzzle flares piercing the shadows and the sudden, desperate silence. Carson felt impacts on the wall behind him, felt drywall sting his face. But nothing struck him, bullets or fists. He snapped his head up, gazed wildly, dazedly about, coughing and gagging.

No ninja.

"Go! Hallway! *Move!*" Dex was pounding across the room, moving with the surprising speed he always managed to muster when there was action. He was already in the hall as Carson staggered to his feet, snagged the chair in his good arm and pelted headlong after.

They hit the first corner at a dead run, bounced off the wall and into a long straight hallway. At the far end, was a tall window, braced open. The ninja stood poised, one leg thrown over the sill, slipping something onto its hands that looked like stubby claws.

Climbing claws.

Carson's brain registered the eclectic fact, remnant of a dozen late night reruns of *Revenge of the Ninja,* even as he charged; even as another part of his brain wondered *why* he was charging and *what* he would do when he got there.

The questions, however, were moot. At that precise moment, Dex planted, drew down and fired. Double tap. This time, there was nothing to skew his aim.

The ninja's body jerked twice, tilted, pitched back into black empty space and toppled out the window.

Carson froze, jaw slack. Seconds later, even from where they stood, they heard the *thud.*

"He... had that one... coming," Carson gasped.

Dex lowered his gun, face a mask of pain and rage. "He... cut me! The *&^%$... cut me!" He lurched down the hall, came up short at the window, stared down into the plaza twenty-five dizzying stories below. There, at the base of the building, a dark shadow among shadows, lay the crumpled form of their attacker. The night air blew softly about them, ruffled the thick curtains and Dex's sweat smeared dreads.

Dex steadied himself with a hand on the windowframe and another on his bloody side, wheezing, breathing hard. "I'll... say this... ninjas *suck!*"

"I'll... say this... that's one less you have to... worry about..."

And then it was getting up.

Stiffly, stubbornly, slowly, relentlessly, but getting up. It fought its way to its feet, turned and limped off into the shadows, leaving behind it an empty plaza, a warm breeze and two men who, for the moment, had absolutely nothing to say.

CHAPTER FIVE

Shogun

"...then we got the bork out of there. Called 911, didn't stop until we hit the medicenter."

There was tapping.

Carson was starting to hate tapping.

Detective Patch Parsons of the Las Calamas Police Department, Homicide Division, leaned back in a distressed folding chair in the cramped 24/7 storeroom, drumming a pen on his notepad. He looked as if he had just taken a spoonful of cod liver oil. The detective tried to stretch his long legs into a more comfortable position, found nowhere to go, pulled them back. "You didn't go back? Didn't talk to anyone, didn't make any other phone calls?"

"No. On the one hand, I wasn't feeling very social after that, and on the other, I figured, 'hey, why take all the fun for myself - leave some for the cops'. After all, it's their *job*."

Carson was starting to feel agitated. They'd been at this for an hour, and it wasn't going well. Parsons had asked the last couple of questions mechanically, as if his job required it, and hadn't even written down the answers. He hadn't, in fact, written anything down in a long time.

Det. Parsons tapped his pen a little harder on the leather binding of his notebook. Carson recognized the book only too well - it hadn't changed since last time. Neither had Parson's long, academic face, the gray sandpaper hair - unless it looked a little more gray - nor his rumpled corduroy professor's suit. And neither had his skepticism.

The man shifted, attempted to straighten his legs again, gave up. With a huff, he rose abruptly to his feet. Dex, positioned almost at his elbow, didn't bother trying to make room. He hadn't even attempted to squeeze himself into one of the old folding chairs, as it was fairly certain how such a contest would have ended. Instead, he leaned against a shelf, affecting an air of interested disinterest, offering a few colorful comments but mostly letting Carson handle their statement. It wasn't helping.

Parsons glanced at his notebook as if by habit, looked disgusted, then aimed a frown at Dex and another at Carson. "Don't tell me my *job*, Mr. Dudley. I know my *job*. My *job* is to investigate murders, not fairy tales." He waved the notebook like it was a dirty diaper. "Last time, it was a giant killer wolf-man. This time, it's... it's... super ninjas?!"

"Yeah. That's right. But this time, I have a witness."

Parsons made a strangled kind of noise. He favored Dex with a withering gaze, as if John Dillinger had just insisted that Al Capone could back up his alibi. "Your 'witness' has troubles of his own. Our department is still investigating Mr. Jackson's role in thwarting a car robbery at a facility where he was providing... services. It seems several of the perpetrators are still in critical condition. One almost died."

"Always happy to help." Dex showed Parsons his teeth.

Carson felt his credibility slip another few notches. "Okay, okay... but the body. You can't argue with a dead body. Right?!"

"No, I can't. When there is one."

Carson stared. "I'm guessing this is gonna be bad news."

"We visited the premises," Parson's cod liver look was back. "Located the office you described - which was vacant, I may add, and has been for the last five months - and had forensics examine it top to bottom. Even checked out the window and the courtyard outside where you last saw the alleged... 'assailant'... fall." Parsons gritted his teeth, unable to bring himself to say *ninja* again.

"And...? And you found...?"

"Nothing."

"Nothing?! But... but we saw... he was..." Carson faltered, flustered. "Did you... did you look *under* the desk?!"

"You should be thankful we looked at all, especially after your last crackpot story. I feel it only fair to mention that I still haven't ruled out the fact that you withheld evidence last time, or that you had something to do with that mess at the slaughterhouse. Don't push your luck."

Carson pushed it anyway. "Did you at least *talk* to someone? Nose around a little? Dust for prints?! Heck, even on..."

"Mr. Dudley," Parsons cut him off flatly. "I should inform you that, if the letters 'CSI' come out of your mouth in the next ten seconds, I will be authorized to use deadly force." Carson shut his mouth. "As I expressed previously, I *do* know my job. Furthermore, I am under *no* obligation to discuss with you the details of this investigation. However, strictly in the interest of bringing this unfortunate interview to an end, let me inform you that I spoke to the CEO of the company himself, a Mr...." he consulted his notebook. "...Fujika. He assured me quite convincingly that nothing out of the ordinary had occurred last night. Even showed me security footage. Normal. Boring. Hours of it. It all checked out. So, unless you can show me a corpse, Mr. Dudley...?" Carson cast about helplessly, looked at Dex who merely shrugged, then back at Parsons. His mouth opened, closed.

"...then it's time we wrapped this up. Anything else you want to share with me?" It was a dare. Parson's eyes were flat and dangerous.

"Er..." Carson thought back to last night, struggling to put the blur of pain and panic into some kind of order, grasping at straws, anything that might help convince Parsons that he was not just a repeat lunatic. "As a matter of fact, there is! He, uh... smelled funny. The ninja. Nasty, really, now that I think about it, almost like you could taste it, so bad. And he felt kind of... squishy. I've never hit anyone with a chair before, but I always imagined it would be a little more, I don't know, cracky. Plus, the chair didn't break, which it always does in the movies. Kind of threw me off. And I'm babbling now, so I'm going to stop. Dex, anything?" He looked at Dex, eyes begging.

Dex shook his head, still smiling. He was enjoying himself.

Parsons snapped his notepad shut. As usual, he hadn't written a thing. He glared at Carson with open hostility. "If I need any more fairy tales, I'll be in touch." The shelves trembled as he stomped out.

Carson watched him go. "That went well."

"Told you he wasn't gonna like it."

"Actually, I believe your exact words were, 'Detective Parsons sucks.'"

"Well?"

Carson watched as Parsons stalked out of the store and threw himself into a waiting patrol car. It roared away in a rush. "Detective Parsons sucks." He sighed, ran a hand through his hair. "You saw his face... he didn't believe a word of it. Again!"

"Can you blame him?"

"I'd *like* to say 'yes'."

Carson slouched into the store, hands stuffed in his pockets. Dex swaggered along behind, still grinning. He seemed unfazed both by Parson's obvious brush-off and his own injuries, a pair of deep cuts which had required numerous stitches. It was a service he would have been happy to provide for himself, but Carson had dragged him to the medicenter anyway.

The thought of it made Carson's own aches throb. He prodded a tender, nasty looking bruise under one eye, winced. "Heck, if it wasn't for this, I'm not even sure I would believe it. It did happen... didn't it?"

"Dude. We fought a ninja."

"And we won, right?"

"Kicked his *&^%$."

"And then, after that, you know, when you shot him - twice - and he fell out a twenty-fifth story window... he got up and walked away, right?"

"We won. Who cares about the details?" Dex wasn't smiling anymore. He snagged a box of powdered donettes as they passed a shelf, caught himself and put them back. "But now that you mention it... that thing about the smell. What you told Parsons. Were you just crackin' wise or did you really get a snootful of somethin'?"

"There was a stink, that's for sure. Didn't notice it while I was, you know, fighting for my life, but afterward, yeah. It smelled like... bad."

Dex considered, didn't like the way his thoughts were going, shook himself free of them. "Probably just that dead guy. When a man dies, he usually has a number two situation, if you know what I mean."

"That's lovely. Thanks for that information, that's great. Next time the Jeopardy category is 'Smells That Come From a Dead Guy', I'm gonna be all over it. And while I'm totally repulsed by this conversation and can't believe we're actually having it, let me just say that it didn't really smell like that. It smelled more like..." Carson struggled to put words to the odor. "Bad."

Dex frowned. "You're startin' to stress me. It's time I hit my rounds. Get a little fresh air." He headed out the door, a muttered string of broken sentences floating in his wake: "...kicked his... drilled that sucka... who cares what he smelled like?! Drilled that sucka..."

Carson slipped behind the front counter, moody. He shook his head. Parsons didn't believe him? Fine. Dex was in denial? Peachy. He knew what he'd smelled. And saw. He didn't understand it, but he knew. It was like Pete once told him: *the eye don't lie.* And neither did the nose.

Only problem was, they didn't always make a lick of sense either. Carson scratched his chin beard, pondering, pacing.

"Everything okay?" Josh looked up from his study of the Omni-Biz 7520. "You guys were in there awhile." He wasn't trying to hide his concern.

"Yeah. It's all good."

Josh didn't look convinced. "That Detective... he looked unhappy."

"Trust me - I've worked with Parsons before. He was way past unhappy."

"Anything I can do?"

"Ever fought a ninja?"

"Um... no."

"Then keep studying. If we can get that till figured out, at least something will make sense."

"I'm on it," Josh gave a grim smile and turned back to the register. Then his face fell a little. "Oh, uh... Kinkade wants to see you."

Carson froze. "He's here?!"

"Uh... yeah. Sorry. He showed up while you were in the back. Said to send you to his office the second you came out."

"How did he look?"

Josh glanced out the window in the direction Parsons had gone. "Way past unhappy."

Carson's shoulders slumped... then squared bravely. "I fought a ninja," he muttered to himself. "And I won. I fought a ninja, and I won."

"Beg your pardon?"

"Nothing." The front door opened, and an elderly couple strolled in surrounded by scampering grandchildren. "You got this?"

"I'll manage." Josh glanced at the till with determination. "Where I come from, that's just what people do."

 80

A few seconds later, Carson was knocking on Kinkade's door. It was still weird. Jack had never had the door closed in the three years that Carson had worked at the 24/7. Not once.

"Enter." It was a command, not an invitation. Carson sighed.

Inside, the office was neat as a pin, the complete opposite of the elegant mess Jack had lovingly crafted over thirty years. Gone were the stacks of ten year old invoices, the half-eaten corn dogs, the dilapidated filing cabinet, the pair of unruly potted ferns, and the *I'M THE BOSS - FILL THIS* coffee mug the employees had given him last Christmas.

In their place was neatness.

Glaring, blinding, eat-off-the-floor neatness. Neat desk, neat walls, neat files, neat shelves. Worst of all was the neat plaque on the wall bearing the Seven Corporation motto: *Eternus Vigilo.*

Then Carson's eyes lit on Ross Kinkade, and he realized he was wrong - the *plaque* was not the worst. Kinkade was staring at him from behind the immaculate desk, fingers steepled. Josh had been right. Way past unhappy.

"Sit."

Carson sat.

He tried to look casual and inoffensive but had his doubts that he was pulling it off. After a moment of enduring Kinkade's gaze, he decided the best defense was a good offense. "Hey, chief. How's business?"

If Kinkade heard, he made no indication. "Tell me what happened at Fujikacorp last night."

Carson hesitated. Although he had just spent the last hour relating those exact details to Parsons, he was fairly certain that, as cool a reception as the detective had given, Kinkade's would be even worse.

"There was... an incident."

"An incident? Please, Mr. Dudley - elaborate."

"We were... harassed"

Kinkade blinked. "And by *'we'* you mean...?"

"Dex... that is, Officer Jackson. And myself. That's the 'we'. 'Us'."

"Did you hurt anyone?"

"Well..." Carson pictured the ninja's inert and crumpled form after his 250 foot swan dive onto the pavement. "Not permanently."

"The detective took your statement?"

"He took it. Yes. And I'm pretty sure what he's going to do with it," he muttered.

"Fine." Kinkade swept the matter aside like an old packing slip.

"Now, on to more important matters. Did you deliver the letter?"

"The... the letter?!" Carson was flabbergasted. "You're kidding, right? I was assaulted... er, harassed! Painfully!" Something tickled his hand, and he looked down at a large black beetle that had scuttled across his lap. He flicked it away, glanced back sharply at Kinkade.

"That's your story, certainly," Kinkade retorted flatly. "And you have made your statement to Detective Parsons, and he will undertake an investigation to determine whether there is any credibility to it. That is his job. And yours, Mr. Dudley, was to deliver that letter. You had a productivity milestone to complete. Did you complete it?"

Carson felt the blood rushing to his face. "You... you're... seriously?!"

"Did - you - deliver it?" The question was still flat, but now it was dangerously flat. And hard. And sharp. Like the edge of a machete.

"Well, I don't know Ross - I guess it might have dropped on the floor of the dead guy's office while I was fighting for my life! I guess, if you count that as delivered, then yeah! It was delivered!"

Kinkade stared at him through his drab boxy spectacles. They suddenly made him look more like a prison warden than an annoying dad. "I see." He picked up his tablet and scribbled on it. Carson resisted the urge to slap it out of his hands. He forced himself to calm down, waiting while Kinkade scribbled more notes.

Breath in. Breath out.

In. Out.

"This will go on your record as a negative achievement. Failure to complete a productivity milestone." Kinkade spoke without looking up. "As for the letter, I hope you know how much extra work and embarrassment this is going to cause Seven Corporation. When the replacement document arrives, I'll have Stanley deliver it. After recent events, I think it's best if you stay away from Fujikacorp. You're not ready for that kind of responsibility."

Carson concentrated on his breathing. In. Out. With effort, his fingers unclenched from the arms of his chair. "Alright," he answered smoothly and somewhat to his own surprise. "Is that all?"

Kinkade looked at him. His face, as usual, was largely unreadable, but there seemed to be just a hint of surprise. His eyes narrowed slightly, dangerously. "No. That's not all. Something stinks around here. Clean it up." He looked back down to his tablet, scribbled some more. "My guess is the alley. See that it's done quickly, and that you treat it with more respect than your previous milestone. And one more thing... have you been in my office?"

Carson shook his head. He didn't trust himself to speak.

Kinkade stared at him, looking every bit the prosecuting attorney who was grilling an accused murderer but didn't have the proof to make it stick. Absently, he touched a stack of papers. "Someone spilled something on these." Carson looked. The papers were yellowed, cracked around the edges, smudged with brown. "A reminder: my office is off limits."

It wasn't a reminder. It was an accusation.

Kinkade turned back to his work, and the room fell silent, except for the incessant scribbling and tapping. Carson got the message. He pushed out of the chair and made a beeline for the door, trying not to slam it on his way out. He managed.

Barely.

Carson waved off Josh's questioning look and busied himself with store duties for the next few hours. It was the best therapy he knew, and right now, he needed therapy. Thankfully, Kinkade left soon after their encounter. Josh followed shortly, his shift over. He left with the operations manual, a commiserating smile and a promise to keep studying hard because, where he came from, that's just what people did.

After that, Carson was alone with his store and the few late-night stragglers. It was a little quiet time, and right now that was just fine with him. It had been a day of unpleasant surprises, following a night of downright awful ones.

The next one came just after eleven.

Carson looked up from stacking Freezie cups as a long black limo slid up to the front of the store. It just kept sliding like there was no end to it, past the front window, filling the whole storefront before pulling a wide, slow, self-important turn and nosing in front of the gas pumps. Carson squinted through the blinds, intrigued.

And suddenly... strangely... edgy.

Something stirred in the pit of his stomach. Something inexplicable. Something dark. He waited.

After a minute, the front doors swished open, drawn back by a pair of dark-suited Asians. One was thick and beefy and the other lean and knife-like. They drifted into the mini-mart, dark eyes alert and probing, checking every corner and cranny before they even looked at Carson. Or through him, it felt like. They had the flat, expressionless features of men who looked for trouble and knew what to do when they found it. A word of greeting died in Carson's throat. Unconsciously, he held his breath. The thugs stood, silent and motionless.

Then, between them, out of the night and into the 24/7, stepped trouble.

The man reminded Carson instantly of the katana hanging in the Fujikacorp lobby - lean, razor sharp and dangerous, with a face that would have been handsome had it not been hawkish and proud. A pencil thin goatee traced his chin, and his black hair came to a sharp point over his head, like the iron sights on a gun. He wore power and confidence over a gray silk suit like he was born with both, like he was used to people jumping to obey his every whim. Immediately. Without question. Carson didn't need the corporate logo on the limo to place the man. He could obviously, only and ultimately be just one person: Ichiro Fujika.

The Shogun had arrived.

Fujika swept the mini-mart with a disdainful look, his dark, almond eyes settling on Carson after a long moment. A derisive smile tweaked thin cruel lips.

"So. You are the one." It was part accusation, part insult. Fujika spoke English with perfect fluency but a thick accent, as if he had stooped to learn this foreign tongue but would not honor it by giving up the inflections of his own.

Carson disliked him instantly. After sorting through a half-dozen smart remarks, however, he decided that it would be best for his job and Jack's legacy to try things straight instead of sideways. He had the feeling things could go sideways with Fujika quickly enough on their own. He squared his shoulders and mentally puckered. He'd already being playing this game with Kinkade for weeks, anyway. It was corporate kiss up time. Again.

"I'm afraid so." Carson flashed a rueful smile, dropping into his disarming 'Regular Joe' act. "You must be Mr. Fujika, right?" He extended a hand which he instinctively knew Fujika wouldn't touch. Fujika didn't. Carson took it back without missing a beat. "Sorry about all the noise at your place last night. My bad."

Fujika let his cynical smile wither Carson for a moment, then turned it against the store by angling his head the barest fraction. He swept the well stocked shelves, orderly rows of goods and colorful marketing posters with a contemptuous gaze, as if he could stare the place into closing by a sheer act of will.

When the Shogun finished his inspection and turned to Carson, he was no longer smiling. He took a single step toward the counter, stopped at the edge of it as if it were his choice rather than because of any physical impediment. A wink of metal caught Carson's eye, and he noted a tie pin bearing a strange three pointed symbol. Something poked at Carson's brain. He felt he should recognize it.

"You interrupted my morning schedule." Fujika spat out the words. It was as if he were reporting a grave offense that could only be made right by Carson committing ritual suicide.

Carson lounged against the nacho cheese tub, smiled apologetically. "Yeah, sorry about that. That's the trouble with schedules... they don't always go as planned." He wasn't going to instigate, but neither was he planning to back down.

Fujika's eyes bored into him like smoldering olive pits. "Mine do."

So much for the corporate kiss up.

Carson stared coolly back. "You haven't been attacked by ninjas recently, then."

"And neither have you."

"Are you thinking that or telling me that?"

"The tale you have told is a lie," Fujika's voice was flat, final. "A fabrication. Your police know this already. They found nothing."

"Maybe they didn't look in the right place. Those ninjas... they're tricky little devils."

"Quite correct. Ninjas are devils. Masters of silent death. I am certain you did not encounter one last night, for if a *ninja* meant to kill you," Fujika gave the word special, almost reverent inflection, "you would be dead."

And now the gloves were off.

Carson was suddenly very, very tired of corporations and very, very ready to get under Fujika's skin. Deep. "Okay, now that sounded a little like a threat. How 'bout a Freezie just to lighten the mood? Guys?" Carson turned to the thugs, offering them each a brightly colored spoon straw. "I hear the Super Maxi-Pad won't be opening any time soon. Whaddaya say?"

Fujika shrugged with an expression. His body made no movement. "Interpret my words as you wish. The truth remains unchanged. The authorities found no *ninja* because there were none to find."

"Uh-huh. And what about corpses? I also saw one of those - are there any of those to find? They must be hard to find, too."

"No. But they are easy to hide."

"Okay. Whoa. Now that *was* a threat. I mean, the other one you kinda danced around, but that one..."

 85

"Excuse me..." A soft voice from the front door interrupted him. A slender, beautiful woman stood waiting subserviently, looking like Fujika's twin in a skirt. She bowed, brandished an important looking legal docket and murmured a few things Carson didn't understand. She had a voice like a silver waterfall.

Fujika silenced her with a curt burst of Japanese. Carson didn't understand any of his words either, but he was certain none of them were "please." The woman bowed again, backed out.

Fujika's eyes, like the deadly barrels of two sniper rifles, turned back to Carson. "I do not threaten, Mr. Dudley. Nor do I attempt to hide my victims. I find, as did my samurai ancestors, that a field of bloody corpses speaks for itself. It makes the next conquest that much easier - as those who witness it tremble and choke on their fear. My latest conquest, for example," he indicated the woman who had just left with the slightest twitch of one hand. "Ah... I do not, however, suppose that you speak Japanese?"

Carson chewed one of the spoon straws disinterestedly. "They had it as an elective in high school, but I passed. It was that or wood shop. I chose wood shop. I still have the duck I made."

Fukija pressed on without pause, showing no signs of irritation. "In that case, I shall translate. My personal assistant has just informed me that a rival corporation has failed to accede to our demands. And so, we strike. As we speak, forces gather to seal the fate of our enemy. I will watch its death throes from the comfort of my limousine."

"Maybe you'd like some nachos, then. They go really well with a hostile takeover. It's the salsa. Spicy."

Fujika studied him carefully. "I came here today," he murmured bleakly. "To take the measure of a man. To survey the terrain of the coming battle. To destroy a thing, one must understand it. And to understand it, one must observe it. Now that I have, I see that all is as I imagined." Dark eyes narrowed. "You are the West. Soft. Weak. Detestable."

"I'm betting you don't have many friends."

"Nor, Mr. Dudley, do I have many enemies."

"Nice. That one was nice. But I gotta tell ya, speaking of the West, you could learn a thing or two from us about threats. You should watch a few Clint Eastwood films, get some tips. You've got the squinty eye thing going, but I think, if you stuck a little black cigar in your pie hole, you'd really be a lot more convincing. Maybe, a black hat... one of those sassy neckerchiefs. Make you look all scary. I've got

 86

one you could borrow."

"Fujikacorp will crush you. And do so easily."

"Hey, now that's catchy! Word on the street is you guys are working up a new slogan for your mini-marts. That one just might work: 'Welcome to the Super Maxi-Pad: We Will Crush You, and Do So Easily.' Say it with me, just to get a feel for it..."

Carson couldn't be sure, but he had the faint impression that last one had hit the mark. Fujika had Kinkade's same poker face, but his voice was definitely his tell. And now, it was as cold and icy as his eyes.

"Take heed, Carson Dudley. I do not threaten idly."

"No, but you do threaten frequently. And just a second ago, you said you didn't threaten at all. Personally, I think you're a little turned around. I think you're getting business confused with war."

"Business, war... it is all the same. You are my enemy now, Mr. Dudley. Make no mistake. Tell me... have you ever read *The Art of War*?"

"No. But I've played the video game. *And* I've seen the movie."

"I read it every day. Study it. Absorb it. I do so for one simple reason: it tells me how to win. In business. In life. In war. It teaches that, to beat your enemy, you must learn the lay of the land. Then, you must use it to control the time and place of battle, turning both to your advantage. And so, the wise general, merely by observation, can win a war..." Fujika's dark eyes held him for a long moment. Staring into their black, shiny depths, Carson was certain there wasn't the barest hint of soul. "...before his enemy even knows he is in one."

Then Fujika turned on his heel and was gone, leaving only the ghost of a malevolent smile. The thugs closed ranks and drifted out behind him, glaring at Carson like two pit bulls looking at lunch.

"Yeah?!" Carson hollered after him. "Well... at least *my* store isn't named after a *tampon*!"

Then, the adrenaline hit, and he was shaking. He stood for a moment, letting nerves and a sudden fury wash over him. Through the front window, he watched as Fujika slipped into the black limousine and disappeared from sight. Then, on impulse, he grabbed his bat and vaulted the counter, heading for the alley. He had the sudden desire to smash the crap out of a couple hundred cans.

Carson was halfway to the back when he heard the shouts.

"Crabapples!" He muttered. "What now?" He wheeled, listening. Raised voices. Coming from the parking lot. He could see the outline

 87

of Fujika's limo through the front window, still parked in front by the pumps, not moving. And there were people - milling - a crowd, gawking, pointing. Carson's brow furrowed. Something was wrong.

Then, through the glass, the sound of raised voices again. This time, he recognized one of them.

Dex.

Carson forgot the alley, forgot the cans, forgot everything and pelted for the front door. He hit the pushbar, moving fast and spilled into the heat and humidity of midnight in Las Calamas. Several things leapt into focus all at once, and Carson stopped short, his brain frantically sorting them. It was a busy, dangerous, crowded scene. And it was primed to explode.

The limo sat right where Fujika had parked it, neatly blocking off both lanes of gas pumps. Several cars had lined up, waiting to enter. A few had started honking, but the limo showed no signs of moving.

Dex stood by the driver's side, blocked by the pair of suited Japanese kneebreakers. The big one stood chest to chest with him, as if squaring off for a Sumo match, while the other drifted slowly, lazily to Dex's left. Dex's hands were up in a gesture of peace, but Carson could tell by the position of his body and the look in his eye that he was thinking something entirely different.

All three stood loose and ready. They were professionals, old hands at a game of human chess in which the slightest move was observed and matched. It was a subtle and delicate game that could lead at any second to a confrontation that was anything but.

"Mr. Fujika is occupied," The big guard's voice fit his size, like a bucket of gravel tossed into a Japanese rock tumbler. His tone was steady and even, but his stance was begging for Dex to make a move.

"I got that, Kato. But, he's occupied in a real inconvenient place. This here's where people get gas. So either pump some... or push on."

"Or what?" The other man with the knife-like face sneered. "You will call your police?" He took another casual step, drifting further toward Dex's flank.

The guard shifted slightly, checking him with his peripheral vision but keeping his eyes locked on the bigger man. "Never had much use for 'em. I don't find many problems I can't sort out."

"Mr. Fujika will leave when his business is concluded." It was the big fellow again, puffing his chest full of threat, holding Dex's attention. They were working him.

"It is concluded. He just don't know it yet." Dex took a step

 88

forward. The big thug shifted his weight back slightly on his right leg, lifting his left hand in a "stop" motion: palm flat, fingers locked, thumb tucked in tight to the side. His right hand made a fist and chambered low on his hip. Carson had seen the same stance on Ultimate Fighting Challenge last week. This was going to go bad.

The smaller guard slipped a hand behind his back, reached for something under his jacket. "Step away from the car," he snapped. "Now."

Carson took a step forward. His bat came up.

"Sure. Just need a quick word with your boss first..." Dex reached past the big Asian to tap on the glass of the passenger window.

It all happened in the blink of an eye.

The big Sumo snatched Dex's outstretched wrist, yanked him off balance and pitched him headfirst into the gas pump, starring the glass. Dex reeled back. As he staggered, the brute drove a foot into the side of his knee, taking it out and sending him to the pavement on the other, then hammered four or five blows in rapid succession using fist, open hand, elbow. The thud of bone on flesh was shocking. The strikes were methodical, surgical, delivered in a way that said he was used to hitting people and that he liked doing it. It was one big man pounding another big man like he really meant it, really wanted to do damage, wanted to put him in the hospital. Or worse.

Only, he'd never hit Dex before.

By the fourth blow, Dex had his steel baton out, and it was there to meet the fifth. It shot upward and caught the Sumo's huge forearm on the way down. There was a crack that wasn't the baton.

Dex whipped the weapon by its handle, backslapping the fellow across the face with enough force to split a two by four, then reversed it and drove the blunt tip straight down onto the flat of his right foot, putting his weight into it. Another crack.

As the thug bent with a grunt, Dex drove the opposite end of the baton directly upward into his nose. The Asian flew back and staggered into the limo, spurting blood.

The man's partner, equally surprised at the turn of events, finally moved with a jolt. He yanked a short black rod from his belt and snapped it open, a telescoping whip of steel segments. Lunging, he came at Dex from his blindside, swiping low and fast for the kidneys. Still on one knee, Dex tilted back with the deceptive speed of a big man who knows how to fight. He caught the blow on his baton. Steel *pinged!* on steel, and before the attacker could swing again, Dex grabbed his arm, twisted his hips and pulled, sending him headfirst into the gas pump. It was the same one Dex had struck seconds earlier. The thug's star was bigger. Much bigger.

Dex levered himself to his feet as the first bruiser came off the car, viciously swiping at blood, limping but ready for murder. To his left, the lean Japanese staggered awkwardly up, though somewhat less gracefully. He shook his head to clear the dancing lights and grasped at the pump hoses for support. The whip-rod was gone. This time, he held a knife. Dex set himself, picking targets...

Then Fujika was there.

"ENOUGH!"

The limo door stood open behind him, cold fury etched into his face. The bodyguards stopped, instantly and completely, as if Fujika had hit a kill switch. They dropped out of stance and stood loose, arms slack, heads down. Dex narrowed his eyes, shot a glance back and forth between his opponents, ready for more scrap but with enough presence of mind to wait and see if it was coming.

Fujika barked a few terse words in Japanese. The guards bowed. Then, all three were gone, swallowed in the dark, voluminous depths of the limousine. Its engine throbbed to life, and it nosed out into the street. Seconds later, it was gone.

Dex's mouth made a grim frown. "Just when things were gettin' interesting."

Carson lowered his bat. He hadn't even had time to take a step, much less a swing. Around him, the small crowd of onlookers chattered excitedly. One of them was on a cell, another snapping pictures. Carson's eye was drawn to a third, a shadowy figure lurking by the far pump. It was a heavyset figure in a tan 24/7 work shirt. A figure with slick 80's rocker hair, yellow teeth and a wicked smile that said someone was going to get in trouble. Big. Even from that distance, Carson caught a whiff of stale cigarettes.

It was Stanley.

Carson had the sudden, sinking feeling that Dex was wrong - things were going to get a *lot* more interesting very, very soon.

CHAPTER SIX

The Good, The Bad and The Rotten

"All things considered, I prefer the *other* Ichiro."

Carson reached up to place a bag of frozen cream-cheese kielbasa dogs on the shelf.

Josh handed him another, shook his head in wonder. "No arguments here. Hey... didn't Stanley say to put these on the bottom shelf?"

"Yeah. He did." Carson stuffed the bag on the top shelf. "You take any heat, just tell him I made you do it. Same for Kinkade."

Josh grinned and passed up another sack. "Whatever you say."

Several days had passed since the altercation with Fujika's goons, and Carson had had plenty of time to reflect on it. Stanley's lecherous grin still burned in his brain, and he knew it was ammunition his opponent wouldn't let go to waste. He had waited tensely for repercussions from Stanley - or Kinkade - or Fujikacorp - but so far nothing had happened. No lawsuits, no reprimands, no news footage. Not a peep. Far from being at peace, however, Carson felt like the hangman was just out picking up a new rope. It wasn't a good feeling.

An even worse feeling came from replaying Fujika's words. Carson kept rewinding the tape, trying to figure out if his threats were the veiled kind or the "I mean it" kind. The more he replayed them, the more they sounded like the latter. In the heat of the moment, Carson had found them easy to dismiss, but thinking back... no doubt about it. Fujika was bad news.

"So that was it?" Josh's question brought him back to the cold reality of kielbasa dogs and the walk-in freezer.

"Pretty much. They all piled into the stretch and off they went, like it was time to go shake down the orphans."

"No wonder they call him the Shogun."

"He's a ruthless suit. That's for certain sure."

Josh hefted the last bag easily, passed it up. "So what do you think Stanley's going to do?" He tipped up the empty pallet and dragged it into the store.

Carson stowed the bag and followed, pondering. "Something bad. Something very bad. But I can't exactly go to Kinky with the story. I've already got one negative achievement on my record - whatever that means - and I'm pretty sure being caught waving a baseball bat at our company rival isn't going to improve things. The security tapes will back up whatever Stanley says, too, within reason. Nope..." he scratched his chin beard. "My only move here is to sit tight and do my job. Frankly, I'm getting a little tired of worrying about how and when other people are gonna shaft me."

Josh nodded his approval. "Where I come from, that's how people handle things. Change what you can, don't worry about what you can't. It'll work out. You'll see." Together they hauled the pallet out into the alley and tossed it on the pile.

Carson paused by the stack, wrinkled his nose. "Wow. Never thought I'd say this, but Kinkade was right. It stinks out here." He sighed, remembering his latest directive. "And I'll give you one guess whose job it is to unstink it."

"Need a hand?"

Carson checked his watch. "Aren't you off?"

"Twenty minutes ago. But I wouldn't mind sticking around for a bit. It'll take you forever to get this cleaned up by yourself. We can go over closing procedure while we do it."

"Eugene, you just earned yourself a Baby Ruth." They turned back into the store, heading for the front counter. "Mama mía!" Carson sniffed sharply and made a face. "That alley's worse than I thought.

Now I smell it in *here*."

"It's bad alright. Of course, where I come from, folks are used to bad smells..." Josh launched into a wholesome recollection of life in rural Oregon. As he did, a strange, faint sound reached Carson's ears. Strange - yet uncomfortably familiar. He cocked his head, listening.

There it was again.

"*Eeeriiiibibibiit.*"

"...and he never did *that* with a skunk again. Know what I mean?"

Carson caught himself. "Er... yeah. Yeah... I think. I mean... what did you say? About the...?"

"I was just saying that I know a man who had a cow..." Josh retold his anecdote, but again Carson's attention wandered. He strained his ears, listening for the sound.

"*Eeeriiiibibibiit.*"

There. It was louder this time. Louder, in fact, than any other time. The stink was worse too. Suddenly, with a strange clarity, Carson realized they were linked. And, while he couldn't place the sound, the smell was starting to ring some bells. Fujikacorp bells. He sniffed again, ignoring the way it made his dinner quiver. No - it wasn't the same. But it was close enough to send a shiver up his spine. And whatever it was, it was time he found out.

"Yeah, I love that part, great story," he piled into Josh's narrative. "And on second thought, let's bag the alley."

"You sure, Carson? It's no big deal, I'd be happy to..."

"Forget it. You've been a big help, why not take it easy tonight?" Carson took a box of industrial strength garbage bags from his hands and gently shoved him toward the door. "It's your time off; you've earned it. Go home and spend some time with Laura."

"Lauren."

"Yeah, her."

"*Eeeriiiibibibiit.*"

Josh stopped, a funny look on his face. "Say, did you just hear...?"

Carson hustled him toward the door. "Yup, my stomach. Boy, am I hungry! Gonna grab some corn dogs, now. See ya later! Say "hi" to Laura!"

"Lauren."

"Yeah, her. Here, treat the little lady to something special..." Carson snagged a package of Twinkies and thrust it at Josh.

Josh paused in the doorway. "Well..." he turned the package in his hands, slowly warming to the idea. "I guess we could use a date night.

 93

I mean, gosh, we're still technically on our honeymoon. But you're not off the hook, Carson - I told you I'd help and I will! Where I come from..."

"... is where you're going. Have a great night - see you tomorrow!" With a final shove Josh was out. Carson shut the door, locked it and put his back to it. The store was his.

"*Eeeriiiibibibibiit.*"

There it was again. But fainter now. Farther away. Retreating. Carson pushed away from the door. Not this time. This time he'd get to the bottom of it, whether he liked it or not. Just in case, he swung by the counter for his bat, then jogged into the middle of the mini-mart and stopped, listening hard.

A *thump* from the back made him start. That was new. There was another *thump*, then a louder *bump* and finally a *bang!* that made him take a step back and bring up the bat.

He wasn't alone.

The knowledge made his heart skip a beat. A whiff of smell hit him, nastier than ever. Carson steeled himself. Cautiously, he crept forward.

Another noise *banged!* through the store and he paused, locating. It came from... he frowned. The bathroom? He could just see the door, standing slightly ajar, between a gap in the shelves. That had to be it. Fitting... but hardly comforting.

Carson eased forward a few more steps, staring hard. Then a few more. A cautious moment later, he reached the door. He waited, tense. No more banging. He put his ear to the door. From inside, a strange, gurgling noise reached him, setting his short hairs standing at attention. He jerked back, palms sweaty. The smell was intense, like concert port-a-potties on a hot day. But he was too close. There was no backing off now. He put his hand resolutely on the door, drew a steadying breath, wished he hadn't. It was now or never. He pushed and stepped, one quick, fluid movement, ready for anything.

He wasn't, however, ready for this.

The bathroom was a wreck. Stinking sludge swirled about the floor or stood in pools, decorated with chunks of flotsam, clumps of soggy white toilet paper and worse. Much worse. A large patch of floor tile had ruptured, showing exposed pipes beneath from which the awful goo was gushing. A wash of sewer smell took his breath away and made him gag. Carson turned away, breathing into his sleeve.

"Cock-a-doodle-do!" He fought back a wave of nausea. After a moment, his stomach settled and he turned back to the room. Staring into the mess in dismay, wondering how any one mop could ever handle it, his ear caught the faint *clack-clack-clack* of porcelain on porcelain. It came from the far side of the room, where the metal stall door stood partly ajar. The sound was coming from behind it.

The toilet.

Carson craned his neck, trying to get an angle, but could see nothing. His sense of curiosity rapidly overcame his sense of hygiene, and he stepped inside. Gingerly, carefully, trying to avoid the largest of the landmines, he picked his way across the floor. It was slick and treacherous; twice he almost went down. He reached the stall door, nudged it open gingerly with his bat. Inside, the toilet was smeared and slopped with murky brown and green. Sludge streaked its sides and bubbled out of the bowl. The seat bounced and chattered like the lid on a pot of boiling water, sending fresh splatters into the stall.

Carson swallowed hard. Something was in there. He knew it.

"Okay, this is stupid," he whispered fiercely. "I am stupid!" He glanced back to the relative safety of the store, then at the unknown of the toilet. "After all the good times we've shared," he muttered at it. "You're not going to do me wrong, are you?" He braced himself, reached in with the bat, stretched...

Too far.

The tip of the bat was still inches from the lid. Carson took a cautious step into the stall, tried to avoid the pool of brown but couldn't, felt it soaking into his once-favorite tennis shoes.

He grimaced. "Well, since I've already stepped in it..." He took another step. Brown muck seeped over the top of his shoe, poured into it. He was close enough now. More than close enough. Carson leaned in, slipped the tip of his bat under the toilet lid, and lifted...

A *blurp* of brown murk marked the disappearance of *something* into the bowl. Carson lurched back with a start, slipped, almost went down, caught himself. Fouled brown water swirled and eddied, sloshed out of the bowl and washed over his shoes, filled his socks. He didn't even notice, just stared, breathless, eyes bugging.

Nothing.

Then... a thick, fat bubble surfaced. It sat a moment. Then popped. Then a few more rose. Ripples spread through the bowl.

It was in there.

Carson licked his lips nervously, tried not to think about what "it" might be. He was fairly certain it was no ninja, but that was a small comfort. Whatever it was, he had to find out. Carson eyed his bat, measuring it against the depth of the bowl, then eyed the bowl, measuring it against his thirst to know what the hell was going on. He looked back at his bat. The faded Louisville Slugger emblem and every familiar notch brought back a rush of childhood memories. He frowned regretfully.

"Sorry..."

Just as he was drawing back his arm for the thrust, the sound of sharp rapping on the front door glass caught his ear. Faintly, he heard the sound of happy voices and musical laughter.

With a silent oath, Carson disengaged and retreated into the store. It was fifteen minutes before he had finished serving a crowd of late show moviegoers and was able to return to the mess. By then, the toilet was silent and still. The bubbles were gone.

He stood staring into the mess for a long time, so engrossed with the mysteries of the last few days that he paid no heed to the stink. A murdered executive. Disappearing corpses. Indestructible ninjas. Shadowy figures. Veiled threats. Not-so-veiled threats. Toilet phantoms. And through it all ran the ribbons of a frightfully realistic dream - a vision - that had started it all off. He racked his brain, replaying all the events, the conversations, the impressions, weighing them against the dream, struggling to make the pieces fit. But try as he might, they wouldn't. It all ended up looking just like the bathroom. A mess.

Carson thumped the wall in frustration. He couldn't even turn to his friends. They had troubles of their own. Sister Becky was up to her frock in kid issues and hostile priests, Dex had the Fujika scuffle hanging over him, and Kiki... well, no one knew what was up with Kiki. Except too much school. True, she had connections, but... Carson stopped short, struck with sudden inspiration.

Kiki's connections.

The police were out - Parsons had made that painfully clear - and if the law wouldn't help, then he'd have to look elsewhere. And he knew just where to start. Carson rolled up his sleeves.

It took almost four hours of hard work to clean up. Carson kept the mini-mart doors propped open, which helped with the smell but made the heat almost unbearable. Still, he kept his head down and pushed through. By then, his shift was almost over. He had just enough time to hang an out of order sign on the restroom and call Kinkade to fill him in before the morning guy showed up. Then, it was grab the bus home, snatch a few quick hours of sleep and back to the 24/7 again for a killer turnaround 10am-6pm shift, part of Kinkade's regimen for the night manager spot. At 6:01pm, Carson grabbed a chili dog and hopped the crosstown bus, getting off curbside at the spacious, sprawling campus of Las Calamas Community College.

Carson stood on the sidewalk for a moment, taking in the well manicured lawns, ivy-covered brick buildings, stately clock tower, scattered groups of co-eds. As he'd told Dex, Carson hadn't the faintest idea of how to contact Kiki. He had known her for over a year now and had never called, written, emailed or texted her - or had to. She had always just *been* there. *Well...* he squared his shoulders. He may not know where to *call* her, but he was sure of where to *find* her. Here. Somewhere. He set out purposefully toward the nearest building.

Unfortunately, by the time he found the registration desk, it had cleared out for the day. Carson was left wandering the grounds, poking his head into classrooms, mostly empty by this time, hoping for a stroke of blind luck. Hours crawled by. At last, frustrated, dejected and overheated, he slumped onto a bench by a gurgling little fountain that did absolutely nothing to buoy his mood. Carson sat in the heat, feeling the sweat trickle down his face and the back of his khaki shorts, watching people go by. It was then he realized that, in the rush and hurry of the day, he had forgotten to change his shoes.

"Perfect," he muttered. "Just perfect."

The sun had just set, and he was beginning to question the sanity of his plan, when he finally, miraculously, spotted a welcome sight - a familiar red stocking cap bobbing across the lawn. Carson lurched to his feet and sprinted for it, half expecting it to be a mirage brought on by heat stroke. It wasn't. It was Kiki.

He caught her just as she hit the bus stop at the edge of campus. "Pardon me miss... I'm late for my embalming class, do you have a few empty jars I could borrow?"

She half-turned. "Hunh?" She stopped, stared. At first, it seemed like she didn't recognize him. She blinked her blue eyes. Carson noted the tightness of her face, the shadows under those eyes.

"Carson?"

"Ta-daaa...!" He grinned his crooked grin.

A smile teased Kiki's face. "What...?" Then it faded, and she looked suddenly self-conscious, staring over his shoulder, glancing about, clutching her pack. "Right! Sorry. About the... I don't usually see you outside the... I mean... what are you doing here?!"

 97

Despite her alarm, Carson detected a note of genuine gladness in her voice. Whatever else was going on, she was happy to see him. That was good enough for him.

"Playing Sherlock. Got a second?"

Kiki checked her watch, an action which, by this time, was reflexive. "Yeah, a couple. But only that. What's going on?"

"Let's grab a cool one and I'll fill you in. You look like you could use it..."

A short while later, they were seated in a quiet corner of the college cafe, sipping iced latte's. Kiki, who usually bridled at even the slightest hint of charity, didn't say a word when Carson plunked down his money. He chalked it up to her academic stresses and made a mental note to pay more attention to her. Later. For now, he needed answers, and Kiki was the only way to get them.

"So, that's the short and skinny." Carson wrapped up his tale. He had rushed through a sketchy account of the ninja incident, his run-in with the Shogun and last night's bizarre bathroom situation all in a matter of minutes. While far from complete, Carson was convinced by Kiki's incessant watch checking that it was the only way she'd sit and listen to the whole thing. But she did. And, as sketchy as it was, it was enough to pique her interest.

Kiki leaned back, weary eyes searching the ceiling as if for answers. Carson listened to the happy chatting of a nearby gaggle of students, losing himself in their conversation for a moment, waiting on Kiki to process. He let the cool of the air conditioner wash over him, shivering slightly after his long time sitting in the sun.

When he looked back, her eyes were closed. "Hey... you with me?"

"Hmm? Oh, yeah. I'm with you..." She sat up quickly, covered a yawn. "Weird. Totally weird. So... all this stuff," she propped herself on an elbow, slowly swirled her drink. "You think it's related?"

"Maybe. Maybe not. All I know for sure is that it's bugging the crap out of me. So, I'm sorry to play stalker and all, but I didn't know how else to get ahold of you. Here's the bottom line: I need help."

"Nothing new there." She managed a peekaboo smile. "What can I do?"

"I need information. Information I can't get from Wikipedia... or any other pedias for that matter."

"I'm listening."

"Last time I was in a jam, you got me some intel. Said you had

 98

connections. Look, I hate to ask, but I'm going nuts here." He paused, leaned in. "You still have those connections?"

"I do."

"Can I borrow them?"

"They don't play well with others."

"I'll take my chances."

Kiki stared at him. Carson knew she was resisting the urge to look at her watch. Her blue eyes, usually sharp and clear, seemed cloudy and dull. Something flickered in their depths. A glimmer of the old Kiki. "Tell you what. Let's go talk to Leet."

"Leet?"

"As in 'L-3-3-T'. As in 'elite'. As in..."

"Yeah, Leetspeak. I know it. Dude sounds hard core... or like C3PO's twin brother. He isn't some artificial intelligence computer brain thing is he?"

"Sometimes I wonder. But he eats junk food and has bad breath, so if he is, it's a damn fine job."

"Good enough for me."

"Plus, he's on campus. Dorms. Right across from Anthon Hall."

"Even better. Think he can help?"

"Well, he's not a plumber, so you're on your own with the Mystery of the Clattering Toilet. But he's dangerously savvy with the tech, has an expensive rig and fewer scruples than Paris Hilton. If anyone can dig up some dirt on Fujikacorp, I'd say he's your man."

"Awesome! You had me at bad breath." Carson knocked back the rest of his espresso. "Ooo... cold. Still very cold." He pressed a hand to his forehead. "Ow. Yeah, that's a good one. Okay, let's scoot!"

"Hey, Carson..." Kiki reached out suddenly and touched his hand. He hovered for a moment, half out of his seat. She never touched him. Or anyone. Her fingers were cool, almost cold, strong, supple but well calloused. And, ever so slightly... trembling.

He sat down again. "What's up?"

She took her hand back quickly, stared at her coffee. When she spoke, her voice was small. "I'm sorry."

"For what?"

"For turning you into a stalker. For standing you up at the beach. For... for not being there when... when you need me."

"Hey, no worries. School sucks. Everyone knows that."

"Yeah. That's the truth." She flashed a tight smile, eyes dipping again. When she lifted them, there was something new there, some

 99

truth looking for a way out. She hesitated, weighing something.

"You know, I..." Her voice weakened, trailed off.

Carson waited. "Yeah?"

"I... I think we should grab a bite sometime. Dinner. To make up for the beach. And everything. Catch up, you know? Like this." She waved to indicate the cafeteria and the moment. "I miss this. I miss... Freezies." She sighed, and Carson knew with that breath that she hadn't let out the something that had been inside.

He smiled anyway. "You bet. Dinner. Sounds like fun."

"And one more thing... are you *sure* you want to do this?"

"Do what?"

"Get involved. After last time... well, wasn't that enough for you?"

"Listen, K - I don't know why this is happening again, and I sure as biscuits didn't ask for it," Carson's tone was matter of fact. "But something hellastrange is going on here, and the plain fact is no one's doing squat about it. A dude is dead. I can't walk away from that." He paused. "I won't."

Kiki nodded, gave him a tired but understanding smile. Then, she wrinkled her nose. "Whoa... what's that smell?"

"It's me, actually."

"It smells like..."

"Yes. I know."

She glanced at his feet. "Is it your..."

"Yes. Yes it is."

"Did you..."

"Yes. Yes I did. Trust me - when I say I've stepped in something deep... I mean it."

"Alright, then. Let's go find out what stinks."

Five minutes later, they were standing in front of a door on the second floor of the dorms. The hallway was clean and tidy, and the drone of several TV's filtered into it. A girl in sweats wandered past, chatting on a smart phone and sipping a cup of microwave soup.

"Hm." Carson glanced about. "Very... hrm... what's the word... normal."

"It's a dorm."

"Yeah, but... your hacker mastermind lives *here*? Not exactly what I expected."

Kiki rapped on the door. "It's me, Leet," she called. "Open up." She glanced at Carson, noted a look of slight disappointment. "What?"

"Nothing. Just... that's it? 'It's me, Leet, open up?' This guy's a

 100

criminal contact... I just expected a code word, maybe. Secret knock at least. How does he know we're not cops?"

Kiki turned back to the door. "And put on some pants!" She looked back at Carson inquiringly.

"Cops would want him to wear pants, too."

The door jerked open. Framed in the doorway was a short, skinny kid in his late teens, with plaid cargo shorts and a black T-shirt that proclaimed *I'M SMARTER THAN YOU.* His hair was shoulder length, black and kinky, eyes sharp and alert behind the lenses of designer frames. His nose was a little large, but he otherwise looked like a fairly normal college kid - a mix of Geek Elite and couch potato. Sounds of gunfire and screams echoed from inside, spilling out around him.

"Kiki! Hey, girl! I didn't think you were..." His voice trailed off, a look of pleasant surprise melting as he caught sight of Carson. "Who's the stiff?"

"A client. Maybe. Can I come in? It's hot out here." She brushed past him into the room.

"You bet. Always a pleasure to welcome the Master-Babe into my boudoir." He promptly closed the door in Carson's face.

"Him too, Leet," came her muffled voice.

The door opened a crack. Leet shot him a critical look. "Don't touch anything." The door opened another crack, and Carson squeezed through. The room beyond was small and comfortably cluttered, well stocked with Lego models, blue-ray discs, comics, Battlestar Galactica action figures and a treasure trove of other über nerd kitsch. Posters of superhero movies and unknown alternative bands covered the walls, some autographed.

Carson glanced back as Leet closed the door and slouched past him. "No lock? I thought you were... you know..."

"I am. And if I was sloppy enough to get caught, I'd get a lock." Leet crossed the room and flopped into a leather desk chair. Behind him, a jumbo widescreen monitor danced and jabbered, parading the images of a bombed out Third World marketplace and soldiers in camo blasting away at each other. Screams and more explosions rocked the room, rumbled the floor. An impressive cluster of computer hardware whirred and flashed blue LED's and made Carson glad he wasn't epileptic.

Kiki stood by an overstuffed couch. "Sorry to break in. You wanna finish that?" She indicated the game behind him.

"No worries. I got a 'bot on it. Just schoolin' some newbs... and

my baby doesn't need me for that, do you baby?" He turned and patted his computer affectionately, then watched as a line of vehement text scrolled across the bottom of the screen. "Ooo... boo-hoo... QQ more, newb." He reached over and switched off the screen. "So what's up, chica? Didn't expect to see you here. Take a load off and tell me your life story. You can lie on the bed if you want... I'll even let you pick the side." He smiled coyly and gave her an exaggerated wink. Carson rolled his eyes.

"Can't Leet," she shook her head. "Gotta get. Places to be, you know. Just wanted to bring my friend by. Carson, Leet. Leet, Carson. This is the guy from last time."

"Oo, yeah. The freebie - charity case. All the crazy bodies over in Belfry. Fun. Another cop job?" His eyes glinted eagerly.

"'Fraid not. This one's Corporate. Should be a kick, though. I'll let Carson give you the details." Kiki shouldered her pack and turned for the door. "Be good to him, Leet."

"Uh..." Carson fidgeted, displeased with Kiki's sudden departure. He shot a look at Leet's sour face and realized it was a feeling they shared. "You mean you're...?"

"I've gotta go, Carson. I'm late as it is. But look... I'll be in touch. I'll give you a call soon. Promise." She flashed a smile, weary but genuine, shrugged deeper into her pack and trudged out the door. It closed with a thump.

"Okay. Well. Bye then." Carson nodded at the closed door. An awkward silence settled on the room. Leet was staring at him like he was a baby someone had just dropped off on his doorstep.

"So," Carson clapped his hands. "You're a criminal contact."

"Not according to my police record."

"Right. Gotcha. So... you're what then... a hacker?"

"Cracker. Although, I wouldn't expect you to know the difference. Or much else."

Carson nodded, still staring.

"Do you have a mental problem?"

"No, it's just that... you're not what I expected. I thought you'd be... taller. I guess. Or at least have a tattoo. Or at least be old enough to vote. Are you old enough to vote?"

"Are we gonna do this crack or should I just freeze your bank account?"

"Yeah. Right. So... how exactly does this work?"

"First," Leet said it slowly, as if explaining to a child. "You tell me what you want."

"Information."

Leet tossed him a phone book "Done."

"No, no..." Carson tried again "There's a corporation in town. Fujikacorp."

Leet hesitated, his next wisecrack hovering. "I've heard of them." A faint glimmer stirred in his eyes.

"I need you to dig."

"How deep?"

"As deep as you can go."

"That's a big target. Corp that size, there's a lotta dirt to dig in. What am I looking for?"

Carson considered. He hadn't thought of that. "Missing persons," he decided. "And... um... recent employee shakeups. Firings, lawsuits... any kind of trouble or anything out of the ordinary. And..." he hesitated. "Anything to do with ninjas."

Instead of laughing at him, Leet leaned in slightly. "Ninjas? What's going on over there?" His fingers started drumming on the arm of his chair. His eyes were shiny.

Carson felt the nibble. Time to set the hook. He looked around carefully, lowered his voice. "That's what we're gonna to find out. Better cover your tracks, too. There's at least one dead body so far. Whatever's going on, it's big." Although he was playing for effect, Carson realized with a sudden electric jolt that everything he said was true. Something very big *was* going on. Very big and very dangerous.

"Alright. I'll dig. But Fujikacorp is a pretty big haystack."

Carson pondered some more. "Start with the twenty-fifth floor."

Leet eyed him skeptically, read the look on his face and shrugged. "Better than nothing."

"Super. Let me know if - when - you find something. Let me give you my..."

"Not so fast. Now we talk price."

"Price?"

"Listen, Charity - Kiki gets her favors gratis. Professional courtesy. She's helped me with some cracks that'd make your head spin. But this time... it's just you and me. So we deal. What are you putting on the table?"

Carson felt in his empty pockets, thought of his empty bank account. "I'd give you my bus fare, but then I'd have to sleep here tonight, and I don't think that's high on anyone's list."

"Agreed." Leet eyed him shrewdly. "But I got a better idea. You work at that mini-mart, right?"

"The 24/7. Yeah."

"You, uh..." Leet licked his lips. "You got Yoo-hoo?"

"What self-respecting mini-mart doesn't?"

"Banana?" It was almost a whisper.

"Cases of it."

"Then, Charity..." Leet sunk back in his chair, fingers steepled in front of a smug smile. He looked like a 19-year-old supervillain in shorts and a t-shirt. "You got yourself a cracker."

Carson hopped the next bus back to Belfry and did some hard thinking on the way. It had been a good day. The best in a long time. He and Kiki were building bridges, there was a glimmer of hope on the Fujikacorp mystery, and the bomb still hadn't dropped on Dex's parking lot scuffle. Even better, when he arrived at the 24/7, it didn't smell like a field trip to the local sewer. The out of order sign was still up on the restroom, and car air fresheners were hung about the store like ornaments on a white trash Christmas tree, but that was the worst of it. The only thing wrong with the day now, as far as Carson was concerned, was the fact that his shoes still stunk. That he could live with.

As he started his shift, he began a happy little whistle. He was still whistling forty-five minutes later when Kinkade strolled briskly through the front door.

"Good evening, Dudley."

"Hey, Mr. Kinkade. Still hot out there?"

Kinkade looked slightly puzzled by the question, as if it had never occurred to him to be affected by something as trivial as the weather. "I suppose it is. Are you ready?"

"Er... ready for...?"

"The alley inspection."

The whistle died. "Umm..."

"You do recall the milestone?"

"Hm? Oh, yeah! Heck yeah! It's just... well... you see... the toilet thing... I had to clean..."

"It's been a week, Dudley. Have you been cleaning the toilet for a week?" It wasn't a joke. With Kinkade, it was never a joke.

Carson laughed anyway, overloud and overlong, racked his brain for a way out. "Ha! Ha ha! No, Mr. Kinkade. Ross. Mr.... I haven't been cleaning the toilet for a week. A week! Imagine! Ha ha...! Just last night, is all. Or this morning, actually. Anytime after midnight is... is morning. Gee, it took awhile. Man, you should've seen it! Reminds me of the time I..."

"I'm a busy man, Dudley. I have a schedule to keep." Kinkade glanced at his tablet, tapped once, glanced back at Carson. "Judging from your behavior so far, you would do well to develop one yourself, as well as a way to manage it. One of these would do you some good." He indicated the tablet.

Carson realized one of those would indeed do him some good. He imagined snatching Kinkade's and bashing him over the head with it. That would do him a world of good.

"Yeah. A tablet. Now *that* is a fabulous idea! So, where did you get yours? What's this little button do..."

Kinkade tucked the device protectively under one arm. "Later. I have an inspection to make and I - for one - value my commitments." Kinkade eyed him with a shrewd, penetrating gaze. "I directed you to complete this milestone immediately. Do you think an entire week is insufficient as a hard stop?"

"I'm sure I could answer that if I knew what a hard stop was."

"A deadline, Dudley." Kinkade blinked at him. "Can you manage deadlines? Honor commitments? Follow through? *That's* the kind of person Seven Corporation is looking for."

Carson mumbled a vague affirmation. More to head off any further lecturing than anything else, he turned and led the way to the back door. On the way, he prodded his brain into furious thinking. It would do him no good to bluff, stall or lie. Or even, for that matter, offer legitimate excuses. Kinkade was immune to them all. Carson was caught, pinned and plugged, and there was absolutely no way to get out of it. Now, he was going to pay the price.

Still, there was such a thing as damage control.

"So, anyway, about the alley..." Carson tossed out airily. "It's not exactly what you would call... well, *completely* done. Yet! I mean, it's a start, sure, but you know alleys," he put his hand on the door handle. "You clean 'em up one day, and the next, *bam*! They're just as full of trash and junk as before. Almost like you never cleaned 'em up in the first place." They stood close together by the big metal door, pressed between the returns shelf on one side and the cooler on the other. Carson looked his boss right in the face.

Carson grinned.

Kinkade didn't. "I'm waiting, Dudley."

"Yeah. Sure. Alrighty. Well... here we go then."

Carson braced himself and pushed.

The alley was spotless.

It took Carson just an instant to wipe the look of absolute shock from his face. "Aw, man..." He stooped to pick up a bottle cap, the only piece of debris he could find. "See what I mean? Getting filthy again already. Sorry about that." He put his hands on his hips and surveyed the scene with modest humility.

Inside, his brain was whirling. *How*?! Bathed in the yellow light of a single bulb, the alley practically sparkled. Trash was gone, boxes carted away, garbage cans neatly stacked, pavement swept... it even smelled good. Not *good* good, but certainly not bad, and a whole lot better than before. *But...* h*ow*?! The question reared up again, and he prayed it didn't register on his face. Again, there was no answer. But it didn't matter. Not now. Time for answers later. Now, it was just the miracle he needed.

Kinkade's expression was equally flat. If the condition of the alley surprised him, he was hiding it as well as Carson. "Hm." The noise he made was non-committal He glanced at his tablet, which had been poised and ready for the strike, tapped once and tucked it under his arm. "Satisfactory. You'll relocate those trash receptacles to this side of the alley, of course."

"Of course."

"Very well, then. Now, you can move on to the restroom."

"What?! Er..." Carson bit off the rest of his words. With effort, he wrestled his surprise into submission. "I'm... I'm not sure I follow."

"The restroom. It's a disaster. It happened on your watch, so it's your responsibility. Fix it. Or call someone who can. Management is more than just stocking shelves and using MOLD. Unless, you'd like me to have Stanley handle it..."

"No sir. Not necessary. Not a problem. Fix the restroom. I can do that. Nooooot a problem."

"And there is one additional issue which requires attention." Kinkade was staring at him. Carson could feel the dark, critical eyes. This time, he wasn't trying to hide his emotions. "Ichiro Fujika."

Carson's stomach sank.

Here it came. He turned to face the man, half expecting to be handed a blindfold and a cigarette. "Yes?"

"It has come to my attention that there was an altercation recently between Officer Jackson and Fujikacorp employees. In our parking lot."

Carson kept his expression blank. He wasn't going to give Kinkade any more ammo than he needed. Not that he needed much. "Yes?"

Kinkade waited, bored into him with his eyes, as if daring him to say more. Carson didn't. Kinkade pressed him. "You were involved."

"I was there."

"You were more than just there, Dudley. I saw the video surveillance tape." Kinkade was on the prowl now, like a tiger, ready to pounce and sink his corporate teeth from Section Twelve of the Operations and Procedures Manual right into Carson's jugular. Carson had never seen him like this. It was unsettling. Still, he held his tongue. If the tiger was going to pounce, he wasn't going to poke it first.

When it became apparent that Carson wasn't taking the bait, Kinkade pushed. Again. "As painful as it was to watch your involvement, it was simply an embarrassment to observe Officer Jackson."

That did it. Now there were two birds on the wire. Carson had to do something. "Look... I can explain. There were reasons...."

"I'm sure there were, Dudley. I'm just not interested in them. I'm warning you for the second time - the last time: leave Fujika alone. You're not ready. You'll receive another negative achievement for your involvement in this fiasco. As for Officer Jackson, we won't even bother."

Carson's sinking feeling became a sick one. "What are you saying?"

"Fujikacorp is planning to file charges. I learned of it this morning, never mind how. There is a way, however, that we may be able to lessen the damage. Officer Jackson is a liability to Seven Corporation, true, but only as long as he is employed by us."

Carson gaped. "You're not going to...?!"

"No." Kinkade fixed him with a level gaze. "I'm not."

It took Carson a second. Then it hit him. "What... *me*?! You want *me* to...!"

"Terminate him."

"That's cruel!"

"That's management. You have one week." Kinkade turned his back to Carson and left him gaping in the middle of the alley.

He stood for several moments in the muggy heat and shadows, feeling the blood pounding in his ears. He wanted to throw up.

Fleetingly, he considered quitting - just bulling his way into the store, storming right up to Kinkade and telling him where to stick his negative achievements, maybe knock a few things over. He'd start with the *Twilight* Freezie display. He hated that thing.

After a moment of pleasantly imagining the look on Kinkade's face, he quashed the idea. The look he pictured was wounded and angry, but in reality, it would probably be just as blank as usual. Or maybe with just a hint of smug triumph. Kinkade was showing a little more emotion lately, but it was all negative. Not to mention the fact that he had started referring to Carson simply as "Dudley". Carson didn't take that as a cue that Kinkade was warming to him.

No. He shook his head resolutely. He wouldn't give Kinkade the satisfaction of quitting. He also wouldn't willingly leave the store - *Jack's* store - in Stanley's hands. He couldn't bear the thought. Besides, quitting wouldn't save Dex. Maybe, just maybe, if he stuck it out awhile longer, he could think of a way to save his friend. Somehow.

Carson sighed. He glanced up, noticed the row of containers Kinkade had ordered moved. He sighed again. He had no idea what the hard stop was on moving garbage cans, but he was certain it would be a lot sooner than whatever he decided. Might as well tackle it now. Slowly he trudged across the alley.

"Well, Jack..." Carson muttered. "I hope you're enjoying the surf."

He hefted the first can and hauled it across, sweat starting out on his forehead even with this slight exertion. He wasn't sure if it was the oppressive heat and humidity that were making him feel smothered and breathless, or the tightening noose of Seven Corporation. Still, he hardly felt it - any of it. Mostly he just felt numb. He moved the second can, turned back for the last one.

And someone was there.

Carson froze. He had taken three steps toward the figure before his brain registered that it was there, standing in the deep shadows on the far side of the alley, just out of sight behind the circle of light. Carson had no idea how or where it had come from, but realized with a sudden feeling that made his skin crawl that it had been there for some time.

Watching.

One thing was for certain - he no longer felt numb.

Carson swallowed past a sudden dry lump in his throat. He'd seen two shadowy figures in recent months, one of them in this very alley. Both still woke him up at night in a cold sweat. He checked the door behind him from the corner of his eye, judging the distance. He edged a step closer...

Then a voice. "Hot night."

It was a whisper, drifting out of the shadows like a shred of mist. Carson stopped. He squinted, trying to make out details. There was something about the voice, creepy as it was, that made him want to listen - made him relax, if only just a fraction. Plus, whoever it was, they weren't trying to kill him. Yet.

"Yeah. Also a good night to sneak up on someone in an alley and scare the crap out of them." Carson took a cautious step, trying to get a better angle, catch a glimpse of the speaker. But the figure had placed itself in the perfect location to prevent just that. He caught a glimpse of a worn trench coat but nothing more. At the same time, the figure made a subtle adjustment of its own, just the slightest shift of weight - but it was enough to let Carson know that, if he made any further moves, the interview would be over.

Carson sensed it, stopped. "Sorry. I've had a lot of surprises lately, and none of them have been very good."

"That's an understatement." There was a hint of a smile in the whisper. "A word of advice - not every surprise is bad."

"I'm gonna need some proof on that one."

"The proof is all around you."

Carson glanced about, but all he saw was the alley. "Yeah, well... I guess I need to use a lifeline, cuz I just don't... wait... this was *you*?!"

Silence was his only answer. It was enough.

"I... I don't... who *are* you?!"

"That's not important. What's important is why."

"Okay, then, I'll bite - why?!"

"For Pete."

It was like a bullet between the eyes. Carson stood for a moment. "You... you knew Pete?"

"Yes. And we know what you did for him."

Carson frowned, bitterness and guilt washing over him. "What, got him killed?"

"Pete got himself killed. You got him respect. That's a lot harder to do."

There was a shift of movement in the shadows. The figure edged forward the slightest fraction. Carson could pick out a few more details now - the coat was dirty and threadbare, but worn with a certain amount of style and self respect. Underneath it was a man, not tall, haggard but still somehow noble. Carson had the impression of sloped shoulders, plain features.

"You've got friends, Carson." It wasn't a whisper now, but a voice, soft and reassuring - at least as reassuring as a shadowy figure in a dark alley could be. "Don't forget that."

Carson said nothing. There was nothing to say.

The figure faded back and, for a moment, Carson thought it was gone. Then, suddenly, the whisper again. "One more thing..." Pause. "Tell Kiki... a ghost says, 'hello'."

"You got it. I... hey... wait! Kiki?!"

But this time, the figure really was gone.

Carson realized with a rush that made his head spin that there was a whole lot more going on in this alley, this city, and most likely the world in general than he was even remotely aware of.

CHAPTER SEVEN
The Yoo-hoo Connection

"24/7, Carson speaking."

"Show me the *Yoo-hoo*!"

"Sorry, pal. Only people who get to see that are my doctor and the future Mrs. Dudley." He reached to hang up the phone.

The voice on the line crackled. "Don't flatter yourself, Charity."

Carson paused. "Leet?"

"It's not just a name... it's a lifestyle."

"So did you misdial 1-900, or are you calling to tell me you've got something?"

"They call me 'Leet' for a reason."

"Yes!" Carson fist-pumped madly. "I knew it!! So what is it?! Yakuza... mad science... alien conspiracy?!"

"No way... not over the phone. How soon can you get here?"

"I'm back on swing tonight. Gimme..." Carson checked the clock hungrily. "An hour."

"Fine. And don't forget the stuff."

The line went dead. Carson hung up, lurched out of his stool and started pacing, bouncing like a freckle-faced teen on prom night. It had been a few days since his alley chat with Kinkade, and Carson had come to realize that Leet was his best chance for saving Dex. A half dozen half-baked solutions had popped into his head, but since each one ended up with Kinkade stuffed in a steamer trunk bound for Singapore, they weren't really solutions. His last, wildest hope was to somehow get leverage against Fujikacorp - make them drop the lawsuit. And that's where Leet came in. Too nervous to sit, he started cleaning.

For the next hour, endless theories, suppositions and imaginings chased through his fevered thoughts. Carson struggled to remain calm, mindful of the danger in letting his mind run free. For all he knew, the only thing Leet had found was that the Super Maxi-Pad was going to beat their price on deep fried pork fingers. No sense in getting worked up until he knew more. The seconds ticked by. Slowly. Agonizingly.

Ten minutes before the end of his shift, Carson remembered the Yoo-hoo. There was a full case in the back, and he breathed a sigh of relief... that quickly changed to a groan. The cash was a problem. He was short this month and knew he wouldn't be able to cover it. He stewed for a minute, then grabbed the box and headed for the front. Payday was coming - he'd make it right then. After all, lives were at stake. He would have just enough time to stash it outside, then he could nab it for the bus ride to the dorms. It was a good plan.

It might have worked, too, if he hadn't run straight into Stanley.

Two steps into the parking lot, Carson bashed Yoo-hoo first into the man himself, just as he was stabbing out a cigarette on the Red Box machine.

For a moment, Stanley wore a look of near perfect surprise that was almost as good as Carson's. As his quick dark eyes took in the scene, however, the look slowly shifted into one of smug self-satisfaction. "Thirsty?" he rasped.

Carson managed a tight smile. "Very. So if you'll excuse me, I'll get started on my bender." He edged sideways.

Stanley blocked him casually. "If you're stocking the cooler, it's that way. But I can't imagine why..." He glanced at the label. "Banana Yoo-hoo? Not exactly our biggest seller." He narrowed his eyes shrewdly, pinned Carson to the case like a beetle on a bug board. "Where you headed, pard?"

"Out. And I can see you're going in. Or should be. Lots to do in there, busy night. There's cream cheese poppers thawing out and some brown nosing you forgot to do earlier. Now if you'll excuse me..."

Carson moved again, starting to feel the weight of the case.

Stanley didn't budge, just peered at him with his little piggy eyes. "You know," he drawled. "Watching you sneak out of here with a case of product makes a guy wonder. It looks a little like... what's the word..." His eyes hardened around the smile. "...stealing."

"None of your business," Carson said bluntly. It was the best he could do. His arms were really starting to ache.

"Maybe it's Kinkade's business."

"Maybe Kinkade *told* me to do it." Carson didn't know what made him say it. He immediately regretted it.

Still, the words struck a chord. Stanley's shrewd look became even shrewder. "Kinkade? What's he want with Banana Yoo-hoo?"

"Why don't you ask him yourself..." Carson lifted his chin to indicate something behind Stanley. Stanley turned sharply. As soon as he did, Carson slipped past him, making sure the pointed corner of the box jabbed him in the ribs on the way by. "...when he comes in tomorrow. Nice night. Gotta jam. Don't forget the poppers. *Big* hit with the ladies. Have a few - find that special someone!"

Carson hurried off down the street without risking a backward glance. There was no sense in going back, even though he still had a few minutes left on his shift. He had enough lumps coming already and spending any time with Stanley was likely to add an assault and battery charge to the list.

Carson still hadn't looked back ten minutes later when he was safely aboard the 316 heading for Las Calamas Community College. He was too busy fuming, berating himself. It had been just plain stupid getting caught like that, flat footed with an armful of contraband. It had been even worse tossing Kinkade's name into the mix. Stanley would ask - definitely. Might even have Kinkade on the phone right now...

But that would have to wait. What was done was done. He had to keep his mind on the now. Carson groaned, glared down at the Yoo-hoo on the seat beside him. "You better be worth it," he muttered. For the rest of the ride, it sat beside him like a big yellow box of guilt.

A short time later, he was seated in front of Leet's computer, peering at a widescreen LCD monitor that was bigger than the TV in Carson's apartment. Leet sat beside him, oblivious. He had uncorked a fresh Yoo-hoo without waiting for Carson to put the box down and was sucking at it like a hamster at his bottle. Every time he took a pull, he made a strange moaning sound that Carson found more than faintly disquieting. So far, he had offered no explanation as to what he'd found.

Carson stared at the image on the computer screen, trying to tune out Leet's addiction and make sense of the picture at the same time. Frustration and nerves gnawed at his patience. "Well?" He finally gave up. "What the frack is this?! What am I looking at, Leet? I'm an angry man tonight, and I just might take my Yoo-hoo and go home. Give!"

Leet took another pull on the bottle, dimpling its plastic sides with his gusto. He wiped at his mouth, made his disturbing little noise. "Don't you recognize it?"

Carson squinted. The image was mostly blobs of color, a room of some kind, perhaps storage, maybe a den. Judging from the time counter in the upper left corner, he figured it was a still frame taken from video footage. The camera angle was odd, though, and the aperture small, making the features of the room somewhat distorted and hard to make out.

He tilted his head. Still, it looked familiar...

Carson pulled back, startled by a sudden epiphany. "Dude - that's the *office*. That's *the* office!"

Leet took another pull on the bottle, kicked back in his leather chair. It creaked, echoing his soft moan of ecstasy. "Thought it might ring a bell." He belched softly, made a lazy grin.

Now that he was oriented, Carson's eyes eagerly picked out details. "That's it! Grandma's garters, that's the room. Son of a gun. That's the place where..." He caught himself. "Um... that's the place... where... um... did you get this?"

"A little luck, a little skill. No, scratch that - it was all skill. After I cracked 'em, I dove into the haystack right where you said. Twenty-fifth floor. And there it was - *bam!* Bandwidth." Another big drink. Another moan. Another belch.

"Bandwidth?"

"There was a spike on the switch up there. Not big, but big enough to get my attention. In my experience - which is vast, by the way - big bandwidth points to big secrets. Plus, all the traffic was internal, not from the cloud or some lame WAN connection - not just an intern grabbing the latest *How It Should Have Ended* off YouTube. So, I did some poking around. Deep. Took some real solutioneering, but I cracked it out. Lotta D there. Some real top level cyber-shenanigans. Somebody wanted this kept a secret - real secret, like way beyond WikiLeaks. Course... such are my mad skills, Fujikacorp didn't stand a chance." Leet was so engrossed in recalling his brilliance that he had momentarily neglected his Yoo-hoo. He noticed it in his hand again and lifted it passionately to his lips. The bottle, however, was empty. He rattled the dregs with disappointment.

Carson tossed him a fresh one. "You've earned it. So..." He turned back to the screen. "You've got the room. That's a 9.5 from the American judge. Now tell me what..."

Leet lifted a finger for silence. He tapped a key on the keyboard. The digital timer on the image started ticking. The film was rolling.

"Quarter impulse, Ensign Charity. We'll get there." Leet kept his eyes glued on the timer. "Wait for it... now."

A man entered the picture. A neatly dressed Asian with a dark suit and a broad face sprinkled with pock marks. It was the man from the room.

The dead one.

Carson's jaw dropped. "That's him," he whispered. It was strange, awesome almost, seeing a man alive whom he had only before seen dead. Like reality backwards. But there he was: moving, sorting papers, flipping through books, jotting notes, sipping tea. Carson watched, enthralled. It was eery, like watching a ghost. Eery, and somewhat disorienting, especially with the awkward point of view.

Carson tilted his head, frustrated, trying to get a better angle. "What's with the camera? How come it's so..."

"Janked? I know. Great feed: super expensive, top quality, all HD. Motion activated, too, auto track and zoom. Slick. But bizarre placement. Why? In my experience - which, again, is so exceedingly vast it's sick - the only reason you stick a bling camera in a place like that is cuz you don't... want... someone... to see it." He arched his eyebrows meaningfully.

Carson pondered. "They spy on their own people?"

"They spied on this guy. There's hours of this stuff. Days." Leet reached over lazily and tapped a key, sending the replay into fast forward. The exec was a blur as he repeatedly moved, sorted, flipped, jotted and sipped almost faster than the eye could follow. The time counter spun crazily, ticking off hours, days.

"No one else came in," Carson murmured as he watched the replay. "No one called. Stopped by. Just him." He stared, wide eyes reflecting the images on the screen, not blinking, absorbing.

"Yeah. And get this - that ain't even his office..." Leet reached toward his desk but stayed rooted in his seat, as unwilling to separate himself from the case of Yoo-hoo as Carson was from the video. He

 115

scrabbled, snagged a piece of paper, flipped it to Carson. "Dude doesn't even work on that floor."

Carson stared at the paper which contained a photo of the dour, pock-marked executive beside a laundry list of employee data. "'Haruki Nubuyuki'," he read. "Sales division. Senior management. Years of service, all good. Lots of acronyms and commendations, I don't understand, educational stuff, blah blah blah. Hm." Carson scratched his chin beard. "You're right. He's supposed to be up on thirty - top floor. Wonder what he was working on here?"

"Beats me. But whatever it was, it was off the books. This office is unassigned. Officially unused - not even in the corporate directory. Even weirder - check out the timestamp," he waved his bottle at the screen. "Dude was always there *after* hours. And always alone. No secretary, no Domino's guy, no hotty little Asian mistress," Leet looked slightly disappointed. "Anyway," he swallowed a mouthful of banana, shrugged. "Whatever it was, he wasn't trying to put the 'I' in T-E-A-M. This kind of solo stuff - I'm guessing corporate espionage. From my experience, which as I might have mentioned..."

"Is vast, yup. Like the ocean. Got it. You think he was dirty?"

Another swallow, another shrug. "Top brass probably did. That's why they set up this surveillance, I'm guessing. Ran it until they had enough to bury the guy. Which must, by the way, have been recently. The footage stops last week."

"Stops? Er..." Carson tried to look only mildly curious. "With what?" He knew the answer already, and judging by the fact that Leet hadn't left the state; he was pretty sure it wasn't on the tape. But he had to be sure. If only there was *something*...

"Nothing. Just stops. One day it's business as usual, then zilch. Done. End of story."

Carson's hopes fell. That meant no record of the attack, the ninja, the murder. Nothing to show Parsons, nothing to back up his story, nothing to get Dex off the hook. He had to keep digging.

"This footage - the surveillance - who made it?"

Leet pursed his lips, ran a finger thoughtfully along the rim of a fresh bottle of Yoo-hoo. Carson hadn't noticed him kill the second or open the third. "That's a little jank too." He stared at the ceiling. "It wasn't stored in any of their main archives. Or backup archives. Or any archives. This little baby was tucked away in a sweetspot - the kind of spot somebody stashes something they don't want found. Ever. Could've been Fujikacorp security, sure. But it could've been somebody else too. Even from outside. I've seen it before - crack in, set up your cams, find a place to stash the vid without drawing eyes..." He shrugged again. "Hard to say."

Carson glanced back at the screen, watched the images still blurring past. After a moment, the feed hit the end and stopped. It froze on an image of Haruki Nubuyuki sitting at his desk, bent low over a book, his face wearing an inscrutable look.

And now he was dead.

Carson shivered.

"Anyway," Leet tossed his empty bottle at the trash, looking for a three point shot. It missed, but he didn't seem to care. His speech was slightly slurred. "That's it for Haruki Nubuyuki. He's no longer on the payroll here in LC, and his office - his real office - has another stuffed shirt in it already. They must've slapped his hand for whatever he was doing and sent him home in disgrace. Lost his face, or whatever. I dug up some travel docs from their AP with his name on 'em - looks like they put him on a plane back to Japan. I'm guessing in coach."

Or in a box, Carson thought. He remembered Fujika's commentary on corpses: *"...they are easy to hide."* He shivered again, looked away from the screen, away from the empty, haunting eyes of the exec.

As he did, a flash of green caught his eye. He looked back, focused on the tiny wedge of color. Carson squinted. It was a file folder, lying open on the desk close to Nubuyuki's hand. As he stared, he half-remembered glimpses of the folder throughout the high speed review: always there, always close at hand. There was something about the folder - the way Nubuyuki kept it close - something important. And now it lay before Carson, just an image on the screen, its contents agonizingly beyond his reach. He could, however, almost make out the writing on the folder's tab.

"Hey," Carson scooted closer. "Can you zoom on that?"

"What?"

"That, right there..." Carson pointed. "The folder."

Leet tapped some keys, jerked a selection box with his mouse. The folder loomed, filled the screen.

"Hm. Looks like... what does that say... Ashes... Ouchies..."

"'Ashi,','" Carson read. "'Ashi Keiyaki'." He blinked, stared at the name. "Who the freak is that? Do they work at Fujikacorp?"

Leet had the hook in his mouth, already working. He brought up a document on a second monitor and entered a search. They waited, watched a blue progress bar crawl agonizingly across the screen. A minute later an empty box appeared, apologized for finding nothing and politely asked if they'd like to change their search terms. Leet did, several times. Again, nothing.

"Nope. Negative." Leet tapped a few more keys. "And apparently, they never did. I don't show any record of anyone with that name ever working for the corp. Maybe Haruki was trying to track down his high school sweetheart," he lounged back. "Or write a musical. You know, get outta the corporate rat race and make it big on Japanese Broadway. Could just be a catchy title. Beats me." He took another big swallow of Yoo-hoo.

Carson could tell that, in spite of his nonchalance, Leet was as intrigued as he was. Unfortunately for both of them, the folder was a dead end. Still no help. "So. Put a pin in that one. What else do you have on Nubuyuki?"

"More dirt, coming up," Leet pulled up new documents. "Already been digging - figured you'd ask. So, let's see... first off, our boy's been busy. And this is on regular company time, mind you, not just behind the scenes in his secret office wonderland. He's quite the rabble rouser, too. A real thorn in the ol' CEO backside."

"CEO... you mean Fujika? Ichiro Fujika?"

"That's the guy. And they do *not* play well together. Nubuyuki was riding the boss pretty hard - questioning decisions, raising Cain in staff meetings, sending nasty emails. Enough to get himself a couple of official wrist slaps: a reprimand, two disciplinary actions and a few... uh... what did they call 'em..." Leet clicked, flicked screens. "...negative achievements."

"I like him already," Carson nodded. "So you said he was questioning Fujika's decisions... what kind of decisions?"

"Investments, mostly. Dude filed lots of paperwork on 'em, trying to get the chief in hot water - misappropriation of funds, questionable business practices, yadda yadda. Never went anywhere, though. Fujika squashed 'em. Hard. Great reading, though. Lotta read-between-the-lines drama. I've got one here," Leet slid a document bearing the Fujikacorp letterhead out of an expensive looking envelope.

Carson blinked. "That's... how did you...?"

"Had his secretary mail it to me. Or at least 'Nubuyuki' did," Leet put quotations around the name with his fingers. "She'll be darned if she can find that email now, though." He grinned.

Carson didn't. "I thought I said..."

"Relax, Charity. I covered my tracks. Just wanted to see if I could get away with it."

Carson glanced over the paper. It looked official enough. "What's this?" He ran a finger along one edge. It showed a brownish discoloration and some crackling. "Looks like it's been pried off the bottom of a trash can."

"Beats me. Maybe that's how they save money. Corps are weird."

Carson handed the document back. "Anything else?"

"Yes. He's pretty good at golf. Decent handicap. Likes his *sake*, too, judging from his credit card statements. And he had a bug problem. Had his office fumigated twice this year. Man, that makes me thirsty. Hit me, will ya?"

Carson tossed him a fresh bottle of Yoo-hoo. He had lost count of the number. "Alright, so they didn't get along. And Nubuyuki was doing something on the side - something sketchy. But Fujika may have something to hide." He shook his head, feeling slightly dizzy. "Or the other way around." Even dizzier. Carson puzzled for a moment longer but came up blank. "I give up. What the frack does it mean?"

"It means I'm getting sick on Yoo-hoo tonight." Leet popped the top and dumped half the bottle down his pipes. He smacked his lips, sighed lustily. "Reeeaaaaal sick..."

Carson left shortly after. He had no real desire to see Leet fulfill his plan and plenty to think about. His head was buzzing the whole bus ride home and during a quick bite of dinner with Granny. He was so preoccupied he almost forgot to snag a plate of her Heaven's Gate double-chocolate-peanut-butter cookies with chocolate and peanut butter chips. As he munched through his third one, the buzzing hadn't settled into any coherent theory.

Fujika had a beef with Nubuyuki. Given. But it wasn't enough to kill him. Or was it? Carson's knowledge of Eastern culture was restricted to *Kung Fu* re-runs and a handful of Bruce Lee films. While entertaining, *Enter the Dragon* was hardly the framework on which to build a case for corporate intrigue and assassination.

Haruki Nubuyuki.

Ashi Keiyaki.

Ninjas.

Phantoms in the toilet.

Ghosts in the alley.

Not to mention, night manager training and the ongoing mystery of the new till procedures. As he tucked himself into bed that night, Carson realized he had, as usual, far more questions than answers.

The next evening he was back to graveyard and pondering the exact same issues. Things were slow, largely due to the heat, which had continued to rise and was leaving record after record shattered in its wake. Kinkade's policy of raising the temperature on the AC continued in the face of all reason, driving away even more customers and even a few employees. Carson had resisted the urge to jack it back down, knowing in the very center of his being that Kinkade would walk through the door the second he touched the dial. He had, however, dared to strip off his regulation 24/7 uniform shirt. It was a little thing, but it made him feel better.

Now Carson sat brooding in a wife beater and jeans, a half-eaten double-fried cheesy burrito and a Freezie next to him on the counter. He hadn't had the appetite or the interest to finish. A fat black fly had, however, and was buzzing hungrily about the leftovers. Carson swatted it away absently.

He shifted on the stool, knowing he should be studying the Operations and Procedures Manual that his feet were currently propped on, but he was just too hot and preoccupied to care. He wished Kiki were back in the game, or that Sister Becky was around, or even that he could trust Josh enough to pull him into the loop. Even Dex was on his weekend and wouldn't be back for another two days. Besides... he felt his stomach churn unpleasantly. He and Dex had other business.

The fly buzzed in for another look, and he waved it off again, a little more vigorously. Carson watched it circle for a moment - lazy, annoying, without a care in the world. It irked him. Absently, he took the employee manual from under his feet, rolled it into a fat tight tube. He had just thought of an even better use for it. As if reading his mind, the insect veered away from him, buzzed out into the mini-mart. Carson settled back. He could wait.

His thoughts returned to Dex and the impending altercation which, if it didn't ruin their friendship, would certainly ruin Dex's career. The big guy had said it himself - all he had left was the 24/7. Carson growled. He hated Kinkade.

Thoughts of the man brought a recollection of the latest in his list of degrading assignments: the bathroom. Carson groaned, then sighed. At the least - the *very* least - it was something he could tackle. As he tried to summon enough strength to reach for the yellow pages, the fly was back, buzzing around in his peripheral vision, hovering over the food. His eyes narrowed. But first...

Slowly, very slowly, Carson lifted his makeshift fly swatter. He took aim, waited, watching from the corner of his eye. Then... *whap!* The manual came down with a thud, and the buzzing stopped short. The crunch meant there would be something to clean off the counter - but at least it was gone. He left the manual where it was and reached wearily for the phone book.

Buuuzzzuuuzzzuuzz...

Carson stopped, cocked his head. *Another* fly? He glanced back at the manual. The muffled buzz came from underneath. No. Same one.

"Super fly," Carson muttered. He lifted the book, intent on giving the thing another good smack... and out it flew, fat, black and shiny as if it hadn't just been tagged by five pounds of corporate how-to's. He eyed the insect in disbelief. It buzzed into the air, swung lazily toward his burrito, then seemed to reconsider. Like it was no longer interested. It hovered for a moment, dropped a foot, then came back up. It veered, hovered, came about... then buzzed, slowly, straight toward him.

Buuuzzzuuuzzzuuzz...

Carson watched it coming. "Changed your mind on the burrito, huh? Can't say I blame you."

The buzz sounded strange. He squinted at the little speck. It was even flying strange. Like it was in slow motion. And it came in a straight line, no wandering, no weaving, no trademark insect flight path. As it loomed closer, he leaned in for a good look... and wondered, in fact, how it was flying at all. The insect was in bad shape. Critical condition. Terminal, in fact. Fat black body crushed, fluids oozing out, one wing bent at right angles, several legs broken or just missing entirely.

"Cheese and crackers," Carson murmured in awe. "I thought I was having a bad week."

And then something long and black snagged it out of the air with a wet slap and sucked it back, and it was gone.

Carson snapped his head sideways and looked full into the milky white eyes of the fattest, nastiest, deadest looking toad he had ever seen. The thing squatted on the counter like roadkill in a hillbilly diner, a foot from his elbow, squirming with maggots and awash in a stink straight from the pits of hell.

"*MOTHER PUSS BUCKET!!!!*" Carson went down with a crash in a tangle of legs and stool, piling into a cardboard box of novelty straws that exploded everywhere. He scrabbled frantically away, slipping and sliding on cardboard and plastic as the thing regarded him with it's baleful dead eyes, two fat pearls in a bowl of rotten green jello.

 121

"Eeeriiiibibibiit."

Then it turned about with an awkward shuffle and leapt off the counter into the store and was gone. Seconds later, Carson was on his feet and clawing for his bat. Vaulting the counter, he set off in hot pursuit. Somewhere in the back of his mind, Carson knew just how reckless, stupid and dangerous it was to chase the thing; knew that he was being swept along by waves of blind panic and not reason. But he also knew something else: he had finally found something he could hit. It was fight or flight, and fight was winning by a landslide.

Carson tore off in the direction the creature had disappeared, heart hammering, sneakers pounding. Too fast. He reached a corner and failed to stop, slipped in a goo trail and skidded into a stack of breakfast cereals. They went down together with a tremendous crash.

Carson kicked free, leapt to his feet, glanced around wildly. He spotted the thing just as it disappeared around a corner, dragging a bent and broken hind leg that showed exposed bone. It moved with an awkward hop-drag, but was still fast - faster than he would have thought possible. Carson gave mad chase.

He skidded around the next corner, slid to a halt, eyes darting again. It was gone. He picked a direction, ran a few steps, stopped, listened hard. Nothing. He ran back, dropped to the floor and checked under shelves, frantically swiping product off with his bat to get a clear view. Still nothing. He stood, eyes wild. On impulse, he sniffed. Hard.

It stunk.

He sniffed right. Same. Left. A little worse? Galvanized, he set off at a run, slid to a halt, sniffed again. Gag reflex. Right track. A few more steps, stop, sniff and listen.

"Eeeriiiibibibiit."

Bingo.

This time he set off at a trot, bat low. He was close. If he could only... up ahead, he caught a glimpse of movement. The restroom door just swinging closed.

The truth hit him hard and fast. The toilet phantom. The bubbles in the bowl. This was his visitor from last week, he knew it instinctively. And it was heading home.

Carson launched himself forward with reckless abandon, caromed off the coffee bar, almost vaulted a display of Sweetie Pies, sending brightly colored cartons flying. He stumbled into the door at full speed, crashed through without slowing, hit the broken tiles, now once more slick with slime, and went sliding out of control straight past the stall door and slammed into the wall. Sneakers squeaked as he backpedaled, arms windmilling.   From inside the stall, he caught the sound of porcelain clanking.

"Eeeriiiibibibiit."

Carson seized the stall door, yanked it open and wrenched himself through. A foot slipped and he pitched sideways into the metal frame, banging his elbow painfully and sending sparks shooting through his arm. He hardly felt it. Inside, the toad thing squatted on top of the tank, staring at him with its dead white eyes. The lid was up. It had a clear shot at the murky brown, and it was ready to go. Pulpy legs gathered for a leap.

It leapt.

With furious effort Carson shoved himself off the wall, lunged forward and swung with all his might. A frantic, ragged, wordless shout tore from his lips and everything slipped into slow motion. The toad hung suspended for a fraction of a second like a grotesque, hideous, pustulent balloon. The bat swept toward it. The thing tilted forward, head down, plunging for the bowl...

But it was a split second too late.

Carson's Louisville Slugger caught the beast full on and, with a meaty wet *smack!,* sent it flying across the stall where it hit like a grocery bag full of rancid meat. The impact dented the metal and left a stain that would be difficult to clean without a hazmat license and a lot of patience. The mash of flesh stuck for a second, then slid slowly downward like a child's splat ball, leaving a trail of sticky black and green. When it reached the bottom, it dropped to the floor with a *plop*.

It lay still.

Carson stared, eyes wild, heart like a jackhammer, sucking air and trying to keep his half of the burrito down. Tingles of fire shot through his arm, but they barely registered. He collapsed against the stall and stared at the thing, dizzy. It lay unmoving. Horrendous.   An aberration. Almost as disgusting in death as it had been in life.

Life?!

Carson shook his head, momentarily overwhelmed with horror and revulsion. How could this *thing* ever have been considered alive? Its flesh hung in ghastly folds, patchy and gaping and showing internal organs, bones and various colors of leaking goo. One of its awful eyes had burst, but the other still pointed up at him, glassy and distended. And most of that had been *before* he hit it.

Buuuzzzuuuzzzuuzz...

"You gotta be kidding me..."

Numbly, Carson's eyes sought out the black tongue, six inches of which lolled on the floor beside the corpse, fearing what he would see. He was right. Undaunted by recent events, the fly was still twitching, struggling to pull itself free from the sticky mucous of the frog's tongue. It was still moving. Still alive. Carson's skin crawled. A cold sweat started out on his body.

It was happening again.

He'd had a vague, nagging feeling for days, but here, at last, was the proof. Carson forced himself to look at the toad, forced his mind to push through his revulsion and terror and to start working. He didn't know what this thing was - didn't have the faintest, foggiest, freakingest clue - but it was supernatural nasty, that was for sure. And if there was one person who knew supernatural nasty... ready or not, his favorite nun was about to get a visit from her favorite visionary.

Buuuzzzuuuzzzuuzz...

But first things first. Carson stepped forward with a set jaw and brought his shoe down on the squirming, struggling, terrible fly.

It crunched.

Buuuzzzuu...

Carson ground his foot. This time, when the buzzing stopped, it didn't start again.

The rest of his shift passed in a blur of cleaning and sanitizing, and it was early afternoon the following day before Carson had time to collect his thoughts. He had made up his mind to take the corpse to Sister Becky ASAP, and that was precisely what he had done. He sat now in the austere but tasteful waiting room of the child care wing at St. Timothy's Sacred Heart Cathedral. The sign over his head read *Little Angels' Clubhouse.* In spite of everything, it still made him smile.

Carson sat quietly with a plastic garbage bag on his lap and tried to keep from yawning. It had been a long, sleepless night. He had kept the freak toad under his bed, tightly secured by a plastic garbage bag and plenty of duct tape. Although he had thought it would help him rest easier having the thing close, he found it quite the opposite. He had lain awake most of the night, alert to even the slightest noise.

The smell hadn't helped either.

Overall, he rationalized, he should have been getting used to terrible odors. But the fact was, it just wasn't the kind of odor you got used to. Out of frustration and exhaustion, after tossing and turning for hours, he had emptied an entire bottle of Granny's Febreze on the thing to try and kill the stink. He could smell it now, wafting up from his lap like the freshest, cleanest, most flowery stench of death he had ever smelled. He wrinkled his nose and tried to think of something else.

Something slammed into the wall behind him, and he would have jumped if he hadn't been so tired... plus, since it happened every few minutes, he had become accustomed to it. The screaming and shouting of children followed the impact, sweeping off in a thunder of rushing feet. The commotion was raucous and unsettling, as if all three rings of a three ring circus had gone mad, and the ringmaster had fled the tent. Carson had heard Sister Becky talk about Father Black, and his intentions to crush her spirit, but had largely laughed them off. Now, sitting here in the middle of it all, he wasn't laughing. What was going down on the other side of that wall could only be described as chaos.

Carson had passed the time fitfully, impatiently, skimming the various announcements on the bulletin board, counting floor tiles and staring out the window at a Japanese tourist who was avidly snapping pictures of the park like grounds. Finally, after almost an hour, he was ushered into Sister Becky's office.

"Mr. Dudley!" She greeted him at the door, clasping his hands in a warm double grip. It was as strong as ever. Up close, though, her aged face seemed even more so than usual, and although her emerald eyes still sparkled, there was a note of bone tired weariness in her Irish brogue. She reminded him of a wilted shamrock.

"Please, dear boy, sit... sit!" Sister Becky swept behind a massive, age-worn desk and settled into a chair. "Do mind your seat, though - that one is a bit damp." She directed him to the drier of two upholstered wingbacks. "Dear little urchins, but very moist, most of them."

Carson took a seat, glancing about at the small, tidy office. An odd counterpoint to the severe, spartan appearance of the old nun, the room was festooned with colorful drawings, piled with stacks of nursery-school periodicals and children's books and littered with toys and stuffed animals. Amidst it all, fingers steepled on the desk before her, sat Sister Becky, swathed and hooded in black, like the one clown at clown college who just didn't get it.

"I like your new digs," Carson commented. "Very... colorful. Yup, lots of color. Downright jolly." He picked up a DVD titled *The Barnyard Bunch Sings the Songs of Swine.* The cover featured a cartoon pig dressed like Elvis singing into a corn cob. "*Very* jolly."

"Yes, well, I thank you for your kindness, Mr. Dudley - but I shall also thank you to keep word of this from Mr. Jackson." She snatched the movie from him and stuffed it into a shelf full of similar titles. "I am quite certain it would only lead to a host of unpleasant new nicknames, and I can assure you that I have quite enough of those already." Another shudder shook the far wall, drawing a dark look from her. "Along with other burdens."

"Yeah. I've been listening to those burdens for almost an hour."

Sister Becky clucked, rolled her eyes in exasperation. "I do apologize for keeping you waiting, my boy. I am short-staffed, over-enrolled and quite up to my elbows in paste and paperwork. As I have previously mentioned, Father Black is determined to make my term of service here as miserable as possible, and he has proven himself quite capable at it. Recently, he has seen fit to accept as many special needs cases as he can: ADD, ADHD, Autism, Asperger's Syndrome... confidentially, Mr. Dudley, I honestly believe we have a victim of demonic possession in our facility."

"What's his name..." Carson cast back. "David, was it?"

Sister Becky made a face that Carson had only seen once before, when they were hunting vampires. She lowered her voice. "I have secretly attempted to exorcise him on two separate occasions. So far, nothing. I still hold out hope." She crossed herself.

The door opened and a young nun entered, looking harried and distraught. There was a massive amount of glitter and hot glue on her smock, and she looked like she was silently begging God to initiate the rapture. "Apologies, Sister Becky, but..." She hesitated.

"Anthony's medication?"

The other nun nodded vigorously. "I know it's not due for another fifteen minutes..."

Sister Becky shook her head with determination. "We must not weaken, Sister Carmen. We have a sacred duty to provide for these dear souls, no matter what hardships we are enduring. We must not falter. However," She whirled, unlocked a medicine box and passed a prescription bottle across the desk. "Hold this until it is time to administer the dose. 'Bread in the hand, while the hungry wait, helps pass the time 'til they pass the plate,' as the saying goes. Now, off with you. Back to the trenches."

Sister Becky watched as Sister Carmen hurried from the room, the sound of screaming voices and chaos flooding through briefly as the door opened, then shut.

"Sounds like a war zone out there."

"It is, Mr. Dudley. It is indeed." Sister Becky sent up a silent prayer, crossed herself again. A rare flicker of emotion flashed across her face - so rare, in fact, that it took Carson a moment to register it: resignation. He'd never imagined the tough lines of her face could rearrange into such a sad, weary, pitiable state. "And I am afraid..." she hesitated, drew a steadying breath. "That I may be its first casualty."

"Casualty?! Wait, you're not...?"

"Ill? Oh, heavens no, my son. Merely a figure of speech. What I am, however is weary... thoroughly, completely and unutterably *weary.*" She sighed, deeply. "It is not the children's fault," she added, in a way that sounded like she had been trying to convince herself of that for some time. "I am simply too old, too tired and too out of place."

"How could a nun be out of place in a church?"

"I may be in *church*, Mr. Dudley, but I am not in *service.* There is a great difference, make no mistake, and it depends entirely on following the direction of our Lord. Where God guides, He provides, as they say, and where He doesn't... well... I have seen absolute maroons rise to remarkable heights when they undertake what God has called them to, and I have seen noble, talented folk falter and crumble when they attempt a task He has not. I fear, Mr. Dudley, that I am now one of the latter. You may as well be the first to know, lad," she eyed him hesitantly. "I am considering hanging up my cowl."

Carson gaped. "Quitting?! You're thinking of quitting?!"

The door opened and another nun poked her head in. She was heavyset, with a flushed red face. A tuft of wild hair poked out from under her hood, which she was either too busy or too distracted to fix. "Sister Becky!" she puffed. "*We're out of cheese sticks!*"

Sister Becky fixed the newcomer with a shrewd eye. "Celery and peanut butter?"

She shook her head vigorously.

"Yogurt squeezers?"

Another shake.

"We have no choice, then. Deploy the graham crackers."

A curt nod. The door closed with a thump.

Sister Becky sighed again, her proud, squared shoulders slumping. She glanced at Carson. "The thought, Mr. Dudley, had occurred to me." The old nun levered herself wearily out of her chair and began to pace, hands clutched pensively behind her back. "I have stood at this crossroads once before, dear boy. Several months ago, as you no doubt recall. Then your rather... inspiring situation presented itself." There

 127

was a faint spark in her eyes. "When Roberta telephoned and spoke of your needs, it was like the Call - the glorious, triumphant voice of the Almighty Himself. And then, the hunt... *magnificent*," she breathed. "It had been so long... I truly believed that the Lord had presented me with a second chance. And now," she lifted her face, as flat and disdainful as her voice. "This." With a disgusted wave of her hand, Sister Becky slumped, defeated, back into her chair.

Carson could relate. "Yeah. Work sucks. Today. But hey..." he leaned across the desk, squeezed her hand. "Yesterday you stood toe to toe with a vampire."

She held his gaze. The ghost of a smile twitched at her mouth. "Once upon a time, Mr. Dudley. But why relive the past? That was a war to which I was called - equipped! This one..." she trailed off, miserable.

Carson had never seen her like this. It made him suddenly angry. "So change it."

Emerald eyes settled on his face, probing.

"Don't quit. Find another way. Tough it out. You say where God guides, He provides. Well... maybe He's about to. If He is, don't you owe it to Him to find out?"

"But... Father Black..." She frowned. "I am a fighter, Mr. Dudley, and always have been. I have made it my life's work to cast down fiends and tyrants. Alas, here is one I cannot. Backing down, living under his tyranny - it smacks of defeat, lad. It feels like... giving up."

"It's not giving up. It's just a... a tactical retreat."

Sister Becky hesitated. Watched him. After a moment, she gave a grudging nod. "I shall take it under advisement." Then she straightened, almost imperceptibly, and Carson knew she would be alright. For a little while longer. He also knew with sudden insight that his little speech had been as much for him as for her.

"So," Sister Becky resumed her businesslike air. "I have troubled you enough with my own sorrows. Tell me... what is the purpose of your visit?"

"My visit... right." Carson suddenly felt the weight of the plastic bag on his lap. The weight of last night's encounter came with it. "I know it's on the shelf and all, but I was wondering if I could interest you in dusting off that calling of yours. Just for a few minutes."

Beneath the weary green pools of her eyes, a greedy light glimmered. "A supernatural matter, Mr. Dudley? By all means. What is it that plagues you?" Her eyes narrowed shrewdly. "Is it Mr.

Kinkade?"

"Er..." Carson hesitated. Something in the way she said Kinkade's name gave him pause. There was an edge to her voice, a coldness... but Carson dismissed it. The man just naturally made your skin crawl. "No. Although I do suspect he's the cause of global warming and war in the Middle East. No, this is something... different."

"Then by all means, Mr. Dudley, proceed. I am both intrigued and enthused to hear something that does not concern itself primarily with the bodily functions of five to ten-year-olds or any catastrophe involving paste. However..." she glanced sourly at the wall clock. "You had best be brief. It is pool day." Sister Becky's hands clenched.

"Sweet. That oughta cure the rugrats of some wiggles."

The nun produced a thin smile. "Mr. Dudley - have you ever attempted to supervise four dozen children in a public swimming pool?"

"No."

"Do not. It creates more maladies than it cures."

"Fair enough. I was having trouble picturing you in a bathing suit anyway." He winked.

"Bathing suit?"

"Um... never mind. Okay, brace yourself - here's your dose of weird for the week..." Carson jumped into his tale, rapidly recounting his recent adventures. He spared few details. He had known Sister Becky a shorter time than he had the others, but ever since Vanessa, he had always felt he could talk to her about anything. There was something about telling a person you thought vampires were real and having them agree that knocked down all barriers.

Finally, he arrived at his bathroom encounter from last night. It all spilled out in a rush, sounding even more fantastic and unreal in the light of day. "So then I let the thing have it. *Splat!* Right outta the park - or the pottie. And you won't *believe* this thing 'til you see it." He slipped on a pair of rubber gloves. "In fact, I've seen it and I don't even believe it. Now, maybe you can tell me..." he reached gingerly into the bag. "What... in the Sam Hill..." he took hold of the oozy, slimy remains, shivered involuntarily. "...is *this?!*" He tugged the thing free of the bag, thrust it toward her. The smell came with it and his stomach gave a heave. He held his breath, clamped down. Sister Becky peered closely at the rubbery, dripping remains.

She clucked, muttered to herself. "It appears, Mr. Dudley," her brows furrowed. "That what you have there..." She nodded with certainty, lifted her eyes. "Is a toad."

"A *toad*?"

"And, unless I miss my guess, a dead one."

"That's it?!" Carson balked. "You... I... a few months ago I said there was a vampire in Las Calamas, and you didn't bat an eye. Now I show you *this*..." he waggled the corpse in a way which threatened to tear loose several appendages and fling them into her lap. "And all you've got to say is... it's a *toad*?"

"I am certain it is not a vampire, Mr. Dudley, if that is what you are implying."

It hadn't been the reaction he'd been hoping for. Carson faltered, wondering whether he had just imagined the whole thing, had finally cracked from too much stress, too much heat and too many chili fries. The toad looked hideous, but in its present condition, he could imagine it losing a little of its impact...

He quelched his frustration, forced his mind into gear. If Sister Becky was going to disbelieve him, she was going to have to work harder at it than that. "Look... throw me a bone here, Sister B. After all, you're the one who told me that testing strangers to see if they were werewolves was a good habit."

"And I still maintain the veracity of that statement. There are far too many werewolves about and proper identification is one step closer to blowing the fiend's brains out with a silver bullet." A tiny gasp drew her attention to the door. "Yes, Olivia, what do you need dear?"

A child of nine stood rooted in the doorway, eyes wide. "Um... nothing," she squeaked. The door closed with a hasty thump.

"As I was saying," Sister Becky turned back. "Proper identification is the key. Last time, Mr. Dudley, there was ample and unmistakable evidence of supernatural presence. We knew the enemy and her purpose. We followed procedure and protocol - even if you were unaware of it. LIPISC."

The term instantly reminded Carson of MOLD and he felt a flare of frustration, struggled to remain calm. "LIPISC?" He forced the question.

"Locate, Identify, Plan, Incapacitate, Stake, Clean Up. Basic hunting protocol. Typically, it is applied to vampires, but it is also useful in hunting other classifications of undead. I stress now, even as I did then, that the Identify step is critically important, both for you *and* your target. And in this case, Mr. Dudley, even though you are possessed of a strange and disquieting aberration," she gestured toward the corpse. "You are still a goodly distance away from proper identification. As the saying goes, if it looks like a toad and croaks like a frog, it is probably not a cow."

"What if it looks like a toad and smells like a zombie?" Carson heard himself say the word, knew it was what he had been thinking, but had been unable to admit. It sounded weird hearing it out loud. Weird, but somehow right.

Sister Becky arched a brow. "A zombie? An animated corpse? The walking dead?"

"Hopping dead. You shoulda seen this thing go. Attack of the freakin' zomphibian."

She tilted her head thoughtfully. "Interesting, Mr. Dudley. Tell me - did it actually *attack* you?"

"Well..." He thought back. "Yes. No. Well... not exactly."

"What then, pray tell, did it do? Exactly."

"It... well... it hopped." He fidgeted. "And ate flies. And tried to get to the toilet."

"To water, then. Not such bizarre pursuits for one of God's creatures. Much like a normal toad."

Carson held up the beast, exasperated. "Does this *look* like a normal toad?!"

"Mr. Dudley..."

"Listen, it's that little girl's pet! What's her name... Hetta, Henrietta, Oprah..."

"Hannah?"

"Hannah! Yes! It's hers, I tell you - the frog from the microwave! You gave it to me; I tossed it in the trash; it got pitched in the dumpster. Then, somehow..." he struggled to fill in the gap, came up blank. "...came back to life! Or death... or whatever!"

A sudden burst of music once again swelled from Sister Becky's robes. This time, it was the stirring notes of the *Hallelujah Chorus.* She struggled to find her phone, stabbed blindly at buttons.

"Haaaaalelujah! Halelu...!"

The music stopped. She spoke briefly into the instrument, fumbled for a moment, snapped it shut.

"My apologies, Mr. Dudley. This device is less vexing since Ms. Masterson's intervention, but still a nuisance. That was Sister Carmen - our sojourn to the community pool is imminent. I do hate to be brusque, but if you would please come to the point." Sister Becky began rifling through desk drawers, pulling out folders, keys, children's sunscreen.

 131

"The point?!" Carson gawked, incredulous. He had just fired both barrels, point blank, and the old nun hadn't even blinked. "The point is... it's happening again!"

Sister Becky arched a gray brow. "Again, Mr. Dudley? A second supernatural incident... once again with you as the afflicted party?" She sounded doubtful, checked the time on the wall clock and reached for a clipboard.

"You've seen your fair share."

"Quite, Mr. Dudley," she smiled softly. "More than that, some would say. But that is my profession," She glanced down at the pair of water wings she had picked up, sighed. "*Was* my profession. For a lay person, multiple encounters... frankly, Mr. Dudley, the odds are... well, they are very poor. I recall one tragic case in which a fellow was thrice possessed by evil spirits. Three different spirits, mind you, on three different occasions. In three different countries, no less. All, as it turned out, completely unrelated. He was not quite the same after the third," she mused. "Seemed to think that if he were a duck, the spirits would lose interest. Started nesting..." She shrugged. "But those cases are rare, Mr. Dudley. Rare indeed."

Carson slumped back in his chair, was about to run a hand through his hair but remembered what he'd been holding. In frustration, he pounded his thighs, or at least intended to, and instead smashed the toad that still lay on his lap. Some kind of liquid squirted out of it onto Becky's desk.

"Oops... crabapples. Sorry! Here, let me..." Carson snatched a tissue from the desk, dabbed at the mess. It only made it worse.

Sister Becky watched for a moment as Carson clumsily smeared the sticky fluid across her desk. The hard look in her eyes softened. She sat. "The maggots, Mr. Dudley. How many were there?"

Carson stopped wiping. "How many?"

"Yes, Mr. Dudley. How many. Three, five, seven...?"

He screwed his eyes shut and thought back, picturing the creature as he'd first seen it.

"Five. I think. Give or take."

Sister Becky nodded, stared at the wall. "Most likely dead then... how long?" she mused. "Weight about three pounds... in this climate... perhaps a week, maybe ten days. Well... I will admit that, given the time frame and your rather exotic experiences, it could, possibly, be Hannah's amphibian, although to conclude that it was of the undead variety is still premature. If you are going to pursue this matter, Mr.

Dudley, you must be open to other possibilities. What other explanations are there that fit the facts?"

"I'm insane."

"Excellent. Always a wise probability to consider in these cases. However, I have been assessing you for just such a condition, and the signs are simply not there. What else, Mr. Dudley?"

"I have unresolved Muppet issues? Or..." Another thought occurred to him. "Fujika."

"Interesting." Sister Becky tapped her clipboard. "He certainly has motive. But what are his means, Mr. Dudley? Unleashing supernatural evil is no minor feat, even with his vast resources."

Carson tugged his beard, forgetting again about the mess on his gloved hand - this time too late. He yanked it away, disgusted. "I dunno... it's a corporation, who can say? Maybe they stumbled onto some kind of zombie-inducing formula or... or accidentally warped the laws of nature and reality by invoking some ancient artifact."

Sister Becky nodded grudgingly. "I must admit, both scenarios sound perfectly plausible."

"Especially when you consider this guy has 'Evil Bad Guy Mastermind' written all over him. He pretty much confessed to knowing about Nubuyuki - that dude the ninja ganked. Did everything except say, 'Yes, I killed him, and I would have gotten away with it too, if it wasn't for you meddling kids.' Of course, he might have, for all I know. How do say that in Japanese?"

"I should think it would sound something like: *Aa, orega yatsuo koroshitanda. Omaera warugaki gaina kereba mitsukarazuni sundanoniyo.* Although I am a bit rusty."

Carson made a little noise. "You speak Japanese?"

"I speak many languages, both living and dead. In my line of work, one never knows when understanding the nuance of a subtle turn of phrase can mean the difference between finishing your tea in peace and eternal damnation."

Carson shook his head, impressed. Then a sudden inspiration poked him, and he fished a yellow sticky note out of his pocket. "Alright then, Professor, bonus question: does the name 'Ashi Keiyaki' mean anything to you?"

She considered. "No. Why?"

"Nubuyuki was keeping a file on him. Must've been important, too. He kept it close. Like he was guarding it."

"Perhaps a rival? Or a contact."

"Maybe, but not around here. We checked."

"Curious, Mr. Dudley. Curious indeed. Some acquaintance from his homeland? Perhaps a criminal element?" She shrugged. "I do have a few contacts left in the Orient. I could make some enquiries." Searching for paper, she snatched up a crayoned masterpiece and flipped it over. Before she did, Carson caught a brief glimpse of what looked like a nun in full habit and a rubber duck floaty standing in a swimming pool. She scrawled the name on the back. "No promises, Mr. Dudley, but at least you'll..."

"*Haaaaalelujah! Hallelujah, hallelujah...!*"

Sister Becky banged down her pen and snatched up the phone. "Now see here, Sister Carmen, I am well aware of..." she stopped, listened for a moment. Her face grew stormy. "Yes. Yes indeed, I shall. Straightaway." She snapped the phone shut. "It seems the pool will have to wait. That was Father Black. I have been summoned to his office. Again." She rose, picked up a thick file folder and headed for the door.

Carson got to his feet. "Remember, tactical retreat. Oh, hey..." He held out the bag. "One more thing - what do I do with this?"

"Just pitch it out with the rubbish, Mr. Dudley, that should suffice." Then she paused, fingers on the door handle. "On second thought... burn it. Just to be safe." She made to leave.

"Sister B..."

"Yes, dear?"

"There are more shadows in this town than there should be."

Sister Becky hesitated, glanced back at him sharply.

"Just..." Carson didn't know what had made him say it - the words had just popped into his head, a fragment from his half-remembered dream. "Just something Pete used to say."

She stared at him a moment, then turned on her heel and left. She didn't say another word. She just looked tired.

Carson was tired too when he clambered aboard the crosstown bus fifteen minutes later. Hot and tired. He was in a foul mood, barely grunting at Joe, the driver, as he offered a friendly "hullo." His meeting with Sister Becky had only depressed him. More dead ends. Carson made his way through the crowded aisle toward a seat in the back. The blazing heat drew odor from his bag magnificently, which had the unexpected benefit of causing everyone nearby to find a new seat. Left alone, Carson turned off his brain and stared out the window at the other tired, sweaty people dragging themselves around in the sweltering heat.

As the blocks rolled by, he dozed. A few moments later, a familiar sound woke him. It took him a minute to place it. His cell. He fumbled for the phone, thumbed *Talk*. "This's Carson - say something interesting or I'm passing out again."

"I gave Becky the *Hallelujah Chorus*. For you, I'm thinking Menudo. Something peppy."

It was Kiki. Suddenly he felt better.

"Woman, the Irish have an old saying - if it looks like a frog and smells as bad as this bag I'm holding, then it's too damn hot."

"What does that mean?"

"It means I'm glad you called. What's up?"

"Dinner. Remember?" She made a kissing noise. "A little suck-up, some groveling, maybe a few h'ors d'ouvres."

"Y'know, I hardly even recall you totally abandoning me at the beach now. But, since you mentioned it... why not. I'm thinking - and I hate myself for saying this, but it was your fault for bringing it up - the Fish n' Ships. I can relive my childhood fantasies about battling the giant squid, present my groundless theories that it's *real,* and you can try the shrimp cocktail. Whaddaya say... let's get piratey."

"Yeah. No. I'm not feelin' it, matey. And the squid's a fake. How about the Taj Palace?"

"Boy, you don't have a clue about this suck-up thing, do you? Alright, Taj it is. But I'm still wearing my eye patch and hook."

Kiki giggled. He liked the sound of it. But it wasn't the only sound. There were other voices on her end, muffled but there - raised voices. And another noise... a droning. Something *clanked* and the phone made a weird crackle. Carson strained to hear over the roar of the bus engines and the chatter of the other passengers.

"Hey, you uh... you at a carnival or something?"

"Hm? Oh, no..." the noises faded. He could tell she was moving, hustling someplace quieter. "I just... I mean, I just stopped in a... at the store. To borrow a land line. So, tonight's good? Seven o'clock?"

"You're on. My shift doesn't start until ten, should give us plenty of time. Shall I swing by - pick you up?" Another odd noise from her side. This one he couldn't place. Then another raised voice. He opened his mouth to ask but didn't get the words out in time.

"Better meet you there. So, hey... before you go, how did things work out with Leet?"

"Leet? Oh... heck, he's a pistol alright. I thought the waiters at the

 135

Fish n' Ships were awkward socially. But I gotta say, as my first criminal contact, he ain't half bad."

"He did the crack, then? Got you some leads?"

"Yes... and no."

"You didn't give him any Yoo-hoo, did you? Once he gets that monkey on his back, he's pretty much useless."

"Uh... well... he's... I gave it to him, yeah. But after. That guy needs help. Anyway, he dug up some stuff on the dead guy. You know, the one the ninja killed?" Carson noticed one of the passengers staring at him, an elderly woman with a feather cap. He smiled cheerily, waved. She turned away quickly. "Turns out he wasn't real popular with Fujika. Some kind of investment squabble. Got me excited for a minute, but then it just dead ended. Kinda sucked. One of those 'more questions than answers' thingies."

"Investments? Like what?"

Carson sat quietly, feeling suddenly like the dumbest kid in French class had just been asked how to say "cat". "Um, yeah. That would be good to know, wouldn't it?"

"That's right where I'd start - follow the money. It's usually where you find answers. Just be careful, okay?"

"Careful as always. I don't suppose you have Leet's..."

Kiki read off the number to him. "And while you're at it," she added hesitantly. "Let me give you another one. I was thinking... I might be a little hard to reach sometimes. So... so listen, if you ever need to get ahold of me, you can leave a message with Lucky Earl. He should be able to get it to me."

"Whoa. Things are getting serious. I'm now allowed to leave messages for you with some guy I don't know who might be able to pass them along to you."

"Just write, stupid." She gave a second number, and he jotted it down. Behind the brief pauses on the other end of the line as she rattled numbers, Carson thought he heard a hissing sound and a low reverberation. It was an industrial noise, almost like a factory.

"Are you there now?"

"Er... no. Why?"

"Just the noise. Sounds wild. Where are you? Sounds like an Arab market. Or maybe Euro Disney."

Then, audible but strangely distorted, a voice said: "*Kiki...*"

The rest was lost. Carson could tell the voice had a thick accent and that Kiki had quickly cupped her hand over the receiver to mute it, but that was all. There was a short conversation, just a few words. Then she was back.

"Gotta go," her voice was strained. "See you tonight. Bye."

And then he had dial tone.

The lady with the hat was staring at him again. She eyed his plastic bag, sniffed pointedly and made a face.

"Yeah. You shoulda smelled my shoes." Carson smiled. The lady changed seats. Carson punched Leet's number into his cell. It rang for a full minute. Carson hung up, tried again, was just about to give up, when someone answered.

"'Lo?" The voice was thick, slurred, hardly recognizable.

"Leet? Wow. Hey, man, this is Carson. You, uh... you okay?"

"Yeah." A pause. "Jus'... jus' a little Yoo-hoo hangover." There was a rattle of empty plastic bottles, as of someone rolling around on a bed littered with them. "Going to sleep... 'bye now..."

"Yeah, well, actually, I need some more info."

There was a pause, more rattling. A soft moan. "Tomorrow. We'll talk..." Leet's voice faded, as if he was hanging up even as he was speaking.

"*Stop.*" The sharpness of Carson's voice surprised even him.

There was a short pause, and for a moment Carson thought Leet had hung up. Then his voice came back. "Little harsh, ain't it Charity? Not really your style."

"Look - people are getting hurt, here. I need answers."

Another pause. "I'm listening."

"You said Haruki questioned some decisions - investment decisions."

"Uh-huh." Bed springs squeaked. When Leet's voice came again, it was slightly more alert. "Made a real stink, too. There was this one in particular, he jus' about went postal - you should read the docs, man, he was..."

"That one. That'll do. I need to know what it was. Where it was."

"'Sec. Got it here. Somewhere..." Carson detected another squeak of bed springs, a muffled groan. Fingers clattered on keys. "Here it is. Looks like... real estate. Commercial property, maybe? There's no name."

"Got an address?"

"Got a pencil?"

"Shoot."

Leet rattled it off, pausing in the middle for a soft belch and

137

another quiet moan. "So... we done?"

"For now. But keep digging. Everything you can find on those other investments. Names, addresses, everything."

"Alright, Charity. Let me jus'... sleep this off a few hours. Then I'll take another trip through Fujikacorp's dirty laundry. See what I can turn up." Silence for a moment. "Okay?"

"Okay. And Leet - is banana still alright?"

"Oh yeah... oh yeah..." Another soft moan. "But no hurry on that."

The phone went dead.

Carson leaned back, staring out the window as the buildings whipped past, blurred by heat and speed. He recognized the neatly trimmed lawns, older residential single family homes, white fences. He was aware that he was getting close to home, but still processing the fact that he had just successfully extracted information from a hostile Yoo-hoo addict with major social hangups. He'd done it without thinking. It had just happened. It felt good.

A moment later, the bus was idle, sitting at the curb outside Granny's house. Carson looked up, heard people grumbling about the delay. In the rearview mirror, the driver's eyes were watching him expectantly.

"Your stop, Carson," Joe called with a friendly nod.

Carson rose, strode to the front of the bus clutching his garbage bag. It suddenly didn't feel as heavy. "On the contrary, Big Joe. I'm just getting started..."

CHAPTER EIGHT

Job Shadows

"Have you got a deathwish?" Kiki stared in awe, shook her head. Behind her, the waiter was just disappearing through the crowded tables, heading for the kitchen. In his hands was the ticket with their order, including Carson's "*4-star-hot-warn-customer*" and a signed waiver the wait staff was required to collect from everyone who dared to request it.

Carson kicked back in the booth and laced his hands behind his head, grinning. "Once you get used to it, it's not that bad. It's like riding a bike. That's on fire. In a volcano. Only, it's all inside your mouth."

"Refreshing."

Carson laughed at her expression, had a drink of Mt. Dew and glanced around the Taj Palace, listening to the sounds of other people having fun. He liked the smells of this place, spicy and exotic; the candles on the tables, even though the lights were on; the attempt at East Indian decor that made him feel more like he was in a tacky import shop than another country.

Kiki smiled back, sipped water and joined him in his reconnoiter The smile was a good sign, and Carson was happy to see it. She had been late, as usual, but Carson expected it by now and the table was ready with drinks on hand by the time she arrived.

With the bustling dinner crowd, it had taken their waiter awhile to visit, and they'd had time to catch up. Carson had been doing the lion's share of the talking, but he'd been prepared for that, too. Even when she wasn't exhausted, which was most of the time now, Kiki was quiet in public, withdrawn, preferring to listen rather than talk. Like tonight. She just sat and watched, eyes roving like a spy in some Third World marketplace. The red stocking cap lent her an even greater air of mystery, pulled down low over her eyes. She'd shucked her pack, taken off the canvas jacket, sat there now in her white tank top, hunched over her water glass. But the hat - even in this heat. People and their habits. Carson had to chuckle.

"What's with you?" She spoke without looking at him.

"Your hat. It makes me laugh. Is your brain really that cold all the time?"

"I don't know." Kiki glanced after the waiter. "Is your stomach?"

"Yup." Carson patted his belly. "I think Homer Simpson said it best: 'Mmmm... hot gooooood.'" He took another big gulp of soda, sucked in an ice cube and crunched his way through it.

Kiki flicked a look his way, took in the details: the jeans with the worn out knee, the worn leather flip-flops, the faded green ringer T with a picture of the Sesame Street gang and the words *Everything I Ever Needed To Know I Learned on the Street*. One leg was propped up on the booth and he slouched as usual, casual, like he was reclining on a divan in a New Delhi hostel. Same old Carson. He could be hopping across the world on a shoestring budget, lazy lopsided smile, scruffy hair and chin beard. But lately... lately there was something else. Something she couldn't quite put her finger on.

"No. I don't buy it," she said, suddenly giving him her full attention. "There's more to you than that."

Carson glanced at her. She was staring at him with a face he new well - the face he'd seen dozens of times before while she was poring over textbooks, absorbed in some technical treatise on virtual servers or voice-over-IP or any of a hundred other things he only vaguely knew the names of. "Okay, professor," he said around another chunk of ice. "I'll bite. What is it?"

"You're an adrenaline junkie."

 140

"Get out of town!" He scoffed, crunching the cube loudly. "Freezie junkie, sure, corn dog maybe... but adrenaline?"

"I didn't see it at first - the pieces are all spread out. But it's clear to me now. The brain freezes, the spicy foods, the beach volleyball..."

"Hold up, House - what's volleyball got to do with it?"

"Everything. For example, it's an action-oriented game, physical, very competitive with limited participants, so it's guaranteed to put you in the middle of the action. It's got a stressful environment, hot, dry, harsh even, not some comfy indoor court. It fits on every level." She sat back, swirled the ice in her water glass thoughtfully. "You may not even realize it yourself - but you're more than just a mild-mannered convenience store clerk."

Carson enjoyed a hearty laugh, more at his own expense than hers. "Girl, you're about as far into left field as... well, as left field."

"Oh? Let's take a look at your childhood, then. High school for instance. I'm guessing you were a popular kid?"

"*Ennhh!*" Carson made the buzzer sound. "Not even close."

"A jock, then?"

"Strike two."

"But you knew them. Both cliques; ran with them, yes?" She was relentless, like a hound on the scent or a scientist on the verge of a critical breakthrough. Carson was enjoying seeing her on the hunt. It made her look less weary and more like the old Kiki. And it had her talking.

"Okay, sure. I'll admit it - you got me. I ran with them. Had some great buds from both crowds. But..." he hastened to add, raising a finger. "I wasn't *one* of them."

Kiki leaned in, fingers interlaced, intent. "Even better. It wasn't just those two, then - you were part of them *all;* weren't you?"

Carson considered. It had never really occurred to him. "I guess. I mean, yeah... I had a few friends, so what? Silver spoons, headbangers, skaters, jocks, preps... even some of your people. Oh yeah..." he pointed his finger at her like a pistol and *clicked.* "I had some nerdies in my circle."

"It fits. Restless energy. A drive to meet new people, experience new personalities. Always looking, never sticking. How about activities... sports, clubs? I'm guessing you kept busy."

Carson shrugged. "Sure, I tried some things. Baseball. Volleyball. Diving. Metal shop. Even did a semester with Glee..." he shot her a warning look. "Don't say it - I know how it sounds."

 141

"Perfect." Kiki nodded, satisfied. "Exactly what I would expect. Lots of involvement, wide range of interest, all of it displaying a thirst for new experiences. Classic adrenaline junkie."

"Alright, then," Carson rose to the challenge. "Riddle me this: why am I still here? LC isn't exactly a hotbed for exotic adventure."

"Interesting." Kiki eyed him shrewdly, wheels spinning. It was a wrinkle. "You're a lifer here?"

"Belfry District, born and raised. Had a chance to cut out when my parents moved during my Senior year, but I passed. They took the sibs with 'em, hit the road, but me... I dunno; it just didn't feel right. So, I moved in with Granny Dudley. Finished out the year, got my tassel flipped and just sort of... hung out after that. Last couple years, it's been pretty much the 24/7 and living the dream in Granny's basement. You know... basic adrenaline junkie stuff."

Kiki slumped back, brooding. The wrinkle wasn't straightening. She hated wrinkles. "That's it? You don't even know what kept you here? No aspirations, no dreams, no goals?"

"Well... I always wanted to kill a vampire." He flicked a straw wrapper at her, grinning. "But now that that's in the bag, I can pretty much coast through the rest of life. So, let's move on to something new. As much as I enjoy playing *Trivial Pursuit: the Carson Dudley Edition*, I'd say it's high time we turned the conversation to you. Let's start with high school. Um... I'm thinking... AV Club, definitely. And... Chess Team? Knowledge Bowl?" He paused, squinted at her. "Cheerleader? You weren't a cheerleader, were you?"

"No." The word was flat, final, as if the conversation had just been dropped from a very high place and fallen to its death.

"Oh. Um. Okay. I see. Not a Barbie. Um... okay. Forget high school. How about the rest of your childhood?"

"Just like everyone else's."

Carson could tell by the look in her eye and the tightness of her lips that it had been anything but. He could also tell it was a bad idea to ask any more questions about it.

Luckily, he was saved from further awkwardness by the arrival of their food. At first, Kiki only picked at her salad, haunted by whatever ghosts his comment had kicked up, but after watching him sweat and whoop his way through half of his 4-star-hot-warn-customer, she loosened up again. The rest of dinner passed in pleasant conversation.

"Man..." It was half an hour later when Carson finally pushed his plate back. "I needed this. Been awhile since I had some solid R&R.

Y'know, maybe you're right - maybe I am an adrenaline junkie. Trouble with the boss, trouble with the cops, trouble with soulless mega-corporations. It's all part of my exciting, thrill-a-minute plan to die of a coronary by age thirty. I tell you, it's killing me. No vids, no TV, no social life. Kinky's had me working like a dog. Did you know tomorrow is the first day off I've had in *two weeks*? I've even been ditching Granny."

"For dinner?"

"For church, actually. I started in on this Sunday night thing with her awhile back. It was weird."

"How so?"

"It was fun."

"That is weird."

"Loud music, drums, you know, like a concert that you don't feel slightly guilty about afterward. Pastor was cool, too - if you can trust a pastor with tattoos. Can you trust a pastor with tattoos?"

"We trust Sister Becky. I wouldn't be surprised if she had a few stashed away."

"I know where you can see her in a bathing suit if you really wanna find out."

"I like to leave a little mystery in life. And while we're on the topic of life's mysteries, what's with the sudden interest in the spiritual ones? You getting that existential itch or just taking precautions against the Burny Place?"

Carson belched softly. "Woo. Speaking of the Burny Place... sorry about that." He fanned the air vigorously. "4-star-hot-warn-customer's-*friends*. Anyway... no, no deep issues. Granny just invited me. She was the one who hooked us up with Sister Becky, after all - I guess after that, she thought I was 'seeking' or something. I was happy to say 'yes', though. You can't watch someone smoke a vampire with holy water and not wonder if there's a little something to it."

"That's a selling point, alright."

"Amen."

"Speaking of liquid diets... did you get back to Leet?"

"I did." Carson paused. Dinner had been nice. Very nice. So nice, in fact, that he was hesitant to bring up the weird events of the past several days, even though part of him had been itching to all night.

"Well?" Kiki pressed. She wasn't making it easy. Her and her darn inquisitiveness. "Did he find anything? About those investments."

"Uh, yeah." Carson nodded grudgingly. "I, um... I had him check

143

those out, just like you said. Wouldn't you know it... he dug up an address on one of them. Follow the money, right?"

"Have you checked it out?"

"No. I..." Carson paused, struck by a sudden idea. "Hey... wanna live dangerously?"

"I'm sitting through your burps. Isn't that enough?"

"I've got the address here. We could swing by on the way home. Check it out. Whaddaya say... for old time's sake?"

"Old time's sake?!" Kiki frowned. "That, my friend, is *not* a selling point. Those old times were almost our last times." She considered for a moment. "But... it is a nice night for a walk..."

"That's the spirit! We can have ourselves a little stroll, chat a bit, scope out the enigmatic danger-ridden mystery spot, and you can see if this whole 'adrenaline junkie' thing is everything it's cracked up to be."

"Again, *not* a selling point."

"Hey, this is our first evening out. I just wanted it to be memorable..."

A short time later Carson and Kiki were making their way into the heart of the Belfry District's commercial downtown. Carson checked street signs and guided them through the maze of tidy strip malls, coffee shops and restaurants. They strolled, chatting, watching people passing in two's and three's, sometimes in crowds, all daring to brave the evening heat in their reckless pursuit of summer fun. The melting pot of the Belfry District was a glad distraction from Carson's ponderings and problems. It always took his mind off things doing a bit of people watching, and there was always a lot to see here: from rowdy teenagers to elderly couples out for a romantic stroll, to noisy biker packs, to the Japanese tourist snapping pictures of the local scenery. Carson breathed it all in, enjoying the warmth of the food in his belly, the pleasant, natural smell of Kiki's hair, the now almost tolerable haze of summer heat.

Gradually, they drew clear of the crowds and energy and pulse and drifted into quieter environs. The buildings were older here, most of them closed at this hour, and people were fewer. An occasional car passed, but for the most part, the traffic dwindled to almost nothing. Even their own conversation lulled.

They walked another block in silence. They could hear the street lights buzzing now, the sound of their footsteps echoing off darkened storefronts.

"How come a relaxing evening with you always includes a trip to a dark lonely neighborhood?" Kiki stepped around a pair of curbside garbage cans, peered cautiously down the mouth of the alley looming behind them.

"Brings back memories, don't it?"

"Yeah. The kind that keep me up at night. You know, the last time we took a quiet little walk together, we ended up at a slaughterhouse. Literally."

"Yup. Kinda exciting. You should be feeling that adrenaline right about... now."

Kiki looked around apprehensively. "Why so sure?"

"Because," Carson checked a nearby street sign against the address on a hand scrawled note. "It's right around this corner." He stopped, looked up and down the street. It was empty. Dark. "And it looks like we've got the place all to ourselves. Whatever it is."

"So, what do you think?" Kiki squared her slim shoulders. "Haunted warehouse, ancient Indian burial ground, condemned tenement that guards the gateway to hell?"

"Haven't the foggiest. Whatever it is, though, be ready for it." He stepped out, and she was right behind him. Moments later, they stood in front of the address. In spite of Carson's warning, neither one had been ready. Not even remotely. They stood staring up at the building, momentarily unable to speak.

Finally, Kiki found her voice. "What... what is that? Is that a..."

"Yes. Yes it is. It's a flower shop."

Kiki snatched the note from his hand, compared the street number to the one on the building. "Well, that's disappointing."

Carson nodded with feeling. "And I'll tell you what else that is, misappropriation of funds. Questionable business practices."

"Hard to argue that one." Kiki leaned in, eyed the perky bouquets and fresh flowers in the darkened window.

Carson stared up at a simple, elegant sign hanging over the door. "*The Orchid Road*," he read. "Yeah. No. I don't get it. Road to nowhere is more like it. This is a *flower* shop." Carson made a small disgusted sound. "I'm a little fuzzy on how this fits into Fujika's plans for world domination."

"Although, they do have some nice arrangements. And look," Kiki pointed to a hand painted sign. "'Ask About Our Exotic Flowers.' Not every flower shop is an *exotic* flower shop."

Carson glowered through the glass, his reflection frowning back at him as he scanned the shop's interior. He was like a kid looking through the toy store window in June willing Christmas to get there already. "Grabthar's Hammer! It doesn't make sense. What would Fujika want with a flower shop?!"

"I'm gonna go out on a limb here... flowers?"

"You're not helping."

"Maybe I am. Some leads take you places, some just send you places. Put this one in your pocket, Carson. It's a dead end." She tugged at his sleeve, snapped him out of his brooding.

"Hm? Oh. Yeah. Yeah, I guess you're right. Lead you places, send you places. Got it. Nice. Catchy. Alright," he sighed. "Dead end it is." He tore himself away from the window, following her slowly back the way they had come. He glanced back, once, frowning at the flower shop. He shoved his hands in his jeans pockets, kicked a can and sent it spinning down the street.

"Well... I don't know what you expected, Carson, but you gotta admit - it's better than last time."

"It won't take as many band-aids, that's for sure." He ran a hand through his hair, shook his head. "I'm just sorry I dragged you out here. It was supposed to be a little excitement and intrigue, and instead, it turned out to be just like a Justin Bieber concert: a whole lotta hype for something that cost me an hour of my life and left me feeling slightly ashamed."

"I don't know. All in all... I'm glad we came." She smiled up at him. Slowly, he felt his frown fade. He smiled back. They walked.

Carson listened to the crowd noise growing again, watched the glow of neon and storefront lights approaching. He was glad too, he realized, even with the wild goose chase. Glad for a break from the stress and craziness of the past few weeks, yes - but also glad for a chance to get better acquainted with Kiki.

It occurred to him, in fact, that he knew more about Haruki Nubuyuki than he did about Kiki. Carson didn't even know where she lived, had never heard her talk about family, hobbies, school, friends. He was just opening his mouth to ask when, with a flash, he remembered his encounter with the strange figure in the alley.

"Oh, hey, that reminds me..."

"What reminds you?"

"Er... nothing. I mean I just remembered... I met a friend of yours the other day."

She glanced up at him sharply. "A friend? Of mine? Who?"

The tone in her voice made him pause. "I... I dunno... exactly. Just

 146

a guy. I ran into him in the alley behind the 24/7. He really saved my bacon, too, cleaned up this super-freakin' mess before... hey, what gives?"

She had stopped. Cold. Her blue eyes drilled holes in his. "He came to your store?" Her voice was low, flat. Coiled to strike.

"Yeah. Well, the alley at least. Did I mention the part where he saved my bacon? You see, Kinky had..."

"His name. What was it?"

Carson groped about mentally, wondering when the ground had suddenly disappeared from under his feet and desperately wanting to get it back. "He, uh... he didn't really give me a name. Just said to... um... 'say hi from a ghost', or something. What do you...?"

He never finished his question. Kiki turned without another word and was gone, storming off down the street in the opposite direction.

He would never, however, forget the look on her face.

Carson could still see it when he walked into the 24/7 an hour and a lot of walking later. Greeting him from behind the counter, however, were two faces he wished he *could* forget.

Ross Kinkade. Stanley Plugg.

And they looked like they meant business.

Carson's stomach knotted, and he knew it wasn't from dinner. He could tell by the way they stood, their expressions, the crackle in the air, that this was an ambush. He stood rooted in the doorway, listening to the fading warble of the sickly door chime. It was like a sound effect from a Saturday morning cartoon, right at the part where somebody got pancaked by an anvil.

Kinkade fired first, maximizing the advantage of surprise. "What did you do with the Yoo-hoo?"

Ordinarily, Carson would have laughed; now, the question made his palms sweaty. Stanley lurked just behind Kinkade, playing the toadie to his schoolyard bully. His smirk was like a slap in the face.

Carson knew he had to say something. "Er..."

"Stanley informed me that you left with a case of it several days ago. There is nothing on the employee purchase log." Kinkade waved the notebook, and Carson winced. He'd forgotten. Kinkade's dark eyes were hard and penetrating. Carson had never seen him quite so agitated. He was so upset, he was practically frowning. "An entire case, Dudley. Gone. Let me ask again: where - is - it?"

"I took it." Carson didn't see any reason to lie.

The confession took Kinkade momentarily aback. He blinked.

"Then, I assume you have a good reason for doing so. A *very* good reason."

"Yes." However, Carson couldn't see any reason to just blurt out the truth, either.

Kinkade stood, arms folded, staring. Silence. In the warmer between them, the hot dogs sizzled and hissed. Softly. Expectantly.

"And that is?" Kinkade's tone was almost sharp.

"Well, it's good; I can tell you that," Carson retorted. "A good reason. A *very* good reason. This reason is, as a matter of fact, excellent and perfectly rational. And it is also one that I am going to tell you. Now. Right now." His brain worked furiously. Nothing came. "And you'll be quite surprised when you hear it, I may add." He cleared his throat. So would he. "The reason, of course, is..."

"The bathroom remodel," said a voice behind him. He turned. It was Josh.

"Er... the bathroom remodel? Um... yes. The bathroom remodel. Yes. That is the reason of which I spoke." Carson forced a plastic grin.

"You might as well tell him the whole story, Carson," Josh ambled up behind him, smiling. "Looks like the cat's out of the bag."

"Right. The whole story. Darn that cat! Ha ha! Um..."

Josh finished wiping his hands on a rag and tucked it into his back pocket. "You know, how you threw in the Yoo-hoo to get things moving with the contractor? Rush job and all."

"Contractor?" Kinkade's brow had the slightest furrow.

"Yup. That's it alright." Carson kept his plastic grin and shifted his eyes toward the restroom door. It was closed, the "*out of order*" sign still in place. As they traveled back to meet Kinkade, his eyes slid across Josh, who stood nonchalantly by his side.

"Let's go take a look, shall we?" Josh turned and headed for the restroom. Carson followed stiffly. It was that or bolt for the door. The others followed closely.

A few moments later, the procession arrived, halted. Josh stood aside, motioned for Carson to take the lead. "After you."

Carson put his hand on the door handle, got a wicked belt of deja vu and was glad he was holding onto something solid. "Thanks. Well. Here we go... again..." He pushed.

The restroom was immaculate.

The pipes had been repaired, new tile laid and a fresh coat of paint applied to everything. Baseboard had been added, as well as a tasteful strip of crown molding. Even the urinal sparkled. It looked classy.

Kinkade's face was implacable, unreadable. Stanley, however, was dumbfounded - his features sagged with the expression of a trained killer who had just missed his shot.

Kinkade tapped his tablet, referenced notes. "You should have checked with me before selecting the paint. Seven Corporation has color guidelines." He tapped a few more times.

"Sorry, my bad. Just trying to put the 'L' in MOLD. You know... 'Lead'. Section Fifteen."

Kinkade looked at him. The expression was cold, blank, and wholly unappreciative of what Carson felt was a helpful point of order. "And your approach was most unorthodox - trading product for services. Even if it was to 'get things moving.' Next time, confer with me first. We aren't a trading post, Dudley." He turned on his heel and strode toward the front of the store. Carson and Josh followed, leaving Stanley still staring.

When they reached the counter, Kinkade rounded, presented Carson with a neatly folded slip of paper. "Now then... here."

Carson took it. "What's this?"

"Your next productivity milestone."

Carson read the note: it was an address, a name, a time and tomorrow's date. "Who's Carl?"

"He's a SME," Kinkade answered, pronouncing the acronym *smee*. He offered no further explanation, as if the word spoke for itself.

"Right. Er... SME?"

"Subject Matter Expert, Dudley. Carl is the night manager of the Valley Avenue 24/7. He is also the regional SME on end caps"

"Valley... you mean the one over in the Romero District?"

Kinkade gave a single, brief nod. "He's your job shadow."

"But this is tomorrow. That's my day off."

"Which is why I felt it would be the perfect opportunity. You won't be here working, so you can be over there learning. Hard workers, Dudley. *That's* the kind of person Seven Corporation is looking for. See that you arrive precisely at 10 p.m. Carl will be expecting you."

Kinkade left without so much as a good-bye. Stanley followed a few moments later, still flabbergasted, muttering quietly to himself and shaking his head.

When they were safely out of earshot, Carson leaned back against the counter and stared at Josh. Josh wore a tiny smile.

"Hard working, clever and resourceful," Carson mused, stroking his chin. "You know, I think you're the kind of person Seven Corporation is looking for." Then his face split into a giant of a grin and he *whooped!,* pumped the air. He clapped Josh on the shoulder, *whooped!* and clapped him again. "You *crazy* Oregonian!" Carson waved his arms with wild, pointless enthusiasm in the direction of the restroom. "How did you...?! When did you...?! That's nicer than *my* bathroom! *Most* bathrooms! That's like the showroom for 'Pimp My Crapper!'" Carson stared back and forth between a beaming Josh and the gleaming bathroom.

"Just a little fixit project. I like working with my hands."

"Wait a minute... you did that *yourself*?! On your own?!"

"Well, Lauren picked out the colors. And the crown molding. She thought it was a nice touch."

"But... why?!"

Josh shrugged. "Figured you could use a little help. I know you've had it rough lately, and I missed out on the alley, so I thought I'd at least patch up the pipe. That went pretty well, so I just sort of... started in on the tile. Rest just fell into place. Nothing to it, really. Hope I didn't step on your toes."

"Yeah, well... next time check with me before selecting the paint. Seven Corporation has color guidelines."

Josh grinned. "Will do."

"But seriously, dude - I don't know how to thank you."

Josh dismissed him with a wave. "Forget it. Where I come from, we watch each other's backs."

"I'll say - backs, fronts and Yoo-hoo's. You even covered that angle."

"Had to fudge that a little," Josh looked regretful. "Hated to do it, but I figured you just forgot to write it down, and it sort of fit the story. I knew you wouldn't steal it."

Carson stared into the friendly, honest face. He shook his head, still grinning. "Alright, that's it. Purple Freezies. My treat. And no foolin' around - we're goin' for the 74 ouncers. They were Jack's favorite, and thanks to you, I just might have a chance at keeping his store out of the toilet you just fixed." Carson snagged two bucket-sized cups and started filling them. "And I'm paying you back for all that," he motioned to the bathroom. "Every penny!" He passed a cup to Josh, raised his own. "To new friends and new bathrooms - may they always be there when you need 'em!"

Carson went home that morning exhausted, yet with a grim sense of

 150

satisfaction. Life was still complicated, hot and messy, but at least now it didn't smell like a sewer, and he could pee while at work without having to go next door. And that was something. Best of all, it felt good to have an ally again. At least now, he had someone at his back. At least now, he wasn't alone.

And then there was the look on Stanley's face.

Carson chuckled as he slipped into his Superman boxers and crawled wearily into bed. Catching Stanley with his pants down - you couldn't put a price on that. He was still grinning as he drifted off.

Carson awoke early in the evening, rested and refreshed. He talked Granny into a game of Wii baseball and took a little time to relax in the relative cool of the basement. The thermometer in Las Calamas remained stubbornly in the triple digits, according to Chuck and Phil, who had started a Mayor Klapp Bikini Watch Hotline. After a quick bowl of cereal, Carson slipped into his 24/7 uniform and headed out.

The bus crowd was light and so was traffic, and he made good time to Romero. Early, for what felt like the first time in weeks, Carson got off one stop short of his destination. He was brimming with energy and fresh enthusiasm and needed the walk to mull over the issues of the day. He let his mind run as he strolled the unfamiliar streets, took in the sights, sounds and smells.

The Romero district was newer than Belfry, more posh, a recent addition in the grand scheme of things. Sprawled neatly at the foot of the upper class hillside residential neighborhoods, it was Yuppie central, crawling with the young money of Las Calamas. Convertibles, sleek electric scooters and even a Segway cruised past him as he walked. The streets were clean, the stores new and the sidewalks broad and well kept. While it lacked the character of Belfry, it had a charm all its own, and Carson let it soak in. He felt his mind begin to kick into gear.

Problem number one: Dex. Carson walked it through step by step. He replayed the details of the fight at the pumps, pondered what he'd learned about Fujikacorp from Leet, twisted and turned the thing from every angle. In the end, though, he just kept seeing Dex on the chopping block - losing his job at the 24/7, losing his job with Gold Shield, and then... what? Carson wasn't sure if it was possible to Twinkie oneself to death, but the thought gave him pause. He shook his head to clear it. Crossing the street in front of a Sushi bar, he gave up on Dex for the moment and switched topics.

Problem number two: the Orchid Road. Why would Ichiro Fujika, feared Shogun of Fujikacorp, youngest CEO in Japanese history, stick his neck out to pick up a two-bit flower shop - even an exotic one? He knew Haruki was watchdogging. Why risk it? What could be *that* important? Carson ticked off possibilities: money laundering? Illegal gambling? Opium den? Underground martial arts bloodsport arena? He shook his head. They were theories but not very good ones - every one sounded like a Jean-Claude Van Damme movie.

By the time he rounded the corner of Valley Avenue, he had worked himself right out of his earlier optimism and back into a general funk. Down the street his eyes picked out the squatty, friendly shape of the 24/7. The *other* 24/7, he reminded himself. It looked a lot newer and a lot more hip than his own, but still... the familiar green and yellow sign blazed above the entrance, like the front porch light of home. He paused, momentarily cheered. Then, he remembered why he was there. The buzz faded.

"Hey, I know what'll cheer me up," he muttered to himself. "End caps!" His shoulders slumped, and he set off toward the mini-mart.

As he approached, Carson was struck by the polish of the place. The parking lot was neatly swept, gas pumps gleaming, garbage cans expertly arranged and spotless, not a lick of trash or graffiti He nodded, impressed. The squeegees were even aligned, all at a proper 45 degree angle. Stepping between the pumps, he moved toward the store.

It was then he noticed the place was dark.

Carson frowned. He checked his watch: 9:55pm.

"SME my fat Aunt Fanny," he said quietly. "What good are end caps if you don't have the sense to turn the lights on?" He stepped over the curb and up to the glass, peered inside. There was a glow from the Freezie machine and several other neon displays by which Carson could see orderly shelves and the trademark 24/7 layout. It felt like home. Home with a big-time makeover and the lights out, but home.

Carson scratched his chin. Probably just a fuse. It made sense - all the AC this time of year drew a lot of juice, plus the place was loaded with a lot more shiny pre-processed-food-warming gadgets than his own. He shrugged and hit the door. *So much for newer is better...*

A wash of cool air struck him, and he was momentarily disoriented by the perfectly healthy non-warbling door chime. Then, he looked up smack into the most elegant, tasteful, well presented end cap he had ever seen. Strategically placed just off center of the entrance, it was masterfully arranged around the cardboard cutout of the star of this summer's action blockbuster. Blue two-dimensional eyes stared him boldly, coolly down, as if daring him *not* to select one of the products peeking over cardboard shoulders. Carson stared, captivated. The layout. The staging. The presentation.

"Alright," he admitted quietly. "That's one hell of an end cap" With some difficulty, he tore his eyes away and took a step into the store. "Hey, Carl?" he called. "Carl?! Yo, Carl my man! Carson Dudley, Belfry 24/7. You here, buddy? Is there a SME in the houuusssse....?"

Then, he saw the figure. It was a man, standing still in the middle of the store by the self-serve espresso machine, leaning on a mop, the water bucket still at his feet. His back was to Carson, and he wasn't moving.

Something suddenly felt wrong.

Very wrong.

A buzzing sound reached Carson's ears. He looked, spotted several fat black flies circling the figure. The man was wearing a standard 24/7 uniform shirt, tan, just like his own. Emblazoned across the back in cheerful orange were the letters C-A-R-L.

"Oh. Er... there you are." Carson cleared his throat hesitantly. "Um... Carl?" No response. "Hey, dude... I'm, uh... I'm here for that... for that job shadow. Looks like you, er... maybe blew a fuse, or something."

Bathed in the multicolored glow of the store's interior signage, Carl looked eery and surreal, the green and yellow neon giving him a gaunt appearance. Carson edged forward another step, flicked his eyes about the shop. Everything else looked fine. Clean, neat and well ordered, a place for everything and everything in its place.

Except Carl.

Carson cleared his throat loudly, tried again. "Hey, uh... Carl! Dude... you okay, bro?"

Carl's hand twitched.

Carson's twitched too. He stopped talking; eyes glued. The figure started to sway, gently, side to side. Carson thought he detected a low, barely audible moan. He also noticed something dark at the figure's feet. Dark and wet.

Carson eased forward another step, palms starting to sweat. "You okay, dude? You don't look so good. I mean, we just met, so I don't know, maybe this is a regular thing for you..." Carson froze.

It was blood.

The pool at the clerk's feet shone bright and red in the reflected

 153

neon. And there was too much, too close for it to be anyone else's or for the clerk's condition to be anything but unpleasant. As the realization hit him like a punch in the gut, the figure's head slowly began to swivel. A low, animal groan leaked out from between cracked lips.

"Nnnnnnn..."

He sounded hungry.

Carson's blood went cold. "Oh, crabapples..."

The mop fell from numb fingers, struck the tile with a clatter that jarred Carson's nerves. He realized suddenly how silent the store was. Silent except for Carl's moan, which was rapidly upshifting into a growl.

Except this wasn't Carl - not anymore.

A face slowly crept into view, peering back over a hunched shoulder. A bleak garish face, shot through with dark protruding veins and cast in a ghastly greenish hue. Carson didn't know if it was from the neon lights, or just a bad bag of pork rinds, but didn't care. All he knew was that the single, milky, dead white eye that looked back at him - at *him* - was one he had seen before, or at least one very much like it. And he didn't want to be in the building any more.

"Nnnnnnn!"

Carson whirled to flee just as Carl whirled to charge, the clerk's speed as surprising and disturbing as the fevered hunger on his face. Off balance and halfway to a full panic, Carson veered too far left and crashed headlong into the end cap, tossing cans everywhere and going down in a clatter. Dead weight piled onto him a split-second later, crushing the wind out of him and jamming him painfully into the cans. Fingers clutched madly at his throat. The horrible stink of the thing that had once been Carl washed over him in gagging waves. It was a smell he knew.

Carson wrestled and fought, tearing at the powerful hands and desperately trying to twist to his back, skin crawling, struggling mightily to maintain his wits. It was deathly still and silent as they thrashed and writhed among the cans; silent except for the low, growling moan that continued to leak from Carson's assailant.

Carson strained, lurched, bucked with all his might, barely able to keep it together as he felt himself slowly weakening beneath the crushing weight that pinned him. The growling moan grew louder, closer, filling his ear. Something hard brushed his shoulder, clicked.

Teeth.

Carson wrenched violently with every ounce of frantic strength he could muster. Carl's body lurched up... then dropped straight back. He was immovable, relentless, clinging like a drowning rat to a plank. The fabric of Carson's shirt pulled tight at the neck as teeth caught and yanked. Carson wrenched again, violently, so violently he felt something pop in his shoulder. A wave of heat and agony washed through him. He yelled, a wordless, unintelligible shout torn from his throat by desperation and horror, and wrenched again with the last of his fading strength. This time, Carl shifted, slipped - not much, but enough. A can rolled under his arm; he slipped a fraction more. Carson shouted again and threw a vicious elbow, smashing into Carl's throat and chopping the moaning growl into a hacking cough. Carl jerked sideways, tilted, teetered...

Carson felt the weight go, and with a final desperate heave, he was free. An instant later, he was on his feet, clutching his shoulder and staggering back into the darkness, looking for a weapon, any weapon. Carl was up in a deuce and hot on his heels, dead eyes fixed, gleaming hungrily out of the shadows. His face was contorted, dark veins popping, jaws gaping. A bit of fabric from Carson's shirt hung from his teeth. He came in crouched and low.

Hungry.

Carson backpedaled, fast, yanking bottles, cans, boxes, anything he could lay his hands on off the shelves and chucking them hard, ignoring the pain in his shoulder. Some missed, some hit, bounced off Carl's head, chest. Carl came on, oblivious, moaning, gaining ground, reaching out, groping... until Carson reached the household aisle and hurled a gallon bleach bottle that bent Carl's head to his shoulder and spun him a half turn around. He crashed into a shelf, and Carson kicked him hard, toppling the man and the unit. He turned and ran then, blind in the dark, heart smashing against his ribcage and threatening to drown the sound of the Carl's incessant drone.

The door! Carson's brain screamed. *Where is the door?!* He whirled, ducked blindly down an aisle, came up against the walk-in freezer. *Back of the store! Good! You've got your bearings. Now, turn around and MOVE!* He did.

Feet pumping, Carson reached the espresso machine, slid out into the heart of the mini-mart and then to a rapid halt as Carl lunged from the shadows across from him, blocking his way. Behind the Carl-thing, beckoning, were the friendly, winking street lights of the Romero District. They might as well have been Mars.

Carl snarled, all bared teeth and clutching hands, put his head down and charged. Carson jerked back instinctively, and his foot nudged wood. The mop. He hooked his tennis shoe under the handle and kicked it up into his hand. It wasn't a bat - but it would do.

And suddenly, he was charging too. Suddenly, something inside him wouldn't let him turn and run, as every other part of his being was screaming at him to do - something that forced him to stay, to fight, to take the thing head on. With a snarl of his own, he lunged forward, bursting with adrenaline and a sudden hot anger.

They came together a second later. Gripping the mop like a staff in both hands, Carson shoved it out straight and hard. The sturdy Seven Corporation handle slipped between Carl's groping fingers and smashed lengthwise across his face, adding the force of his lunge to Carson's own. Carl's neck snapped back, and he lifted off his feet, crashing down hard from five feet off the floor. The mop handle broke with a loud *crack!* Off balance and unprepared for the success of his attack, Carson stumbled forward, carried by momentum. He slipped in the pool of blood and crashed painfully to his knee. Fireworks sizzled up his thigh and his leg went numb.

"Nnnnnnn!"

Clutching fingers scrabbled on his jeans, snagged hold of the leg and pulled. Carl, on the floor, dragged himself forward, grasping, trying to get his other hand a hold as well, mouth yawing crazily. Carson caught a glimpse of a horrible wound on the man's throat. He yelled again, grabbed the counter for support, slipped, then realized he was still holding the halves of the mop handle. Weapons. He turned with a roar and laid into Carl with both at once, a savage, furious beating, raining blows to the thing's face, neck and skull like the kid from anger management finally getting a crack at the piñata.

"You wanna manage some end caps?! I'll show ya how to manage some end caps!" Again and again, in a frenzy of rage and fear, Carson lashed out, smashing away at the horrific features, the clutching hands. Under his furious assault, one tore loose. Then, Carl's head took a vicious crossing shot, and his other hand jarred loose, and for the second, time Carson was free. He surged to his feet, backed wildly into the front counter and felt a painful jab of metal in his back. Painful, yet familiar.

Spickets. Freezie spickets.

Carl had rolled to his belly, was recovering quickly. His face oozed dark juices from a dozen gashes and welts, but he crawled forward relentlessly, swiftly, slithering on the blood-smeared tiles. Carson's brain screamed at him again to flee, but again he crushed the thought. Instead, he seized the heavy Freezie machine and heaved. His shoulder screamed, but he kept on with furious resolve. Carl was at his feet now. Grabbing at his sneakers. Carson heaved again. The machine tilted, teetered ponderously... then plunged off the counter and straight down onto Carl's head, striking full on one corner with a sickening crunch.

Carson scooted back, waited, breathless.

The moaning had stopped. The store was silent.

As he stared down at the horrific site, Carson's wild eyes caught a sticker on the side of the machine declaring proudly *"It's always the right time for a Freezie!"*

"You can say that again..." He backed away, banged into a shelf, turned, staggered for the front door, still clutching one half of the mop handle. Outside, the night air hit him like a blast furnace, and he sucked it in, lungs burning. As he stood, panting and gasping, his eyes darted across the quiet night scene of the Romero District, desperately seeking something normal to re-anchor himself to reality. The empty street. A trendy clothing store. The big fancy windows of a luxury car dealership. He forced himself to relax, to breathe. His eyes drifted up the front of the dealership, up the letters of the giant red sign.

Something was there.

He froze, skin tingling. Something was clinging to the side of the man-sized letter "L" in the *"Lexus of Romero"* sign. Something clothed entirely in black. Something that hung like a spider, a slice of shadow. Something he had seen before.

The ninja.

And above it, another something... only this one far more sinister. Carson felt it first, before he saw it - standing on the rooftop just above the sign. It was a gaunt, night black figure, tall, wrapped in a tattered, hooded cloak that rustled in the scorching night air. Only, it didn't feel hot any more. It felt cold. Icy cold. Waves of it washed over him, and Carson realized dimly that it was not a natural cold but a spiritual one - like the concentrated chill of death.

Then Carson's jaw tightened The little spark of whatever it was that had made him charge Carl flared once more. He lifted the mop in both hands, setting into a batter's stance and wishing fleetingly that he had retained the handle end and not the one with the dirty mop head. But it didn't matter. He had a weapon. He had an enemy. And he had

had enough.

So engrossed was he, however, that Carson failed to notice a shadow behind him. A shadow that crawled slowly across the pavement as another figure, unseen, approached him stealthily from behind. The shadow touched his ankle. Ran up his calf. Then across his back. A ragged breath. A hand reached out...

"You guys got Freezies?"

Carson started and whirled, almost smashing the mop into the face of a pimply teenage kid in a Transformers T-shirt. The boy's date dropped her smart phone with a gasp, and it clattered to the sidewalk, stopping cold a giddy text to her BFF who was eagerly awaiting news of a magical evening out. She wouldn't get it.

A foot away the boy gaped, speechless and terrified. Carson stood fiercely, glaring, mop ready.

r u there?!

The words flickered across the face of the phone on the pavement, insistent in green.

Carson blinked, shook his head. He whirled back to the rooftop.

There was nothing.

They were gone.

He lowered his mop. Tension and anger drained away, leaving only the haunting echo of fear, the ache in his knee, the burning in his shoulder and a pair of stunned tweens who finally had something worthwhile to Facebook about.

"Yeah, kid," Carson answered slowly. "We got Freezies. But tonight... they're on Carl."

CHAPTER NINE

Grave Digging

"What... is... *wrong* with you, Mr. Dudley?!"

"Well... my knee's a lot better, but my shoulder hurts like crazy. You wouldn't have any Icy Hot, would you Detective?"

A pencil snapped.

"That's it. Get out."

"I'll get out when you find a body!"

"There *is* no body!"

"Did you look? Did you even look?!"

"We looked!"

Beat.

"Did you look under the Freezie machine?"

"Everywhere, Mr. Dudley! We looked everywhere! Believe it or not, we've looked for dead bodies before! And we're pretty good at it! But funny thing - when we look for *your* bodies, we don't find anything. Ever! No body, no blood, no fibers, no trace evidence, nothing!"

"Well... what about Carl? He's still missing, right?"

Beat.

 159

"Well?!"

"We'll find him."

Carson snorted. "Great. The one thing I know you'll never find is the one thing you're looking for."

"I don't like the tone of your voice, Mr. Dudley. You'd best mind your step. This is the third time I've seen you this year. The third homicide - *alleged* homicide - and you know what I think? I think you saw the first dead body, and it knocked a screw loose - now you're seeing them everywhere. I don't know what's broken in you, but get it out of here and get it fixed. It's sad and it's wasting my time!"

"You think I *want* to look like a lunatic?!"

"Yes!"

Carson paused. "I... I don't know where to go with that."

"I'll tell you where to go - *out*!" Parsons was on his feet now, eyes bulging. "*Out* of my office, *out* of my precinct, *out* of my life! And be thankful you're not going *into* jail! Do not return - I repeat *do not return* - and do NOT speak to me again unless you pull up in front of this office with a corpse in your trunk!"

Beat.

"I don't have a car."

"*OUT!*" The blinds rattled. Heads poked out from other offices down the hall. Carson was, strangely enough, not as upset as he thought he'd be. The body was gone - again. Parsons thought he was nuts - again. There were dire supernatural forces at work in Las Calamas that wanted him dead - again. In a strange way, it just seemed like everything was finally fitting into its proper place.

Again.

Carson rose without comment and limped out, resisting the urge to slam the door on the cluttered little office. He limped past the gauntlet of gawking cops, down the broad steps of the precinct building and out into the swelter of mid-morning Las Calamas. He had his cell phone out and was already dialing Dex. It was time for an ally. Any ally.

Dex answered on the seventh ring, sounding groggy. "Yo..."

"I just fought a zombie."

"I'm awake now."

Carson related the story as he strode down the wide sidewalk, past the community park where happy civilians who had not recently been assaulted by the undead frolicked and splashed in the public pool. He left nothing out. "After that," he concluded, "I jammed out of there and made a beeline for the cops. Made 'em get Parsons out of bed which, in

 160

hindsight, might not have been the best idea. He had me sweating it in containment all night. Didn't even take my statement until this morning, and you can imagine how well that went."

"I can. What'd you tell him?"

"That I went to the store for my job shadow, found the place busted up and Carl dead when I got there, and then ran like hell. Parts of it are very close to true."

"That's it?"

"What was I supposed to say... that I got jumped by a zombie?! That I killed Carl, but it's okay because I think he was already dead?! Uh-uh! No way, forget it! I tried playing it straight with Parsons - twice! - and now he thinks I'm mental. Dude... I am *never* talking to the cops again. Ever!"

"Always been my policy," Dex rumbled. "Cops suck. So... Parsons checked it out, yeah? He must've gone by the place at least. And I'm guessin' by your general attitude that he didn't find anything."

"He didn't find Carl, that's for sure - or anything else for that matter. According to Parsons, it was evidence free. Which means somebody doesn't want this getting out and sanitized the place. Unless, of course, Carl revived, pulled the Freezie machine out of his skull and tidied up a bit before staggering off to the nearest graveyard. He *was* supposed to be a model employee."

"Negative," there was concern in Dex's deep rumble. "You drop a dude like that, he don't get up - whether he's dead already or not. We're in some wicked supernatural *&^% here."

"Maybe. Or maybe it's just us - maybe we're doing something wrong when we cap these guys. Knock one out a window, he gets up and walks off. Drop a hundred pounds of stainless on another one, he gets up and walks off. Maybe these guys were only *technically* dead. We gotta start trying for *completely* dead."

"I like your thinking." Dex paused. "Wanna know what *I'm* thinking?"

"You're thinking Fujikacorp."

"Damn straight. I say we go over there and shake the tree. I ain't had breakfast yet, but I can wait on Corn Flakes..." his voice trailed off ominously. It sounded like a lawsuit waiting to happen.

Carson recalled the details of their last encounter with Fujikacorp and didn't need Kinkade to tell him what a terrible idea it would be to put in another appearance at corporate HQ. Along with those thoughts came, unbidden, a recollection of his assignment to fire Dex. With a jolt, Carson realized that he was out of time. His week was up. Today was the day.

"No. Uh... not yet. I'm gonna do some poking around. Check out a few leads. Sit tight, and I'll let you know what I find out. The, uh... the tree shaking thing... just give it a bit."

"Your op, your call," Dex sounded disappointed. "But if I miss out on some head bashing, I ain't gonna be happy. I got bruises from them Fujikacorp *&^%! that ain't got a thank you note yet."

"You'll be the first to know." Carson paused, mustered his courage. "Hey, uh... you gonna be in tonight? There's something I gotta talk to you about."

"You can tell me about a zombie attack over the phone, but there's something else you gotta tell me to my face? Is Hostess going out of business?"

"No, it's just... I'll tell you tonight. Gotta go." Carson hung up and stuffed the phone into his pocket. He stopped for a moment, listening to the splashing and laughing coming from the pool. He stared through the chain link fence that protected the happy swimmers from the outside world. A kid in blue shorts stood hesitantly for a moment at the top of the big slide, looking nervous. Then, throwing caution to the wind, he jumped aboard, shot down the chute and plunged into the sparkling, crystal clear water with a mighty splash. Peals of delighted, carefree laughter filled the air.

Carson knew he, too, for some strange reason, was once more standing at the top of his own slide. Staring down, down, down the long, twisting, slippery slope. Only the outcome wasn't guaranteed to be such a pleasant surprise. Not by a long shot. He was about to get into it again. Deep.

But unlike last time, he wasn't just going to sit around and wait for it. This time, he was going to meet it head on. Four months ago, he had come face to face with a savage, bloodthirsty vampiress. He had also, and of infinitely greater importance, come face to face with something else: a deep, primal connection with a force that had pushed him on in the face of overwhelming terror and impossible odds.

Purpose.

Carson stood for a moment, letting the feeling wash over him once more. As he watched the kid in the blue suit zoom down the slide again, he realized that he should be wishing he was that kid: carefree, fun loving, without a worry in the world. But he wasn't.

Purpose.

It was the same as when Pete first told him there were vampires. He'd known right then that he was going to do something about it. And now he knew there were zombies. It was their turn.

Carson stepped away from the fence and set off briskly down the street, heading for the nearest bus stop. As he walked, he tugged Pete's faded red bandana out of his jeans and tied it around his neck. There were things to be done now, steps to be taken. He had formed his plan last night, knowing, somehow, that Parsons would be no help. It was just as well. If Parsons and his team had checked the store more carefully, they might have noticed that there was something missing besides Carl: several cases of Banana Yoo-hoo.

Carson fished his bus pass out of his pocket, checked his watch. It was almost 10 a.m. Good enough. Leet would just be getting up or would be after a phone call. Carson would direct him to look outside his front door and, when he found the single bottle of Yoo-hoo there, Carson would tell him what he had to do to get the rest.

He waited for a dump truck to pass, cut across the street to grab a breakfast burrito from a street vendor and parked himself at the bus stop. The rest of the passengers crowded together under the shade of the awning, and Carson joined them. It had been a long night, would be a long day, and he would need to conserve his energy. He munched slowly, tuning out the idle chatter around him.

First, talk to Leet. Second, chase down some evidence. Third, call the Gang and lay it all on the line - circle the wagons, get the posse together. Together. It was how they'd taken down Vanessa. It was how they'd get through this little pickle too. His phone was out, and he was dialing.

Leet answered on the first ring. "Creepy. I was just gonna call you."

Bingo.

"Talk to me."

"Whoa. Smaller bites, man. Sounds like you've got a whole chihuahua in there."

"Sorry - breakfast."

"Yeah? Well, I hope it's a hearty one. I've got some goodies for you."

Carson forced a swallow. It hurt. He ignored it, reached into his pocket for a pencil stub. "You've been busy."

"Yeah. Turns out, this is a lot more fun than erasing parking tickets. But first things first - what did you find at the mystery spot?"

"A flower shop."

"A *flower* shop? Why the heck would Fujika buy a flower shop?"

"Dunno. Place was closed, but I'm headed back to check it out right now. See if I can get some answers. Now... what've you got?"

"Plenty. I backtracked some of our friend Haruki's traffic through the system, found some files he'd been snooping through. Not his stuff, definitely someone's dirty laundry. Buried deep, man, real deep. Don't know what they are, exactly, but he was real interested in 'em."

"And?"

"And... I don't know. It's all in some kind of code. Encrypted. And it's in Japanese. Did I mention it was in Japanese?"

"I heard Yoo-hoo is re-releasing Chocolate Banana."

"I've always wanted to learn Japanese."

"Awesome. Get crackin'."

"Thought you'd say that. Already started. Got another address."

Carson looked around for something to write on, settled for the greasy wrapper of his half-eaten burrito. "Gimme."

Leet rattled it off. "And that's just for starters. I'll keep on it - shoot you some more as I go. Okay... now for the weird stuff."

"Shoot."

"What do you know about ninjas?"

Silence.

"You still there?"

"Yeah... just dropped the phone. Did you say 'ninjas'?"

"Bet your Bushido I did. Turns out Haruki was nuts about 'em. Practically gaga. Remember those books piled on his desk? Half of them were about ninjas. Other half was weirdsville too, real kooky stuff: mythology, necrology, demonology and some other -ologies I've never even heard of. Incidentally, I never cracked library records before, turns out it's pretty easy. Oh, and there's something else," Leet was rushing now, spilling it all out in an excited tumble. "I poked through his Web browsing history too - he was spending a lot of time in online issues of the local tabloids. *Word on the Street, LC Confidential, Las Calamas Daily World Planet*, you know the ones. But - here's the brain bender - they were all running the same stories. A series of break-ins by... drum roll please... ninjas!"

"You're kidding?!"

"If I'm lyin', I'm dyin'. These guys picked some truly weird spots to hit, too, old school weird. An antique store, a museum, an apothecary... I don't even know what that is! What the heck's an apothecary?!"

Carson's brain reeled. "Ninjas on the loose in the streets of Las Calamas?! Why haven't I heard about this?" He made a mental note to read more tabloids.

"Think about it; any headline that reads '*Ninja Robs Apothecary*' isn't exactly gonna end up on the front page of the Las Calamas Daily Tribune." The phone was silent a moment. "Or..."

"Or?"

"Or someone wanted it buried. Someone rich. Powerful. Influential. Someone with a great batting average. Wink wink, nudge nudge, say no more."

Carson processed furiously. Leet was right. The whole thing stunk to high heaven of coverup. But coverup of what? He considered going back to Parsons but discarded the idea almost the instant it was born. That door had closed long ago. Besides, he was fairly certain that announcing to the detective he had hacked into Fujikacorp's corporate database wasn't the ideal way to reestablish his credibility.

"...so they're tied in to Nubuyuki's beef with Fujika, somehow..." Leet was still going, hadn't even paused for breath. "...but I'll be minced if I can figure out how. Ninjas, man! This is out there! Freakin' outer space! What was this guy *doing*?!"

"You don't wanna know what I think. Look, great work. Top flight. Now keep digging. When you find something else, call me. And Leet..."

"Yeah?"

"Open your front door. You've earned it."

Carson snapped the phone shut. Things were starting to click now. A tingle of excitement raced through him. He could practically feel the rungs of the ladder under his hand as he climbed to the top of the slide. He glanced at his watch. His shift started at 10 p.m. Just over twelve hours. Plenty of time. Now - finally - he was getting somewhere.

By that evening, Carson had discovered exactly where it was that he was getting - lost. It had been a confusing, flustering, whirlwind day, and his brain was foggy with exhaustion and the oppressive, muggy heat. His feet hurt, his seat hurt, his shoulder hurt, and he was sticky and smelly from pounding the pavement. He shifted, trying to make himself more comfortable as the 420 bus cruised toward the outskirts of Belfry.

The day had definitely taken its toll. Leet had texted him a steady stream of addresses, a dozen in all, and he had tracked them down, every one, putting a severe strain on his energy and the "ride all month

 165

for free" promise of his bus pass. He rubbed his throbbing shoulder, wishing he had time for an ice pack and something stronger than the aspirin he'd bummed off a fellow passenger.

Carson's first stop had been the flower shop, and although the employees hadn't been much help - the Chinese proprietor spoke only a few words of English - Carson had managed to piece together some sketchy details. Shortly after the sale of the shop, the new owner, who more or less matched Fujika's description, had made a single appearance. He came for only one thing - a rare flower. A lotus. Judging by the excited, enthusiastic gestures and wild expressions of the employees, Carson gathered it was more than just "rare". It was downright priceless. One-of-a-kind, not even for sale.

Interesting, yes. Helpful, no. Carson had moved on.

The other addresses had proven even more confounding. Some were obvious real estate deals, just like the flower shop. Recent acquisitions to the Fujikacorp holdings; although for the life of him, Carson couldn't figure out how they fit into a corporate power scheme. There was a boardwalk oddities shop, a hole-in-the-wall antique dealer and a creepy private museum. Some were recently closed, by the look of it, for good. But at a few, Carson found people and managed to gather the same basic details as at the Orchid Road. Shortly after the sale, someone roughly fitting Fujika's description made a single appearance and left with something. Something rare.

The rest of the places on the list were an even bigger mystery, since they hadn't recently changed hands. These were as eclectic and varied as the previous set: an herbalist shop, an exclusive, high priced Indonesian import/export firm and even a few nameless warehouses with dour-faced, silent attendants, where management was "unavailable". While the buildings themselves hadn't been purchased by Fujika, Carson felt certain that *something* had. If the proprietors knew anything, however, they were tight-lipped about it. Any questions about recent strange transactions or a description of Fujika usually brought an intense reaction and an invitation to leave.

In the end, after a long, hot, wearisome day, Carson had few concrete conclusions. But that didn't matter. He may not have answers, but he had information. Enough to call in the cavalry. Enough to bring the Gang back together.

And so, as the sun sank low over the ocean, Carson had made his calls. The meeting was set for tomorrow night. Or at least, so he hoped. Sister Becky and Kiki had both been voice mails; Dex was the only one who'd said he'd be there for sure. And that answer might change after tonight. Carson felt hollow, thinking about the unavoidable unpleasantness that awaited him and Dex. But after that... well, that would be Dex's call.

In the meantime, Carson had work-related problems of his own. He glanced at his watch. 10:15. Fifteen minutes past the start of his shift. That was bad news. He was pretty sure *late* wasn't the kind of person Seven Corporation was looking for.

His phone rang.

It was Leet. "How's the weirdo express?" Leet's voice was thick and slurred. There was a noisy slurp, chased by a satisfied sigh. Carson had long ago given him the location of the Yoo-hoo stash.

"I'll tell you one thing - it stops at some places you don't find on a tour bus."

"Izzat so? Get me any souvenirs?"

"No - but someone did. These addresses you found, they look like stops on a shopping spree. I don't think it was about the real estate, I think someone was picking up goodies. Probably Fujika. And if this is his shopping list, it's gonna be one bizarre Christmas."

"How bizarre?"

"Fingernails from a dead emperor, a root from some plant I can't pronounce, ceremonial bones, a sorcerer's bag from the Muramachi period... all of it ancient and most of it not for sale."

"No monkey's paw?"

"Wait a sec..." Carson checked the list he'd scrawled on the crumpled burrito wrapper. "Yep, there it is - monkey's paw. Little hard to read. Some crazy shop in Chinatown."

"You were in Chinatown?"

"I was everywhere."

"Yeah? Well, I know one place I've been that you haven't, Ichiro Fujika's personal files."

Carson sat up straighter. "Speaking of Christmas..."

"Told you I was good - turns out that's an understatement; I'm freakin' *awesome*!" Leet belched softly. "Followed another one of Haruki's digital rabbit trails, but he got stone cold stopped by this one - couldn't get through the door. Awesomeness problems, obviously. Something I don't suffer from. Took me a bit, but I cracked 'em. Files were locked down tight, it was sweet! Multiple security layers, overlapping protocols, wicked encryption, too, used a 128 bit..."

"Leet. Focus. I'm on the way to work, and I could very well be torn apart by a wild corporate suit when I get there. Give me something to keep me going."

"Hm? Oh, right. Gotcha. So, a lot of it's boring business stuff, insider trading and that, but there are some nuggets. For example, why would you keep the lights on in a store that wasn't open?"

"I wouldn't."

"Exactly. But Fujikacorp does."

"Say what?"

"The big Super Maxi-Pad - the one down in Romero? Supposed to be all fancy and stuff, their flagship or something... and by the way, it does look sweet. I've got some of the blueprints here..." Fingers tapped keys. "Sweeeeeet..."

"Leet. Rival store. Trying to crush us. Sensitive subject."

"Oh... yeah. Sorry." He could hear Leet take a discrete slurp of Yoo-hoo. "Anyway, it hasn't opened yet. Waiting on some zoning snafu or something. But you couldn't tell it from the power bills. It's got lights, AC, refrigeration... sucking down water and sewer too."

"Maybe they're just training..."

"Uh-uh. No payroll records. Got shipments coming in, too."

"Shipments... to an empty store?! What kind of shipments?"

"Dunno. Manifests are real vague, just list everything as 'goods'."

"What the frack does that mean?"

"It means either Fujika has a heck of a sweet tooth, or he's stashing stuff at the SMP he doesn't want found. And you know what?" Another sip, a soft moan. "I think it may be people."

"People?! How could you possibly know that?"

"I don't - so don't get your knickers in a knot. It's totally just a guess. But I backtracked those shipments, and the trail stops at this shady international shipping company. A company which, I happen to know, ships a lot more than just paper lanterns. We're talking white slavery. Human trafficking. You're wondering how I know, right? Well see, I did a job for a guy once..."

"Leet - is this going to put me on the witness stand if I hear it?"

"Potentially."

"Then skip it. I've got enough problems."

"Suit yourself," he heard Leet shrug. "Bottom line is, I'm not sure what your pal Fujika is up to, but it's not good. In fact, it could be very, very bad. Really very bad. And that's just the stuff they're shipping *in*."

"Hold up... they're shipping *out* too?!"

"Yeah. And just because I know you're gonna ask, I don't know

 168

what, and I don't know *where.* There's a private trucking company doing the transport, and I can't find any specifics. Again, the trail is covered up good."

"Leet... none of this makes any sense."

"I know. It's like the final season of *Lost.* But if it makes you feel better, whatever's going on, I think it's stopped. They used to send out a truck every couple days. Then one a week. Now... I haven't seen anything for the last two."

Carson made a small noise. He tried to find words to put behind it, came up with nothing.

"Thought you might feel that way. Oh, and one more thing..." Leet belched. "Sorry, not that - I found one more address. Haruki had a question mark by this one, not sure what it is. Doesn't look like Fujika bought the place, just made a purchase there, maybe. Weird thing is, it's down by your mini-mart."

"The 24/7? What's the address?"

Leet read it off.

Carson frowned. "That's our street, alright." He closed his eyes, pictured the neighborhood. "But what's..." He froze. His eyes snapped open. He knew exactly what that address was, didn't need a GPS or a map to confirm it. He'd stared at the place a hundred times. He'd even seen it in his dreams.

It was the Curio Shop.

A dizzy feeling swirled in the pit of his stomach, as if he had just dropped off the end of the slide and was hanging suspended in mid-air. Beneath him, fathomless, inscrutable and waiting to swallow him whole, was the deep end of the pool.

Leet's voice crackled. "You still there, Charity?"

"Yeah, yeah. Just... are you sure about that address?"

"Sure as shootin'. That's where the transaction went through."

"Leet... that can't be. I know that shop; it's not even open! I've never even seen..."

The air brakes kicked on, and the bus heaved to a stop. The door swished open. Carson realized they had arrived. The heat of the night rushed in, mixed with the chill that was running up his spine and made him feel slightly sick. As he glanced out the window, he saw something that made the feeling even worse, a sleek black BMW parked in the manager's spot. It was Kinkade.

"Hang on, Leet. I'll have to call you back. Things are about to get interesting." He rose and headed for the front of the bus, snapping his phone shut on Leet's reply, eyes scanning the store through the front window. He caught a glimpse of brown suit. His stomach churned. Kinkade was posted by the front counter like a sentinel - one eye on the door, the other on his tablet. Stanley lounged nearby, chatting like they were old friends, but Kinkade was only half listening. Carson could feel Kinkade's prison warden stare from there.

Damn.

"'Night, Carson. Have a good shift!" The driver tipped his hat, same slow grin as always.

"Thanks, Big Joe. It may be the shortest one of my life." Carson dropped down the steps two at a time and hit the sidewalk. He headed straight for the front door in spite of the inclination his feet had to take him in the opposite direction. There was no sense in postponing the inevitable. Carson hit the door, stepped from the heat of the night to the heat of the store.

Before the sickly door chime could even begin, Kinkade was on him. "My office, Dudley. Now."

As usual, Kinkade's voice was flat and efficient, as if expending energy on an angry tone or elevated volume wouldn't have a beneficial ROI. But it didn't sound happy, either. If anything, it was extra flat and extra efficient, and that could only mean trouble. Carson wished Kinkade would yell, shout, wave his arms, maybe throw a stapler or two. It would almost be preferable, show that he was human instead of the mechanical, robotic, mirthless, ruthless corporate automaton that he truly was. Carson sighed. It was like getting lectured by the Terminator. Suddenly, he was tired of getting lectured.

Kinkade led the way and Carson followed. An insect - some kind of winged beetle - buzzed out of nowhere and zoomed for his face. He swatted at it in irritation, trailed Kinkade into his sterile, bureaucratic lair.

Kinkade seated himself behind the desk without bending. He laid his tablet carefully in its designated space, squared it with the edges of the desk. Carson fidgeted. It felt like he had been called into the principal's office. He was tired of that, too. He felt himself getting mad.

Kinkade indicated a chair. "Sit."

"No."

Kinkade flicked his gaze up at Carson.

"Thanks," Carson added.

Something faint, almost like surprise, registered on Kinkade's face.

 170

Carson was certain he saw the man's eyebrow quirk. It was the closest thing yet to an expression.

"You're late." Kinkade dropped the accusation, then waited, staring. It was the kind of ridiculously obvious comment a boss made when he wanted to put an employee in his place. Carson knew he should apologize, grovel a little, maybe even offer to make up the time. But right now, he wasn't in the mood. He was hot, achy, exhausted, starving and frustrated. He was also very tired of corporations.

"Yes," he answered bluntly. "Yes I am."

Kinkade blinked. For a moment, he seemed uncertain of how to proceed, as if all the buzzwords and acronyms and corporate handbooks hadn't prepared him to handle the simple, honest truth. But for a moment only. He bent over his tablet, tapped and scrawled. "And you're out of uniform."

"Yes. But think how late I would have been if I'd stopped to grab it. You can't have it both ways." Carson smiled as if he were trading pleasantries with a neighbor over the backyard fence.

"And that bandana... it's not regulation." Kinkade spoke without looking up, just tapped and scrawled.

"It's the red, isn't it? I know, people say it's not my color. I'm more of a Summer."

This time, Kinkade did look up. There was a little furrow on his brow that Carson had never seen before. He regarded Carson for a moment, unblinking, like an owl staring at a shadow on the barnyard floor, trying to decide if it was a mouse or not. Then, he looked back at his tablet and tap-scribbled. "These are actionable items. All three will be going on your employment history as negative achievements." Kinkade looked up again, contemplating him. "I must inform you, young man, that you are in serious jeopardy of uncompleting this promotion. Considering your recent transgressions, I am starting to realize why this store was in such a shambles when I arrived."

"Hey..." Carson bristled. "Cut me down all you want but don't diss the 24/7. She's a good store."

"Based on my observations, however," Kinkade clipped on, unfazed. "The blame is only partially yours. I've been going through the books. Jack wasn't much better himself. Sloppy. Careless. Undisciplined. I haven't seen a wiener inventory this out of balance in fifteen years."

Carson could feel himself getting hotter. "Jack made this store what it is." His eyes narrowed, stabbed at Kinkade. "You didn't."

Kinkade hadn't tapped or scribbled for several moments. His eyes were locked on Carson's. "I don't think I like your tone, Dudley."

"Funny... the cops didn't either." The bug was back, suddenly dive bombing Carson's face. He swiped at it angrily, then turned back to Kinkade, ready for another shot. Amazingly, the man had bent back over his tablet and was again tapping away.

"Yes. The police. I understand you had reason to contact them again last night. Something about your job shadow."

"Damn straight. And since you brought it up, let me tell you about my little deep dive with your buddy Carl..."

"There's no need. I spoke with Detective Parsons earlier today."

"Yeah? And what did he have to say?"

"He asked if we enforced mandatory drug testing." The way Kinkade said it made it sound like he was considering the idea. "He also told me the basic elements of your statement."

"He told you about Carl?"

"He told me everything I needed to know."

Carson knew right then that further discussion was pointless.

Kinkade was tapping again. "In light of this, I am also giving you a fourth negative achievement. Failure to complete a job shadow."

"What?!" Carson clapped hands to his head. "How was I supposed to... the dude was *dead*!"

"Every productivity milestone has its challenges, Dudley. Going on in the face of all of them, finding a way... *that's* the kind of person Seven Corporation is looking for. For all we know, you made up the whole thing as an excuse for avoiding the assignment."

"Now you... you think that... you're accusing me of...?!"

"Your record is hardly exemplary, Dudley. People do strange things under stress. When pushed to their limits, it is difficult to predict how they will react. Wouldn't you say?"

"And what about Carl?! Did I kill him too, just cuz I didn't feel like going to work?! Maybe next time you put me on swing shift, I'll just blow up the freakin' store!"

"Now you're being ridiculous."

"Ridiculous?! No, ridiculous would be making all that up! Why wouldn't I just play sick?! Say I lost my bus pass?! Look, I saw it; it's the truth - the store was smashed up, Carl was dead!"

"Dead, Dudley?" Kinkade eyed him dubiously, a tiny crinkle of doubt lodged between his eyes.

"Yeah..." Carson planted his knuckles on the desk and leaned across. "...but you'd be happy to know his end caps looked real nice."

The little crinkle became a definite crease. "End caps are no laughing matter, Dudley."

"Neither is a dead employee!"

"And can you show us one?"

Carson faltered. He felt the redness in his face, didn't want to back down but had no answers. "No." He ground the word out through clenched teeth.

"Then, until you can, the matter is closed." Kinkade gave his tablet a final, authoritative *tap.* It was the bang of the judge's gavel. Carson forced himself to think about Jack and the thirty years of his life the old man had invested in this place. The love, the care, the passion for all things fried. He forced his breathing to slow, unclenched his fists, leaned back. He fumbled for the chair, sat. He pictured himself sitting on the beach beside Jack in Hawaii. Sipping a Freezie.

A yellow one.

Cool.

Refreshing.

The bug zoomed him again, and he swatted it fiercely.

"Now then," Kinkade had already moved on. "I have prepared your final productivity milestone." Kinkade thrust a large important looking packet labeled with large important looking letters at him. "The Disaster Preparedness Plan. You and Stanley will both craft a uniquely tailored safety blueprint for this store based on the Seven Corporation guidelines in Sections Twenty through Twenty-Five."

Carson felt the weight of the packet. It pushed what was left of his soul down into his sneakers.

"I cannot stress enough the importance of this milestone. My decision on the night manager position will depend heavily upon it. Stanley has already received his packet and, I am certain, is well under way, so you have a bit of catching up to do. Be thorough. Disaster preparedness is a serious matter. Oh, and there is one additional matter, more of my paper has become... damaged." Kinkade picked up a stack of paper that was crispy yellow around the edges.

Before he could continue, a booming voice reached them from inside the store. "Cheese, sucka... I said *cheeeeese*!"

Dex.

Carson felt a jolt of despair. Just when he thought he'd hit rock bottom, it turned out there was little ways left to go.

"Ah..." Kinkade set aside the stack of paper. "Officer Jackson.

The perfect opportunity for you." He rose to his feet, picked up his tablet and tucked it under one arm. "A disappointing week, but at least, you have the opportunity to finish on a high note."

Carson gaped. "What... now?! In front of... everyone? Shouldn't we... I... at least... call him in here...?"

But Kinkade ignored him, marched through the office door and out into the store. Carson heaved to his feet and pursued.

Dex was by the front counter, carefully overseeing Stanley as the clerk poured liquid cheese onto an order of nachos.

"More... a little more... that's it, don't be shy! Load me up, sucka! C'mon... look at that poster you got hanging up over there... look at the *cheese* on that picture! That's what I'm payin' for! Yeah, that's the ticket... over here now, that chip looks a little lonely..." Dex glanced up. "Hey, Dud!" His grin lit up, broad white teeth like a shark's.

Only tonight, Dex wasn't the predator. Carson was.

Carson's face flushed. Kinkade drifted to the side, lifted his tablet, looking for all the world like he was trying to find an unobstructed view of the guillotine.

Carson swallowed. "Hey, dude." His voice sounded hollow.

At last satisfied with his order, Dex swept up the bowl. "Put it on my tab, Whitey." Dex grinned at Stanley, crunched a huge bite in his face.

Stanley caught a glimpse of Kinkade, read the look on Carson's face, sensed what was coming. He turned back to Dex with a grin of his own. "I don't think that'll be necessary."

Carson fidgeted, shuffled his feet as Dex strolled over. The guard stuffed another big bite into his mouth, oblivious. The crunching was unbelievably loud. Carson glanced about, praying for a crowded tour bus, an armed robbery, a plane crash, a stray meteorite, anything. But all he saw were a few customers wandering idly through the shelves.

"Hey, bro..." Dex's voice dropped. "How'd the snoopin' go? We ready to shake them trees?"

"No." Carson's answer was terse. He shot a glance at a couple of young parents cruising the baby aisle. The store suddenly felt crowded, and he wished everyone would just go away.

Dex's grin slipped. "Alright then." He glanced at Kinkade, who stood nearby, watching, his dark suit and white shirt making him look like a vulture in fancy shoes. "So... there was something else. Something you wanted to talk to me about. Something we had to do in person."

 174

"Not now."

"Yes." Kinkade said. "Now."

Dex turned his great head to face the man. His grin was still showing on his face, but it was no longer showing in his eyes.

"Hey, Pops. Dud said it would keep. Why don't you just lay off?"

"Dex!" Carson's voice cracked like a whip. "Cool it!"

Dex turned hard eyes to his friend. There was no sign of the grin now, anywhere. "You got something to say?"

"He does. Dudley... do it." Kinkade held his tablet out in front of him, poised to tap. Carson had the almost overwhelming impulse to knock it to the ground.

"Yeah, Carson," Stanley rasped. "It ain't gonna get any easier." His voice dripped with mock sympathy.

Carson had the almost overwhelming impulse to knock him to the ground too. "Shut up, Satan... Stan." The beetle thing was back, buzzing loudly in his ear. Carson swatted at it, missed. Without thinking, he used his bad shoulder, and it sent hot sparks up his neck.

An older fellow in a faded Hawaiian shirt approached the register but stopped, suddenly aware of the tension gripping the room. He clutched his fountain drink and a box of Triscuits protectively, glancing between the tight expressions. He looked uncomfortably like Jack.

"Proceed, Dudley."

"Give me a sec..."

"Do it."

"Yeah," Dex rumbled. "Maybe you should just do it."

Carson stood in the big man's shadow, had forgotten how *big* he really was. "Dex, look, you don't know..."

"Now, Dudley."

"Yeah, man... don't make the dude suffer..."

"C'mon, Dud. Let's have it..."

The bug was back again, this time tickling his ear. Carson slashed at it, missed again. Again, his bad shoulder. More sparks, and this time a gasp of pain. He looked up, and the room seemed to freeze in time.

The young couple, staring from the baby aisle.

Hawaiian shirt unmoving, eyes glued to the scene from behind his box of crackers.

Kinkade, cool and unemotional.

Stanley, leaning in, hungry.

Dex, glaring down, a drip of cheese on his chin.

Everyone watching.

 175

Waiting.

Carson felt detached, strangely, light headed from lack of sleep, stress and a day in the triple digit heat and bus fumes.

Then the words just came out. "You're fired."

Dex's nachos hit the floor. He swore.

"Dex... dude, I..."

"You *&^%$!"

Dex turned on his heel and headed for the door without another word. The look he gave Stanley on the way by, however, didn't require words. Stanley stumbled back, went white.

"Now then..." Kinkade stepped forward, tapped once on his tablet as if checking off a to-do list. "Let's get back to the matter of my papers, shall we?"

With a start, feeling returned to Carson's limbs. His fingers tingled uncomfortably, and his mouth felt dry and stale. He tasted bile. And he had never, ever before in his life felt so little concern for his job. "Screw your damn paper."

Kinkade blinked, stopped in mid tap. "I beg your pardon?"

"I said... screw - your - paper!" Carson took a step towards him. "You're so damn concerned about your damn paper! Here's a little tip - *you don't even use paper*!" He took another step. He was very close now. "You're always tap, tap, tapping on that damn tablet! Tapping, tapping, tapping, always tapping... I'm expecting Edgar Allan Poe to jump out any damn minute!"

Kinkade blinked at him. "Mind your tone, Dudley. There are customers in-store."

"Well screw them, too! You just made me fire my best friend!"

Kinkade clucked disapprovingly. "I'm afraid I'll have to assign you another negative achievement..."

"I am *sick* of your negative achievements!" Carson exploded, his face as red as his bandana. "*Sick* of your damn milestones, *sick* of your damn CWBS, *sick* of your damn TLA's and *sick* of your stupid freakin' damn tablet! And you know what I just realized? CWBS isn't even a TLA! It's got *four* letters! Four! You want a *real* TLA?! I've got one for you... *KMA*!"

Kinkade stared at him for a moment. His mouth made a tiny, puzzled frown. "I'm not familiar with that one." Mechanically, he bent over his tablet and started to tap.

For the hundredth time, Carson was struck with the overwhelming urge to knock it from his hands.

Only this time, he did.

Before he could think, feel, hesitate or weigh the consequences, he felt his right hand lift high, swing down and smack into the device. It leapt from Kinkade's grip and drove straight into the clean, hard, unyielding tiles below. Carson heard the unnerving, unforgiving and absolutely irreparable smash of plastic and glass. Pieces slid and spun away across the floor, scattering in all directions.

It all happened in a heartbeat.

In its wake, there was silence. A terrible, awful, unbearable silence.

Then...

"Go home, Dudley."

"Mr. Kinkade... I..."

"Go home."

Without another word, Carson left.

CHAPTER TEN

Night of the Living Dead

"You going back tomorrow?"

"He said 'go home'. He didn't say 'and don't come back'."

"Wasn't that sort of implied?"

"I'm scheduled. I'm going. I'm no quitter. At least that's *one* quality I have that Seven Corporation is looking for. Of course, I don't know if I'll have a job waiting for me, but, the way I see it, I really haven't had enough suspense in my life lately. It's a welcome change."

"I'll try to stop by. If you're there, I'll celebrate your survival. If not, I'll talk really loud about that nice clerk who was always so helpful and how he was the only reason I ever came in and why I'm now taking my business elsewhere. And maybe I'll knock some things off the shelves."

"You're a real comfort. Tape?"

Kiki passed him a strip, and he anchored the corner of a newspaper clipping. He and Kiki stood in his basement apartment, putting the finishing touches to the makeshift evidence board he had erected. It was an old screen door that he'd found in the storage shed, the screen rusted and punched with holes and the frame festooned with faded stickers. He remembered carefully applying each one when it hung on the back of the garage, when his grandpa was still alive. Grandpa had just chuckled when he caught Carson and his brother in the act, ruffled their hair and sent them on their way for one of Granny's chocolate chunk macaroon smackerels. They had expected punishment and found forgiveness.

Now, a plaster of clues, scribbled notes, crude maps and tabloid clippings all but obscured both the stickers and the fond memories. Staring at the jumble of data, Carson couldn't help but think that, this time, punishment would be much harder to avoid. Much.

But if it was coming, let it.

"Hit me again."

Kiki dutifully passed him another strip of tape. As he took it, she kept a grip for just a moment, forcing him to look up. "By the way... and for what it's worth... I'm sorry."

"Yeah. Me too." He tried a smile, but it was wholly unconvincing. Still, it was an effort and enough to show Kiki that there was at least a remnant of the old resilient Carson buried somewhere deep inside. She released the tape.

Carson turned back to the board. "But the one I'm sorry for the most is Jack. He was the one guy I didn't want to let down in this whole thing, and now I've kicked mop water all over him. And the 24/7. Makes me sick to think what Stanley and Kinky are gonna do to her when I'm gone."

"Don't take it so hard. Jack would understand. He'd have hated Kinkade."

"You think?"

"The only question he'd have is why it took you so long to play pattycake with his tablet. Guaranteed."

Carson gave her a quick guilty smile. "I've been wanting to do that for a looooong time," he confessed and smiled a little more. Then, he let the matter drop and stepped back to admire his work.

The screen door was propped up on two old chairs in a corner of the basement. It tilted badly because one chair had only three legs and was shorter than the other. But it would do. Kiki stifled a great yawn. It triggered one in Carson, too, and he stretched gingerly, feeling the tightness in his injured shoulder.

It had been a long night, following right on the heels of his previous long night and killer day, and Carson was feeling every

179

moment of every one. He had hardly slept a wink, tossing and turning all night, tortured with dreams of chasing Dex around the store trying to fire him while Kinky and Stanley turned into zombies and beat him with tablets. Giving up on sleep, he had rolled out of bed shortly after noon and began prepping for tonight's meeting. It had been hard to concentrate. He spent the whole day on pins and needles, dreading the phone call that would end his career at the mini-mart. But it never came. Far from reassuring, however, it felt ominous. Very ominous.

Still, Carson had done his best to squash such thoughts and stay focused on the business at hand. He was eager to reveal the fruits of his investigations to the Gang, and it had helped keep him on task. Whatever was going to happen at the 24/7 was going to happen, he told himself; that was the plain of it. He'd done what he'd done, and the straw was in Kinkade's Freezie now. There were bigger fish to fry in Las Calamas.

To that purpose, Carson had spent the remainder of the day engaged in a largely unfamiliar pursuit - research. He had tracked down print versions of the various tabloid articles about ninja thefts and tacked them on the board along with the list of sites and items from yesterday's fact-finding marathon. After that, he had stopped by the Belfry Library and checked out every book he could on all things zombie and zombie-related. The clerk had been all too willing to help, a somewhat unusual experience for Carson lately but welcomed.

During a fevered recounting of his exploits in a zombie-themed video game, the pimply kid had loaded Carson up with bags full of material. There was fiction, non-fiction, hardback, paperback and magazine, books about voodoo, Haitian culture, cannibalism, monster movie trivia, zombie survival guides and even the first volume of some graphic novel called *The Walking Dead*. In his zeal, the clerk also loaded Carson up with a stack of books on chronic skin conditions, infectious diseases and radical dermatology, including the critically acclaimed *What Everyone Needs to Know About Syphilis* Carson had even ended up with a few DVD's of "classic" zombie movies which, in the opinion of the kid, were far superior to today's fare and should be studied for their social and moral commentary as well as their horror value. Carson was sure he already had plenty of horror value, but he'd taken the lot.

Kiki drifted to the couch and slumped down onto the faded flower cushions, stifling another yawn. Carson noted the dark circles under her eyes. She looked even more tired than before - like Alice Cooper on a bad day. She'd been very late, too. Even so, she was the first to arrive.

As for the rest, Carson was worried. Sister Becky had finally called an hour ago to say she was on her way. He hadn't heard a word from Dex and wasn't surprised. What *would* surprise him was if the big man actually showed. Carson scooped up a toilet plunger and started pacing, still limping slightly on his tender knee.

"You got a clog, or are you just getting ready for what life's got coming next?" Kiki smiled wearily at him, head resting on her fist which rested on the arm of the couch.

"What... this?" Carson waggled the plunger. "It's my pointer." He demonstrated, jabbing it at the crooked evidence board. "Classy, eh?"

"On CSI, they use a laser pointer."

"Amateurs. Ever try to unclog a toilet with a laser pointer?"

A noise at the top of the stairs stopped them - the opening of a door. The chatter of voices spilled down the stairs, a small crowd by the sound of it. Steps creaked, and, a moment later, Granny Dudley descended into view, a pleasant gray-haired woman in her wake.

Granny beamed a wrinkled smile, held up a plate piled high with cookies. "Sorry to barge in, dear, but I thought you and your friends might like a snack."

"Like one? I'd kill for one!" Carson shoved a stack of books to one side of the scarred old coffee table, making room. The other woman bore a pitcher of ice cold milk and some plastic cups. Carson inspected the cookies, sniffed. "Mmm... especially when it's Granny Dudley's Belfry-District-Street-Fair-Award-Winning Double Chocolate Fudge Slaps. Just what the doctor ordered." He grinned and snagged one, even though he was far from hungry. Recent events had filled his belly with a gnawing uncertainty and guilt that didn't leave room for food. But he didn't want Granny worrying, so he took a bite.

Granny patted his injured shoulder, beaming. "Oh, you shouldn't make such a fuss! Just an old Dudley family recipe, you know. Although, I do add extra vanilla and a few secret... oh, sakes, forgive me! Where are my manners? Kids, this is Annie..." Granny indicated her companion. "She's new to the book club. Tonight is her first meeting!" Granny made introductions, then turned aside to chat with Kiki.

Carson shook Annie's hand. She had a nice, friendly face and wore a shirt with a teddy bear on it.

"Book club, eh?" He smiled his lopsided smile. "Welcome

181

aboard. You're in for a wild ride."

"I certainly am... and I couldn't be more thrilled! Roberta has been asking me for months to attend, and I'm just tickled to finally get the chance. Reading is my passion!" She glanced down at the stack of books on the table. "Oh! Are you having a book club meeting too?"

Carson blinked. "Yeeeeessss," he answered slowly. "In a way...."

"What are you reading?" Annie eagerly snatched the top book off the stack, her eyes scanning the title with interest: *What Everyone Needs to Know About Syphilis* She made a small gasp.

"Um..." Carson took it gently from her. "We're still deciding."

"Erh," Annie said. From the cover of the next book, the ghoulish features of a zombie glared up at her. Its brain bulged from a split skull, and bits of flesh dangled from broken teeth. She edged away.

Suddenly, she seemed to notice that Carson had a plunger slung over his shoulder. Her eyes widened. From the plunger, they drifted to the evidence board behind him. Words jumped off the board at her: "five maggots means dead for a week", and "Carl - did he really want to eat me?", as well as the covers of various tabloids splashed with overdramatized artist renditions of ninjas slicing the heads off old ladies. Her eyes widened more.

Just then, there came a smart rap at the basement door. Seconds later, it swung open, and Sister Becky swept into the room with a billow of dark robes. "Apologies, Mr. Dudley!" she clipped. "Heartfelt apologies for my tardiness, but it simply could not be helped. Work, you know; the little darlings don't discipline themselves... though that does provide food for thought. And the paperwork! St. Peter's Pepper! You have no idea!" Her eyes found Granny. "Well Roberta, this is a pleasant surprise! Good evening dear; it has been ages...." Sister Becky embraced her friend and chattered away happily. Beneath her smiles, though, Carson could see the weariness and frustration.

Then a shadow filled the doorway.

It was Dex.

Carson's breath caught in his throat. For a second, the big man just stood there. Not moving, not speaking, a glowering mountain of foreboding and ill will, like an executioner who had forgotten his axe and was trying to decide whether to go back for it or just improvise. Then he scowled, stalked inside and planted himself in the far corner, facing the wall, huge arms folded tightly. He wasn't wearing his uniform, just a black button down and shorts. It was a bad sign.

Carson wanted desperately to rush over, apologize for last night,

   182

beg for forgiveness, ask about Dex's job with the Gold Shield... but he didn't dare. Carson's wild, momentary hopes for forgiveness crashed against the reality of Dex's attitude - it was rolling off in waves so hostile and intense, he was certain it would curdle the milk.

It also had an effect on Annie. With a small sound, she turned and fled up the stairs.

"And this, Rebecca, is my friend..." Granny turned. "...oh. Well now, sakes. Where did she go?"

Carson pointed up the stairs with his plunger.

Granny chuckled. "She does love her books! Well, enjoy the sweets and have a nice chat. If you get tired of these youngsters, Rebecca, just pop upstairs. It should be a lively discussion tonight!" She beamed a smile at them and toddled off up the stairs.

The moment she was gone, Sister Becky wilted. In an uncharacteristic display, she plopped down beside Kiki on the sofa, sprawling in exhaustion. An exasperated sigh escaped her thin lips. "My deepest apologies once again, Mr. Dudley, Ms. Masterson. It is Father Black... *again*." Her face soured with the memory. "The man seems determined to shape my life into a living hell, and I must say that, so far, he is succeeding heroically."

Kiki helped herself to a cookie, took a small nibble. "Don't you have someone you could go to? A mother superior or something?"

Sister Becky sat up, composed herself. She smoothed the front of her robes, sniffed. "I could indeed - but I shall not. It is simply not my way, dear child. 'Do all things without grumbling or complaining' is what Paul advised the Philippians, and it is advice I shall adhere to as well. Complaining never improves a situation."

From across the room, Dex snorted. It startled them all, like an angry bull lurking in the shadows. "Not from lack of you tryin'," Dex rumbled softly. "For not complaining, you're doing a damn fine job." It was the first words Dex had spoken. Carson found himself no longer wishing fervently that the man would speak and, instead, wishing fervently he would stop. But he didn't. "Hell, I take Black's side," Dex sneered. "If I had to work with Attila the Nun, I'd be making a *&^%$! ruckus too."

Sister Becky stiffened. She had been reaching for a cookie, but her hand froze. "I shall thank you to keep your opinions to yourself, Mr. Jackson. I have one great torment in my life already, and I am not in need of a second." She was so flustered she didn't even chastise the guard for his profanity. "At any rate... I am comforted solely by the fact that, at this point, my career can sink no lower." She reached again for a cookie.

Dex smirked from the shadows. His great arms, folded across his chest, squeezed so tight it was a wonder he could breath. "Why not just pray yourself up a new one?"

Sister Becky stopped in mid bite, glared at him. "God is not a piñata, Mr. Jackson. One does not simply prod him with a stick and expect good things to rain down. He has His purpose in allowing misery and discomfort, I can assure you. And I am most thankful for that, since I am now in them up to my knickers... oh, Zion's trumpet!" A blaring guitar riff erupted inside her robes, and she started, dropping her cookie. The sound of raging strings and pounding drums filled the room with the chorus of AC/DC's *Highway to Hell.*

Sister Becky dove a hand into her habit, fished about frantically, came up with her phone. Snapping it open, she checked the number, sighed, snapped it closed just as the caller started to speak.

"It is only his eminence attempting to draw me out," she reported. "There is a tiresome issue of creamy vs. crunchy peanut butter over which we resolutely disagree. It has quite consumed him lately." The phone continued to buzz and ring loudly.

Kiki gave it a pained look. "Your ring tone... er..."

"Yes, dear. David again - my little Philistine."

"Do you want me to..."

"No, my child," she sighed and patted Kiki's hand. "It is time for me to accept my fate. I appreciate your continued efforts, but, unfortunately, this little heathen," she crossed herself vehemently "...is not only ruthless but also apparently unstoppable. I have battled 3,000 year old mummies who were less persistent. No, it is best to simply live with it... even though this particular tune is most obnoxious. Do any of you recognize it?"

Kiki opened her mouth, shut it. "Um... no. Nope. Can't place it."

Carson clamped his lips tight, shook his head. Dex just smiled another smile, more evil than his last.

"Well," Carson headed off further discussion "Let's get started. I'm glad you all could make it tonight. I know how hard life has been lately, and I really appreciate..."

Dex shoved away from the wall and lumbered straight at him. Carson stepped back in spite of himself, shocked and momentarily frightened At the last second, the big man veered around him and headed for the tiny bathroom, disappearing inside. The door slammed behind him, rattling Carson's Wii controllers across the room.

The others stared in mute surprise. Inside the restroom, the fan kicked on, rattling and chattering. As noisy as it was, however, it was completely unable to mask other much louder, more disquieting sounds.

Kiki started, her face contorting. "Is... is he...?"

"I dunno. Let's just let him..."

"Oh my."

They sat in silence for a few minutes, an awkward, uncomfortable silence. The sounds grew more candid and more disturbing.

Carson cleared his throat loudly. "He's, uh... change of diet. Kinda... off the wagon. Has a... it's a... personal thing." Carson checked his watch, considered turning on the radio.

Finally, mercifully, there was a flush. Then another. Then a third.

The door rattled open, and Dex lumbered back across the room, avoiding eye contact. "You might need that," he muttered darkly, glancing at the plunger in Carson's hands as he passed.

Carson looked at the tool, then at the bathroom. He shuddered. "Uh... yeah. Right. Okay. So. Unless anyone else needs to...?" Heads shook. "Alright. So thanks for coming..."

Sister Becky's phone rang again, carrying away his words on a fevered rock anthem. Becky sighed, glanced at the caller ID, then laid it back in her lap. She didn't even bother to shut it off. "My apologies once again, Mr. Dudley. Do continue."

"Right. So... uh..." Carson struggled to regain his focus. "I should just... get to the point, I guess..." He set off on a rapid, rambling review of his discoveries over the last few days. It was awkward, disjointed and, at times, painful. The plunger made a poor pointer, and the evidence board had a tendency to slip and threaten to topple on his listeners. His thoughts wandered, the right words just wouldn't come, and he couldn't seem to take his eyes off Dex, expecting him to explode at any moment and storm from the room. And every time he got on a roll, it seemed, Sister Becky's cell phone would erupt and take them all on an unnerving journey down the *Highway To Hell.*

Altogether, it was a lot less impressive than he had planned.

Finally, he stumbled through the last bit of evidence. "And so..." he tapped the stack of library materials with the plunger - the wrong end, he suddenly realized, and reversed it quickly. "Er... yuck. And so... I bet you're wondering what all this means. Well... I think I know." He paused dramatically. It was the moment he had been waiting for all day. The zinger. It didn't matter how bad everything had been up to

 185

this point; this, he knew, would make up for it all. "I've been staring at this all day, and it finally hit me - I finally realized something totally huge, something completely mind-blowing. I finally figured out what's *really* going on here. You see, the truth is the zombies..."

"Alleged zombies, Mr. Dudley," Sister Becky corrected him. "Remember: LIPISC."

"Er... yeah, okay, 'alleged' zombies. Anyway, the truth is that the zombies... er... alleged zombies... *are coming after the 24/7!*"

It was silent. Immediately, he felt foolish. His conclusion had seemed so clear, so inescapable earlier today. Now, staring at the jumble of evidence and trying to collect his scattered thoughts, it didn't seem that way at all.

Apparently, his friends felt the same.

There were a few moments of intense, awkward silence, during which he could clearly hear crickets. Then, Dex gave the first feedback, and he gave it plainly: he snorted, rolled his eyes and shook his head.

Sister Becky was a bit more tactful. "Hm. Yes. Well. All... er... well and good, Mr. Dudley. That was... succinctly put. But tell me - precisely *why* would these alleged zombies do so? 'To a pig, the mud is purpose enough,' as the saying goes. But what possible purpose would the living dead have to persecute your store?"

"Yeah," Kiki yawned. She was slumped back on the couch, too tired even to finish the half-eaten cookie in her hand. "What's up with that? Even if the zombies..."

"Alleged zombies, dear."

"Even if the 'alleged zombies' *were* attacking the 24/7, I don't get it. Why just the mini-mart? Don't zombies run around in mobs, or something?" She lazily tapped one of the coffee table books with her boot. "If this is the Zompocalypse, why aren't they everywhere?"

Carson glared at her. "Who's side are you on?!"

"Sorry." Kiki looked chagrined.

"Look," Carson groped for words. "I don't know... I don't know why; I don't know how, but I know they're coming after the mini-mart! Some supernatural bad dude - Fujika, maybe - is trying to slap the hoodoo beatdown on the 24/7! It started in Romero, and now it's coming for me... for us. Everyone tied to the store is in trouble! Sure, I'm probably not lucky enough for it to go after Kinkade or Stanley, but you guys are in danger too! I can feel it! I don't have all the answers, but take a look at the facts!" He jabbed at the evidence board, grazing

 186

it. It wobbled precariously. "They're..." Carson grasped at his scattered thoughts, waving the plunger. "They're scary facts... bad facts! And... and you can't argue with facts! Sister B..." he rounded on the nun, desperate for support. "What do you think?!"

"Well, dear lad..." Becky cast about, looking as if she had just been asked whether or not she liked the world's ugliest shirt. "I suppose there is some... er... interest... to what you have uncovered. The list of ingredients for example," she indicated the evidence board. "They are certainly... curious. I can think of many rituals and dark magics that might implement such items. Although to be fair," she added, "I can think of many benign uses as well..." She glanced at Carson's scowl and hurried on. "And, of course, there is your altercation with this 'Carl'. It is certainly suspect; although, I should like to see the body before making a final determination as to his condition."

"His condition?! His condition was he was trying to kill me!"

"Of course, Mr. Dudley, of course. However, there are many reasons for trying to kill someone. Mania, narcotic-induced psychotic episodes, latent sociopathic tendencies..."

"But those are... he was... are you saying you don't believe me?!"

Sister Becky leveled her gaze at him, her voice compassionate. "Mr. Dudley. It was dark. You were under mental duress. The things you have seen recently sometimes enhance one's awareness of supernatural foes and sometimes cloud it. I am not saying that I doubt you, only that it would be wise to doubt yourself. Sometimes, in these situations, doubt can be a powerful ally."

"You *are* saying you don't believe me!" Carson clapped a hand to his forehead. "I don't believe it!"

"I am merely calling attention to the first steps of the hunt: Locate and Identify. These are the first because they are the most important..."

"Look... just forget LIPKISS for a sec..."

"LIPISC, dear."

"Whatever! Just... just forget all that for a minute! Just... just *assume* I'm onto something here. Tell me what to do next!"

"Quite. Well then, taking you at your word, Mr. Dudley, we shall *assume,* as you suggest, that the Identification phase has been successfully completed. I must point out, however, that you are still out of order in your process. 'Locate' is actually the preferred first step, and while we are speaking strictly in the hypothetical, in that regard, you are still sorely lacking."

"Lacking?! Haven't you been... what about...!" Carson waved the

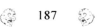

plunger at the board but was too close and struck it instead, knocking it off the chairs and sending it crashing to the floor. Pages of evidence tore free and floated gently to the ground. He snatched up one or two, tried in vain to stick them back to the board, but the tape was spent, and they wouldn't stay. He gave up, staring down at the sad, pathetic mess. In desperation, he whirled back to his friends. "Kiki...there's gotta be a pattern. C'mon girl, don't let me down, tell me you..." his voice trailed off. He stared.

Kiki was asleep.

Head pillowed serenely on the couch cushions, hat pulled low over her eyes, breathing soft and steady.

"Kiki?" Carson's voice was choked with disbelief.

"Ahem," Sister Becky cleared her throat, prodded her gently. Kiki didn't budge. "*Ahem!*"

This time Kiki stirred, woke up. She sat up slowly, blinking. "Oh. Um... sorry." A massive yawn stretched her jaws. "I was just... what... what were you...?"

"A pattern," Carson repeated numbly. "Do you see... anything?"

Kiki stared at the board with glazed eyes, struggling to focus. After a minute, she blinked. "I got nothing."

"Nothing... nothing?!?!" Carson didn't even ask Dex. The look on his face said it all. "I can't believe this! You're all just gonna *sit* there?! You guys are worse than the zombies!"

"Alleged zombies, Mr. Dudley."

"Alleged my little red wagon!" Carson finally blew. He banged the plunger on the table but the rubber head hit instead of the stick, making a soft *fump* and not the furious *smack* he'd hoped for. "They're out there; they're real, and they're coming after the 24/7! This is just like *Night of the Living Dead*..." he threw his hands in the air, exasperated. "Only *you're* the dead!"

"Mr. Dudley," Sister Becky said coolly in, what Carson assumed was, the voice she reserved for temper tantrums at the *Little Angel's Clubhouse*. "As passionate as you are, you must face facts. You still have no clear adversary and no clear evidence. We simply have no direction in which to proceed. I know you have been under a great deal of stress lately, but then, so have we all. We have each had our own pressing matters to attend to..." As if on cue, her phone rang again. Again, she sighed. "And I have neglected mine for long enough. I must apologize yet again, Mr. Dudley - but it is time I took my leave." She rose, smoothed her habit and inclined her head politely. "I fear that

Father Black will not be dissuaded. Do not trouble yourself showing me out. I know the way."

Kiki rose, too, quickly. "Better call it myself. I've got... late night... there's a... stuff." She mumbled excuses and good-byes, crowding after Sister Becky as the nun bustled through the door, "yes"-ing and "no"-ing into her phone. Dex didn't say a word, just stomped out after them.

Then they were gone.

Carson stood in the middle of the room, his evidence board forgotten, the plunger still in his hand, his brain numb. As he stared out the open door that no one had even bothered to close, it finally hit him.

He had suspected it, felt it, denied it, even fought against it.

But now, he knew it.

He was alone.

CHAPTER ELEVEN

Rush Hour

"Well, at least you're not alone." Josh smiled, plunked down a box of frozen mini-tacos.

"Just don't say anything about job security - I'll punch you. And get those minis on the heat, stat. Alrighty, four pizza sticks..." Carson jammed buttons on the cash register, shot a glance across the counter at twins in concert T's, their hair plastered down with sweat. "And I'm guessing something to drink."

The girls giggled in stereo. They ordered pink Freezies, and Carson rushed the sale through, shoved cups and bags at them and hollered over the noise. "Next!"

The line to the counter wound through the mini-mart like a hungry, impatient, dehydrated serpent in desperate need of an energy drink; around aisles and shelves and the coffee island; it's tail just touching the cooler. The line for the restroom was almost as long.

"What happened even?!" Josh called over his shoulder as he hustled to fill the warmer. "Why are they all stocked up here?!"

"A concert, I'm guessing," Carson called back.

 190

"You got it, man!" The middle-aged rocker next in line head-bobbed his way to the counter. Carson could hear raging music spilling out of his ear buds. He sported a similar shirt to the twins, but his was faded and worn with years and memories. "Only it wasn't just *a* concert... it was *the* concert!"

"Rock on, dude!" Carson flashed the universal rocker sign, rang him up and sent him on his way.

"Does it get like this a lot?!" Josh swooped past, pulling on plastic gloves and taking position beside the hot food section like a riot cop on the front line.

"Depends. You shoulda seen it when Weird Al was here."

"Crazy?"

"He came into the store, dude. Sang *Eat It* a-Capella right next to the muffins."

"No way!"

"Way. Of course, the week after was the Milli Vanilli comeback tour."

"What was that like?"

"A regular night."

Josh laughed, and they were back in the mix.

It was nights like this Carson would miss. Really miss. He loved the hum and hustle of the summer concert season, the drive and energy and excitement of the crowd, still buzzing and singing snippets of songs and hungry for food and a willing ear. Any ear. They had him sweating, running crazy, but they needed food, needed to refuel, to keep the moment alive just a little longer. And that's what the mini-mart was. That's what he loved. He may not have been part of the concert, but being part of the afterglow was every bit as good.

But, now those days were over. Carson felt a quick pang but let it go. It wasn't time for that now. Not yet, anyway - there was still work to be done. They still needed him. The next group was up, a couple of tweens and their parents, eyes glazed and talking too loud from the music, and they were full of questions about what came on the fully loaded nachos and which of the burritos had beans.

It had been like this for almost an hour. Carson had slunk into work around eight. It was Stanley's night off, and there was no sign of Kinkade - no Beemer out front, office door closed and locked. There were no other ill omens, either: no notes on the bulletin board, no padlock on his employee locker and no pink slip. Just Josh, halfway through his restock and full of the usual easygoing good cheer. He apparently hadn't heard of Carson's altercation, and Carson didn't clue him in. There was no point in ruining the mood. Before he could start worrying, the rush hit, and he was too busy to care. Much.

They kept hard at it after that. Just before ten, things tapered off to a nice steady stream. Carson had just let Josh take over the till when he spotted Dex. The guard had slipped in unnoticed, something of a feat for a man his size. He lurked by the pre-owned DVD's, hands stuffed in his polyester pockets, head bowed. The moment he saw him, Carson was moving. He didn't hesitate, didn't think. He'd had plenty of time to do both already.

"BRB, Josh. Hit that till like you mean it." Carson slipped through the counter and made a beeline for Dex, didn't stop until he was directly in front of him. "You're right. I was a *&^%$!" He held his breath.

Dex looked up from the movies. His eyes had been pointed at the titles but hadn't been registering them. He blinked at Carson. "You gotta be more specific. I use that word a lot."

"Right here. Two nights ago. I was the corporate stooge; you were the humiliated security guard..."

Dex's confusion unraveled. "What? You thought...?! Naw, man... that wasn't for you. That was for Kinky."

Carson breathed again. A weight lifted, and he felt like turning a cartwheel. "Alright... you may not have called me that, but I still fit the description. I'm hating myself right now. It wasn't right."

"No worries." Dex shrugged ruefully. "Brought it on myself, goin' after them Fujikacorp punks."

"You were just doing your job."

"So were you. I figured Kinkade dumped it on you. Kobayashi Maru, bro."

"Guess I'm no Captain Kirk."

"Who is?" Dex's grim expression cracked just a fraction.

Carson grinned. "C'mon. I gotta get back up front. At least let me buy you a Freezie." He clapped his friend on the shoulder and led the way. "And if you need a job recommendation from a former mini-mart night clerk, I'll give you a sterling one."

"Former? I leave too early?"

"Kinda got into it with Kinky after you left."

"I did leave too early. Miss anything good?"

"Let's just say, he won't be using his tablet to document the incident." Carson stopped, picked up a fragment of plastic he'd just spotted. "They don't work too well without all the parts. Here's a little souvenir" He dropped the bit into Dex's hand.

Now Dex was grinning too. "My hero."

They reached the counter, and Carson slipped behind it. Josh waved a 'hello' to Dex, then hurried off to the freezer for more stock.

"So," Carson took his place behind the register. "What brings you in tonight, big man? Y'know, now that you're... well..."

"A civilian? Just came to grab my stuff. Had a few things stashed in the store room." Dex glanced wistfully around the mini-mart. "Gonna miss this place. Ain't gonna miss Kinky, though, that's the upside. Man, what a square - the suit, the glasses... it was like having Buddy Holly give you the stink eye."

Carson chuckled. "Speaking of bosses... I hate to ask, but how did Rodney take the news?"

"We'll see when I tell him." Dex ran a hand along the glass counter as if for the last time. "Ain't had the heart just yet." Carson noticed Dex's uniform shirt wasn't buttoned or tucked, and his badge was absent. He seemed to be wearing it more out of habit. He was also jingling the same something in his hand that Carson had seen the night of their trip to Fujikacorp. He knew better than to ask about it, though, or to press the Rodney issue. Right now, Dex was still employed, and that was about the only good news anyone had. He wasn't going to jeopardize it.

Josh reappeared, dropping a load of munchies. He fixed Carson with an even gaze. "Look, I hate to eavesdrop... but did something happen the other night I should know about?"

Carson smiled wanly. "Eavesdrop... just don't ask. You're a great trainee, and the best thing to happen to the 24/7 since Jack left - which is why you should keep your nose out of it. I'm toxic, dude. Poison. And probably history. Just talking to me will probably get you a negative achievement. And *that* goes on your permanent record."

"Just paper."

Carson narrowed his eyes, trying to read the expression on Josh's expressionless face. "You could lose your job."

"I've been out of work before."

Carson whistled. "They sure grow 'em gutsy in O-re-gon. Tell you what, I'll... *ay caramba!*" He jumped, slapped at a crawling tickle under his pant leg. With a couple of frantic stomps, he dislodged something, something small and black that rolled out of his jeans onto the floor, tiny legs flailing as it lit on its back.

Carson bent to pick it up. "Dang. Bug or something. What is it

193

with this place...?"

"Uh-oh." Josh cocked his ear, nodded toward the door. "Another rush." Outside, a small crowd was hustling across the parking lot, heading for the 24/7 and sanctuary from the scorching heat.

"The 420," Carson assumed his game face. "Right on time. That's Big Joe for you. Yellow alert, Ensign Decker. This is no drill."

They took their places behind the counter, ready. As the crowd hit the store and dispersed, Carson caught a glimpse of something both familiar and welcome - a red stocking cap bobbing through the press.

"Kiki! Hey, girl!" He waved a greeting.

Kiki made her way to the counter, cautious as always in a crowd, careful not to brush against or stray too close to the others. Carson's spirits lifted a little. He hadn't expected to see her after last night's meeting. After she had dozed off and then abandoned him, he reminded himself. He felt a quick sting of betrayal but resisted it. What was it Sister Becky had said? *"We have each had our own pressing matters to attend to..."* Whatever Kiki's were, they were pressing hard enough all on their own. The last thing she needed was him adding to the burden. Besides... it was probably the last time he'd see her walk through that door. He didn't want to spoil it.

When she hit the counter, Carson was smiling. "You made it."

"So did you. Congrats. Didn't see the gallows outside, so I thought I'd pop in. Dex." She nodded at the guard, who had taken up position nearby, staring gloomily about the store. A lift of the chin was his only reply.

"Yeah, well..." Carson shot a glance at Kinkade's door. "Don't start the party just yet. I've got the feeling this judge is a hanging judge. Sorry, guys," he glanced over Kiki's shoulder at a couple of men standing behind her. "What can I get you?"

"Oh... er, sorry. They're with me." Kiki turned. "Meet some friends, willya? Guys, this is Carson. Carson, this is Mike and Ben. From... um... school."

"School buds, eh? Awesome. Glad to meet you." Carson shook hands. "You guys friends of Leet?"

The two exchanged glances.

"No." Mike shook his head. He was the taller of the two, with a thin beard, glasses and a sharp eye.

"Me neither," Ben was wiry and enthusiastic and resplendent in a vintage Iron Man T-shirt. "What site is he..."

"Different circles," Kiki cut in. Her smile looked strained. "You

 194

guys should grab something - the transfer will be along in a few." Mike and Ben disappeared into the store as Kiki turned her attention crisply to the warmer. "I'll take a corn dog. Extra mustard."

"Coming right up." Carson slipped a corn dog into a sack. "What's with the escort?" He added a couple of potato wedges on the sly. Kiki was too distracted watching Mike and Ben to notice.

"Hm? Oh, them. Car trouble. They've got a LAN party tonight, and Mike's car is in the shop. They're bus newbs. Just showing them the ropes." She glanced at them again, looking nervous and fidgety.

Carson eyed her for a moment. "Relax. I'm sure they won't get off at the wrong stop while they're inside the store."

"Eh? Oh, yeah." A thin smile. "Right. It's just... they don't get out much."

"I think they can handle a mini-mart." Carson smiled, amused, as she absently unwrapped her corn dog. It was then he noticed her pack. Ordinarily, it was a lean, tight package, holding just her laptop and a few school books. Tonight, it was stuffed with something.

"Going camping?" He gestured.

"Er... no. Just... stuff. I gotta... there's a little..." The rest of her reply was cut off by the huge bite of corn dog she stuffed in her mouth. She munched slowly, keeping her eyes on the floor.

A steady stream of customers flowed past the counter after that, and Carson and Josh kept busy. Kiki's friends brought up the rear of the line, dropping their goodies on the counter. Dex, who had been buried under his melancholy up to this point, perked up as the snacks hit the glass. He eyed them with whimsical envy.

Carson scooped up a six-pack of Code Red Mountain Dew and a package of chocolate donettes. "Dew and donuts. Midnight snack of champs. A little fuel for the LAN party?"

"Actually, no." Mike fished for his wallet. "It's for breakfast tomorrow. Saves me a stop on the way to work."

"Yowza. I hope you work at a cardiac center."

"No," Mike smiled. "Actually we..."

"Hey, weren't you telling me about that raid in *Warcraft?*" Kiki intruded. "I gotta split in a sec; you better finish your story."

"Oh, the PUG," Mike took his bag from Carson. "Yeah. So anyway... things started fine. Came to the first pull, and I put up the raid markers. I'm on crowd control, and I sheep mine... then all hell breaks loose. Somebody missed a mark, pulled the whole pat! It was a mess. So, I just cut loose. Man. You wouldn't believe it - my DPS was

 195

twice everyone else's... *combined*. I even popped mirror images to drop aggro, but it didn't help."

Ben twisted the top off his own 20oz Mountain Dew. "Anybody survive?"

Mike shook his head. "Full wipe."

"Ouch. Minus 50 DKP! I had the same thing happen in STO. It's a shame when newbs can't play their class."

In spite of his apathy, Dex was carefully observing the conversation, like an anthropologist among chimpanzees. His face registered a look of curiosity. "What language are they speakin', Dud?"

"Massively Multiplayer Online-ese. It's easy to pick up, but oh-so-hard to put down."

Ben overheard the comment, grinned. "And it only costs fifteen bucks a month for lessons. You play?"

Dex grunted. "Only for keeps. And I got my own language for that." He patted the beefy automatic on his hip. "Gat, shooter, piece, pistol, heater, peacemaker..."

Kiki wrinkled her nose. "And you're making fun of *them*? C'mon... 'gat?' Why don't you just say 'gun'?"

Dex looked at her. "Cuz I don't. Same reason the shotty in my car is called a shotty."

Ben nodded sagely. "Shotgun. Right on. You loading slug, buck or bird?"

"Bird."

Now all the men nodded sagely.

Kiki frowned. "Should I even ask?"

"Bird," Dex said off-handedly. "Y'know... as in bird*shot*. Not slugs, not buckshot - bird."

"Then why don't you just say 'birdshot?'"

Dex shook his head. "Chicks don't understand guns."

"Gats," Carson corrected.

"Whatever."

Kiki just rolled her eyes.

"Anyway, speaking of ordinance... I gotta go drop some. S'cuse me." Dex lurched upright and set his sights on the bathroom.

Shortly after that, the store was empty once more. Kiki was first out, slipping away in her usual mysterious exit. Ben and Mike drifted out a few minutes later with the rest of the crowd, heading for the bus stop. Afterward, the store was silent.

Silent except for Dex.

After a few minutes, Carson switched on the radio to cover the noise. Chuck and Phil from KBRZ prattled and joked, completely oblivious to the carnage taking place in the restroom as Carson and Josh tidied up in the wake of the rush. Soon, they were finished and settled back on their stools.

"Busy night." Josh fanned himself with a flattened hot dog tray.

"Yup. Rush hour. That's where the magic happens." Carson sighed wistfully. "It's like I can still hear the bus..." He paused. His brow furrowed. "Wait... I *can* still hear the bus. Is that the bus?" He reached over and switched off the radio. "Weird. Is that... do you hear that?" Carson cocked his head. He could just make out the rumbling idle of a diesel engine.

Josh listened hard. He nodded. Slipping off his stool, Carson headed for the front door. Josh was on his heels. They pushed out into the sweltering evening, stopped beside the pumps and stared down the street. The Belfry District was quiet and deserted at this late hour. Nothing moved, and the streets were empty.

Save for the city bus stopped dead in the middle of the street three blocks away.

Carson and Josh stared at it. Red tail lights stared back at them out of the blackness. They could hear the thrum of the engine clearly now, rippling through the still, muggy air.

"Yup." Carson's eyes narrowed. "That's a bus." He felt suddenly uneasy.

Josh shaded his eyes against the glaring streetlight overhead, peered down the street. "I didn't think there was a stop down there."

"There's not. It's back that way." Carson jerked a thumb behind them. For some reason, standing there in the hot August night with Josh, he was suddenly reminded of the first time they'd met. It had almost been in this exact spot. Only that time, Carson had been staring down the street after something else. A recollection of the shadowy figure in the tattered cloak swam through his mind. He knew with a sudden, disturbing clarity that it had been the same figure he had seen at the Romero 24/7. On top of the building across the street. After Carl...

A shiver ran up his back. He glanced around quickly, probing the shadows, half expecting to see the figure again. But there was nothing. Nothing but the bus, idling away in the middle of the street without a soul in sight.

"Hey, uh... keep an eye on the store, okay? I'm gonna... I'm gonna go see if everything's alright."

"Uh-huh. Sure." Josh was staring at the bus, too. "You really think that's a good idea?" He glanced around, checking shadows. Whatever was in the air, he was feeling it too.

"Oh... oh yeah. No prob. No big - somebody probably scarfed one of our deluxe inferno green-chili-bean chalupas and chucked their cookies. It happens. Least I can do is help clean it up, right?" Carson forced a smile, took two steps down the street. Then he stopped, turned and trotted back to the store. He popped out seconds later with his bat.

"Wouldn't paper towels be better?" Josh asked.

"You haven't seen someone toss one of those chalupas," Carson muttered as he trotted past. Then he was off, the bus growing bigger and steadily more real as he drew closer. He slowed as he reached the rear of the rig, holding his bat loose and ready. A few more steps and he pulled up short, listening.

Nothing. Just the soft, rumbling idle of the engines.

This in itself, Carson realized, was thoroughly disquieting. Nothing meant no screaming, which was good, but also meant no chatting, laughing or complaining about delays. Which was bad.

He moved on, slower now, gliding carefully along the side of the bus. The smell of diesel and hot pavement filled his nostrils - that and something else. Something he couldn't quite place. Something unpleasant. He stood on tiptoes and peeped inside, but it was no use. The windows were all up, sealed against the heat, and either darkened by tint or plastered over with portions of a giant-sized ad which showed Phil and Chuck armed with squirt guns blasting away at a ferocious cartoon Mr. Sun shooting heat beams from his eyes.

Carson squinted. It was dark in the bus, no reading or running lights. He could see shapes - silhouetted outlines - but that was it. There were people on board, but they weren't moving. He glanced around again, tapped his bat on his leg nervously. He considered for a moment, hesitated... then turned abruptly and headed for the door.

Carson stopped when he got there. It was shut tight. Inside, he could see the driver sitting behind the wheel. Big Joe. Motionless. Still. Just like the rest. Goosebumps tickled up his arms. He reached up and tapped the glass with his bat. "Joe?" he called, softly at first. His voice sounded faint and fragile against the churning of the massive engine. "Hey. Hey!" He raised the bat, tapped again, harder. "Big Joe! You okay?!"

Nothing.

Carson dug his fingers into the rubber door trim and pulled. He fought it for a second, then felt the door give way with a sigh. It collapsed on its center hinge and slammed back with a *crash!* that made Carson jump, even though he knew it was coming. Big Joe didn't even flinch. Carson swallowed hard. Up in the driver's chair, Big Joe was slumped over the wheel. He couldn't see much more than that because the bus had stopped precisely in between two street lamps and was just out of range of both. Everything inside was shadows. Carson craned his neck, trying to see. Various scenarios raced through his brain.

Heart attack? Heat stroke? Aneurism?

Sure. Maybe Big Joe. But certainly not...

"...the whole bus?" Carson finished the thought out loud. He leaned in a few inches, peered back into the dark, cavernous expanse of bus. Nothing moved. He hesitated. For a moment, he flashed back to Romero. The other 24/7. Carl. He shook free of the grisly memories. That was different. Carl had been up. Moving. Joe was neither. And he may be hurt. At any rate, there were no answers outside the bus.

Well...

Carson lifted his foot to the first step, hesitated again. Then, with a deep breath, he caught the hand rail and hauled himself up.

The smell of diesel was fainter inside, but the mystery odor took its place now, making his nose wrinkle. He reminded himself that buses usually smelled that way and pulled himself up another step.

"Joe...?" Carson could see part of the man's face now, just under the brim of his ever-present driver's cap. The cap was askew, knocked out of place. Carson paused for a moment, listening, but all he could hear was the banging of his heart and the rumble of the engine. Cautiously, he set his bat down, leaning it against the stairwell. He reached up toward the driver and slowly, carefully, pressed his shoulder.

"Hey, Joe? Buddy?"

No response.

Carson knew, vaguely, that he should take a pulse. It was what they did on TV. He mounted the final step, hesitant. He turned, swept the dark interior of the bus with his eyes, probing, searching, nerves tingling. He could just make out the commuters in their high backed seats, slumped and slouched like bus passengers did on the night bus. And yet... not. Carson strained his eyes but could make out no other details. Just dark, huddled shapes in the shadows. The center aisle seemed to stretch miles back into that blackness. He couldn't see the end.

All was still. Still as a tomb.

"What do you see?"

The whisper shocked him, and he jumped. "Josh!" he hissed. "What are you doing here?! You scared the frack out of me!"

"Sorry!" Josh hovered just behind him, perched on the top step, eyes gleaming nervously behind his glasses. "It's just that... well, where I come from, we don't let people go wandering off alone in the middle of the night. Besides, I'm EMT certified. If someone needs help..."

"I admire your lack of common sense," Carson cut him off. "I really do. But there are things..."

"I also brought a flashlight."

"Where were you four months ago?"

"Pardon?"

"Never mind... just get it up here!"

Josh hauled himself up beside Carson and flicked the switch on a sturdy pocket flashlight. The brilliant white beam stabbed down the aisle, picking up arms, legs, shoulders, patches of skin. Colors exploded under the brilliance: yellow, blue, purple, green... and red. Lots and lots of red. In pools, drips, puddles, red everywhere. Too much red.

Carson couldn't move, couldn't think. Could only stare. His voice choked out in a hoarse whisper. "They're dead!"

"No!" Josh stiffened, pointed. "That one's still alive...!" He brushed past Carson, heading for a middle-aged Mexican in a faded flannel shirt. The man's head had just started weaving, slowly, side to side. A low, animal groan spilled from red lips.

A familiar groan.

"Josh, no!" Carson grabbed his arm, yanked back, ripping the sleeve in a sudden panic.

"Hey! What're you...?!"

"Get off the bus... now! Go!" Josh struggled, not understanding as Carson pulled, shoved him toward the door. Around the Mexican, several other passengers were starting to sway and groan as well. The whole bus was coming alive now with murmurs and rustlings. Toward the back, someone stood up.

"What...?! What are you... that man... he needs medical attention!"

"CPR's not gonna help him, Josh... not anymore!"

"But...!"

"Move!"

Josh tumbled down the steps, still protesting, a wild, uncertain look in his eye. Carson was hot on his heels. He was just starting down after Josh when he heard a soft creak behind him. Carson whipped about, heart in his throat, caught a glimpse of movement at the top of the steps.

Big Joe.

With a pallid hand, Joe threw the heavy lever that operated the bus door, and it crashed shut before Carson like a drawbridge gate.

He was trapped.

But, there was no time to think about it as Big Joe launched out of his seat with a snarl and was on him. Carson tried to twist aside but big hands caught at his shirt in a frenzied grip and yanked him backward. He slammed into the side of the stairwell and pain lanced through his injured shoulder. Hot breath washed over him, and he caught a glimpse of dark green flesh spiderwebbed with black veins, a gaping mouth, teeth, dead white eyes glaring from under the ledge of the driver's cap.

A sense of deja vu swept through him that was so powerful, it almost made him sick. Carson thrashed, shouted, felt his feet slip on the steps and went down, slamming his backside onto the stairs. One of Big Joe's meaty hands pulled loose, and Carson surged to his feet again, swinging wild. A fist smacked face, and he shoved hard, pulled free but slipped sideways in the process, dangerously off balance. He pitched down the stairs and crashed against the door, shoulder screaming. Joe flopped back into his seat like a 250 pound sack of meat, banged his skull against the window, then lurched stiffly up.

Outside, Josh was shouting something Carson couldn't hear, banging on the glass of the door. Carson whirled back, panic seizing him as Joe prepared to lunge again, looming from the top of the stairs like a gargoyle, arms spread wide. Carson's brain fired commands, too many and too fast to obey: *Get away! Run! Scream! Fall down! Find a weapon, a tool, something, anything...!*

His bat.

It was there, right where he had left it.

Carson's hand shot down, missed the handle, scrabbled a moment, then caught the sturdy leather-wrapped grip. Big Joe lunged, and Carson drew back and swung fast, a cross body blow that was fueled by pure adrenaline and raw terror. Hampered by the cramped conditions but still packing plenty of force, the wood smacked into the side of Joe's head, sent it flying into the front windshield where it broke the glass and left a tuft of hair.

Desperately, Carson lifted his foot and jammed it out at the door release lever, struck it hard, dead center. The door gave way behind

 201

him, and he was in free fall, arms windmilling as he plunged headfirst onto unforgiving concrete. His bat skittered away, and his head smacked down, sending fire and light dancing through his brain.

When he came to seconds later, Big Joe was hunched in the stairwell, blood streaming from his skull, poised to attack again. A hellish growl ripped from his throat. He lunged.

Just as Joe's foot hit the bottom step, a metal garbage can smashed into his face, sent him stumbling sideways. Josh. Josh leapt in and struck again. Again. Big Joe went down.

Josh hurled the can at him, lunged for Carson and hauled him to his feet. "You okay?!"

"You'll have to... ask my therapist..." Carson weaved unsteadily, trying to blink away stars. "Let's... beat it!" He snatched up his bat, and they staggered quickly away, Josh taking much of his weight. Behind, they could hear a chorus of fearsome groans and the sound of feet on pavement as the bus disgorged its contents. The noises did wonders for Carson's recovery. In seconds, he had shaken off his head injury and was running on his own, sprinting neck and neck with Josh for the 24/7.

"What's going on?!" Josh threw a wild look over his shoulder.

"The truth?!"

"Now's a good time!"

"Monsters are real!"

"Got it!"

"And they wanna eat you!"

"Got it!"

"Any more questions?!"

"They can wait!"

They dodged between gas pumps and hit the door, Josh first, Carson pausing a half second to watch their backs and check the progress of the mob. It was coming. Fast.

He ducked inside, slammed and locked the door, heart hammering, sucking gasps of air. "Barricade!"

Josh nodded, grabbed a magazine rack and upended it.

"Dex!" Carson hollered, seizing the frozen treats mini freezer and dragging it over. "*Dex!*"

Seconds later, the first zombie hit the door - the Mexican in the flannel shirt. It skidded to a halt and banged headfirst into the glass. Others joined it seconds later: a young woman in a Denny's uniform, a big man in mechanic's coveralls and several others. They hammered on the glass, bit at it, smearing it with saliva and something green, dead eyes staring hungrily. Carson and Josh toppled one last display in front of the door, then lurched back in horror.

Their voices rose in stereo: *"DEEEEEX!"*

From the restroom, there was the sound of cursing, then an angry flush. The door burst open, and Officer Jackson stood revealed: his shirt untucked, belt undone and a dog-eared magazine clutched in one hand. He looked mad. *"What?!* Can't a guy drop a deuce around here without..." He glanced at the front window. "*&*&^!" The magazine hit the floor.

"Guns!" Carson barked. "Now!"

"Shotty's in the car..." Dex's eyes were locked on the grotesque masquerade outside the store. The horde was swelling, moaning, yammering, pounding, a dozen or more in all. Shelves shook. The employee bulletin board dropped off the wall with a clatter.

"That's *not* gonna help us!"

The barricade shuddered. Glass cracked.

"Dex!!"

"Yeah... yeah I'm on it." Dex shook himself and stepped up, drew his .45 and thumbed off the safety. He swore. "Guess this is what you was..."

"Yup."

"And we shoulda..."

"Uh-huh."

"And I kinda..."

"Yeah."

"Alright, then. I'm a bad friend."

"I've had worse."

"And we're in deep *&^%!"

"That part we agree on."

The three formed a line, shoulder to shoulder in the center of the store. Carson held the middle, taking warm-up swings with his bat, staying loose, bouncing on his toes and trying to ignore the burn in his shoulder. Beside him, face a mask of determination, Josh brandished his mini flashlight.

Dex glanced at it, did a double take. He reached down to his ankle with a quick grunt. Velcro ripped, and the big man passed a compact, matte black automatic to Josh. Josh glanced at his flashlight, then at the gun. The light hit the floor. A second later, he was racking the pistol's slide, sighting at the mob.

Carson shot Dex a wounded glance. "Hey...?!"

"I already gave you a shotgun. Ain't my fault you don't bring it to work. Besides... I've seen you shoot."

With a shatter of glass, the door gave, jerked open a foot before the makeshift barricade stopped it. Faintly, over the inhuman racket of the howling undead, the sickly warble of the door chime could just be heard. The barricade tilted, slipped. A breach was imminent.

Carson shook his head in a mix of terror and dismay. "I'm starting to get a real *I Am Legend* feeling here!"

"I love that movie," Josh muttered. "Just never thought I'd... hey! *I Am Legend! I Am Legend!*"

Dex flicked a look at him, disgusted. "So much for Eugene. He's lost it. Looks like I gave my gat to the wrong guy. Again." He sighed, leveled his weapon at the door.

"No!" Josh was almost frantic. "The movie! The end... the tunnel! The back door! *Our back door!*"

Carson's brain, momentarily derailed by the zombie panorama, suddenly clicked. "Yes!!! Back door! Why are we standing here?! We have a back door!" As he wheeled to run, the barricade pitched and toppled, crashing to the floor in a tangle of shelves and product. The door swung wide, and several ragged green moaners slipped through, spilling onto the pile and scrambling and clawing over it.

"Go!" Josh yelled. "Make sure it's clear - I'll hold them off!"

"No way!"

"I've got a gun!"

A look into his eyes told Carson there was no arguing. "Don't be stupid!" He turned and ran. Behind him, Josh planted and drew down.

Seconds later, Dex came up short against the wall beside the big metal back door, weapon up and ready. Carson slid straight into it with a crash, bounced back with his fist already on the handle.

Dex took a deep breath. "Ready?!"

"Steady!"

"Go!"

Carson yanked. He wished he hadn't. *Something* had been shoving against the far side, hard. The door crashed into him and tossed him roughly to the floor. A blur of green lunged inside, staggered, launched at Carson with a snarl.

Dex snap-fired, point blank. The *boom!* caught the thing in the side of the head and threw it to the floor, where it slid to a halt at Carson's feet. The head lolled to one side, and Carson recognized the face.

"Aunt Jemimah! That was Ben..." Carson stammered. "Kiki's friend! You... you just...!"

"Your point?" Dex's look was anything but apologetic.

"Er..." Carson shot a wide-eyed glance at the corpse, back at Dex. "There were two!"

Then Mike was lunging through the door, donettes and Code Red still in hand, and Dex whirled. The muzzle flashed again, roared a double-tap. There was a burst of red mist, which probably wasn't the Mtn Dew, and Kiki's second former friend flew back out the doorway.

Dex poked his head into the alley after him, covering, checking corners. "Clear! Let's evac!"

"Josh!" Carson surged to his feet. "Book it, trainee! We are *leaving!*" As he looked back, a fierce smile died on his lips. Josh stood stock still in the middle of the store, sighting down his barrel at the trio of zombies who were nearly on top of him. He would never make it.

Then he fired.

Three shots rang out. Three zombies hit the floor.

Carson froze in mid panic, jaw dropping. "Shazam!"

Josh lowered his weapon. "Where I come from," he called. "That's how we kill zombies!" He smiled humbly.

It was the last time he ever would.

A wave of green bodies surged from the side aisles and slammed into him as the rest of the zombies arrived. He disappeared instantly under the press of flesh. Carson saw clearly as yellow teeth sank into his neck, his arms. Josh's gun boomed once, twice... again... again.

"*Noooo!*" Carson charged without thinking, Dex right behind him, and they hit the pack of undead like an All-Star offensive line.

The zombies, fully occupied with dispatching Josh, were unprepared for the counterattack and were caught completely unaware. Carson smacked and swung in a fury of wrath, knocking the fiends left and right, splitting skulls and smashing bones. Dex waded directly into the action like the very angel of death, taking his shots at point blank, sending lead flying with lethal accuracy into every snarling face he met, sometimes dropping two with one shot. The melee swirled about them, bodies lunged and fell, arms swung, shelves crashed.

Then, abruptly, it was finished. A stunned, shaken stillness descended on the store, filled with the whining hum of gun noise and echoes of the zombie's ghastly moans. Whirling and gasping in the center of the bodies, it took Carson a minute to realize there was nothing left to hit. He shook himself, staggered to the dogpile where they'd last seen Josh. He grabbed a biker's leather vest and pulled it's owner clear, desperately searching the tangle of limbs. His eyes caught a glimpse of tan uniform, and he gave a shout.

"Dex! He's here!"

Dex joined in, and seconds later, they had pulled Josh's body free. It was covered in blood, fluid and far too many wounds. They laid him out carefully on the floor. Dex checked for a pulse while Carson waited, numb, hoping and praying. But from the condition of the body, the diagnosis was never in doubt.

"Sorry, Dud." Dex looked up, his face stony. "He's gone."

"Sonofa...!" Carson turned, face twisted in fury. He kicked one of the corpses savagely, then banged away at it with his bat, cursing and shouting.

Dex let him vent. He slapped in a fresh clip, wiped the sweat off his brow and looked around for more targets. Nothing moved. Satisfied they were safe, he eased himself wearily down onto a stack of energy drinks.

It was a minute or so later when Carson dragged himself over, slumped down beside him. "Man," he sighed heavily, wiped some goo from his face. "That freakin' sucks. Same spot where Pete bought it, too. Is it me?"

"Best not to dwell on it. Damn shame, though. I liked that guy - good with a piece."

"Shoulda seen him with a cash register," Carson shook his head sadly. "Best trainee we ever had."

"To Josh." Dex popped the top of one of the cans and sucked down half of it. He belched, shook his head. "It ain't fair."

"No, it's not. It's not fair at all!" Carson's anger swelled again, and he took a furious whack at a nearby corpse. "Why him?! Why is it always the *good* ones?! Why *Josh?!*" The senselessness of it all made him feel suddenly nauseous "And for that matter, why her?" Carson poked his bat at the tangled corpse of a blonde in a bikini top. "Or him? Or this guy?!" At his feet was the body of a Japanese man in a red silk shirt. The corpse still clutched a camera, face a frozen mask of mindless hunger. "I mean, this dude dodged death once already, just last week! You'd think he could catch a break..."

Dex frowned at the body. He turned his head sideways, trying to get a better look. "Dodged death... you know this stiff?"

"No. Well, kinda. At least... as well as you do."

"Say what?! I never seen this mutha before! I do not know him!"

"Well, maybe not officially. But you almost became *very* well acquainted with his lawyers."

"Make some sense, fool."

"You remember - it was just last week, when you picked me up at the beach. You hopped the curb with your car and almost smacked this guy at the crosswalk. I'll never forget the look on his face."

"I dunno..." Dex squinted. "A lot's happened to it since then."

"Granted. But it's the same shirt. I remember because it was red silk, had that cool dragon pattern..." Carson's voice trailed off. Something tugged at a corner of his exhausted, grief-stricken brain. Something he needed to remember. Something about that pattern...

"No! No way!" Carson slipped off the stack, squatted quickly beside the body. He rolled it onto its back, examined the pattern on the ripped, blood spattered shirt. "Dex... I *do* know this guy! Only..." Mental images flashed, disconnected and hazy at first, but coming rapidly into focus with each passing second. "...it wasn't *just* from that day at the beach! He was at St. Timothy's when I stopped to see Becky... and outside the Taj Palace with Kiki! He had this camera, every time - he was taking pictures! Dex... he was tailing me!"

Dex was up now. "What the hell..." He knelt and patted down the body. A moment later, he yanked a wallet out of the pants pocket and was flipping through it. He stopped, storm clouds gathering on his brows. Big fingers slid a card out of the wallet, an official-looking picture ID with a logo they both recognized immediately. "This guy's security," Dex rumbled. "*Fujikacorp* security."

"But..." Carson's brain struggled with the implications. "Oh, man..." On impulse, he snatched up the man's camera bag, yanked the zipper and dumped its contents on the floor. Inside was more than just camera gear: glossy photos and black leather notebooks spilled out. Carson snatched up the first picture he could reach.

It was him. At the beach. Playing volleyball.

"He was doing more than just tailing me... he was full-on spying on me! On *me*! Why was he spying on *me*?"

Dex had one of the notebooks and was thumbing through it with a professional eye. "These are contact logs... phone transcripts... surveillance photos. Looks like he had eyes on you for weeks."

"Yikes. Not just me..." Carson held up another photo. "Isn't this your car?"

Dex squinted, snatched at the picture. He cursed.

 207

"And here's Sister Becky... and Kiki! What the H-E-double-hockey-sticks is going on here?! Why were they tracking all four of us? If this is about the 24/7, why..." He froze, shot a look at Dex. "Did you say phone transcripts?" Dex gave a terse nod. "Jehoshaphat!" Carson jumped up. "They know! Fujikacorp knows! They've been listening in; they know I know something; and, even though I don't know what it is, they do; and now they're trying to cover it up with this hit; and if they're hitting us, they're also hitting..." His stomach gave a sick lurch.

Dex was on his feet, digging for car keys. "I can get to St. Tim's in fifteen. You got a twenty on Kiki?"

"No. But I know someone who does. Or at least did..." Carson snatched the notebook from Dex and rifled through it. "You said contact logs, right? There's gotta be... sassafras! This one's all you..." he threw the book down, grabbed another. "Wait... yes! Kiki. This is her! Okay, let's see... c'mon, tell me you... yeah, lookit!" Carson jabbed a finger at a column of dates and addresses. "Here! Contact lists, just like you said!" He scanned the data, rapidly flipping pages. "Check it out! Here's an address she's at almost every night! Weird..." he frowned. "Whatever it is, she spends a lot of time there."

"Think she's there now?"

"Only one way to find out..." Carson tore out the page and made a beeline for the door. "Get over to Becky's as fast as you can - I'll go for Kiki. And pray to God we get there in time! We'll meet up at Granny's!"

Dex was hot on his heels, moving with the surprising speed he always managed to muster in times of crisis. They ducked through the wreckage of the door and hit the parking lot at a run. Dex broke left toward his car. Carson swerved right without slowing.

"Hey!" Dex called after him. "How you gonna get there?!"

"How else?!" Carson broke into a sprint, heading for the long dark shape idling in the street several blocks away. "I'm taking the bus!"

****

The huge white brick of a bus eased to a stop with a hiss of brakes. In the driver's seat, Carson leaned forward, peered out the front window at his destination. He checked the address again.

"It can't be," he muttered. He had arrived. He just couldn't believe where he was. Carson glanced down for the hundredth time at the torn slip of paper. "No way. Not here..."

Directly before him, massive and still, was the Fish N' Ships.

Carson forced his whirling brain to slow, took a deep breath and stared around the shadowy street, probing every nook and cranny. Plenty of places for something to hide. No way to be sure. He shut off the bus, slipped out of the seat and pulled the door lever. A second later, he hit the street. Before him sat the hulking shell of the restaurant of his youth - faded, weatherworn plank boards, the bow of the pirate ship thrusting from the restaurant's facade, the silly buccaneer clinging to its mast with a giant french fry waving in his fist instead of a cutlass, and all of it still badly in need of a paint job. Carson squinted, checking for signs of life. The closed sign hung in the door, but there was still a light on inside. He took a deep breath and ducked across the street.

It had been a quick trip cross town, in spite of his unfamiliarity with the ponderous vehicle. A jerking, clutch-popping, white-knuckled trip but fast. Apparently, no one cared when a bus drove crazy. The sparse traffic was only too happy to get out of the way, and he had made excellent time to the waterfront district in which he now found himself. At this time of night, it was almost as deserted as Belfry.

On the way, he had also made a few frantic phone calls to anyone and everyone he thought might be in danger. Granny was out of town, up the coast to see her sister, but he'd left a voicemail with her anyway to take a few extra days. He'd tried to make his voice sound casual and to keep the squealing of tires out of the message. Leet was next and had picked up on the second ring. He was practically out of the house by what would have been the third. Apparently, Leet was accustomed to "get-out-of-the-house-and-do-it-now" calls in the middle of the night. Carson didn't care, just as long as he didn't ask any questions. He hadn't.

After that, Carson had even considered - grudgingly - calling Kinkade and Stanley but was quickly forced to abandon the idea. He had no way to contact them and no time to find one, not if he was going to get to Kiki in time. They were on their own.

But, then, so was he.

Carson paused before the door, staring though the grinning pirate painted on the glass that beckoned him on with a hearty *All Lubbers Enter If Ye Dare... To Eat All Ye Can!* Through the faded picture, he could barely make out the cluttered little lobby with its waiting benches shaped like longboats and the crow's nest courtesy booth. Cargo netting hung down from the ceiling, casting weird spiderwebs of shadow through the gloom. He sucked in a breath and stepped inside.

Immediately, a jaunty chorus pealed from hidden speakers, heralding his arrival: *"Yo-ho-ho and a bottle of tartar..."*

"We're closed!" a voice called from the restaurant floor.

"Yeah, hey!" Carson called back, padding warily across the foyer. "I, uh... I think I left my bowling ball in here earlier." He checked shadows, jumpy as a cat. If something was coming, it might already be here. Nothing leapt out at him, but he kept alert and moving.

A second later, Carson edged out into the main room and stopped. The once-familiar sights of his childhood washed over him with a tangle of emotions, a weird mix of wistfulness and apprehension. Tidy clusters of captain's chairs, tables shaped like pirate ship steering wheels, yards and yards of more cargo net, jaunty pirate paintings, spyglasses, treasure chests, a few sharks and everywhere, everywhere Jolly Rogers: on flags, bibs, menus, coasters, napkins. And there, in the very heart of it all, even bigger than he remembered, the centerpiece of the restaurant and the one thing that made every kid absolutely *have* to have his birthday party here again and again and again.

The giant squid.

As big as an elephant, the thing was submerged in a massive tank in the center of the restaurant. Long purplish tentacles stretched out and twined about various architectural elements - pillars, the salad bar, and the rear half of the boat from the restaurant's facade, which jutted into the restaurant from the opposite side of the wall. A second pirate leaned off the stern of the ship, brandishing a harpoon in one hand and stuffing a great piece of beer battered fish into his mouth with the other.

Carson peered at the squid. Without the bright lights and the chatter of happy families, the effect was much less whimsical than he remembered. He caught sight of a submerged eye, as big as his fist, staring sightlessly out through the murky tank water. *Much* less whimsical.

He shrugged off his feelings and slipped into the restaurant, searching for the owner of the voice. Someone in pirate bloomers, wearing a Jolly Roger dewrag and an eyepatch, was mopping the floor - a waitress. A green parrot perched on her shoulder, staring at the roof through plastic eyes, its stuffed body askew and several feathers missing.

"Sorry to bug you," Carson called. "But it's league night."

The waitress glanced at him wearily. "Where were you sitting?"

"There..." He gestured vaguely, twisting his head, peering into shadows, searching for any sign of Kiki or the undead. "Or maybe, there..." His eyes flicked across the waitress. She had stopped mopping. She was staring at him. He could tell she wasn't buying it.

"Okay, look... you got me. I really just came in looking for my friend. Thought she might be here. She's about..." for the first time, he met the waitress' lone unpatched eye. It was bright blue. "About..." Something about her looked familiar. "About..."

"Hi, Carson."

It was Kiki.

Carson felt like he'd been punched in the gut. He stood stock still, stunned and gaping. The sensation was more disorienting than the zombie rush. Kiki flipped up the eyepatch and leaned wearily on her mop, looking demoralized, sheepish and deeply embarrassed all at once. Her eyes grazed his face but couldn't meet his gaze. "Aaaarrrgh, matey," she muttered. "Welcome ta the Fish N' Ships."

It took a second for Carson to find his voice. "*What...* in the name of Davy Jones... are you *doing* here?!"

"I work here."

"But... but... why?!"

"Why does anybody work? I need the money."

"But... but... why?!"

"I'm not going to school, Carson," her voice was quiet but firm. "I dropped out."

"But... but..."

"That's getting old."

Carson shook his head to clear it. It didn't help much. "Uh... okay. How about, 'But... but... I saw you at the college."

"Coincidence. I was just there selling some books back. Rent was due. Next?"

"What about your job? Lucky Earl's? I thought it was a good gig."

"Keeps a roof over my head. Leaky, but a roof. And enough left over to keep me from starving. But that's it - school is the rest of the iceberg, and it's a big one. As in Titanic."

Carson took a breath. He was beginning to regain some control. "Don't you have... you know, loans? And stuff?"

"I did. But they don't last forever. I've been at this for awhile now, Carson. Finishing my GED, getting my pre-req's, it's been a slow process." She settled back against the edge of a table, propped one boot on a chair and slumped against her knee. "Some of the loans came due... it's complicated."

"Uncomplicate it for me."

"I missed some deadlines. Important deadlines. The fight with Vanessa came at a bad time."

"There's a good time to fight a vampire?"

"Turns out, some are worse than others. Anyway. I missed a final. That hurt my grades. Cost me one of my grants, another one played out... I got into some trouble. So, I took the summer off to work. Try to get caught up." The circles under her eyes looked twice as deep in the shadowy restaurant. She looked silly and sad in her clown pirate suit. "Just minimum wage, but, with the hours, I can still pull double shifts and get to my work study in between."

"I've been there, sister," Carson rolled his eyes. "That's a tough act. Double... whoa! Hold the phone... work study?! On top of this?"

Kiki sighed, set her forehead on the mop handle. "A requirement for my program. It's past due already, but the chair gave me an extension, says he might let me back in if I can get it done. Been working as an intern out at Palm Hill School District. Grunt tech stuff."

Carson was quiet a moment, letting it all sink in. Everything was starting to click. Kiki's exhaustion, the clock watching, always dashing off in a flurry, the secrets, even... "Mike and Ben," he murmured. Carson remembered seeing a Palm Hill High logo on Mike's polo shirt.

Just before Dex shot him.

"They're not, um..." Carson tugged his beard uncomfortably. "...friends, then, are they?"

Kiki shook her head. "'Fraid not. Co-workers. Part of the IT Dept. Ben's a tech and Mike's the director. My boss."

"Not anymore."

"Huh?"

"Let me put it this way: there might be some openings out there in IT real soon."

Kiki stretched, yawned, too tired to ask how he knew. "Yeah, well, it won't do me any good without a degree. Which is why I'm here..." she waved a hand half-heartedly at the darkened restaurant. "In paradise."

They stood for a moment, listening to the hum of the distant refrigeration unit, the soft burble of the filter on the squid tank. Kiki looked frail and pathetic. Carson wanted to put his arm around her, tell her it would all be okay, but he knew better. Instead, he pulled up a chair and sat facing her.

"Kiki..." His tone was gentle, but he had questions he needed answered. "Why didn't you tell me?"

She looked away, face flushing pink. "Because. I... you're my... friend." The mop handle twisted in her hands. "My good friend. And there are things about me I don't... didn't... want you to know. I don't have much, but I still have... or had," she muttered, shooting a glance at the plastic parrot on her shoulder. "... my pride."

"You lied to me."

"I know!" She was in anguish. "I know... but if it makes you feel better, I lie to a lot of people. Almost everyone, actually. You're one of the few I tell the truth." Her voice dropped, along with her eyes. "Most of the time."

"But why not *this* time?! Don't you trust me?"

"I haven't had a lot of experience with that word."

Carson waited, said nothing, watched the emotions on her face as she wrestled with them. Finally, she spoke.

"You want the truth?" The words were soft, almost a whisper. "Alright, here's the truth." She stared hard at the floor. "I'm not a very nice person, Carson. I've... I've done things. Bad things. Things I'm never going to tell you. Things I've had to do to survive. I'm not making excuses, and I'm not proud of it. But I *am* proud of one thing..." Blue eyes flashed as they hardened into diamonds. "I'm still here. I've been through hell and back, just me, all by myself, and I'm *still* here. No one can take that away from me!" Her shoulders squared, and she looked fierce for a moment in her pirate garb. Then, the emotion faded, unable to hold its own against a wave of fatigue. "You have no idea..." her voice broke. "...how hard it is." Carson didn't - but, for just a second, he caught a glimpse.

It was quiet a moment. Carson watched her; his heart squeezed. It was a side of her he'd never seen. A frightened little girl, far from the tough, self-reliant, streetwise, sassy co-ed who changed out trannies like other people changed their socks and got by on one corn dog a day, no handouts, no complaints, no apologies.

"But, those days are over." Kiki stiffened, her old resolve returning. "Now, I'm in school... or will be again, soon. I've got a place. A job. A future. I've got..." she peeked up at him. "Friends. For once. Finally. And as much as this bites, it's the best it's ever been. I may not have come very far... but I'm not going back."

Carson studied the floor himself. Something she had said was bouncing around his brain. "All by yourself, huh?" He echoed her words, and it suddenly hit him what that meant. "You've been that way a long time. Haven't you?"

Kiki made a ghost of a nod. "I never had a lot of what you'd call family support. Mom... she died when I was ten. And I had... problems... with my dad." Her body went rigid, lips pulling tight in a piano wire line. Carson didn't push her. He kept his mouth shut. But he couldn't keep the question out of his eyes.

Kiki read the look. Her answer was brittle. "He missed my mom." She looked away. "A lot." Her eyes fixed on a painting of a storm-tossed ship at sea. She stared at it a long time, but the ghosts in her blue eyes kept her from seeing it. "Anyway. Dad's dead. Or as good as. Or I wish he were. Pick one. I don't care..."

She turned her back then. Carson heard the dry sobs, saw her shoulders jerk, felt his squeezed heart breaking. Again, he ached to reach out to her, throw his arms around his friend, pull her close. He didn't.

When Kiki turned back a minute later, a quick sniff and a swipe at a tear was all that betrayed her breakdown. Her eyes were sharp and tough and her jaw set. The vulnerable little girl was gone, and Carson could tell that would be the last he saw of her tonight. Or maybe ever.

"So..." Kiki rose, one hand on her hip, one on the mop. "What brings you to the Fish n' Ships? I'm guessing it's not the shrimp."

Suddenly, in a flash, memories came piling back: the bus, the zombie rush, the Fujikacorp snoop, Josh. Carson jumped to his feet. "Great horny toads! What am I doing sitting around here gabbin'?! We got troubles, girl... we gotta go!"

"Go?" She blinked. "Go?! I can't just *go*! As meager and degrading as this is, it's my job. If I walk, I lose this... and, if I lose this, I lose everything. I'm not going anywhere without a darn good reason."

"How about death?"

"I'm listening."

Carson spilled the story in a rush. He was mindful again of the danger, and, even though things seemed quiet and still, he knew, somehow, they wouldn't stay that way for long. It only took him a minute to sketch out the encounter at the 24/7. "...and so I only know where you are because *they* know where you are, and that means trouble! Now, let's hoof it!" He turned for the door.

But Kiki had other ideas. She stood planted right where she was. "So. That's it?"

"I hoped at least for a 'whoa.'"

"Whoa."

 214

"That was sad."

"Sorry. Right now, it's all I've got."

To Carson's absolute and utter amazement, Kiki sat.

"What are you doing?!" Carson stared. "Didn't you hear a word I said?! Zompocalypse, woman! Zom-poc-a-lypse! We gotta make tracks. We gotta hook up with Dex and Sister B. and..."

"Hold up, hero. Just... hold up."

With difficulty, he rooted himself to the floor, clamping down on his rising impatience. "What? What is it?!"

"I'm tired."

Carson nodded vehemently. "Check. We're all tired. So, let's get to Granny's. You can rest there and we can..."

"No, Carson. I'm *tired*." She stared at him meaningfully, but even that effort seemed almost too much, and she gave up, slumping further back into her chair. "Just give me a sec, willya? Let me think. Maybe we can... maybe we can figure this out..."

Carson stared into her eyes. They were haunted, harried, bone weary. He could tell that she was caught up in life and debt and darkness and the past and too overwhelmed by all of it to want any more burdens to bear. She was desperate for this to be something other than what it was. So was he. The problem was she was wrong.

"Kiki," he leaned forward, gripped the arms of her chair, pinning her to the back of the seat with his intensity. "Listen to me." It made her uncomfortable; he could tell, but it was the only way. "There is nothing to figure out. I am *not* imagining this. I am *not* making this up. This is *not* the result of an overactive imagination, too many violent video games or moonlight reflecting off swamp gas. There are monsters in this town - first *vampires,* now *zombies.* I know it's weird and awkward and makes it really difficult to punch a time clock or stick to a schedule, but it's also *really* happening. They're absolutely freakin' legit and they want... to... kill... us. *Us.* Not just me, or Dex, or Sister Becky, but *you, too.* Us!"

"Maybe..." she mumbled. "...and maybe I don't care." She edged sideways, but he blocked her stubbornly, refusing to let her escape.

"Maybe you don't have a choice!"

"There's *always* a choice." She tried to duck the other way and again found herself blocked. "Now get off me...!"

"Sassafras, woman!" Carson shook the chair, his patience faltering. "You need help! Take it! I am *not* gonna stand around and watch you die!"

"Die?!" Kiki flashed angry eyes around the restaurant. "From what?! Look around you, Carson! What *exactly* is going to kill me in here?! What kind of lame, miserable creature would make *this* hellhole its lair?!"

"Well... well...!" he sputtered, helpless in his frustration "I don't know! But the dead... the dead are rising!"

"*What* dead?!" Kiki scoffed. "That crab leg?" She pointed. "Fishsticks? Maybe the catch of the day?!"

"No - that squid!"

"The squid?! How could it be dead?! *It's not even real*!"

"Oh yes it is!"

"Oh no it's not!"

"Yes it is!"

"No it's not!!"

"Actually... I'm pretty sure it is." Carson's voice was suddenly small. Kiki stopped cold, stared at him. He wasn't looking at her anymore. His eyes were fixed on something over her shoulder.

Her words were a breathless whisper as a sudden, inexplicable chill rolled up her spine. "How do you know?"

"It just blinked."

Kiki turned, following the direction of his stunned finger and stared directly into the eye of the squid, mere inches away, magnified to volleyball size by the thick aquarium glass behind her.

For a moment, it just sat there, still and lifeless.

Then, slowly, ever so slowly, it rolled in its socket. Stared straight at her. A puffy, white, milky, dead eye. With a sudden, ponderous, impossible shudder, the leviathan shifted and began to rise.

Kiki screamed, toppled over in her chair, and, suddenly, the air was filled with whipping, lashing tentacles as the thing heaved, water spilling and sloshing over the sides of the tank in a tainted green tidal wave. Tentacles pulled taut, still gripping beams, straining as the great beast hauled itself upward. The sharp crack of wood rent the air as lumber splintered and snapped, tilting the monstrous thing against the side of the tank. A fresh wave poured out as the glass ruptured with an ear-splitting report, sending sheets of spray halfway across the room.

Carson caught a wave of water across the knees and went down, just as a tentacle whipped past and smashed a chair into slivers. Jarred from his daze, he scrambled madly under a table where a second wave caught him in the face. He coughed, spluttered, spat putrid water, wiped furiously at his eyes. Another tentacle hammered down on the table, split off a third of it, then yanked back for another blow. As it came whistling in, Carson flung himself clear. The table disintegrated.

Carson rolled, crawled and dodged, staying under tables, frantically keeping just a second ahead of the groping grasping arms that blindly sought his form. Furniture flew as the squid sewed a trail of destruction in his wake. Carson hit the wall, shot out from under the last table and dove under the heavy stainless steel salad bar, curling into a tight ball. The tentacles tore and pounded at it, hammering huge dents in the frame, but it was anchored securely to the floor and stubbornly refused to budge. The tremendous beating continued for a moment; then, like a storm at sea that had blown itself out, the thunder and noise abruptly stopped. The fearsome arms whirled away and were gone.

The great eye had spotted Kiki.

Rolling its mammoth bulk across the floor, the monstrous thing fixed on Kiki, who lay half-stunned where she had fallen. As she looked up, it filled her vision, a wall of sickly purple and black, pulsing with dark veins. Kiki screamed, rolled to her feet and dashed across the jumbled wreckage of the floor. She leapt one tentacle, skidded to a halt just as another crashed down before her, twisted past a third and then dove headfirst for the foyer, sliding behind the crow's nest podium. Seconds later, three tentacles whipped in and pulverized it.

Carson, peering around the edge of the salad bar, felt his heart leap into his throat. The tentacles fished about in the wreckage for a moment, shoving aside splintered boards, and came up with a struggling, kicking form. The squid had Kiki by the leg and had her tight. She shrieked in terror and mindless fury, lashing out with her bare hands.

Carson moved.

Shooting out from under the salad bar, he was on his feet, running, desperate to reach her... until a glint of metal caught his eye. He slid to a halt before a pair of crossed cutlasses hanging on the wall. His brain clicked. Costume swords. Cheap imitations.

Good enough.

He snatched one and was off at a run.

Seconds later, Carson was there and swinging. He batted aside one tentacle, lunged up and slashed down hard at the one that gripped Kiki's leg. Costume or not, the blade cut. It sheared through moldering flesh, neatly severed the limb. Sticky black sprayed out in a gush, and Kiki came free, flew through the air, bounced off an upended table and hit the wood deck. Hard. Tentacles yanked back, thrashing the air as the great bulk of the monster quivered in a silent scream.

Carson was at her side in an instant.

"Ow..." Kiki lifted her head groggily, eyes unfocused.

"Sorry!" Carson yanked her to her feet, and they ran. They didn't get far.

A half dozen steps and a purple log smashed down in front of them, blocking the way. Carson shoved Kiki back, brandishing his weapon, retreating. Another tentacle crashed down behind, cutting them off. They whirled to flee in the only direction left and slid to a halt, staring straight ahead into the massy, pulpy, fleshy center of the thing. A great horny beak the size of a watermelon snapped and cracked, reaching for their flesh, as around them a forest of tentacles drew close.

Carson hesitated a single second, eyes locked in horror on the clacking beak. Then, he charged. A ragged shout tore from his lips, cutlass swinging high. He got three steps before a tentacle lashed into his chest and knocked him flying.

The attack also opened a split-second escape route for Kiki, and she took it. Diving between flying arms, she flung herself clear and rolled into open space. Behind her, Carson struggled to rise, sucking air, dazed fingers clutching for his cutlass even as the squid's arms clutched at him. Kiki jerked upright, took a step toward him, stopped, knowing it was suicide. Instead, she whirled, searching madly, forcing herself to think. If she didn't, Carson was dead.

Then she saw it.

With a choked gasp, Kiki dodged into the restaurant, brain working feverishly, calculating angles, momentum, timing. A quick glance showed that Carson was already hopelessly ensnared, almost smothered under putrid purple flesh. The fiendish beak clicked and cracked savagely as the arms dragged him nearer and nearer. He was halfway to dinner already. It would be close.

Kiki judged distance, pushed hard, ran up the splintered ramp of a table, leaped... and barely caught the edge of her target with desperate outstretched fingers - the rail of the pirate ship. Thrusting from the wall into the open space of the restaurant, it loomed almost over the top of the monster below. At the very tip of the stern stood the pirate with the fish stick. And the harpoon.

As Kiki's weight hit the ship it creaked, snapped, dropped an inch, stopped. She kicked wild, pulled down, desperately plying her supple body against the stubborn ship, bouncing, jerking, swearing. She spared a glance over her shoulder. Carson had the sword now, somehow, slashed awkwardly and lopped the tip off a tentacle. Another snaked in, clamping on his sword arm. The thing pulled hard, and he slipped forward right to the beak, jamming his foot into its fleshy underbelly and nearly losing it in the process.

Kiki bounced hard. "Come *on!*" she shrieked.

Then, with a screaming and tearing of wood, the boat ripped free and shot straight down like the end of a see-saw. As it's keel slammed into the floor, the heavy pirate statue was jarred loose by the impact and sailed through the air, plowing smack into the enormous squid. The harpoon punched straight through its quivering flesh, just off center of dead on, and deep into the hardwood floor on the other side.

Instantly, slimy arms loosed Carson and whirled back to grapple with the heavy statue. Kiki staggered to her feet from where she had landed, coughing dust and debris. Clouds of it filled the air. She found the wall and put her back to it, casting about desperately for Carson. She spotted him quickly, back against the wall with a straight shot to the door. He was free. Staggering, reeling, bruised - but free. She sagged with relief. Carson was safe. Now, it was her turn.

As she got her bearings, Kiki's relief quickly faded. She stood now at the far side of the restaurant, opposite Carson, the great bulk of the stricken squid between them. Her maneuver had saved Carson but had cost her. There was no way past.

Carson took in the scene with a glance. "We've gotta kill it!" he shouted over the sound of furious thrashing. "It's the only way!" Somehow, he still had his cutlass, and he tossed it toward her in a high arc. Kiki pushed away from the wall, chased it as it clattered and spun across the floor. Carson broke the glass on a fireman's axe and yanked the weapon out.

Kiki stared at the squid, then at their puny weapons. They were like toothpicks. "How?!" she hollered.

"The brain... hit the brain!" Carson darted in and out, chopping and hacking. "I'll distract it!"

Kiki shook as a crazy rush of adrenaline surged through her. Most of the tentacles faced Carson. The great bullet-shaped head was toward her, unprotected. It just might work... She gripped the hilt of the sword, edged closer. One of the monster's eyes was smashed, and great gouts of blackish-greenish fluid squirted from its wounds as it heaved to get free. Dark veins stood out like cords on its hideous flesh, pulsing with nameless fluids. And it smelled. A horrible deathly stink. Like a blue whale dumped on the beach and left to rot. Kiki felt sick. Gritting her teeth, she hurled herself forward, drew back the cutlass and stabbed.

Black blood squirted, tentacles thrashed, and the quivering bulk heaved. Kiki stabbed again, wildly. More blood, more thrashing. The third time, she came at it meaning business, stabbing and stabbing and stabbing until black ick washed the floor, making it slick and treacherous. The squid didn't even slow. She staggered back in dismay.

"What are you doing?!" Carson bellowed. A tentacle swished dangerously close to his head, and he batted it away.

"I can't find the brain!" she screamed. Frustration clutched her. "Where's the brain?!"

"How should I know?! Keep trying!"

She lunged in, poked again. Another spurt of blood. No effect.

"Any time!"

"Will you *stop it*?! This isn't as easy as it looks!"

"Wait! I remember something... Discovery Chanel! The brain is... it's very small!"

"That's *not* helping!" One of the arms reached over, groped blindly for Kiki, and she squealed and jumped back. With a wrench, the squid shifted sideways, and the statue gave a sickening jerk. The harpoon was loosening.

"This isn't working!" Kiki threw down the sword in despair. "It's too small! I need..." Her eyes lit on a long gash one of the tentacles had left in the floorboards. From inside, poking up through the splintered wood, a stretch of flexible metal hose winked at her. "...something else!" Kiki rushed to it, took hold and pulled. The broken wood gave easily, and a coil of hose came free in her hands.

Catching up the sword again, Kiki whacked the pipe once... twice... the third time, it parted, hissing gas. Yanking and tugging, she dragged it toward the squid, tearing up more floor as she went. The beast rolled again, pulling another few inches of the harpoon loose. Kiki didn't wait to see if it would come free - just lunged forward with a grimace and jammed the hissing pipe deep into rancid flesh. It slapped against her face and arms, quivering and shuddering beneath her. Her stomach lurched.

A tentacle swung around from Kiki's blind side, groping, and brushed her back. She gasped, twisted away, slipped in blood, went down, scrambled up and lurched clear. Breathing hard, she snatched up a tablecloth, quickly bundled it. An oil lantern had crashed nearby, and she swiped the cloth through the sticky fluid. With shaking fingers, she dug a butane lighter out of her pocket.

The great bulk of the squid wrenched again, rolled toward her. With a sickening *pop!* the harpoon pulled free. Kiki leapt back, came up short against the wall.

"Carson... get me out of here!"

"I'm on it!" Carson charged a few feet and hefted his axe, taking aim at something. "Get ready... boo-yah!!" He swung. The axe sheered through the anchor rope of a wrought iron candelabra that hung overhead, now almost on top of the squid. It dropped with a rotten squelch onto the heaving monster, neatly trapping most of its tentacles.

They wouldn't stay trapped for long, but Kiki wasn't being picky. She lunged forward, scrambled up the salad bar, banged her shin on the candelabra as she crested the beast and tripped, plunging and spilling down its far side. She looked up in a daze - straight into the cracking beak. A tentacle popped free, lashed out at her, groped her arm... then Carson was there, slashing and cutting and dragging her to her feet.

"Wait...!" She touched her lighter to the tablecloth and it burst into flame. Without bothering to aim, she whirled and let it fly directly at the beak. Then, they were dashing, chasing, crashing madly across the floor for the front door. They burst out into the night, feet pounding, arms pumping, charging clear.

A heartbeat later, the Fish N' Ships exploded.

The restaurant erupted in a thundering fireblossom, lifting off the roof, blowing out the front windows and setting off car alarms for a half mile in every direction. The french fry sword from the jolly pirate on the store's facade tore loose and sailed over two blocks, where it punched through a Weight Watchers billboard and stuck, quivering, in Jessica Simpson's smiling mouth.

Gasping, reeling and shaking, Carson and Kiki lay on the sidewalk as pieces of wood, decor and squid rained down about them. For a moment, neither one spoke. They just stared in awe at the wreckage. Black smoke billowed into the sky. Flames crackled.

"Well..." Carson managed. "I'd say... you found... the brain..."

Kiki didn't answer. She gazed at the smoking shambles of the Fish N' Ships, then down at her tattered pirate costume smeared with sticky black. Somewhere during the battle, the stuffed parrot on her shoulder had been ripped away. Only the feet remained, clinging forlornly to her shirt. Kiki reached up wearily, pulled them off and tossed them into the gutter.

She sighed. "I hated this job anyway..."

CHAPTER TWELVE

The Art of War

"Y'know, I always wanted to fight a giant squid."

"Your bucket list is like some weird reality TV show."

"*20,000 Leagues Under the Sea.* I loved that movie. Watched it a hundred times as a kid. The über submarine, Ned Land the fighting sailor, Kirk Douglas, James Mason... used to play it in the backyard with my sibs all the time. Squid battle. Sounded great."

"And now?"

"It wasn't as much fun as I thought it would be." Carson held up his forearms, showing angry red welts. "I've got tentacle rash. Zombie squid tentacle rash. Kirk Douglas never had zombie squid tentacle rash."

Kiki stared from the couch. "I really don't have words."

They were silent for a moment, letting the events of the past hour wash over them yet again, trying to adjust to the reality of now. It was hard. Carson paced, unable to sit still, and even Kiki looked wide awake and alert for the first time in weeks.

They had fled the scene in the borrowed bus and driven directly to

Granny's. Or almost. On Kiki's suggestion, they had ditched the bus several blocks away and walked from there, in order to throw off any pursuit. They had arrived at an empty dark house.

No Dex.

Again, Carson felt a squirt of worry shoot through his gut. He stopped, forced himself to relax. They'd only been back for fifteen minutes. Dex was a big boy. Patience. He started pacing again.

After a moment, Kiki rose and padded to the stairs, glanced up nervously. "Is it safe here?"

"As anywhere. Judging from those surveillance journals, they know everything about us. I forgot what I had for breakfast this morning, but after a quick peek in there, I'm hungry for pancakes again. On the bright side, they probably think we're dead, so we might be safe for a bit. Even here."

"I wish you'd grabbed one. A journal. We might have been able to find something useful." Kiki's mind was in gear, eager for data.

Finally.

It was a good sign, and it made Carson smile. "My bad. But don't even *think* about going back there. The only thing you'll find is a store full of dead zombies and possibly a very angry boss who's even more lifeless and terrifying than they are."

"You'll never make night manager with that attitude."

"Look who's talking. All I did was leave a few corpses lying around. You blew up your whole store. If you're trying to make me feel better, it's working."

"I'm not ready to joke about that yet."

"Gotcha. But can I at least say 'I told you so' about the squid?"

"No. And you owe me a parrot. Those costumes were rentals."

The banging on the door made them both jump. Before he knew what he was doing, Carson had rushed over and yanked it open.

Dex pushed past him, glanced over his shoulder, tense and almost frantic. His shotgun was in hand. "Is she here?!"

Carson quickly shut the door behind him. "Who?!"

"The Old Goat! Becky. You seen her?!"

"No. She wasn't...?"

Dex shook his head, his face shiny with sweat. "Negative. She's AWOL. I reconned the whole place. Somethin' went down there, somethin' heavy. Her office was all busted up. There was blood."

Carson could see the whites of Dex's eyes, hear the strain in his voice. He felt his own panic rise and quickly squelched it. The news

223

wasn't good, but having a loose cannon get looser wouldn't improve matters. "Roger that. But let's get a grip. Sister Becky can take care of herself. Maybe..."

Another knock made them jump again. Dex's shotgun snapped to his shoulder, and Carson's bat popped up as if it was spring-loaded.

"Someone follow you?" Carson whispered hoarsely.

"Negative! I checked."

"Relax," Kiki slipped past them. "Bad guys don't knock." She lifted on her tip-toes and peered through the peephole. "It's Becky!" She yanked the door open, and the old nun bustled through, a small black doctor's bag under one arm and a bulky plastic-wrapped object under the other.

"Thank you kindly, Ms. Masterson," Becky clipped. "It has been a strange evening to say the least, and I am most gratified to be among friends once more..." she glanced at the weapons trained on her. "Or perhaps not."

The weapons lowered. Dex's look of relief was quickly replaced by one of suspicion. "But where did... how did you...?"

"Quite simple, Mr. Jackson. I followed you."

Carson poked him gently with his bat. "Dude. She followed you."

Dex spluttered. "You mean you *saw* me?! Why didn't you just *say* somethin'?!"

"I had to be certain that you were not turned Mr. Jackson. In these uncertain times, one cannot be too cautious."

Dex's scowl deepened. Gone were all signs of worry over the old nun's safety. Now, he just looked mad. He let loose a string of curses under his breath and shouldered his shotgun. "Fine. Don't trust me. But at least tell me what happened. Your place was like a war zone."

"Certainly." Sister Becky stepped up to the coffee table, and the plastic-wrapped bundle came down with a thump. "Father Black and I," she announced, "have finally resolved our differences."

Three pairs of eyes riveted on the bundle.

"Um... am I the only one who thinks that's shaped like a head?"

"I should hope not, Mr. Dudley - for that is precisely what it is."

Kiki made a small gasp and covered her mouth. Carson blanched. Even Dex looked a little startled.

"Right. Okay... and are you telling us... is that...?"

"Correct again, Mr. Dudley. That is Father Black."

"You cut off his head?!"

"Of course not." Sister Becky smoothed the front of her habit. "It merely became separated from his body during the course of our altercation."

"That's one heck of an altercation."

Becky sniffed. "Let us not make more of the event than we should. It was as much of a surprise to Father Black, I imagine, as it is to you."

"I imagine. What the hoo-hah happened?!"

"Well..." Sister Becky seemed uncharacteristically ruffled, and she paced for a moment, gathering her thoughts. "It all began earlier this evening. I had made up my mind to have things out with Father Black, once and for all. When I went round his office to lay down my chips, I found him dead. Face down on the oak. Cold as a cellar stone."

"Already dead?" Kiki's eyes narrowed. "How?"

Sister Becky shrugged. "I had little time to examine the body. As I was beseeching our Lord and Savior to be merciful on his immortal soul, he quite abruptly arose from his chair and attacked me - 'he' being Father Black and not our Savior. I must confess to being somewhat surprised. At any rate, I defended myself. The struggle carried us as far as my own office, where, as you know, I keep various tools of the trade. Out of habit, mostly, just a few comfort things. 'Tis a sore foot that lacks a boot when the snake decides to strike,' as the saying goes. A handful of stakes, my best mallet, a collection of crucifixes, a crossbow... and a machete. It was there Father Black met his end." She paused. "Again."

"Well, that's Attila's homicide for the night." Dex turned to Carson and Kiki. "What happened to you guys?"

"I've a whale of a tale to tell you, lad. A whale of a tale or two."

"Say what?"

"Before you begin, Mr. Dudley," Sister Becky interrupted. "I should like a word. I am eager to hear of the evening's developments - *most* eager, based on my recent experiences - but I am afraid I have a matter of grave importance to deal with that is long overdue. It cannot wait a moment longer."

"Er... sure. Shoot."

"I should like, Mr. Dudley, to apologize."

Carson blinked. "For what?"

"For failing you." There was remorse in her eyes, genuine and compelling.

It made Carson slightly uncomfortable. "Hey, no worries..."

Sister Becky held up a hand. "Please, Mr. Dudley." He shut his mouth. "It is clear that I have misjudged the situation in Las Calamas.

 225

Gravely. That misjudgment almost cost me the lives of three people for whom I care a great deal. I was blinded, Mr. Dudley. Blinded by my pride, my selfishness and my own troubles. Blinded by life. And by *this* cursed thing..." she fished under her robes with a look of sour distaste and came up with her cell phone, then flung it violently against the wall. It crunched, not entirely unlike Kinkade's tablet, and dropped to the floor. For a few seconds, the phone struggled sadly to play *Highway To Hell* one last time. Sister Becky watched it coldly until it expired.

When she looked back, some of the wrinkles had smoothed from her face. "I failed you, Mr. Dudley. When you needed me the most. I shall not do so again."

From the tone in her voice, Carson knew that she never would.

"Better put me on that list too." Kiki slid up beside Sister Becky.

"That makes three," Dex loomed behind them. "I suck."

They stood that way for a moment in front of Carson, all of them wrapped in Dex's shadow.

Sister Becky smiled gently. "Forgive us."

"You're forgiven."

Dex straightened. His shoulders moved out of the path of the lamp and lifted his shadow from the group. It was like the sun coming up. Carson felt his spirits lift with it. Something clicked.

The Gang was back.

Carson stepped forward and threw his arms around them. "Group hug!" He squeezed tight. "C'mon, let it out! Oh, sorry about the smell. It's just the zombie squid."

Sister Becky shook her head in wonder. "You are a remarkable man, Mr. Dudley. You simply do not relent. Even when opposed by vampires, zombies... or stubborn old nuns."

"For the record, I'd rather face vampires and zombies."

"Indeed."

"So!" Carson clapped his hands. "Story time?"

"Quite, Mr. Dudley. And this time, my dear boy... you have my *full* attention."

"Awesome. I'll get my plunger..."

It took some time to relate the horrifying events of the evening, from the bus attack to their narrow escape at the Fish N' Ships. Carson left nothing out. Dex and Kiki provided color and the odd detail, and, when they were finished, they fell silent, waiting.

Sister Becky tilted her gray head back and stared up at the ceiling.

She tapped a bony finger on thin lips, leveled her gaze at Carson, then fired. "Were you bitten?"

"Um... what?"

"Bitten, Mr. Dudley. Did any of these creatures put their teeth to your flesh?"

"I... I don't think so." He checked himself, patting his arms and legs. "The whole thing was pretty painful, so it's hard to tell. And there was a lot of splattering. Very juicy. But I don't think... no. No bites."

She examined him closely, scrutinizing. "Very good." Satisfied, she turned her gaze to the others. "And the two of you? Are you unmarked as well?" She checked Kiki over, clucked in satisfaction. then turned her inspection to Dex. It lingered especially long.

Finally, Dex swore. "Damn, Old Goat! I ain't been bit! Turn them green searchlights on somebody else!" He made a fist, threatening.

Sister Becky scowled, narrowed her eyes. "Please contain your angst, Mr. Jackson. This is a slightly more pressing matter than checking for ticks. I am attempting to determine whether or not..."

"Yeah, yeah, I know. I seen the movies."

"This is no movie, Hittite!" she snapped. "This is life! *Real* life! And I guarantee that the Desecration/Remortification process is one you have no desire to see lived out in your own flesh!" Satisfied at last, she turned away. "And I shall, as usual, Mr. Jackson, thank you to withhold your profanities while in my company. If manners were as accurate a test for zombification as putrefaction, I should have already assumed the worst and made you a place beside Father Black!" She shot the head-shaped bundle on the coffee table a meaningful glance. "I brought extra bags."

Dex gave her a mean look, opened his mouth, shut it. He switched to Carson. "Did she just call me stinky or rude?"

"Alright," Carson pushed past the brewing argument. "We're clean. Peachy. Sister B., it looks like you're the resident SME on the walking dead. So, sharing time. What're we up against?"

Sister Becky gave a curt nod. "Right. Well, first of all, I believe we have now satisfied the conditions for Identification..."

Dex snorted. "Ya think?!"

Sister Becky ignored him. "It is safe to assume that we are facing Functional Corpses. 'Zombies', to use the vernacular." She gestured to one of the books still lying on the coffee table, opened to a picture of a fiendish ghoul with gaping jaws and hollow eye sockets "And no longer 'alleged,' I daresay, Mr. Dudley." She started pacing, arms clasped behind her back. "Our next order of business is to determine how the affliction is spread. There are many possibilities, each more vile and blasphemous than the last. Transference by bite is the most common, and, though we should continue to take precautions against it, I do not believe that is the case here. Based on what you have related to me, and what I have myself observed, I believe what we are dealing with is a Remortifier."

It was quiet.

Carson cleared his throat. "Let's just assume that we don't..."

"Something that brings the dead back to life, Mr. Dudley - if one can so dub the dark and sinister state in which these wretched creatures find themselves."

"So how does he... it... do it?"

"That much remains uncertain. Whatever is behind this, it seems to have the power to Remortify creatures either long dead - such as your squid - or recently deceased. Father Black, for instance, or the poor souls on the bus. I would surmise that they were terminated for the sole purpose of Remortification, after which they fell under the power of their new master, who then sent them to pursue his fiendish purposes." The lines in her face deepened. "Murder and corruption of the innocent. This is the worst kind of darkness."

"Build-a-zombie workshop. Yeah. That's bad."

Dex fidgeted, looking suddenly worried. "How far? I mean... how... how far away does this kind of thing... spread?"

"Not far, I should guess. The effect is typically fairly localized, and the Remortifier seems to be choosing his targets carefully."

Dex's shoulders relaxed, ever so slightly. "Good."

Sister Becky eyed him shrewdly. "Mr. Jackson... if I may be so bold - what is it that gives you cause to ask such questions?"

"She's dead." Dex's tone was flat. "What does it matter?" Carson caught a quick glimpse of the necklace in his big fist.

"My apologies, Mr. Jackson," Sister Becky's face softened. "That was most insensitive of me. If you wish to talk..."

Dex's fierce gaze answered the question.

"As you wish." Sister Becky dropped it.

"Okay," Carson jumped in. "Get killed, come back as a meat puppet. Got it. We'll try to avoid that. Anything else?"

"Yes, Mr. Dudley," Sister Becky brooded. "There is much left to consider. These... *ninjas*, for example," she indicated one of the tabloid clippings on the prostrate evidence board. "They are doubtless

Functional Corpses as well. But also something more..." she leaned in, peered closely at the vague, grainy photo.

"Wait," Kiki lifted a hand. "The ninjas are zombies too?"

"I believe so. Unlike their brethren, however, they appear able to think for themselves, to pursue tasks beyond the need to simply feed and sow destruction." She turned thoughtfully to the evidence board again, eyes roving. "The one you battled even had enough judgment to make good its escape."

"Escape, hell," Dex muttered defensively. "I blew that sucka out the twenty-fifth floor. He was runnin' scared, that's what he was, licking his wounds, thanking his lucky zombie stars..." his voice trailed off into various deprecations, and he lowered himself onto the couch, sulking.

"Yes, yes, quite. No one doubts your prowess, Mr. Jackson. But we shall have to learn more about them when we may and, until then, take great precautions. It is also vital that we determine the cause of this unfortunate condition: supernatural, spiritual... even biological. With a corporation involved, one can never be certain."

"So how do we tell?" Kiki asked. "Whether it's bio or hoodoo?"

"There would be signs. If the matter were of supernatural origin, there would be definite indications. Mr. Dudley, you have been at the center of every occurrence. Think, my lad - have you encountered any unusual circumstances recently?"

"You're kidding, right?"

"Begging your pardon, Mr. Dudley - I meant beyond the obvious, of course. Strange omens, bizarre weather conditions, odd behavior in animals, the souring of milk... anything unusual or out of the ordinary."

Carson pursed his lips, threw the plunger over his shoulder and thought hard. "Well..." His gaze strayed, chanced across a hapless moth butting against the overhead light. It jarred a thought. "What about bugs? There's definitely been a lot of creepy crawlies around lately."

"A possibility." Sister Becky stroked her chin. "A definite possibility. I have seen similar infestations drawn to sources of great evil - especially those of a decomposing nature."

"Speaking of decomposing, here's another whack thing for you: the stink. There's been a lot of stinking lately. In the bathroom, the alley, Carl... *especially* Carl. Not to mention at the Fish N' Ships, on the bus... everywhere."

"Foul odors often accompany foul deeds, Mr. Dudley. I should think that was another sign indeed. Any others?"

"Yeah. One more thing: paper. Kinkade's been bellyaching about his office papers getting messed up. Turning all brown and crispy around the edges, old like. I didn't think anything about it at the time, but now... well, I'd say it registers about a nine on the weirdometer."

Sister Becky nodded, pleased. "Excellent! Very perceptive, Mr. Dudley. Corruption of inanimate objects. Paper does, after all, have its origins in living matter. I have witnessed this effect before, though not often. And always, I hasten to add, in the presence of great evil. Great evil indeed."

Her tone gave Carson chills.

"Okay, so we're going with supernatural." Kiki had been studying the evidence board, her analytical mind sorting, categorizing, hunting for patterns. "The worst part is, it's all leading up to something."

She had their attention.

"Proceed, Ms. Masterson."

"There's a purpose here, a plan. I can feel it." She squinted at the board, rearranging, sifting clues, struggling to see the picture without all the pieces of the puzzle. "There's someone - some*thing* - pulling strings. This Remortifier. I'm guessing it's this tattered figure you've seen..." she quizzed Carson with her eyes. "Twice, now?" He nodded. "He's up to something. And part of his agenda is getting us out of the way." She folded her arms, blue eyes full of business. "And Fujikacorp is right smack in the middle of it."

"Old tatters..." Carson tugged his beard. "Yeah. He's gotta be the boss man. Totally. I got a real chill when I saw him. Way beyond goosebumps. I could *feel* him, if you know what I mean, all the way across the street and right in my bones. Icy wind through the soul, cloudy breath, the whole bit. Anyone who can do that in *this* weather is major league scary."

Sister Becky drew a somber breath and let it out heavily. A shadow crossed her face, making her look even older. "You speak the truth, Mr. Dudley. Perhaps more than you know. All of this serves to confirm some recent suspicions of mine. Suspicions concerning *Ashi Keiyaki.*"

Carson's brow lifted. "No way... you found out who he is?!"

"Not *who*, Mr. Dudley. What."

"I'm not gonna like this, am I..."

"No, Mr. Dudley. No, you will not. I confess that I had forgotten the matter almost entirely until late last week. I stumbled across your note while tidying up the remains of a dozen eggs and an exploded jar of peanut butter from my desk," she held up a hand to ward of his question. "A long and exhausting tale, Mr. Dudley, with no happy ending nor joy in the retelling. A blister on a bunion, as the saying goes. Suffice it to say that I discovered the note and was immediately stung by my inattention to your plight. So, I placed a call. As I mentioned, I still have a few colleagues in the Orient."

"And by colleagues you mean..."

"They are in the trade, Ms. Masterson. Deeply in the trade. Even they, however, were unfamiliar with the term. I returned to my duties and dismissed the matter entirely."

"But I thought you said..."

"Until yesterday."

"What happened yesterday?" Carson leaned forward. He sensed that something was coming. Something big.

"They called back."

"And?"

"Something about the name had stirred unrest in my colleagues - enough to make them continue their research. It led down some very ancient, very obscure, very dark paths, Mr. Dudley. And, in the end, to some answers. My colleagues were most insistent about sharing what they had learned regarding the *Ashi Keiyaki*. And quite concerned to know how you had stumbled across it."

"I'm guessing it's not a rare origami fold."

"Far from it, Mr. Dudley. The *Ashi Keiyaki* is a contract. A binding legal document between two parties. One of which," she paused. "Is infernal."

"Infernal?"

"A demon, Mr. Dudley."

Silence fell. Sister Becky's gray face clouded, deep in the shadows of her hood. After a moment, she spoke again. "After tonight's revelations, I believe we may make some educated guesses. I submit that someone in this city has made a pact with the Damned and, through it, has gained the power of Remortification. And that 'someone' is making busy with it like a potter with three hands."

"You're right," Carson said. "I don't like it."

Kiki tugged pensively at a lock of hair. "That gets us started. But we still don't know what he's up to. What does he want?"

Sister Becky lifted her chin resolutely. "That, my child, is what we shall attempt to discover. Questions we have aplenty. Answers will come in time. As of this moment, there is one thing of which we are certain, and that is enough; whatever lies behind this is an abomination of God's Creation. It must be stopped."

"Agreed!" Carson thumped the plunger onto the coffee table emphatically, and it stuck. He struggled for a moment to break the suction. "Uh, sorry..." It came free with a pop. "Right. So, uh... how do we do that?"

"A timely question, Mr. Dudley. First, we Locate," Sister Becky joined Kiki at the board. "Shall we, my dear?"

"Okay..." Kiki screwed up her concentration. "Let's start with Fujikacorp. There's pretty much a neon sign pointing right at 'em. But, we can't just march up, knock on their door and demand to see the Remortifier. There's gotta be something else here. Another angle." She pursed her lips, scratched under her hat. "Carson... didn't you say something last night about the Super Maxi-Pad? Something Leet told you?"

"Yeah - it's their big store, the flagship one in Romero. Whole lotta wackiness going on over there."

"Wackiness?" Kiki stared at him like a yellow lab when a duck toy comes out. "Define 'wackiness'."

"For starters, they keep the power on. Lights, refrigeration, all of it. And the store's not even open. Really got my Spidey-sense tingling, that's for sure. And get this - they're doing shipments and deliveries. Leet tried to find out what it was but ran into some real shady roadblocks. He thinks there may be human trafficking involved."

Dex frowned from the couch. "That makes Dex mad."

"I'd say we have our Location." Kiki nodded.

"And I say," Carson's face was grim, "we pay it a visit. Like it says in the *Art of War,* 'know the territory'. That's why the Shogun came to see my store. It's time we went to see his."

"Long as I get to shoot somethin'," Dex clambered to his feet. "'Bout time we stopped yakkin'. I'm ready to go put some o' them bodies back in the ground!"

"Roger that," Carson knelt by the sofa, groped beneath it and pulled out the King. He patted the worn wood of its chopped stock affectionately. "When the only tool you've got is a shotgun, pretty soon every problem starts to look like a zombie."

"And we got plenty of tools." Dex racked the pump on his own weapon with a meaty *sh-shack!* "In fact, I don't even know if we should haul you along on this one, Attila," he leered at Sister Becky. "The faith whammy had some pull with vampires, I'll give you that... but zombies? You're outta your element."

"We shall see, Mr. Jackson. The Scriptures may suggest otherwise."

"Say what?! What'd the Book ever have to say about zombies?"

"The 'Book', Mr. Jackson, has a great deal to say about a great many things, for those who care to listen," Sister Becky drew herself up. "For example, Revelation 9:6, 'In those days men will seek death and will not find it; they will desire to die and death will flee from them.' As accurate a description of Functional Corpses as you will find. Scripture also discusses witches, skeletons, homicidal maniacs and a variety of monsters. It is the first hunter's guide, Mr. Jackson, and an often overlooked tool."

"Fine. Darth Becky's gonna trust the Force, so I guess you're the only one left, little mama," Dex turned to Kiki. "Need a gat?"

"Assuming you mean a 'gun', yes. There wasn't much call for them at the Fish N' Ships. Well... until tonight. I'll take what you've got."

Dex dug through his ever-present black gear bag like he was going through the Halloween candy, passed her a compact automatic and several clips. She tucked it away behind her belt, pulled on her canvas jacket and checked that it was covered.

Carson followed her lead, slipping into a black hoodie and stowing the King inside of it. He observed himself in the bathroom mirror, making certain the shotgun was concealed. It was. As he turned away, his reflection gave him pause. He looked dangerous. Carson flipped his hood up. Now, he looked really dangerous. From the corner of his eye, he caught Dex's reflection in the mirror behind him.

The guard was staring. He was no longer smiling. "Bro. You can't fight evil in a hoodie."

"Why not?"

"Cuz you look like one of the bad guys. Check it out - you're the the damn Unabomber!"

"Alright, I'll bite. What's the well dressed zombie hunter wearing this summer?"

"Army jacket." Dex fished a rough looking, well worn, military issue jacket out of his bag. "Lots of pockets, tough as rhino hide, and it comes in every flavor of camo you can think of." Dex tugged on the jacket, then dug back into the bag and produced something else Carson had never seen before: a long, curved oriental blade.

Carson puckered. "What, in the name of Sho Kosugi, is that?"

"Katana." Dex busied himself tucking it into his belt.

"Okay, next question," Kiki chimed in. "*Why* is that?"

Dex shrugged dismissively. "Ninja used one against me - I figure it's fair game. Y'know... fight fire with fire."

Carson grinned. "I wish you'd fought the guy with the mop."

"Do you even know how to use that thing?" Kiki studied him doubtfully.

Again Dex shrugged. "How hard can it be? It ain't exactly rocket science."

"It is, however, military science, Mr. Jackson," Sister Becky looked up from a quiet prayer she had just completed. "And one in which you seem woefully uninformed. The traditional weapon of the ninja is the *ninjato.* What you possess, Mr. Jackson, is a *katana,* a samurai's blade, and a shoddy replica unless my eyes deceive me. Note, if you will, the obvious shortness of the tang, the insufficient folding indicated by the edge wave." She belittled the weapon with a glance. "And those designs on the scabbard are hardly period." She bustled off to the evidence board, catching up the plunger.

Carson clapped a scowling Dex on the shoulder. "She also speaks Japanese. So, let's talk tactics, Sister B. We tussled with these guys once and owned face, but I'm betting part of that was beginner's luck. What are we up against?"

"I am delighted you asked, Mr. Dudley. First and foremost, do not underestimate this enemy!" She brandished the plunger pointer. "In small concentrations, they may be managed well enough, but their strength lies in numbers. When mustered in force, they are extremely deadly. Keep moving, stay clear of enclosed spaces and keep your eyes open. Avoid being bitten and any contact with bodily fluids, if it can be helped."

"And keep an eye on your *&^%! gray matter!" Dex tapped his skull with the barrel of a .45.

"I doubt very much, Mr. Jackson," Sister Becky said peevishly. "That they are interested in your brain."

"Well I'm interested in theirs - at least as far as puttin' a bullet in 'it. Only way to nail a zombie."

"At last, Mr. Jackson, a point on which we agree. All sources confirm that violent trauma to the head is the best, most effective way to destroy a Functional Corpse. Or even, in extreme cases, to sever the head entirely." Her eyes shifted to the package on the coffee table.

"Or blow it up," Carson added. "Blowing it up works too."

"Quite."

"Hold up a sec," Kiki looked puzzled. "Why the brain thing?"

"C'mon, it's zombies," Carson looked at her like she was the weird kid on the bus who just asked how everyone knew Santa lived at the North Pole. "It's always the brain thing."

"But..."

"Perhaps, Ms. Masterson," Sister Becky interjected as she made ready to leave, "given the lateness of the hour and the long road still ahead, we might table this particular discussion for another time."

"But don't you think it's important? It could be the key to what drives them... and if it is, how to stop them."

"Let it go, Kiki," Carson fetched his bat, hit the lights. "It's just the way of things. You shoot them in the brain, they try to eat yours. Zombie 101."

"Okay, that's another thing! Why would they want to *eat* our brains?! It's not like they're getting any smarter. It *must* be important..." she frowned stubbornly.

"One does not ask a lion why it stalks a gazelle, Ms. Masterson," Becky was genuinely impatient now, attempting to edge toward the door. "I suggest you simply accept it."

"Well, I can't." Kiki stood planted resolutely in the center of the room. "I won't. There's got to be something to this, something scientific... something we can use to our advantage."

Sister Becky sighed. "Very well, Ms. Masterson. If you insist on plundering the secrets of my vocation, no matter how dark and twisted, I shall divulge them. But have a care - the powers of darkness guard their secrets well." She gathered her robes authoritatively. "The brain, you see, is the source of the Dark Seed."

Kiki studied her intently. "Dark Seed. What is that?"

"Little is known of this mystical force, but it is said that it exists in all of us, a remnant of Adam's original sin. It waits to be ignited by great evil and is thought to provide the unholy spark of reanimation for the walking dead - and thus their craving for it. The secret of the Dark Seed is one of the greatest mysteries of my Order."

"There now," Kiki flashed the others an *I told you so* look. "*That* makes sense. So what are we waiting for? Let's go find its source!" She hurried out of the basement, Dex hustling after her.

Carson held the door for Sister Becky, who was last to leave. "Dark Seed... didn't I hear that on the Friday Night Horror Flick?"

"She is moving, is she not?"

CHAPTER THIRTEEN

Death of a Salesman

Tires squealed.

Helpless against the forces of gravity and Dex's driving, Carson's body shifted sideways and mashed painfully against the side panel as the irresistible presence of physics attempted to reshape his body into the contours of the interior of a two-door compact. The King dug into his ribs so hard he expected it to fire.

Then, the little car straightened with a jerk, and he flopped back. The lap belt yanked tight, brought him up short and nearly cut off his circulation from the waist down. Carson struggled mightily, wriggling the shotgun into a position that was only slightly less likely to cause the weapon to discharge into his groin.

Beside him, Kiki was faring a little better. She was nearly a foot shorter, a good deal lighter and almost fit her seat. She grinned reassuringly, but it was the grin of an airplane passenger who had just told the guy next to her that they were more likely to die in a car crash than a plane crash and didn't really believe it. Dex gunned the little motor, shoving them back into their seats. The G-forces peeled the grin off Kiki's face and wedged Carson's head against the ceiling.

With a whine and a jerk, the straining motor upshifted, and the ride momentarily evened out. Carson knew it wouldn't last, but he took the moment to quickly massage feeling back into his legs.

Kiki watched with sympathy. "You could have ridden up front, you know."

Carson twisted, trying to find something to brace himself against. "I thought if I already *had* a shotgun, I wouldn't have to call it. Besides..." he jerked his head toward the passenger seat, indicating Sister Becky. One of her booted feet was braced against the dash. "This would break her."

They had left Granny's in a hurry, with no options for transport other than Dex's car. Even though he knew the risks, Carson had volunteered for the back seat. It had taken him precisely one block to decide that riding in the back was even worse than riding in the front.

Balding tires stuttered as Dex took a hard right and squeaked against the curb. The car lurched and Carson's belt popped loose for the thousandth time. He desperately wrestled it back into place. The back seat was so cramped he wasn't sure he needed it to keep him in the car, but riding without it just felt - for lack of a better word - dangerous. The buckle clicked. For the thousandth time. It also pinched a fat chunk of skin. For the thousandth time. He yelped.

"Crabapples! I tell ya, we're gonna have to get a cooler ride if we're gonna keep saving the city!"

"I'd settle for saving us," Kiki replied.

"I'd settle for leg room."

"You don't like it, you can walk," Dex stated from the front seat. "In case you forgot, we're on our way to a zombie shoot. I just thought we should be on time." Dex's seat, as usual, was in nearly full recline, jamming Carson back mercilessly into the exposed springs of the back seat. Carson was about to deliver a snappy retort when another quick swerve from Dex planted his face on the side window. Before he could recover, they were there.

All passengers extricated themselves immediately. Carson and Kiki staggered and lurched about the sidewalk, stretching and groaning, while Becky and Dex reconnoitered They were parked down the block from their target in the shadow of a silent furniture store. From there, they had a good view of the stately flagship of Fujikacorp's mini-mart armada.

The Super Maxi-Pad stood majestically in the middle of the block, as handsome and eye-catching as any convenience store could hope for, proudly declaring its unfortunate name in six foot tall red and blue letters. It was big, nearly twice the size of the 24/7, and its style made it look more like an upscale bistro than a mini-mart. Whitewashed and pristine, it had a festive, fun air, strutting a clean stucco finish and a tiled walkway that lead to the front entrance. Lined with ceramic planters brimming with local greenery, the walkway ended at an elaborate door flanked by floor length windows. These, like all the windows, were plastered with signs declaring the goodness and affordability of all things inside. They also blocked any decent view of the interior. There were no vehicles, no lights and no signs of life.

"That's a nice lookin' store." Dex nodded.

"Thanks," Carson rubbed feeling into his legs. "Thanks for that."

"I mean, it's probably zombie central... heart of darkness and all. But it does look nice."

Kiki stretched her back. "Good colors."

Carson grunted. "Let's go lift its tail and see if you still wanna take it home."

They walked slowly down the street, four abreast, approaching warily, senses on full alert. The wide sidewalk gave them plenty of room, and they used it, halting just across the street for another reconnoiter. A few blocks away, the light turned green, and a single paper delivery truck trundled through. Nothing else moved.

Carson gazed warily at the snappy, gaily colored window dressing. In spite of the happy consumers and tasty morsels pictured there, he felt a growing sense of unease. He glanced left. Right. Saw nothing. The others felt it too; he could sense it. Fingers flexed. Feet shuffled. Someone cleared their throat.

Carson looked back at the storefront, was about to take a step and stopped. "Whoa!"

"What... what?!" Dex's finger tightened on the trigger, eyes darting.

"*'There is no stopping the satisfactory flow,'*" Carson read the text off one of the posters. "*That's* their new slogan? Man... it *still* sucks." He shook his head. "Alright. Let's do this." Squaring his shoulders, he led the way across the street at a trot, bat in hand.

When they reached the store, they fanned out, peering in windows. Dex alone held back, planting himself behind them, facing the street. His head swiveled slowly, covering every direction. He was a granite boulder in an army jacket, shotgun cradled and ready.

Carson shielded his eyes from the glare of the street light, struggling in vain to see past the posters cluttering the window. His breath fogged the glass, and he swiped it clear, then wiped his palms on his jeans. They were sweating, and it wasn't from the heat. "I can't see frack! Too many posters." Inside, he could just make out the shadowy shapes of counters, shelves, other blobs and furnishings in the black. The place looked empty, but with the carefully arranged screen, it was hard to tell. "It's like they did it on purpose. Anything...?" He pulled back, glanced at Kiki, did a doubletake as he registered the marketing blurb on one of the posters. "...besides a *great* deal on Super Maxi-Burgers. Cripes. This is a good store."

"No." Kiki stood up from a crouch. "Not a thing."

"I do not see - nor do I sense - anything untoward, Mr. Dudley. I propose we enter." Sister Becky stepped briskly to the swinging glass doors and tried them. They didn't budge. She clucked as she inspected the discrete but obviously sophisticated electronic locking mechanism. A single red light winked at her in silent warning. "If the hens in this coop are worth the latch, then they are laying golden eggs." She regarded the portal severely. "It is well secured. And alarmed."

"Don't you worry, Darth," Dex dug into one of his voluminous pockets. He flashed a small explosive charge and a palm-sized remote detonator. "A little C-4 should cook those chickens."

"And our gooses, you great heathen!" Sister Becky flashed him a look twice as severe as the one she had given the door. "Merciful heavens, man! Do you wish to bring the entire constabulary down upon our heads?! Explosives?!" she fumed. "St. Timothy's toaster! There are times when I think your entire purpose on this Earth is simply to make as great a noise as possible!"

"Look who's talking about noise."

Sister Becky shot him a dark look. It was like a slap. "Explosives..." she mumbled. "Indeed!" She took a breath, adjusted her hood and her patience. "Ms. Masterson... if you please."

Kiki dropped to one knee and slipped out of her pack. She studied the device for a moment, wearing an expression of intense concentration. "Card reader..." she mused. "...four point... counter switch... Markberg 200... electronic lock..." The red light on the panel glared back at her, unblinking, like a tiny fierce cyclops daring her to try and enter its cave. She leaned back, tapped the light as if to accept its challenge. "Alright, little fella... you're on."

A moment later, an assortment of gear had appeared from Kiki's

pack: a battered laptop, a pile of cables, a small duct-taped electronics box, a bulky magnetic card attached to a wire ribbon. She laid out the pieces on the sidewalk, started plugging parts and tapping keys. Her fingers were a blur, the LCD glow lighting the intensity of her features.

Carson watched in fascination, dividing his attention between Kiki, the store and the street. He half expected the shadowy form of a ninja to dart from the night at any second, but all was silent and still. Minutes dragged by. Carson stretched his neck, worked his shoulder. He loosened Pete's red bandana, fiddled with the knot. The waiting gnawed at his nerves. He glanced down at Kiki. "Pretty fancy security for a mini-mart, eh?"

Kiki didn't answer. Her blue eyes were locked on the laptop screen, a cold, logical determination on her face. She tapped a key, reached up and swiped the card attachment through the reader. The little cyclops remained unchanged. Red. She grunted and resumed typing.

Carson watched her work for a moment. "I'm not gonna ask how you know how to do that."

"It's okay if you ask," she said absently, then swiped the card apparatus again. This time there was an authoritative *beep* followed by a loud *click* that sounded a lot like an electronic lock being hacked. The light turned a cheerful green. "...just don't tell." She flashed him a triumphant smile. "We're in."

As Carson watched Kiki pack, it suddenly occurred to him, yet again, how little he knew about her. Her words from earlier echoed hauntingly in his mind: *I've done bad things. You don't know me.*

She was right. He didn't. But he was learning.

Carson stowed his thoughts. Time for that later. "Alright, people. Stay frosty..." The door swung easily on well oiled, noiseless, expensive hinges. He sighed. Even the door was nice. An instant later, he was inside.

It was dark.

"Um... anyone bring a..."

"Yup." Beside him a strong white beam licked out. Kiki played a flashlight about, illuminating the store.

"I was gonna..." Carson mumbled. "...back at my place..." his voice trailed off as he started forward, letting Kiki light the way. He moved cautiously, taking it all in: the clean new fixtures, the neat orderly layout, the wash of cold air across his skin. "AC's on," he whispered. "Feels good." He nodded, appreciating the store's atmosphere and efficiency, then winced as a pang of guilt squirted through him. "Sassafras.. I feel like I'm cheating on my girlfriend."

Then the smell hit him.

His nose wrinkled, and he brought up a sleeve to ward it off. "Ugh! That's more like it. Dead cat?"

"Dead somethin'," Dex was at his elbow, "that's for sure. But there's nothin' in here, dead or otherwise." He stared around at the bare shelves, the bare counters, the bare end caps It was odd, entirely odd, like a huge, brightly decorated piñata that was empty inside.

"Back door," Kiki's murmur snagged their attention. She jabbed the flashlight at a red access door at the back of the store. Dex led the way, boots thumping on spotless tiles. They stopped, drew up in front of it in a semi-circle. The smell was stronger.

"Odd," Kiki eyed the door, then the room behind them, estimating. "More than half the store is behind there, I'd say."

Dex put an ear to it, listening. After a moment, he scrunched up his face, listened harder. "Sounds like... something. Strange. I dunno." He wrapped a giant paw around the doorknob and jiggled it. "Locked." He stepped back, eyed the handle. "No fancy alarm here. Just a plain old lock. I got just the thing..." He drew his katana with a whisper of cheap steel.

Before anyone could stop him, Dex took aim and chopped down with all his strength. The instant it struck the handle, the sword sheared in half with a metallic *ping!* Two feet of blade spun off into the store and clashed down noisily several aisles away.

"Damn."

Kiki dug a small leather case out of her pack and knelt by the lock. "I guess I can try." Beside her, Dex hurled the hilt of his sword to the ground and settled into cursing and muttering under his breath.

Carson watched Kiki work the lock, staring at her as if she were a total stranger. "You can pick locks too?!"

"If it makes you feel any better, I'm a little rusty."

Carson clamped his mouth shut.

In less than a minute, the lock clicked. Kiki backed off, stowing her kit. "It's all yours, boys."

Dex crowded the door, shotgun ready, looking as if he were eager to use it. Carson eased up beside him as Kiki flattened against the wall, flashlight in one hand, pistol in the other, ready to spot.

Sister Becky, gripping a heavy ornate crucifix in each hand, breathed a quick prayer and crossed herself. Emerald eyes glittered.

"Let us see what mischief awaits!"

Dex shot a glance at Carson, hand on the knob. "Ready?"

"Steady."

"Go!"

He pushed.

Kiki's light splashed across a trio of zombies filling the doorway.

Dex yanked the door closed again. "Wasn't expectin' that," he licked his lips, waited, tense, one hand still clamped on the knob, the barrel of his shotgun keeping a tight bead on the door. But there was no rush. No sound. Everything was silent and still.

Dex frowned, dreadlocks shaking in the shadows. "Don't make no sense. Why ain't they comin'?"

Carson quickly wiped his sweaty palms on his jeans and adjusted his grip on the King. He shrugged nervously. "I dunno. Maybe they're nearsighted."

"One way to find out," Dex rumbled. "Mystery door, take two..." He turned the knob and pushed. The zombies were still there, so close they could almost touch them. And still, they were motionless... except for a slow, almost imperceptible side-to-side sway, like rotten trees stirred by an invisible breeze. Silent... except for a soft, practically inaudible moan, like the drone of a funeral dirge.

Dex kept the barrel of his shotgun trained carefully on them. He squinted, trying to make out details in the harsh white beam of Kiki's flashlight. "Whatchyou think?" he whispered.

"I think they're dead," Carson muttered, at a loss. He leaned forward slowly, cautiously, trying to get a look into the room beyond. "Holy cow!" His whisper was explosive. "Take a gander... it's freakin' Zombie-Palooza!"

Just past the trio of zombies was a wide, open room filled with darkness. It was also filled with zombies. Completely filled. Kiki's light played across a forest of ghastly green faces in various stages of decomposition. All of them resembled the trio before the door: arms slack, eyes half-lidded, jaws gaping, and swaying, ever so slightly, side to side. The stink was almost overwhelming, wafting on the cool winds of the air conditioner. The motor kicked on just then, making them start. It joined the soft, eery moan that rose mournfully from the room full of dead.

The four intruders stood for a moment, letting the strangeness, the stark, otherworldly horror of the scene wash over them. They shivered, awestruck. It was a moment before anyone spoke.

"Hey..." Carson pointed to the wall on their far left. "What is that?" From the depths of the shadows, a very out-of-place framework could just be seen hugging the wall. Kiki's beam snapped to it, illuminating a tall skeletal structure made of old boards and metal pipe. It spanned the entire wall, the far end of it butting up against a large container truck that squatted in front of an industrial garage door that was shut tight and locked. An old mine cart perched on the very top of the framework, astride a rusty track. Beside the cart, a short A-frame structure had been erected with a pulley attached. A rope descended from there and stopped halfway to the floor at a large wooden bucket.

"A scaffold of sorts, Mr. Dudley. But as for the bucket, I am at a loss. Ms. Masterson, if you please?"

Kiki obediently panned her light down from the bucket. The forest of gently swaying zombies blocked the room mostly from sight, but, peering closely, the four could just make out a smudge on the floor close to the center. A wide, dark smudge.

"A hole," Carson breathed. "A pit. Didn't see that one coming..." He leaned into the room a few more inches, straining to get a better look. The gaping black opening was some eight feet across and had been cracked straight through the tile and the foundation beneath. It offered no explanation as to its purpose. "I wonder what's down there?"

Kiki shuddered. "I don't." She turned the flashlight away from the hole, played it once more on the zombies. "But I'm betting they dug it." They studied the crowd of undead with a mix of interest and disgust. All were gaunt and disfigured, dressed in loose-fitting pants and sleeveless t-shirts, stained and smeared with brown. Dirt.

"Must be a hundred of them," Kiki whispered. Her voice quavered, although from awe or nerves Carson couldn't tell. "Mostly men. They look... Asian. Don't they? And I think... it looks like... they've been *living* here." The flashlight danced across a collection of tools and cook pots just visible around the edges of the room and lingered on a handful of straw mats, dirty blankets and a few other personal effects. "Awhile."

"They're different - from the ones we've seen so far," Carson tugged his beard. "They seem... what's the word..."

"Squishier," Dex rumbled. "Like they've been here a long time. A few days, at least, maybe longer. How 'bout it, Attila? Whaddaya make of these fellas? Give 'em the ol' professional sniff."

Sister Becky stepped forward abruptly into the room, causing the others to draw sharp breaths and tighten grips on weapons. "Laborers," she muttered, lost in her ruminations. "Judging by their accoutrements and these crude furnishings, they are lower class... if that. Slaves, I daresay, or as good as. Poor, dear, wretched souls. It would seem Mr. Leet's suspicions are well placed. I would surmise that the lot of them were smuggled into the country, forced or enticed to dig this hole... wherever it may lead... and then disposed of."

The gravity of her theory settled about them like a dark cloud.

"We're dealin' with one sick mystery *&^%$!"

"Sick, yes," Carson muttered. "Mystery... maybe not. Kiki... give us some light up there." She complied, following Carson's finger. The light picked out a large, smeary glyph on the wall - a strange, three pointed symbol.

Carson glanced at Dex. "That look familiar to you, big guy?" His voice was a grim whisper.

Dex rumbled deep in his throat. "Fujikacorp! That was on the flag hangin' outside Fujikacorp! *And* on the dead security dude's ID card!"

Sister Becky squinted at the marking. It was crude and appeared hand-painted, done in a glistening red substance that looked ominous. "Are you certain, gentlemen? That symbol bears a strong resemblance to a *mon*, an ancestral clan symbol of Japan."

"I'd stake the King on it. But it doesn't matter," a grim frown shaped Carson's beard into a furry exclamation point. He was mentally shifting gears. "What does matter is *what the hoo-ha-hey is going on here*?! I don't get it!" He swept the scene once more, looking for anything that made sense. "Fujika smuggles these guys into the country and enslaves them - making himself the lowest form of life on the face of the Earth - then sets them to work. Digging. But digging for what? Or to where? And why go to all that trouble just to make a hole?"

"At least we know why the juice was on... and what they were shipping out of here." Kiki jerked a thumb at the container truck hulking in the shadows across the room. "Dirt. Up the bucket, into the cart, down the track, into the truck." Their eyes followed the path as she described it, picturing a much busier, much more lively scene from weeks gone by. "And they didn't want anyone knowing, either..." she indicated a pair of thick steel doors standing upright and open on the back of the container truck, like trapdoors on a ship's cargo hold. "Special hauler. With those shut, no one could see inside. They'd never think twice." Between the doors, the deep valley of the bed yawned open to receive more cargo. But none would ever come.

"An excellent deduction, Ms. Masterson," Sister Becky nodded.

"One question answered... yet countless more presented. Such as the strange state of these Functional Corpses." She peered closely at the nearest of the swaying, moaning creatures. "Most intriguing. I have never seen the like. Even when..." her whisper trailed off, the thought unfinished except for haunting reminiscences that flickered in her eyes. After a moment, she snapped back to herself. "But we shall not know the chunks of this stew until we have put a spoon to it, as the saying goes..." She strode forward, now mere inches from the closest creature. Again, the others drew breath, tensing.

Sister Becky thrust out one of her heavy iron crucifixes, arm stiff as a rod, unwavering. The holy symbol gleamed in the light, reflecting the zeal in her eye. *"In nomine Patris, et Filii, et Spiritus Sancti!"* Her voice was soft but carried through the moaning room with a powerful, quiet intensity.

The creature before her seemed to shudder. Its eyes flickered, and its moan changed pitch, squeezed upward into a tortured whine. The thing still swayed but now markedly to one side. Away from the cross.

Sister Becky lowered the crucifix, turned to her companions with a knowing nod. "It is as I suspected. And feared. This is no mere biological contagion. This, dear souls, is a *spiritual* affliction."

"Spiritual?!"

"Without a doubt, Mr. Dudley. You have just witnessed the reaction of this poor creature to a demonstration of faith. Recall also the nature of the *Ashi Keiyaki*. Make no mistake, this malady is spawned of powerful forces from the blackest pits of hell. It is dark magic, sorcery, necromancy of the lowest order."

"You're saying this... all this... " Carson waved the barrel of his shotgun at the assembled horror. "...comes from the Hot Place?"

"It is dark magic, Mr. Dudley. Where else would it come from?"

"You kiddin', right?!" Dex scoffed. "Zombie gets the hiccups, and you start goin' all preachy on us! Spiritual affliction my *&^%! You wanna know what I see? Old Ichi just cooked himself up a batch of experimental bio-goo - anti-aging cream or some crap - and shot these fellas full of it. But it went wrong, turned out to be zombie juice, and he has 'em buryin' it here in his back yard to cover the whole thing up. That's what I see!"

Sister Becky favored him for a moment with a steely gaze. Then, she whirled toward the room, thrust both crosses boldly in front of her and spoke in a loud, authoritative voice that made Carson quickly check the safety on his shotgun. *"Pater noster, qui es in caelis, sanctificateur nomen tuum!"*

This time, a dozen zombies shuddered and leaned away, their moans rising to pained groans. Several took shuffling steps away, jostling their neighbors and sending ripples through the crowd.

"There is your proof, Mr. Jackson!" Sister Becky whispered fiercely. "Faith the size of a mustard seed can move mountains. It takes much less to shrug off this rabble!"

"That's cruel," Dex shook his head. "Just plain cruel. Now you're just playin' with 'em." He lifted his shotgun, pointed it at the nearest zombie's head and fired. The roar of the gun shattered the stillness, sent thundering echoes crashing about the room. The body jerked and dropped with a wet thud. "Least when I go at 'em, they don't feel a thing."

Dex calmly racked the pump on his shotgun. To everyone's great surprise and boundless relief, the rest of the crowded mass of dead stood silent.

"Will you guys cut it out?!" Carson pressed a hand to one ringing ear. "If you don't quit playing 'Let's Wake the Zombies' you're gonna get us all killed!"

Sister Becky looked slightly sheepish. "You are correct, of course, Mr. Dudley. My apologies." Another withering glance went Dex's way. "Now then, let us proceed with our examination. We must determine how the condition spreads and if it is infectious."

"It's infectious," Carson answered.

Sister Becky blinked at him. "My dear boy... how ever could you know that?"

"Because there's Josh."

Becky followed his stunned gaze. A figure had been revealed by the felling of Dex's victim, hemmed in by the crowd of corpses.

It was Josh.

"Sonofa...!"

"St. Peter on a pogo stick!"

"I'd like to leave now."

Josh's head was down, desecrated skin green and clammy, black veins pulsing. He still wore his glasses, now askew, and the remains of his tattered, blood spattered 24/7 work shirt, the logo still visible through the gore.

Carson set his jaw. "You want answers, Sister B., well here's two: first, this thing spreads. And second... your Remortifier is recruiting. We left Josh at the 24/7, dead, and now he's here, deader. Something *brought* him. Here. Along with plenty of other poor schmoes. Check it out - these aren't all imports." Indeed, they could now see that many of the creatures were dressed in normal clothes: office workers, housewives, waiters... people from all walks of life, united now with the Asian laborers by their unfavorable condition, part of a mindless, faceless, blank eyed, swaying, stinking, moaning mob of death.

"This is an army," Carson stated flatly. "And they're prepping for war. Fujika said it himself - business and war are all the same to him. Where and when it's gonna start, I dunno. But I do know it's gonna be soon. I can feel it." He faced his friends, fiercely resolute, his features cast in red from the light of the Super Maxi-Pad sign outside. "And we're gonna stop it." They stood silently, staring at the unholy scene before them, knowing Carson was right and letting that truth - and all that went with it - sink in.

"At least," Kiki said in a small voice. "They're not... awake."

Suddenly, every single zombie stopped swaying. The moaning ceased, as if a switch had been flipped.

A beat.

Three feet away, the nearest creature's head snapped up, and its blank eyes locked on the intruders. They jumped back, shouting, weapons waving wildly, the flashlight beam swinging in wide, crazy arcs.

It took a moment to regain their composure, and, when they did, they had hustled almost to the front door. By some miracle, no one, specifically Dex, had fired a shot. They settled their breathing as Kiki wrestled the flashlight beam under control, hands shaking. It hovered, a white blob on the red door. In their hasty retreat, someone had knocked it closed.

"There's too many to fight," Kiki breathed. "If they come...!"

"Let 'em." Dex gritted. "Y'all get clear. I'll cover."

"You will not be alone." At his side, Sister Becky raised both crosses, drawn up to full height.

They waited, weapons trained on the door, nerves taught.

But nothing came out.

Slowly, Carson edged out, leading the way back across the store. From beyond the door came a new sound, a shuffling, shambling rustle. Carson stretched out the tip of his gun, heart hammering, placed it on the door. He pushed. Slowly, it swung open. He held his breath.

Inside, the zombies were moving. Every last one was now aware and active, awakened as if by some unearthly, inaudible cue. But, they were not moving out of the room. They were moving into it.

Carson stared. "They're... they're going..."

"Into the hole." Sister Becky's green eyes narrowed to slits, her voice a hiss. "They are going into the hole."

"Then, that's where we go." Carson hoisted his gun.

Before he could take a step, Dex's hand clamped on his shoulder. "Hold up, bro. Let me make something very clear to you..." he leaned in. "There is no way in *hell* I am goin' down there."

"Chill out, big guy, I just wanna take a quick peek. Besides, these sleepers just woke up; if they're anything like me, they won't be fully functional 'til they've had their first cup of brains." Carson shrugged off Dex's hand and stepped into the room.

The second he did a cluster of undead whirled and lunged for him, their snarls filling the air. But Dex was ready, yanking Carson back through the door. Sister Becky's dual crosses held the pack back for a vital moment as Kiki kicked the door shut.

"Whoa!" Carson's eyes were wild. "Thanks Chewie," he patted Dex's arms, still wrapped tightly around him. "I owe you one."

They listened for a moment as the zombies banged and hammered on the door. Gradually the noise subsided, then ceased.

"Unexpected," Sister Becky mused. "Most unexpected. Their rest state has ended, most likely in response to a summons that is outside the ken of our mortal senses. In short - the Master calls. And the creatures answer. This does not bode well."

Carson eased back to the door, bouncing with nerves. He listened for a moment, opened it a crack and peered through. "Alright, it's clear," he turned back to the group. "So, here's how I see it - this bodes worse than not well, it bodes just plain crappy! Any time you dig a big secret hole and jam a bunch of zombies into it, it just can't be good. We *gotta* find out what's down there!"

"I already told you, fool... I ain't goin'!" Dex had his feet planted and there was no budge in his expression. Beside him, Kiki shook her head silently, frowning in agreement.

Even Sister Becky's wrinkled features expressed concern. "It does seem fairly foreboding, Mr. Dudley. 'Only a fool or a bear follows another to its lair', as the saying goes."

Carson cast about, exasperated, caught on the horns of common sense and the overpowering need to find out what in the world was really going on. "Snap my drawers!" He thumped the wall in frustration. Several zombie heads swiveled dangerously, and he ducked back, lowered his voice. "Alright," he conceded. "Hole - bad idea. But if we're not going, neither are they. I'm ready to start monkeying up someone's plans."

"Hoo-rah!" Dex's gun came up. "And I say we do it the messy way! Holes suck!" Sister Becky lifted her crosses, an eager light in her eyes, and, for a dizzying moment, it seemed all hell was about to break loose.

"Wait... just hold up!" Kiki stepped in front of them. "Am I the only one who passed the psych screening here?! I don't know how many bullets you've got in your army pants there, shooter, but I did some quick math: *there's too many*! You can't kill them all, not before they overrun us!"

"We can't just sit here! We gotta stop 'em!" Carson jabbed his gun at the milling crowd. "Lookit - there's a couple dozen down the chute already!" Indeed, the room had noticeably thinned of zombies. Carson edged forward, eager to be doing something, regardless of how reckless, and dangerously close to starting.

"Agreed. But how are we gonna do that *and* stay alive?"

It was the million dollar question. Brows furrowed. Tension sizzled.

"We block the hole!" Carson blurted.

"Block the... how?!"

"With that!" Carson nodded toward the dim outline of the container truck. "We'll just back that sucker right over the top of it and shut down the march. No way they can move that."

Dex squinted into the darkness at the massive rig. "How you gonna drive that, bro?"

Carson reached over to a row of pegs just inside the door. He lifted off a set of keys. "With these, I'm guessing." Several hardhats hung there as well, along with a few shovels, out of sight up to this point in the shadows.

Kiki frowned, dubious. "Will that work?"

"As long as none of them can drive a stick," Carson was already tucking his bat into his belt.

"Okay, okay, just put the brakes on. Let's assume it'll block the hole," Kiki studied the scene, looking increasingly worried. "There's a little matter of the Zombaree out there. How are you gonna get past them?"

"Simple. I'll use the scaffold. I'll just sneak around the outside of the room - should be enough breathing room by now - shin up, run to the other side and drop down into the bed of the truck. Worked for the dirt." He rapidly slung the King, already edging into the room.

"Up that?" Kiki gave the scaffold a wary eye. "It looks pretty rickety."

"It was safe enough for these guys."

"Carson... they're dead."

"Then, they should have unionized. Look, what other choice do we have? There aren't a lot of options here." Carson checked his weapons. "Wherever they're going, they're going fast. If we're gonna monkey, we need to do it *now*."

Kiki bit her lip. Her eyes were full of doubt, but, for the moment, she had nowhere to go with it. "Just... be careful."

"No argument there." Carson pulled his hood up. "I still look like one of the bad guys?"

"Close enough," Dex rumbled. He stared at the scaffold uncertainly, then down at his considerable belly. "Look... I'd go with you, but..."

Carson dismissed him with a wave of his hand. "No way. This is a solo op. Plus I need you down here in case things go screwy."

"I'm on your six."

"And do me a favor - if this does end up backwards, don't let me live out the rest of my life dead, okay?" Carson's lopsided smile showed from the depths of his hood.

"I said I could take you. Don't make me prove it." Dex thumped him on the arm.

"Ow. Alright. Wish me luck..."

"We shall do more than that, Mr. Dudley," Sister Becky's head was already bowed in prayer. "Godspeed!"

With a deep breath, Carson was moving. Hugging the wall, he slipped quickly and quietly toward the scaffold. Kiki aimed the light at his feet, careful to keep the beam low to avoid attracting attention.

"Just for the record, I don't like this," she whispered to no one in particular. "I don't like it at all!"

Carson stepped around a cast iron pot, stirring up a batch of flies, then ducked behind a cardboard shelter and out the far side and was at the near end of the scaffold. He flashed a quick thumbs up, found a handhold and pulled himself upward. The framework creaked loudly and gave a nasty sway. Kiki's fingernails dug into her palm, but the flashlight beam held steady as a rock, picking out Carson's form where he clung to a section of pipe. Several zombies turned their heads to the noise, eyes bulging, teeth bared. But that was all. None broke formation. Carson didn't wait to see if they would. Working quickly and carefully, he started up.

"So far so good, bro," Dex breathed. "So far so good..."

Carson climbed quickly and, in less than a minute, gained the top. He rose gingerly to his feet and tested his balance, swaying fifteen feet above the milling zombies. After a moment, he nodded back at Kiki. Slowly, she advanced the beam of light along the track, guiding Carson's steps. Once or twice his shuffling feet struck a dirt clod that bumped and clanged its way down the structure. Zombies turned, but none investigated.

After a few moments, the rickety boards earned Carson's trust, and he picked up speed, arms spread wide like a tightrope walker. He passed the halfway point, skirting the chest-high rope and pulley structure. He was moving faster now, covering distance, the beam of light laser-focused and unwavering. Carson had just edged around the pushcart near the far end when his foot slipped on a scuff of dirt and off the outside edge of the platform, and he tilted, pitching out into space.

Kiki gasped.

Carson lashed out wildly, grabbed the edge of the cart and checked his fall. He held tight, frozen, shoulders hunched, teetering... but safely anchored. Slowly, carefully, he pulled himself back onto firm footing. Safe once more, he whooshed in relief and slumped against the cart.

Dex lowered the shotgun from his shoulder, swore softly. In his shadow, Sister Becky crossed herself and sent up a prayer.

Up on the scaffold, Carson shook out his hands and readjusted his weapons. He smiled down at them, made an exaggerated motion of wiping mock sweat from his brow. Then, he turned and, in the split second that the flashlight beam hovered in space behind him, it clearly picked out the zombie that sat up from inside the cart.

The beam found Carson again then jerked back to the zombie as Kiki's brain processed what her eyes had just seen. She squeaked. The thing lurched out of the cart, put bare feet on the planks and dead eyes on Carson. It was big. And Carson was oblivious.

"Hey!" he hissed faintly from the darkness above. "Kinda need the light...!"

In her panic and excitement, Kiki switched the beam back to Carson, catching him directly in the face. They saw his arms go up, eyes squinting shut as the powerful beam blinded him. The zombie lurched closer. It was within arm's reach.

251

Kiki couldn't speak, couldn't move.

"On your nine!" Dex rasped. "Weapons free!" While too soft for Carson, the warning did manage to grab the attention of a pair of nearby undead. The zombies turned, moaned, and lurched toward the doorway. Sister Becky shifted to cover, crosses ready.

Carson and his attacker were close enough now to share the same pool of light. A dead clutching hand reached for him, brushed his sleeve as he staggered, blinking, straining to hear if Dex should speak again.

"No...!" Kiki choked.

Dex's shotgun came up, and he squinted, breathed out slow, trying to draw a bead as the platform swayed, and the flashlight swung, and the bodies tilted and leaned.

Finally, Kiki broke. "*Zombie!!*" she shrieked above the moaning and the whir of the air conditioner and the thick blanket of terror that had settled on the room. Carson reacted instantly. He jerked back, staggered a step and yanked out the King, blinking furiously. Sensing movement, and without waiting to see what it was, he fired, point blank.

Boom!

Muzzle flash lit the terrifying scene for an instant and seared it forever into their eyes: a bright blob of red, the image of shock etched into Carson's face, the hulking shape of the zombie as it lunged.

Immediately, there followed the crack and snap of wood, the sound of flesh and bone banging off pipes and a sick thud. The room erupted with barking, frenzied growls and frantic scuffling as the crowd broke and charged in every direction, and it was impossible to see or hear what was happening.

Dex swept the others behind him with one huge arm, crowding them back through the doorway and out, shotgun waving menacingly at anything and everything. "Off... *off*!" he snapped at Kiki, and the light went out. After that, they made no noise, save for Sister Becky's whispered torrent of fervent prayers. They stood in a huddle just outside the door, rubbing their eyes frantically and struggling to control their panic.

Agonizing seconds ticked by. Slowly, steadily, like the receding tide, the zombie angst began to fade. The noise and commotion ebbed back to moaning and scuffling. Kiki surged back for the door, but Dex caught and held her, finger to his lips. She waited, straining, face white and taught. Finally, after what seemed an eternity...

"Alright. Go..."

Kiki's finger had pressed the button before Dex finished. The beam stabbed out wildly, flashed in a zigzag across the scaffold, found the push cart, then tracked quickly sideways to where Carson had last been.

Nothing.

Kiki whimpered, moved the beam. It skipped over a lump on the platform... she stopped, jerked it back. The lump moved, rolled slightly. A lump in a black sweatshirt. Slowly, the hooded head turned to face them. Carson blinked, stretched, made a show of checking his watch. With an exaggerated yawn, he clambered to his feet.

"*&^%* ham!" Dex blew out his air. "Lucky *&^%* ham!" He shook his head with a nervous chuckle.

In the main room, the zombies had returned to their mysterious pilgrimage as if nothing had happened. Kiki sagged, leaning against Dex's massive frame, taking strength from his strength, momentarily forgetting herself in an immense wash of relief.

Carson, meanwhile, had gingerly chambered another round into the King, trying to make as little noise as possible. He slipped a shell out of his hoodie, reloaded the weapon... then quickly put his hand back in his pocket. Frowning, he checked his jeans, then his hoodie again. After a moment, he slung the King and eased himself cautiously to his hands and knees. He groped about anxiously over the platform.

"What's he...?" Dex craned his neck, trying to see. "I don't..."

"The keys, Mr. Jackson," Sister Becky murmured softly. "He has dropped the keys." There was worry in her voice.

Kiki took several steps into the room, risking the attention of the nearest zombies, many of whom had wandered close in the noise and confusion. She held the flashlight up, quickly twisting the lens to wide beam, trying to illuminate as much of the scaffold as possible. Dex and Becky crowded beside her, covering. One of the zombies nearby stopped. It swiveled toward them, half its face obscured in the shadows, the other half showing a pitted rotten cheek and a portion of jawbone. It took a shambling step.

"*Nnnnnnnn....*"

One of its mates, lean and shirtless with a lolling tongue and leaking abdomen, turned as well. Sister Becky slipped aside to face them. They were only a dozen feet away.

"Be on your guard," she muttered. "We are not alone..."

"He sees them!" Kiki's excited whisper cut her off. The flashlight shook slightly as it held on Carson, lying on his belly on the scaffold

 253

above. His grin told the tale, and his finger pointed the way - down into the framework beneath him. As he shifted to lower himself into the maze of pipes and planks, Kiki's light dipped to light a path.

And froze. She gasped in terror.

Carson's altercation had not gone unnoticed. A half dozen zombies were directly beneath him. They were climbing.

Already halfway up the structure, they were spread out in a ragged line, some in front of Carson, some behind, like rotten rats crawling over a decrepit dock. When they gained the top, he would be trapped.

In the lead was Josh.

Kiki drew breath to hiss a warning, but Carson had already spotted the climbers. He scrambled to his feet, abandoning his quest for the keys. Casting about the bare scaffold, he looked desperately for anything that might help - a defensible position, a hiding place. There was nothing.

As they watched, Carson started to unsling his shotgun but hesitated, eying the room full of zombies below. With a quick headshake, he left it and drew out his bat instead.

Kiki could clearly see the worry on his face, made almost ghastly by the shadows from the flashlight. Her breath came quickly, a sharp stab in her lungs that almost doubled her as panic laid hold. "No...!" she whispered fervently. "No!" She took a staggering step forward, fumbling for the pistol in her belt with numb fingers.

"This ain't good," Dex muttered, his eyes showing white all around. "Not good at all. Damn! Brother's gonna need our help..."

"As might I, very shortly, Mr. Jackson," Becky murmured through clenched teeth. The pair of zombies had picked up friends and were drawing closer, eyes hungry, fingers clenching, looming inexorably out of the darkness. They had a scent now, or a feeling, or whatever it was that drew them. They were coming.

The rest of the dead had also sensed something was happening and had paused in their exodus. One by one, they were beginning to move now, slowly, toward the intruders, turning their backs to the hole. Dex swore, shifted position, head jerking back and forth between both ends of the rapidly unraveling situation.

Up on the scaffold, Carson's situation was even worse. With nowhere to run and nowhere to hide, he set himself beside the squat A-frame structure that held the pulley, using it for whatever meager cover it could provide. Kiki jerked the light between him and the room, trying to cover everything at once.

"Easy..." Dex murmured, edging his friends back slowly, giving way inch by inch as the moaning, drooling horde approached, buying as much time as possible. "Easy does it..."

Sister Becky whirled as a rustle caught her ear. A flanker hobbled from the shadows, mere feet away. It wore a rumpled business suit, one shoe missing along with the foot and much of its skin. She split her focus coolly, without a word, turning one cross to face the new threat and keeping the other on the horde. They were running out of room.

Running out of time.

Back on the scaffold, Carson was out of both. Zombie Josh had made the climb quickest and clambered to the top ahead of the others. Hauling himself over the edge with a throaty *"Gurrrrrrr!"* he reeled to his feet and weaved for a second, plucking at the end of the bucket rope that had become tangled about his head and shoulders during the climb. A second later, he gave up and staggered toward Carson.

Carson gave way, teeth clenched, the muscles of his jaw working as he clamped down on his fear. "Don't, Eugene... don't make me do it!"

Josh banged his knees against the pushcart and came up short. He glanced down, moaned his annoyance, then hoisted a leg stiffly and clambered into it. Carson gave another step, checked the progress of the other climbers. They were just now clutching the top plank, broken yellow nails scrabbling for purchase, their dead eyes fixed on him. Meanwhile, Josh had moved to the near edge of the push cart and was climbing out. In seconds, he would be close enough to touch.

Carson shook his head reluctantly, took an anxious breath and cocked the bat to swing. "Sorry, Josh old buddy. Ordinarily, I'd be proud of you - first to the top. But in this case, I'd say it's time for a hard stop...!"

Carson swung.

Then, in a rapid, surreal, almost dreamlike procession, several things happened that would forever change the course of many lives.

The bat whistled through the air with home run force, dented Josh's skull at the temple and lifted him up and back. His body crashed into the push cart, the tremendous momentum sending it shooting down the tracks. The bucket rope, still tangled about his shoulders, snaked out behind him like a dirty umbilical cord.

Seconds later, the cart struck the end of the ramp and tilted sharply up, ejecting its passenger. Zombie Josh flew threw the air like a sack of dead rabbits, arched high and plunged down into the bed of the container truck with a meaty thud. The bed shuddered. Rocked by the impact, the heavy steel doors kicked loose and swung ponderously downward. On the way, one of them snagged a loop of the rope tangled about Josh, and, as it sailed home, it gave the cord a tremendous yank.

Still frozen in his follow through, Carson watched as the rope snapped tight against the A-frame beside him and jerked it free like a pulled tooth, ripping away a large section of the scaffold as it went.

For a second, nothing happened.

Then, the scaffold gave a tremendous, irreparable groan and a single, mighty, unforgettable shudder.

Carson had just enough time to look down. "Oh, snap..."

With a sickening lurch, the entire structure collapsed. Carson, zombies, push cart and everything else dropped, with a fearsome, deafening crash, straight down into the gaping hole beneath.

"*NOOOOOOO...!*" Kiki's anguished scream was swallowed by the thundering clamor of splintering boards and clashing pipes. She was on the move in an instant, Dex and Becky the instant after that.

Desperately, they plunged into the noise, the flying splinters, the choking dust and the press of green bodies, blasting away indiscriminately and swinging wildly at anything that moved. Kiki was in the lead, frantic with fear, gun barking and flashlight beam swinging madly in the dark. Dex pumped and fired, pumped and fired behind her, clubbing violently with the stock when he couldn't see a clear target, his training and precision taking as much of a toll as Kiki's blind ferocity. She was still screaming. Behind them both, a grim specter in black, Sister Becky swept along, warding off all attackers with fierce shouts of holy wrath and viciously clubbing any who lunged from behind or who were too slow to clear her path.

And then, they were there, through the savage, terrifying melee. The white beam of Kiki's light just stopped them from pitching into it in their haste:

The hole.

Choked with wreckage and half-obscured by clouds of dust and debris, it was a scene of devastation and catastrophe. Kiki threw herself at the pile with a sob, frantically searching for Carson in the tangle of bodies that were crushed and pinned beneath it. There was no sign.

"Get back!" Dex roared as he unloaded his last shell at a looming figure, throwing it back into the dark with a boom and a flash. He took a step and launched a massive kick at a section of planks and pipes. A second kick, a furious third and a large portion of the wreckage tore free and flung back, opening a path below.

"He'll be down there... *Go!*" Dex was breathing hard, sweat pouring down his face. He thrust the butt of his shotgun at Kiki, and she seized it, threw her pistol and flashlight into the inky black below. With wild abandon, she swung downward into the unknown. Dex planted his feet, grunted, felt her weight come free as she dropped. Becky was there in an instant.

"*Back!*" she crowed, swinging a crucifix high. "Back to death, or face the wrath of the *true* Risen One!" A trio of zombies shook, stumbled back as if struck. Becky turned with a swirl of robes, dropped crosses into the hole and swung down on the end of the gun with a grace that belied her age. A second later, she had dropped and Dex was flopping to his belly and wriggling back into the hole, his movements long since planned. Catching the edge of the section of scaffold he had kicked clear, he let his weight pull it down with him as he fell. With a clang and a crack and a shower of wood, it crashed into place above him, once again crudely blocking the opening.

Dex slammed down an instant later, legs buckling and spilling him sideways into the dirt. He rolled, momentarily dazed and disoriented, struggling to find his bearings, hands swinging wide to ward off any unseen foes. Then, his eyes focused on the beam of the flashlight, and he righted himself, struggled to his knees, shotgun ready. There were boards and pipe and rough dirt walls and plenty of dust filled the air, but no green. None that he could see. That was a good sign. Dex lurched to his feet, turned toward the light.

His eyes focused first on Kiki. She knelt in the dirt nearby. Dex took a step toward her and stopped. She wasn't moving. She was just kneeling there, gun in the dirt, flashlight forgotten beside her. Something lay in the tangled mess of boards and rusted pipes.

It was Carson.

From his belly jutted six inches of bloody, inch-wide pipe.

Carson rolled his head weakly, face ashen. His mouth twisted into a faint lopsided smile. "This... is *not* gonna help... with my promotion..."

Kiki's shoulders shook as quiet sobs wracked her body. Sister Becky sat nearby, cradling Carson's head in her lap.

Dex dropped to the dirt beside them like a stone, his legs suddenly failing him. He could only gape, his belly empty and sick. His fingers wouldn't function, wouldn't feel for the shells he knew he should be shoving back into his gun. The noise of the zombies thrashing and crashing against the barricade both above and around them came only as a faint echo, faded and distant. Dex lifted his eyes briefly, saw their fevered, contorted faces pressing through the wreckage, desperate to reach them. He searched their eyes, found nothing, felt nothing. He turned numbly back to Carson.

"Which... one of you... wants to say... 'I told you so'... first?" One of Carson's eyes was red, filled with blood. As Dex watched, a crimson tear welled and rolled out of it, tracing a slow trail down the dust on his cheek. His grin faded, melted into agony as a sudden spasm gripped him. Carson's body twisted, shook, pulling unconsciously against the awful, horrid, undeniable reality of the pipe thrusting up through his middle. A part of Dex's brain, the soldier part, detached and unemotional, could see that the pipe wasn't budging. It was still firmly attached to the tangle of boards beneath and wouldn't be coming free. They wouldn't be taking Carson off of it either. The damage was done.

And there was no undoing it.

Sister Becky smiled softly, murmured, stroked Carson's forehead until the spasm passed, and he fell back limply. His eyelids fluttered, eyes glazing. They slipped closed.

Inside Dex, a sudden surge of deep, animal rage welled up, and his own face twisted with pain of another kind. *Damn the training!* He didn't care what it told him. "We're gettin' you out of here...!" He shifted his weight, made to rise.

Beside him, Kiki's tear streaked face lifted, her eyes unfocused, hazy. "Yeah... yeah, babe, don't worry..." She fumbled for her gun in the dirt.

Carson's eyes flickered open and found his friends, read the look on their faces in an instant. It wasn't hard to do. It led to places of darkness where more people died.

"Wait...!" he gasped. Another spasm shook him, but he gritted his teeth and clamped down on the pain. A spurt of crimson gushed into the growing pool in the dirt beneath him, and, when he spoke again, his voice was weaker. "Wait..." He clutched at Kiki's hand, at Dex's jacket, his fingers feeble. "I've... I've got a plan...!"

They hesitated, tense, on the edge of action and self-destruction. Somewhere above them, a board broke, and a hand reached through, clutching, sending a shower of dirt.

"Talk fast, Dud..."

"Let them... take me!" Carson gasped out the words.

Dex shrugged him off, struggled to his feet. "*&^%$ that! We're goin' right through 'em...!"

"No, listen...! Just... let them in. Let them... convert... me! Josh... remember Josh! We know... it... spreads! They'll give it to me... then you..." Carson's face contorted, and he was wracked by a vicious cough. "... find the... head zombie... and kill... it! That'll... turn all the zombies... back. Save... me...!"

"Say *what*?!" Dex exploded. "Kill the head...?! That's vampires, fool, not zombies! And it didn't even work with them!"

"Know it sounds... crazy... but Josh was... converted, he followed... something here. There's a... Mas... Master... Beck said!"

Dex's face was fierce, unconvinced. He cursed vehemently. "That's more than crazy..." he muttered. "That's ape *freakin'* crazy..."

Kiki didn't even waste time arguing. She just gripped Carson's hand tightly as if she never intended to let go. "I'm *not* leaving you!!"

Carson tried to raise himself on an elbow but the pipe tugged at his insides. He grimaced, fell back. More blood spurted. He was desperate now, but not for himself. He knew what they all knew - if his friends stayed, or tried to get him out, they were dead. All of them.

"It'll... work!" he gritted. "I *know* it! Sis' Beck... tell 'em!" He tilted his head, locked eyes with the nun. She stared down into his face, their green eyes sharing pain, fear, remorse... and something else. She watched a moment, watched as the life ebbed from him. Then, the lines in her weathered features softened. When she looked at him now, it was with the ghost of a smile, sad and friendly and fond. Like letting go.

"Perhaps, Mr. Dudley is right." She looked at Dex and Kiki firmly. "This may be our only chance to track down the source of this blight." She glanced down at Carson. Again, the ghost of a smile. "A tactical retreat."

Silently, Carson squeezed her hand.

"Still gotta get clear of here," Dex mumbled uncertainly. He jabbed his shotgun at a pair of zombies that clawed at them through the shadowy wreckage, banging against it in frustrated hunger. "I don't see that happenin'..."

"Shack..." Carson gestured weakly. A clapboard workers shack, rough but sturdy, lurked just at the edge of the flashlight's glow, tucked away in a shallow tunnel twenty feet away. "Hide... wait 'em... out... then jus'... jus'... follow me... to the Remurtefly... Remortifly... Remortifier... it's a... snap!" Carson tried to snap but failed.

Kiki was weeping openly, sobbing, sagging, clutching at him. "But even if... when... how...?! How will we find you?!"

"This...! Use... this!" Carson scrabbled feebly for his back pocket, and, when he couldn't reach it, Kiki fumbled for him, pulled out a battered yellow GPS. "You said... said we... should keep... in touch... said I... might need it... you were... right, kiddo..." Carson's grin was ruined by a cough. It sounded wet. He fought it back. "Still got... yours? Show me... girl..."

Kiki turned dazedly for her pack, fingers fumbling on the straps, digging for her mated GPS.

Dex watched, wavering on the edge of wild abandon. He swore violently, dug a handful of shells from his pocket and began thumbing them furiously into his weapon. "No! *Hell* no...!"

Carson caught sight of something glinting in the big man's palm. He gritted his teeth, shifted against the tug of the pipe, felt it move inside him. Ignoring the pain, he reached out, caught Dex's thick fingers in a dead man's grip. He felt the bite of metal in Dex's palm and held on tight.

"Dex..." Carson pleaded with his eyes, his voice a harsh whisper. "Dunno... who she was..." he nodded weakly at the hand that held the mysterious *something*. "...but I know... she was... special. Don't let... it happen... to me...!" Carson slid his gaze to indicate Kiki, who was blindly tearing through her pack, oblivious to all else.

Dex stopped as if slapped. His eyes locked on the thing in his hand. Both he and Carson clutched it now, and, for a moment, it was as if they were connected by it. Anger faded, replaced by a hollow, aching acceptance.

Carson's hand slipped free. Dex leaned in suddenly, opened his palm and dangled a silver necklace before his friend. A name band hung from it, decorated with once-beautiful purple butterflies, now chipped and worn almost smooth with age and care. "If you see my daughter, tell her I love her..." Dex's voice caught. "Name's Tia."

"I'll tell her... the old man's... doin' fine. Gonna start... a new... diet..." Another cough shook Carson, and a spurt of blood burbled from his lips, coloring his smile. "Ooh..." he fought to maintain his lopsided grin. "That can't... be good..." His eyelids flickered, but he fought them open again. He nudged the King weakly with his elbow. "Better... give this... back too... careful... 's loaded..."

Dex picked it up. "I'll hold it for you. It's a gift, Dud - you can't give it back."

As he lay back, Carson locked Dex's eyes with his own. "One more... thing... remember... promise... if this goes... backwards..."

Dex nodded. Once. It was enough. On impulse, the big man reached down and cradled the back of Carson's head, just for a moment, tenderly. Then, he pulled back and fumbled for his gun.

"Here!" Kiki lurched past Dex, spilled into the dirt at Carson's side. She clutched her own green GPS in her hands. "I've got it!"

"Sw... sweet...! We're all... set... then... plan... good..." Carson gave a feeble thumbs up, made an effort to grin. "Just... one last..." he struggled with Pete's bandana. "...hold this for... me... willya? Can't... win... 'thout this... 's... good luck..." Kiki fumbled with the knot, blinded by a fresh flood of tears. Above them, another board cracked, and the wreckage lurched precariously. Dex shot a glance upward, mindful once more of the danger. Kiki swayed, sobbed, overcome.

Taking advantage of the distraction, Sister Becky leaned in over Carson, her voice a quick whisper. "Are you certain, Mr. Dudley? Are you ready?"

Carson nodded feebly. "Yeah... 's... th'only... way. Take... care of 'em... and finish... this... willya?"

Sister Becky squeezed his hand.

With sudden inspiration, Carson reached to the neck of his hoodie and tugged weakly. He drew out the tiny, rugged iron cross that Sister Becky had given him what seemed ages past. It dangled in the air between them, much as it had that summer night four months ago. "Guess... you're... right... too... I did... need... this..."

Another board snapped, and a pipe clanged and jangled down through the wreckage, striking the dirt beside Dex. A chorus of hungry howls erupted, filling the air. It would only be seconds.

"Now get her... out of here!" Carson stabbed a look at Kiki. Dex lurched to his feet and caught her by the arm, dragging her toward the shack as more wood broke, and a wave of zombies struggled through the gaps, spilling into the dirt, clawing forward.

In spite of the plan, in spite of the logic, in spite of the danger, in spite of everything, Kiki fought him. She fought with everything she had, her face a mask of silent rage, tears burning, nails clawing, legs thrashing. Sister Becky gently laid Carson's head to rest and then was up and running, dodging past groping hands from above that brushed the hood of her habit, to gain the shack door just as Dex and Kiki disappeared inside.

The door slammed, more planks splintered, pipe jangled and, an instant later, came the rushing, pounding thump of bare feet on earth and after that the pounding, hammering racket of fists and nails tearing at the door, the walls, the roof.

Somehow, the shack held.

Outside, above the inhuman storm of hammering and snarling and howling, they could hear Carson's voice, rising above it all, weak and faint but still strong enough to carry.

"Welcome to the... Super Maxi-Pad, fellas! Sorry, we don't... have Freezies... that's the 24/7... they *rock!* All we've got is... mortally wounded... white guys... the other... other... *other* white meat!"

Then, there was an agonized, heartrending cry.

Then, nothing.

Inside the battered shack, the three survivors stood in the sheltering darkness, heads hung, listening, numb, as the storm raged outside, and their friend died. They were hopeless, helpless and utterly broken.

There was no way to know how long the banging, crashing fury outside lasted. No one moved, no one checked a watch, no one cared. Eventually, it slackened, settling into an eery scraping and scrabbling, punctuated every so often by a fierce blow against the boards.

After a time, Sister Becky raised her head and edged to the door of the cramped hut. She drew a careworn wooden rosary from her pocket and began to murmur softly, making the sign of the cross slowly and sadly in the direction where Carson had fallen.

"Stop that."

Kiki's voice came from the shadows, flat and dangerous. She had stopped crying some time ago, only her boots visible where she crouched in the far corner of the shack. Something sounded wrong. Very wrong.

Becky turned, tried to pick out her features in the dark. When the nun spoke, her voice was gentle. "My poor, poor, dear child..."

"I said *STOP!*" Something went *bang!* and Kiki lunged forward from the shadows, face contorted, fists balled. There was no trace of sorrow, no trace of fear.

No trace of Kiki.

Her gun lifted slowly, rested on her shoulder. When she spoke, her voice was cold and lethal. "You act like he's dead."

A moment passed.

Sister Becky watched her, face twisted with anguish and pity. But the nun said nothing more.

Without a word, Kiki turned and faded into the darkness of the shack.

CHAPTER FOURTEEN
The Warlord of Death

Blip.
Blip.
Blip.

The terrifying noises outside the shack had long since died away, leaving its exhausted occupants to their own dark thoughts. The only sound now came from the far corner, where a faint blue glow illuminated the stark features of Kiki's face as she crouched, animal-like, eyes glued unblinking to the screen of her battered GPS. She had not moved for over half an hour.

No one had.

Blip.
Blip.
Blip.
Bling!

The tone changed. Subtle, but distinct. Unmistakable.

"He's moving," Kiki was on her feet and headed for the door in one fluid motion, slinging her pack, eyes still locked on the screen.

"Hey, uh... wait up, girl..." Dex rose stiffly, eyes switching uneasily from Kiki to the door. "We don't know what's out there..."

Kiki drew up her leg and kicked hard, bursting the latch and flinging the door wide. Sister Becky surged to her feet, fumbling for her crosses.

Outside, the tunnel was empty, dark and still.

Kiki lowered her gun. "Now we do." She flashed a look at Dex, her face half-obscured in the dark, and it almost made him take a step back. Turning, she was out the door and into the tunnel, flicking on her flashlight, heading straight for the mangled wreckage of the scaffold.

The zombies had cleared a path, exposing a long, pitch-black tunnel that burrowed straight through the earth and off into the inky unknown. Kiki halted beside the patch of dirt where Carson's body had been, the pool of blood still sticky and the earth trampled. She let her peripheral vision skip across it, not looking directly, just to confirm that Carson was gone. Then, she was headed for the tunnel.

Dex slipped out of the shack, checking shadows warily, unconvinced of their safety. He exchanged a worried glance with Sister Becky. "Uh... maybe you better... um..."

Sister Becky nodded. "Ms. Masterson..." she lifted her voice, advancing quickly. "I admire your courage, my dear, but I believe it would be more prudent to take up the pursuit by motorcar. I am certain you would agree that it would be more..." she stared down the tunnel with a healthy amount of apprehension. "...practical."

Kiki froze at the threshold of the long black empty. She scowled, squinted, pondered. Her head bobbed once, curtly. She didn't look at them. "Fine. Just shake a leg. He's moving fast."

Kiki retraced her steps, stopping only to catch up Carson's bat from where it lay in the dirt. She looked up to find the others starting at her. She stared back. "He's gonna need this." Without another word, she turned and climbed quickly up the broken scaffold. Dex and Becky exchanged another worried look.

Once up the hole, the three hastened through the store and out into the street, making rapidly for Dex's car. There was no one in sight, living or dead. The engine revved, and tires chirped as Dex threw the little auto in gear and sped away.

Kiki sat up front, eyes glued to the GPS, clipping off orders as they went. "Faster. Turn right... no, not here! *Next* right. Stop. Slow down... now left..."

A few times, they were forced to stop and wait as the green blip paused or moved under a building. Each time Kiki squirmed, fidgeting with the red bandana she had tied about her arm and muttering quietly to herself. After fifteen long, agonizing minutes, the white compact nosed out into the grand sweep of Webber Plaza.

"There," Kiki stabbed a finger at a towering highrise across the way, glittering and indomitable. "That's the place."

Dex didn't need the the mammoth gleaming sign to know where they were headed. He guided the car across the plaza and eased up before the entrance to Fujikacorp's corporate headquarters, senses on full alert. He craned his neck out the side window, scanning for threats. "It's dark. That's a good sign. Looks like some lights on up toward the top, but that's about it. So... how we gonna play this?"

Kiki opened her door. "We go in." It slammed behind her with finality. She was moving, gun ready, eyes on the GPS, heading for the front entrance. Behind her on the seat, forgotten, lay her backpack. Dex glanced at it. It was a bad sign.

He swore, popped his seat belt and lurched out of the car, almost closing the door on Sister Becky as she struggled to extricate herself from the back seat. Dex yanked his heavy gear bag from the trunk and hustled after Kiki. They had to run to catch her.

They did just as she grabbed the front door.

"Wait!" Puffing, Dex reached out a hand.

Kiki yanked. The door swung outward slightly. There was no lock, no alarm, no sound at all.

Dex let his air out, relieved. "Alright... just march on in the front door... I got it, direct approach... fine... but look, let's just... take this down a notch, okay? Let me get... my wind..." He squared his shoulders, took a few deep breaths. "Now, here's how this... goes down. When I'm... set, I'll say 'ready', and you..."

"Whatever."

"No, no... you're supposed to say..."

Kiki yanked the door open and ducked inside.

"Or we could just barge right in." Dex swore again, shook his head and plunged after her, Sister Becky crowding his heels. "This is *not* gonna go well," he muttered viciously. "I got the feelin' I'll be needin' Jerry before this thing is over."

Sister Becky jerked an eyebrow as she scanned the shadows. "*Jerry*, Mr. Jackson?"

"If it comes to that, I'll introduce you." He shook his gear bag suggestively. "Just pray it don't come to that."

They hustled after Kiki, already a vague silhouette halfway across the lobby. For a moment, they followed the faint red smear of her cap, eyes squinting in the dark, hurrying... then Dex stopped dead in his tracks. His eyes had caught a faint glow from the opposite side of the vast lobby - the light from the antique armor display. And in it, a shape. His gaze narrowed. It was a tall, lean shape. A shape in a dark suit.

"It's him!" Dex's lips peeled back in a snarl, teeth showing in the dark.

"Who, Mr. Jackson?!"

"Fujika... the Shogun! Damn! *Finally* a break!" He shifted directions, gun coming up. The figure's back was to them, hands moving stealthily inside the open display case, apparently oblivious.

"Caution, Mr. Jackson!" Becky hissed. "We tread the unknown... and where is Ms. Masterson?!" She cast vainly about the shadows. Kiki had disappeared.

"Hell if I know. But she's gonna have to find her own bad guy to thump on. This one's mine!"

Dex set off with single-minded purpose, his jaw clenched in fury. He made a beeline for Fujika, making no effort to mask his approach, boots thudding on marble. Bathed in the low, eery glow from the case, the Shogun withdrew something long and narrow from inside; then he cocked his head, half turned at the sudden shaking of the floor. With a fluid motion, he turned and rose, showing stark, cold features and the sharp slash of goatee that made him look like all he was missing was a pitchfork and horns. Fujika drew himself up, his black eyes locked disdainfully on the approaching guard. He made no attempt to flee.

A low growl began to build in Dex's throat, teeth grinding, fists clenched. Seconds before the black freight train arrived, a second shadow detached from the inkiness just outside the pool of light, gliding on silent feet. Dex saw it, planted and pivoted and came face to face with the beefy Asian - the one from the gas pumps. The Sumo. The man was swinging already, a lightning, lethal knifehand aimed straight at Dex's throat and a crushed windpipe.

Dex's shotgun was there to meet it. A short chop with the barrel broke several fingers. Dex jammed the butt into the man's face, smashing his nose and cracking a cheekbone. He felt the shotgun slapped from his hands, with a kick or fist he couldn't tell and didn't care, and ignored the pair of quick followups that drove into his face, hardly feeling them. Rage surged through him. This time, he wasn't a security guard. This time, the gloves were off.

Dex stepped in and drove a fist into the heavy muscles of the Sumo's belly, then again, felt them give under his bowling ball blows and followed up with a hammer to the injured face. Something came loose under his knuckles. The Asian fired a quick, off center front kick that thumped into Dex's own gut and squeaked him back several inches on the marble, breaking the exchange and drawing a fierce grunt.

Dex came up squared, fists clenched. Blood streamed from the Sumo's face, but he was set in stance and ready to fight. They poised for a heartbeat, measuring each other, two juggernauts on the edge, ready to unleash.

Then Kiki was there.

Her gun barked, once.

The bullet caught the big Asian in the right thigh, kicked his leg out from under him and dumped him face first on the marble. Blood spattered.

Kiki stepped to Fujika, lifted the gun to his face, finger tightening on the trigger. He stared back at her, unblinking, face etched with nothing but a cold, hard disdain. She squeezed...

"Hold, Ms. Masterson!" Sister Becky swept between them, filling the narrow space, blocking the path from bullet to brain. "If you value Carson's memory, stay your hand! There is more here than meets the eye..." she turned that eye to regard Fujika. It was the cold, practical eye of a hanging judge, hungry for justice but tempered by wisdom. She studied the man closely, carefully. For a moment, no one breathed.

Then, almost reluctantly, Becky drew back, hands folding. "You may lower your weapon, Ms. Masterson," she made a soft noise, almost a sigh. "This man is *not* the Remortifier."

"Make me care," Dex rumbled. He casually covered the sweating, moaning Sumo at his feet, shotgun once more in hand. The look behind it indicated that would be difficult to accomplish.

"There are no insects." Sister Becky gestured to indicate the surrounding area, where it was conspicuously clear that nothing crawled or flew or wriggled. "Neither is there a chill. And no stench of death. None of the signs that Mr. Dudley identified. This man may be the Shogun... be he is *not* the Master."

"Maybe not," the tone of Dex's voice was like the cocking of a gun. "But that doesn't mean he don't need killin'. And he sure as hell don't need this..." Dex stepped over the bleeding thug and grabbed an ancient, antique katana, still in its sheath, from Fujika's hand.

Fujika's haughty features, unchanged til now, cracked into wrath.

He swore hotly in Japanese. "My ancestral blade!"

Dex stopped. He leaned down to stare Fujika in the eye. Kiki's gun barrel still pointed at his face, peeping around Dex's shoulder like a menacing black finger. "You want it?" his voice was thick with menace. "Come get it." The Shogun's eyes narrowed to hateful slits, but he said nothing. "You got a helluva stack of payback comin', and this pig sticker is just for starters." Dex rattled the sword under his nose. "You kill..." he shot a quick look at Kiki. "...hurt my friend. You better thank those ancestors that you ain't joined 'em... yet."

Fujika hesitated. Then, slowly, the boiling hate simmered, faded until it was barely visible in the black recesses of his eyes. He made no movement, but the tension seemed to melt from his sharp features. Dex leaned back. Reluctantly, Kiki's gun barrel wavered, dipped.

"Keep it," Fujika murmured. "Perhaps it will help fill the void left by the loss of your friend." He swept the little group with a disinterested look, his gaze coming to rest, finally, on Kiki. "I warned Carson Dudley. I do not threaten idly."

Kiki didn't say a word. She just looked at him. The gun came up.

"Ms. Masterson..." Sister Becky's voice was a caution, not to be trifled with. "We need him alive."

A muscle twitched in Kiki's cheek. A massive internal struggle waged beneath the stark, deathly white of her face. For a moment, the outcome was uncertain.

Kiki lowered the gun. "Alright. We need him alive. Do we need him healthy? How about I loosen some teeth," she tapped Fujika under the chin with Carson's bat, sharply, so that his teeth clicked. "Then, maybe we could get some answers... 'start the satisfactory flow,' eh?"

Fujika shoved the bat away with a quick movement. For a moment, he looked as if he would strike her, and Kiki looked as if she was begging him to try. Again, with an effort, Fujika calmed himself.

"There is no need," he looked down at Kiki along the knife edge of his nose, without tilting his head. "I will tell you everything you wish to know. The time of keeping secrets is past. All, you see, is lost." He paused. The faintest furrow appeared between his brows. "The Warlord of Death has returned."

"Warlord of Death?!" Dex snorted. "You tryin' to tell us there's some *other* mother back of this besides *you*? If you expect me to swallow that sushi, fool, you better bust out some pretty sweet wasabe!"

"You need not take my word. The proof is at hand." Fujika made a barely noticeable gesture, indicating the open display case.

Dex noticed, for the first time, that it was empty. "Hey... where's the stuff?" The bare bones of an armor stand and a few polished pegs stared back at him.

"I have told you. The Warlord of Death once more walks among the living. He has risen, claiming the trappings of war. And his host marches with him."

"You're startin' to piss me off, Jack," Dex's eyes were flat and dangerous. "Talking all *Twilight Zone* like that. Maybe, I should let this little girl open up that can on you after all. See if we can get some straight answers once your smile goes crooked."

Fujika's face was implacable. He was an iron statue in a dark suit. "Do as you will. But know this - you have a greater enemy now than me. Darker and more deadly than you could possibly comprehend. Words cannot encompass the horror that now walks this earth."

"But they may keep you from gettin' busted in the mouth."

Fujika's shoulders twitched in the faintest of shrugs. "As I said, there is no reason for secrets. It is already too late to stop him, so you may as well know the nature of your foe." He inclined his head the barest fraction toward the brass plate beside the empty case. "In life, he was known as Hironagi Tomoru, leader of the Tomoru Clan and a powerful warlord in the service of the Ashakagi Shogunate. A cunning strategist, a fierce warrior and a ruthless opponent, it was by his hand that the Shogun Ashakagi Yoshiteru came to power. The plaque will tell you that much."

"What it will *not* tell you is that Hironagi Tomoru was more than a petty warlord. He was also a necromancer - a devotee of the dark arts, steeped in ancient lore, mysticism and black magic. He pursued it with single-minded passion. Death was his fascination. His religion."

"A blasphemous and horrifying religion," Sister Becky interjected darkly. "Stained with the blood of innocents is my guess. And one, no doubt, that led its follower on a quest for forbidden knowledge... to the *Ashi Keiyaki*."

Fujika flashed her a nasty look, displeased both with her interruption and her insight. He inclined his head a fraction, grudgingly, as if she had just scored a point in a lively game of table tennis. His expression said he did not intend it to happen again. "As you have surmised. Hironagi was not content merely to serve in the shadow of his Shogun. His thirsts were greater. Much greater. To this end, he plotted to undertake a powerful and forbidden ceremony known as the *Kuro Shikiten...*"

Sister Becky drew a sharp breath. "The Black Rite...!" her eyes narrowed to green slits.

"...through which he intended to contact the Ashakagi clan's patron demon, Ashihitokage. Hironagi planned to strike a bargain - one that would grant him endless life. Despite his formidable prowess, however, many of the materials required for the rite were outside his grasp. Great relics of old, the bones of those long dead, a black lotus said to have sprung from a drop of demon's blood... the list was long and daunting."

"To acquire these items, Hironagi was forced to turn to the Shogun Ashakagi himself. Ashakagi agreed to help, but, in return, required a costly pledge: eternal service. Hironagi agreed readily, taking an oath to forever answer when his Shogun called. This, in the end, proved his undoing." A hard thin smile sliced Fujika's face. "For the very instant the *Ashi Keiyaki* was concluded, the Shogun's samurai, lying in wait, cut Hironagi down. He was murdered in cold blood."

"For the Shogun, it seemed, had found a way to transform his already formidable asset into something truly fearsome. Bound by the dark powers of the *Ashi Keiyaki* and his oath of eternal service, Hironagi Tomoru passed, and in his place rose the Warlord of Death - a fearsome specter imbued with supernatural power and unlife by the demon Ashihitokage. Whenever his Shogun called, the Warlord would return from the grave to do his master's bidding, sewing death, destruction and horrors beyond description. Driven by hate and the bitterness of his betrayal, his reign of terror was monstrous."

"Now just hold up..." Dex frowned. "You're tellin' us that this dude came back from the dead?! Started tearin' up Japan like... like... Bruce Lee meets *Night of the Living Dead*?!"

"You asked for information. I am providing it. I expect you neither to accept nor comprehend it. For your limited Western minds, it must be difficult to grasp."

"Yeah, but you're not." Dex's fingers flexed, itching to do harm. "So finish your little ghost story... before I decide to finish *you*."

Fujika regarded him coldly, but continued. "The Warlord of Death served his Shogun for years, slaying all before him in complete obedience, while in secret searching for some way to undo the agreement. That quest went unfulfilled. Eventually, Shogun Ashakagi was slain - assassinated - and the Warlord, with no one left to call on him, slipped into oblivion. The secret of his summoning, known only to the Shogun, was lost. And thus, so was the Warlord."

"But now," Sister Becky intruded again, "he has reawakened. And by some twist of fate, it is *you,* Fujika-san, who finds himself sitting atop this particular elephant." She brushed past Dex and squinted at Fujika's tie tack. "An interesting *mon,*" she noted, indicating the queer, three pointed design. "A scorpion, unless I am mistaken? The same symbol which also appears on your corporate crest... and also, I suspect, on the flag of the Ashakagi Clan."

Fujika inclined his head slightly. "My family was a loyal faction of the Ashakagi Shogunate."

"And eventually, I surmise, usurped enough power to elevate your status over the Ashakagi. As CEO of Fujikacorp, this makes you, in effect, the new Shogun. Your appellation is more than mere whimsy. The Warlord serves *you* now."

Fujika responded with a cold smile. "He is bound by his oath and by the contract."

"The *Ashi Keiyaki...*" Sister Becky murmured. The glow from the display case seemed to flicker at her words. "You have it?"

Fujika's only answer was a flat, blank stare from the shadows.

Sister Becky's hand was out. "If you please, Fujika-san."

Fujika hesitated, dark eyes searching hers.

Dex fondled his shotgun. "Oh, please, make her ask again..."

After a moment, Fujika gave another of his twitching shrugs. He reached inside his jacket and drew out a folded yellow parchment that crackled with age. He held it carefully, almost reverently, before her. "Very well. It is of no use to you now." He hesitated a moment, then handed it over.

"Perhaps." Sister Becky tucked the parchment away inside her robes. "But there may yet be something here that will help us. And now, I have questions. Time is short, and we must know the full of the tale. How did you awaken the abomination? Even with the *Ashi Keiyaki* in your possession, it must have required no small effort."

At this, Fujika looked vaguely troubled, as if the question was a single missing puzzle piece in an otherwise complete set. "I... do not know." He made the admission grudgingly. "Hironagi's remains have been in my possession for years, as has the contract. I had tried unsuccessfully to wake him on many occasions. Why he did so here, now... I only know that it happened shortly after we arrived in Las Calamas."

"Let us away with the particulars, then. He is awake now. That is the plain truth of it and nothing to be done. So then... once awakened, you began to use him."

"He is a highly effective tool. An apt pupil of modern affairs and quite eager to serve. I found the legends of his powers to be true, every one: Shadow Walk, Black Breath, Touch of the Grave..."

"Touch of the Grave?" Dex smirked. "You're just makin' that up to sound scary, right? Sounds like a damn Pokemon card."

"You mock what you do not comprehend. With a mere touch, he draws the very life from his victims."

"Yes, yes, quite impressive, blue ribbons straight across," Sister Becky steered him back. "And he has other resources as well, I warrant. Such as his servants."

"Yes. The Shadow Sect. *Ninja* assassins. And his Shadow Samurai as well, all gifted with undeath by the Warlord's own Black Breath. Powerful and devoted servants in life they were, and even more so in death. As I have said... the Warlord proved himself a great asset."

Becky's eyes narrowed shrewdly. "For what, precisely?"

"To gather information, at first. Then, eventually, he became useful in removing certain obstacles, dealing with delicate situations when other, more conventional, methods proved too cumbersome or time consuming."

"Yeah," Dex rumbled. "Obstacles like Haruki Nubuyuki."

"Leveraging a tool like the Warlord of Death leaves an unfortunate trail. Nubuyuki stumbled across it. Things became complicated."

"Then, me and Dud dropped by that night, and things got *real* complicated. We tossed your little pajama boy out the window, and you got all funked about it. Started keepin' tabs on us, didn't you?"

"I know my enemies."

"Yeah, I bet you knew us real good. Especially Dud. Didn't take you long to figure he was onto you." Dex drifted closer, filling Fujika's limited personal space. His voice was dangerously soft. "Couldn't put one over on ol' Dud, couldya? He knew you were dirty. So, you decided to turn up the heat. Decided to make it personal."

Fujika fell silent behind the thin tight line of his lips. In his eyes, however, something stirred. Sister Becky caught it.

"No," she cocked her head, eyed him quizzically. "Not you. The Warlord of Death. Pressing Mr. Dudley was not your idea... it was *his*."

Shadows seemed to draw about Fujika's face, but he kept his voice even. "You show remarkable insight. For an old woman."

"Then, let this old woman share a wee bit more. As soon as Mr. Dudley entered the picture, the Warlord began to change. Yes?"

"Yes. He took a personal interest in the matter, became obsessed.

 272

Apparently, he perceived the 24/7 as a direct threat to my Shogunate - insisted we take steps. He became more difficult to control. Brash, aggressive. Misinterpreting orders. Making messes." They could hear the distaste in Fujika's voice.

"The attack on the Romero 24/7?"

The ghost of a nod. "Among other things."

"The properties Mr. Dudley investigated," Sister Becky guessed. "The collecting of artifacts..."

"The Warlord had always taken an interest in such trinkets. His appetites grew more insistent, but I thought nothing of it. I had other concerns at the time. Even when he demanded a place to work, alone, in total privacy, I still suspected nothing."

"You refer to the Super Maxi-Pad. And the tunnel beneath the city, the one that led us here... it was constructed at the Warlord's behest?"

"He was most insistent about it. A way to come and go as he pleased without fear of detection. Or so he claimed."

"These labors he was undertaking - what was their nature?"

"He told me he was preparing a plague - an illness of some kind to unleash against our enemies. In truth, I cared not. The Warlord had become erratic and unpredictable, and I welcomed anything that kept him at a distance, anything that made it more difficult to connect him to Fujikacorp. So, I granted his request."

"And you never dropped by to check?!" Dex bristled.

"It was a plague. Why would I?"

"Boy, you're somethin'," Dex's forearms corded dangerously. "So, you just went right along with the whole Secret Tunnel to Hell plan, and found the strongbacks to do it. Chumps that wouldn't ask questions. Slave labor. Not that a heartless *&^%! like you would give a rip, but have you seen how well that worked out for 'em? They're dead!"

Fujika's shrug was implied. "They were peasants."

"They were people!"

"Of which this world has an abundance."

"You keep talkin' and it's gonna have one less."

"I do not apologize for my actions. In war, one takes risks where one must," he glared at Dex. "And removes them where one may."

"Oh, you piece of crap," Dex made fists. "This is the part where you put a hit on us."

"On the Warlord's counsel, yes... although to be candid, I had already arrived at that conclusion on my own." Fujika paused, flashed another ghost smile. "Merely a business decision. Nothing personal."

"Except you were being duped," Sister Becky took up the interrogation again. "The Warlord was merely using Mr. Dudley as a convenient distraction, a ruse. It was the Shogun who was being controlled by his Warlord, not the contrary." Sister Becky stroked her narrow chin. "Although the why of it eludes me..."

"As it did me, for a time. It might interest you to know that it was Mr. Dudley's own research, in the end, that led me to the truth. While the three of you were busy disbelieving him, I was not. He was right all along, you know. You just didn't listen." A sudden cruel smile flitted across Fujika's face, and it twisted like a knife. "It was all a cover, a deception - the Warlord's erratic behavior, his obsession with the 24/7, the plague, all of it. And it had but one purpose: to collect ingredients."

"I know I'm gonna hate the answer," Dex glowered. "But ingredients for what?"

"The *Kuro Shikiten.*"

"You going backwards now, brainless. That Heronoogi already..."

"Yes. But the Warlord seeks to work the Black Rite *again*. A *second* time. And he plans to do so soon. This morning, I uncovered a chamber in the executive suites on the top floor. A place he kept secret even from me. It is there, I am certain, that he intends to hold the ceremony."

"I don't get it... the first time he got screwed. Why would the fool try it again?"

"To renegotiate the contract. It is simple business." Fujika made a dismissive flick of the wrist. "The first time Hironagi was a mere mortal. Now, his powers are vast and dark, and he bargains from a position of increased advantage. The demon will demand an even greater price than before, death and destruction on a truly massive scale. And once again, Hironagi will be only too happy to pay it. Even now, he gathers his army." Fujika glanced at the floor. At the tunnel.

"Mr. Dudley was correct!" Sister Becky's face tightened. "The Super Maxi-Pad was a breeding ground. A staging point for attack!"

"One among many, I am afraid. I have, in the last few hours, discovered another four throughout the city."

"Shogun my *&^%!" Dex ground out the words. "You got played like an eighth grade crush!"

"Lord Hironagi was a genius. A brilliant strategist, manipulator and tactician. Death has made him only more cunning. He may have been new to our society, technology and culture, but he learns quickly."

Kiki spoke for the first time in a long while, her voice a quiet growl from the shadows. "You sound proud of it, you SOB."

"There is no shame in strength."

"Yeah," Dex cocked a fist, "but there's plenty of shame in being a *&^%$ bonehead! This thing came back from the dead... made a deal with a demon... and you trusted it?!"

"Your scorn is of little concern to me. What is of concern is the Warlord. His forces are marshaled His will has gathered. The *Kuro Shikiten* will begin soon. Tonight. Then, he shall seal a new bargain and cast me aside and have no master, save his own black heart. He will take the city first. And from there..." Fujika trailed off. His head made a microscopic shake. "But enough. I have told my tale, in full, as you requested. My only intent now is to flee. So either kill me... or release me."

"I am unsatisfied with either option," Sister Becky clipped. "And thus, I propose a third." She tucked her hands firmly into her sleeves. "You will take us to him."

For the first time that night, Fujika registered surprise. Genuine, complete, unabashed surprise. The expression seemed awkward on his stony features. "Take you to... the Warlord?!"

"Indeed. He is a blasphemer of the worst kind, a biscuit plucked from the Devil's own pantry, and he cannot be allowed to perpetrate his evil any longer. He must be stopped. This chamber you spoke of - this secret sanctum on the uppermost floor - you know where it is, and you shall lead us to it."

"What do you intend to do?"

"What do we intend to *do*? What do we intend *to do?!*" Sister Becky's voice suddenly resonated with cold, merciless fury. "We intend to *destroy* him! We intend to visit upon him such ruin that 'we may plunge our feet in the blood of our foe, while the tongues of our dogs have their share!'" The old nun seemed to grow a foot taller. "We shall confront this Warlord of Death and *slay* him! Reverse his evil machinations! And by his destruction shall we undo the dark magics he has wrought!" Her savage glare dared Fujika to deny her.

"Slay him?" Fujika's eyes narrowed ever so slightly. Ever so shrewdly. "Perhaps..." his murmur was so soft they half thought they imagined it. He fell silent and, for a moment, said nothing more. He seemed to be considering. Weighing.

Then, quite abruptly, his sharp chin lifted a fraction. "Very well. As I presume that I have no alternative, I shall accept. Let us be off."

He made a small gesture toward the brass elevator doors behind him, and with that the discussion was over.

As Dex fetched his gear bag and Sister Becky knelt briefly to attend to the injured thug, Kiki took the moment to approach Fujika. She stepped close, locked eyes with him and poked her automatic into his ribs. "You and me..." her voice was a snake, a cold whisper in the dark. "We're not finished." She left him with the lingering memory of it and a cold blue stare.

Minutes later, all four were rushing noiselessly toward the top floor, the numbers on the mahogany elevator panel flashing past.

Fujika stood in their midst, implacable, arms clasped behind his back as if he were merely on his way to another board meeting. "I must warn you - the Warlord's servants are everywhere. They know me, however, and that I am not to be harmed. Remain close or die."

"I'm givin' you the same advice." Dex prodded him in the back with his shotgun. "I don't trust you. Not one *&^%$ bit. I keep hearin' 'Shogun' this and 'Shogun' that, and if you aggravate me, fool, I just might have to *show* you *my* gun. So jus' remember where it's pointin'."

Fujika said nothing. They rode in silence, floors speeding by.

Dex glanced down at Sister Becky. "'While the tongues of our dogs have their share'?" he muttered. "That's a little harsh, ain't it? Even for Attila the Nun."

"I was merely paraphrasing Psalm 68:23. I was feeling enthusiastic."

"Finally... some Bible learnin' I can get behind." Dex shifted, readjusted his weighty gear bag. One end swung into Sister Becky, jabbing her in the ribs.

"Honestly, Mr. Jackson," she glowered. "Must you cart such a load? I have known oxen to carry less."

"You won't be fussin' if we need Jerry," Dex patted the satchel. It clanked ominously. Sister Becky rolled her eyes and edged away. Her gaze settled on Kiki, wedged into the corner, eyes glued once more to her GPS.

Blip.

Blip.

"Anything, dear?"

"He's up here." Kiki looked up briefly, noting their progress. "Close." She checked her clip, thumbed off the safety of her pistol. "Lock and load."

The lift eased smoothly to a halt, tickling their stomachs with more than just a sense of gravity. Fujika's hands came to his sides. Even though he was their prisoner, he was suddenly in command.

"Stay close. Follow my lead."

Silently, the doors slid open. Immediately outside were a pair of leering, rotten faces, looming from the shadows of a darkened hallway. The zombies turned toward them with rising moans of hunger, fingers reaching... then slowed and relaxed. They slouched back, their growls fading into reluctant animal disinterest.

Dex slowly lowered his gun. "Ain't that somethin'... finally found someone doesn't wanna kill you." The pair of walking corpses shambled off, mingling with a dozen or so others up and down the hall. After a quick glance, Dex unslung the King from his back and passed it to Kiki. She took it, wordlessly. Fujika stepped into the hallway and moved away briskly, Kiki right on his heels, wary and alert.

Sister Becky lingered by Dex as he gathered his bag, watching Kiki's dead man's grip on the gun. "Are you certain that was wise, Mr. Jackson?"

"None of this is wise, Grandma. Not one damn thing. And while we're on the subject..." he checked that Kiki was out of earshot, then flashed Sister Becky a quick glimpse of his palm. In it was the electronic detonator Dex had brandished at the Super Maxi-Pad. "Anything happens to me, I want you to use this."

She blinked. "Use it? On what, pray tell? I hardly think a door will be of any concern to us now..."

"This ain't for no door."

Becky's eyes narrowed. "Mr. Jackson... where have you placed the charge?"

"Back of Dud's head. Stuck it there when he was dyin'."

Sister Becky sucked air through her teeth.

"I made a promise," Dex said stubbornly. "I'm gonna keep it." He moved off. Without a word, Sister Becky followed. There was nothing to say.

The Shogun weaved his way with certainty and speed through a maze of hallways, offices and lounges, past meticulously pruned bonsais, towering vases and elaborate water features, all of which looked garishly out of place against the backdrop of the milling dead, like a mass grave in a Zen garden. Several times, they had to wait for a cluster of zombies to pass, but, otherwise, they made their way quickly and unmolested. Fujika never hesitated, never slackened his pace, moving like a prowling tiger through the shadows and pressing the others to keep up.

Finally, he drew up before an imposing, highly polished door. There was a chill in the air, and the very sudden sense that they had arrived. "This is it," Fujika's face showed no flicker of fear, no ripple of uncertainty, just stone cold aloofness. "The sanctum of the Warlord of Death. I have never seen inside. Ready yourselves." Without letting them so much as draw breath, he reached for the handle.

"Hold up, fool!" Dex stopped him with one meaty hand, panting, sweat streaking his face. Things were moving far too fast, and so was Fujika. "Just... hold up! You tried to... kill us... once already!"

"I concur," Sister Becky checked their flanks warily. "This is most reckless. After all that has transpired, you expect us to trust you?"

"No. But I am certain you can find new guides who will take you to the Warlord, if you wish..." An eerie moan floated down the hall as a pair of staggering zombies passed. Close.

Sister Becky pressed her lips together tightly. Fujika was somehow, once again and quite unexpectedly, in total control. She traded looks with Dex. He knew it too. She gave a curt nod.

Fujika turned the handle.

Immediately, an almost palpable sense of death and darkness washed over them, along with a red glow cast by flickering braziers and hooded lanterns and the nearly overwhelming odor of rotting flesh. For a moment, it was hard to breath, and they stood reeling as their senses struggled to absorb the harsh reality of the scene.

Everything was dark iron, shadows and pitted wood, hard edges and grim intent. Tapestries smothered the walls, scenes of war and death and bloody torment, as well as banners displaying the *mon* of what was undoubtedly the Warlord's Tomoru Clan. Fujika's own *mon* was nowhere in sight. It was an ominous sign. In the center of the room stood a low wooden platform, painted with strange symbols. Torch stands marked each corner, burning with a low, smokeless light that illuminated three small altars, their tops littered with bizarre and disturbing artifacts.

Even more grim were the room's occupants. A score or more of the walking dead hunched in staggered ranks facing the dais, as if assembled for inspection. In front of them was a military line of fully armed and armored samurai, a half dozen or more, standing at full attention. Red light licked the surface of their battle-scarred black *o-yoroi* and gleamed ominously from pitted *naginata* spears. Fierce hawkish features were made even more foreboding in death, stamped into a mummified cast of dessicated yellow-green flesh. Milky yellow eyes roved restlessly, more alive than the blank pools of the lesser zombies, but also, somehow, more dead.

Before them all, at the front of the dais, stood the Warlord of Death.

The intruders started as their eyes met the lean, fearsome figure towering above the others. An intense chill pressed their flesh, a burden of the soul that sucked at their breath and numbed their fingers. The zombie Warlord was a fierce and commanding presence, haughty and ominous in decaying *o-yoroi* armor, a broad pitted *kabuto* helmet casting shadows over a rusted iron *menpo* mask. Twisted in a hideous, savage snarl, a warrior's scream of death and fury, the mask mercifully hid the features beneath - all except a pair of sinister night black eyes. Flies flickered and buzzed about the thing, and insects of every variety could be seen crawling, wriggling and skittering across the dais at its feet. All light seemed drawn inward toward the figure, so that further details were made vague and uncertain, shrouded in a clinging veil of darkness.

If its details were obscured, however, its actions were not. As the four stood rooted in the shadows of the doorway, the Warlord of Death reached out with gory fingers and clasped the head of a man they had missed before - an executive in a rumpled black suit. The man shuddered and tried to pull back, but was held tightly in place by a pair of samurai.

An awful, hissing rush of sound began to build in the room. The victim whimpered and struggled as a long black tendril leaked from the mouth of the Warlord's *menpo* mask, writhing, intangible, like living darkness. It reached out, caressing the executive's terror stricken features. The hissing sound rose to a peak, and, as the watchers stared, transfixed, unable to move or speak, the shadow tendril leaked into the captive's mouth and eyes. The man gasped, screamed, his body shaking and spasming. Then, abruptly, he stopped. His head fell forward, shoulders slumped. The samurai released him and stood back. Slowly, ponderously, the Warlord's victim began to sway, gently, side to side. A moan slipped from green cracked lips. When the man lifted his gaze again, it was no longer that of a man - it was with dead, white eyes.

"Behold," Fujika's tone vibrated, his face cast with the brimstone hue of the lanterns. His expression was very close to pride. "The Black Breath!"

With effort, Dex shrugged off the spell of horror that had settled on them as the soldier in him once more took charge. "Look sharp - we got ninjas, three o'clock." Motionless in the shadows at the far end of the dais lurked the lean, black forms of the Warlord's assassins. "Damn. We need a plan, and we need it quick. So, listen up: I'll take the... hey! Hey!!"

Fujika had stepped forward into the room. The great armored head of the Warlord lifted, black eyes regarding the Shogun coldly from the shadows of the mask. They stared. Then, after a moment, the Warlord inclined his head a fraction and moved to bow... until he caught sight of the others standing in Fujika's shadow. The creature snapped erect.

A grisly hand reached for a katana.

"Now is your chance, fools!" Fujika murmured. "Unless your fear is too great..."

"Fear? Oh yeah," Dex gave a mock shiver. "I'm all shook up." He shouldered past Fujika, lifted his shotgun and fired.

The gun roared, exploding fire and lead straight into the face of the Warlord a dozen steps away. The blast tore the mask loose and kicked the helm sideways, throwing the gaunt figure back. The thing stumbled, crashed into an altar and collapsed in a shower of candles and grisly artifacts.

Dex turned back to face the others. "Head shots," he racked the pump. "Gets 'em every time."

Sister Becky opened her mouth to speak, but the words froze on her lips along with a look of triumph. Behind Dex, the towering, armored figure was rising. Slowly, hauntingly, the Warlord of Death clambered back to his feet. A savage growl built in his throat as he turned the horror of his face, now fully visible, upon them, the dark pits of his eyes tearing at their sanity. The hunched form shuddered and shook with rage, and all light dimmed as shadows gathered and pulled about it.

"Ah," Fujika seemed unperturbed, almost bored. "Perhaps, I neglected to mention one of the Warlord's greatest assets..." the thin gash of a gloating smile split his face. "He cannot be killed."

Dex swore and fired again. Lead pinged off the helmet and tore at the hideous face, but, this time, the Warlord barely flinched.

Sweeping his great katana from its sheath, he gave a rasping cry that shook the torches with a voice like gravel over plate glass.

"Kougeki shiro!"

And the dead were upon them.

The rush hit with a brutal, deafening whirl of chaos, sweeping the

 280

three intruders back into the hallway. Dex roared, pumping round after round into the mass of green, knocking bodies and limbs flying, while Sister Becky laid about with her crosses, dropping faith like a hammer. Knowing escape was their only option, they fought furiously for an opening, a chance to break free of the fearsome press. For a frightening moment, they lost sight of Kiki, who alone seemed intent on staying to finish the battle. With a lunge, Dex snagged her tank top and yanked her clear, pulling her out of clutching, grasping hands.

They ran.

Bodies swarmed and jostled, fingers clawed and grappled, and the deadly blades of the samurai sang and slashed, mostly cutting air but finding flesh more than once. Bodies dropped, muzzle flashes lit the night, and the tangled press of the dead was everywhere. The three companions stumbled, smashed into walls, knocked over priceless vases and laid waste with wild abandon.

Suddenly, somehow, they were free - free and running like mad, pounding down a corridor, the howling, moaning, snarling mob scattered but regrouping, already in pursuit. Dex took the lead, Fujika's katana in one hand smeared with sticky green and sticky red, shotgun in the other. Sister Becky ran close behind, but slowed after only a few yards, glancing back breathlessly. Kiki had stopped dead, coldly thumbing shells into the King.

"Mr. Jackson!"

Dex thudded to a halt and whirled. "Kiki! Woman!!" She ignored him. "Get a move on, sister!! *The dead are comin'*!!"

Kiki slipped a last shell into the King, lifted, pumped and fired straight into the face of a rushing zombie. She pumped, fired again, mechanically, methodically, without emotion, and dropped another. Then another. Still they came, a staggering blitz from the shadows. Dex swore violently, took a step.

Then Sister Becky's strident voice tore the air like a sheet. "*Ms. Masterson!!*"

Kiki's head snapped around. She stared, turned back to the horde, blasting another with her last shell, then turned and ran, pulling her pistol and blazing away into the cavalcade of hell bearing down behind her. Dex set off at a run.

Skidding around a corner, he led them across a broad executive lounge, past a serene fountain and a coffee bar, turned another corner and came face-to-face with a handful of wandering zombies. Unable to stop, Dex plowed straight into them like a runaway freight train, caught his leg and went down.

Sister Becky was there in an instant, smashing one assailant back with a vicious head strike, then planting herself beside Dex, crosses up, eyes flashing. *"In nomine Patris, et Filii, et Spiritus Sancti!"*

Pained groans filled the air, and the lurkers flinched back. Kiki dropped two with her pistol; then, Dex cut loose from the floor and blew the legs from under a third. Before the rest could attack, they'd hauled Dex to his feet and were off, dashing away blindly in the semi-dark. They fled breathlessly across a hall, through an intersection and around another corner.

There, Sister Becky slid to a halt on the smooth marble. "Here!" she rasped. "Make haste!" She ducked through an open door and, when the others had slipped inside, closed it swiftly and silently behind them. Seconds later, a thudding, moaning horde passed by on the other side. The fugitives held their breath, pulses pounding, lungs burning. Sounds of pursuit continued for a moment, then faded. Finally, they were gone.

Dex let his breath out with a huge *whoosh!* "Damn!" he gasped. "Damn! Hey... what the...?!" He felt Sister Becky's fingers on him, busy in the darkness, probing and patting. "Lay off, old woman! Get offa me!" He shrugged her off, trying to reload around her groping hands.

"I am checking for bites, Mr. Jackson! As much as I dislike your company, I should find you even less agreeable as an undernourished Functional Corpse! Now, if you would please hold still..."

Dex shoved her away, roughly. "I'm clean, Old Goat, go check someone else for ticks!"

"Safety first, Mr. Jackson. Now, this gash here looks severe..." she pointed to a deep slash on one shoulder that was bleeding freely, soaking his sleeve with blood. "Ah," she clucked, nodding. "Just a sword stroke I believe - perhaps a naginata. Far too clean for a bite. Now then, let's have a look at this wound on your forehead..."

"I said, *get the *&^%$! offa me!*"

"Very well, Mr. Jackson. But I warn you, if you should be infected, I shall not hesitate to..." Sister Becky's voice trailed off as she wheeled to inspect Kiki. "Hold - where is Ms. Master...?"

And then, the ninja was there.

It struck without warning, without a whisper. Just the glittering silver flash of steel in the shadows. The sword struck Becky in her middle, came away red. With a sharp, short cry, she fell.

Before Dex could blink, it was on him, slashing, leaping, kicking, rolling, a blur of shadow in shadow. Dex felt the blade cut him as he tried to parry, crudely, desperately, with his own blade, his shotgun lost somewhere in the first few strikes. He stumbled, banged against a desk, knocked something over, felt another slash on his leg, a nick on his neck. Sparks struck from his katana as he clumsily blocked, but the blow knocked his blade wide, exposing him. He caught a silhouette of the ninja as its blade whirled, could see it's yellow eyes shining from the black. His brain took the action into slow motion, body overwhelmed, not responding. The next blow would gut him. He was helpless.

In days to come, if asked, Dex would firmly believe but always deny that he saw a flash of light as Sister Becky stepped between them. She held a single cross high and bright, and her voice was a cold, furious lash of power as it reached out and smote the ninja like a sledge.

"*Iesus Christus!*"

There was a terrible, fearful pressure, a *presence,* a sensation of heat and light... and then the zombie fell.

Dead.

Stone dead.

Sister Becky slumped, the arm which had protected her middle hanging limp and red at her side, blood soaking her habit. She favored Dex with a weary smile. "Overconfidence. It was ever the ninja's curse. As the saying goes, Mr. Jackson: 'Fell a wolf with just one blow, 'tis peril waits the...'"

A bone jarring kick to the skull cut her short and sent her crashing into the wall, and a second ninja was there. A lightning flurry of brutal, hammer-like blows shivered Dex's body. He swiped once with the katana, missed, took a shot to the face from what felt like a rawhide bone, swiped again, missed again, took three more shots and, this time, woke up on the floor, spots and stars dancing before his eyes.

He heaved sideways, struggled to his hands and knees. Before him, bathed in moonglow from a small skylight, a cadaverous face loomed - the ninja, its facial wrappings slipped, empty yellow eyes staring from pulpy orange-green flesh. Dex shoved himself backwards, came up hard against a wall. The thing stalked forward. A *ninjato* whispered from its sheath. The razor edge caught a glint of pale moonlight. Dex patted holsters, fingers clumsy, brain ringing.

Nothing.

"Damn..." he mumbled. "It's not my day..." He set his teeth, stared the monster in the eye.

 283

From behind it, Dex heard a sharp *ch-chack!*

It was the pump of a shotgun.

"Gotcha."

A *boom!* lit up the room, and the ninja's head disappeared. For a moment, its body stood in place, still crouched and ready to strike. Then, slowly, it slumped sideways and pitched into the shadows, revealing a lean figure in a red stocking cap. It was Kiki.

Dex gaped. "You... you were here the whole...?!"

"Had to wait for it to make its move." Kiki reloaded the King mechanically. "Let's move." She padded across the room and put her ear to an adjoining office door, listening.

Dex sat for a moment, staring at her back. Then, he shook his head dazedly and heaved himself to his feet. Sister Becky staggered into view, hair amiss and hood awry, clutching her bleeding arm.

"Is it just me..." Dex flicked his head at Kiki, "or is she scarier than the zombies?" Becky said nothing. Gathering their weapons, they joined Kiki at the door.

When they arrived, Kiki had her hand on the knob. "All quiet. Let's go." Kiki opened the door and stared straight into Carson's face.

She gasped, frozen. Carson reached out, black nails grasping for her throat, a growl on his dead lips.

With a cry, Becky clutched Kiki's bloodstained tank top and yanked her back. They fell in a tangle, and, before Carson could lunge, Dex was there.

He stood, tense, fists up, staring Carson full in his sickly green face. Their eyes met, Carson's dead white, Dex's panicked brown.

"Don't do it, bro. I don't wanna hurt you!"

"Nnnnnn....!" Carson lunged.

Dex swung a right hook like a dinner ham, caught Carson in the side of the head. Carson stumbled, crashed into the wall. His skull dented sheetrock.

"Sorry! I'm sorry, man!" Dex danced nervously, fists still up, face twisted in an agony of worry.

"Nnnnn.....!" was Carson's only reply. He righted himself and lunged again. This time, Dex swung harder, a look of sickness and desperation on his face. His fist crunched into Carson, knocking him off his feet and sending him flying into a filing cabinet.

"I'm sorry!" Dex wailed, nearly frantic. "I'm *so, so* sorry!" He danced back, almost beside himself. "Just stay down, bro... *stay down!*"

Again, Carson rose, lurched forward, fingers clutching. Dex cast about furiously, boots squeaking backward on bamboo hardwood. His eyes lit on a bronze urn, and he caught it up by the neck just as Carson charged.

Dex swung. Hard.

The metal made a loud, dull *bong!* as it bounced off bone. Carson's moan cut off like a switch, and he dropped, thudded to the floor and lay still.

Dex stood, chest heaving, eyes wild, the brass urn, now splattered with red, clenched tight. He looked as if he was about to be sick.

Carson didn't move.

A tortured whimper came from Kiki, and she crawled quickly toward the crumpled form.

Dex swallowed hard. "I... I didn't mean to... I was tryin' to...!"

Kiki slowed as she approached, hesitating, fearful of what she would find. She reached out slowly, not wanting to look.

"Is..." the whites of Dex's eyes showed all around. "Is he...?!"

Kiki bent low over the body. She was a smudge in the dark as she hovered over it, desperate to check for signs of life and completely at a loss on how to do so. Her red cap bobbed.

"Nnnn......" a soft groan slipped from Carson's lips.

Kiki slumped, relieved. "No. He's not. He's okay." She looked back wearily at Dex.

Then Carson reared up and reached for Kiki's throat.

"Nnnnnnnn....!"

With a gasp Kiki rolled clear, Carson's fingers scrabbling across her shoulder and catching on her pant leg. She jerked free and scrambled awkwardly to her feet.

"Crap!" Dex brandished the urn, backpedaling. "Whadda we... how do we...?!"

Suddenly, the dark form of Sister Becky appeared behind Carson as he struggled to his feet. She waved sharply and yanked open a closet door. Dex didn't stop to think. He charged, shouldered into Carson and shoved hard. Teeth snapped inches from his ear, and then Carson was stumbling across the room and plunging straight through the waiting door. Sister Becky slammed it shut behind him and clicked the lock.

They all stood stock still for a moment, breathing hard, trying to wrap their heads around what had just happened.

"I... I almost..."

"But you did not, Mr. Jackson."

"Should we...?"

 285

"He will be as safe here as anywhere." With effort, Sister Becky bent to retrieve her cross. "But we will not. Come. We have made too much noise. We must make haste from here."

But, it was already too late. Pounding, lurching footsteps sounded through the open door, accompanied by low growls. Kiki flung it shut in the faces of a host of gaping dead-eyed fiends, snatched a chair and jammed it under the handle.

"Back!"

She waved Dex and Becky off, covering the door with her pistol. No one argued, and they tumbled back the way they'd come, banging shins and dodging wreckage as they headed back for the hallway. Just as they reached the door, it burst open, more growls filling the room. Dex lunged, hurled the urn into the face of a grisly samurai and then himself against the door, slamming it and snapping a thrusting katana in half. Dex threw the lock, staggered backward as a barrage of blows shook the door. He whirled about, desperate. They were trapped.

"Sonofa...!"

"Stiff upper lip, Mr. Jackson," Sister Becky, unruffled, passed him the sword he had dropped during the fight with Carson.

"*Screw* that!" Dex hurled Fujika's blade aside. "Katanas *suck!*" He ripped off the tattered, bloody remains of his jacket. "And screw zombies, too! Zombies *suck!* And screw this whole *&^%$! rotten night!" He reached for his black gear bag. "It's Jerry time!"

Dex swiped the contents off a littered desktop and slammed his bag down with an ominous *thud*. As he worked, the banging and hammering continued on both doors unabated. One of them cracked and splintered. In the corner, Kiki coolly fed bullets into a spare clip.

Sister Becky drifted up to stand beside Dex, looking on with thinly veiled interest. "As there is the distinct possibility that all of us shall perish here, Mr. Jackson, and I am in considerable doubt that our final destinations shall be the same; I shall rise to the bait: 'Jerry?'"

Dex found the zipper. "Uh-huh."

"As in...?"

"As in 'Jerry Lee Lewis.'"

Becky blinked.

Dex blinked back. "'The Killer.'"

He yanked down the zipper. Inside the bag, nestled among clips and sidearms, lay a rugged, gleaming, very dangerous looking chainsaw. It was cherry red.

"Ah. *That* Jerry."

It started on the first pull.

Seconds later, a samurai leg kicked through the door, and Dex lopped it neatly off.

"*That's* what I'm talkin' 'bout!" his voice thundered over the roar and the smoke. Arms reached through the hole, and he set to work on them as well. As Dex busied himself with the carnage, the other door gave a great jerk and popped half out of its frame. Kiki stepped up, guns ready.

As the battle raged, Sister Becky took a moment to quickly knot a torn strip of robes about her wounded arm, wincing as she pulled it tight. Her face was drawn and pale, and her hands trembled as she tied, but her green eyes remained alert and surveyed the room as she worked.

"Mr. Jackson!" she shouted over the din, careful to stand clear of his swinging chainsaw. "We find ourselves at a disadvantage! Perhaps, you and Mr. Lewis might be good enough to fashion us another exit!"

Dex grinned and revved the engine, his shirt smeared with ick. The tool kicked eagerly in his hand as he stepped toward the wall.

Moments later, they were clambering through a gaping hole into the next room, ducking the ends of severed conduit and coughing drywall dust. They tried a door there but were forced back by another mob of undead. Kiki toppled a mini-fridge across it as Dex attacked another wall, cutting into a racket ball court and from there into another office. Again, their exit was blocked by a knot of zombies.

As Kiki secured the door, Dex hit the kill switch on his chainsaw. He shook his head in frustration. "It's no good!" His voice was overly loud in the sudden void, and he was wheezing hard. "Jerry... got us outta one... scrape, but we're right back... in another... there's just too many! Pretty soon, we're gonna... run outta walls. Or gas." He checked the tank. It was already half empty. Around them, the hammering and moaning intensified.

"Then, we take 'em all!" Kiki sounded shrill and strained. She stood with feet widespread, commanding the center of the room, gripping her pistol fiercely. Carson's bat was tight in her off hand, the King loaded and ready across her back. There was death or madness in her eyes; they couldn't tell which.

Sister Becky stared hard at her. She felt suddenly very, very tired. A wave of dizziness swept over her, and she tilted against a filing cabinet, cradling her crippled arm. She closed her eyes, breathed a quick prayer. "I admire your zeal, Ms. Masterson... but by the time we did... were it even feasible... it would likely be too late. I fear the *Kuro*

Shikiten is already underway. Think - why would the Warlord send this rabble to pursue us and not come himself? The wolf is in the hen house, my child, and we are nowhere near to stop it. If we do not, and soon, then any small victory here will have no meaning. All shall be lost."

Kiki seemed oblivious, pacing from door to door, wild and dangerous. Her bosoms heaved, shirt soaked with sweat and blood, Carson's bandana jumping as the muscles in her arm twitched.

Dex glanced at her, shuddered and looked away. "I'm open to ideas."

Sister Becky forced herself to look about the room, but her head spun, making it difficult to focus. The dizziness threatened to topple her, and she slid a few inches against the filing cabinet, head dipping... then, suddenly, she pushed off, eyes hard on a spot high in the far wall. "If we cannot go *through* the walls, then let us go *over* them."

Dex followed her gaze. It was fixed on the white grate of a ventilation duct. He glanced down at his massive frame, back to the small opening. "You got kicked in the head, didn't you?"

Becky's face fell. "My apologies. You are quite right, Mr. Jackson..."

"Quite fat, you mean," Dex's expression was lost in the shadows, but his tone sounded almost amused. "Don't sweat it, Darth. You two go," he hefted the chainsaw to his shoulder. "Reckon I'll just stay here for a bit and make me a little distraction. You two get back to ol' Gruesome. Finish this."

Sister Becky opened her mouth to argue, then closed it. She looked at him, bloody, battered, wheezing... and yet undaunted. A small, sad smile touched her face. On impulse, she reached out and placed a hand on Dex's arm. "Godspeed, Mr. Jackson."

Behind them wood splintered. The growls grew louder.

"You best be gettin'. I got work to do." Dex hefted the chainsaw and planted himself. "I'll catch up when I'm done here." He loosened his shoulders and put his hand on the pull start.

Kiki, however, didn't budge. She stood rigid and immobile, gun trained and eyes blazing with self-destructive fury. Her voice was a deadly croak. "Give me one good..."

"Vengeance, Ms. Masterson," Sister Becky replied quietly. "Vengeance."

Kiki stared. A second later, she was crawling onto a desk and tearing at the vent cover. Within moments, she and Sister Becky had wormed their way into the cramped, echoing confines of the ductwork.

Behind them, Jerry roared to life. They could hear the noise of the mayhem for some time as they bumped and slid down the long, dark, aluminum throat, guided by the swinging beam of Kiki's flashlight and pushed from behind by the aching realization that they had left yet another of their friends at the mercy of the zombie horde.

The ducts seemed endless. They wormed and wriggled their way along, Kiki in the lead. She moved rapidly at first, then with increasing care, hesitating at every grate and crossroad, face screwed tight in concentration. Sister Becky dragged herself doggedly behind, one arm limp and all but useless, numb save for when she banged the wall and sent fire and pain shooting through it.

Finally, gasping, overcome with lightheadedness and nausea, Sister Becky could go no further. She collapsed full length in the duct and pressed her face to the cool metal. "A moment... Ms. Masterson..." she gasped, "...if you please. Just enough... to gather..."

Kiki whirled and glared her into silence, a fierce finger to her lips. The flashlight, Becky noted vaguely, was off. Kiki turned back to a grate. From outside, an eery, red glow seeped through.

With effort, Sister Becky dragged herself forward, peered past Kiki. "Father in Heaven!" she breathed. "The Warlord's inner sanctum! But, how did you know?"

"I've been in vents before." Kiki slid the King up beside her in the dark, cradled it to her breast. Her eyes were hard on the scene below, like a sniper picking targets. "Now... how do we kill it?"

Sister Becky breathed deeply, taking in the room with her keen eyes. Not much had changed, with the exception of its occupants. The Warlord stood alone on the dais, and only a pair of Shadow Samurai remained, standing guard beside Fujika near the door. Fujika looked displeased. Sister Becky took another breath and forced her mind to work.

"We seem to be in time, praise our Lord and Savior," she murmured. "Although our cushion is slim. See... even now the Warlord performs the *Kuro Shikiten.*" Their eyes fixed on the grim, shadowed shape of the Warlord hard at work below, shuffling relics about the altars, muttering chants, kneeling and supplicating. His *kabuto* helmet had been removed and rested now on a stand beside the dais, exposing his ghastly visage. They could hear his voice clearly, rising in a haunting cadence, an eery chant of death and despair.

"Still, it will take time," Becky continued. "Precious time. The

289

Warlord will not - *must* not - risk missteps. He must prove his devotion to the Infernal through this vile obeisance," she wrinkled her nose in disgust and crossed herself. "But very soon, the summons shall be complete. The demon will come. Yes, Ashihitokage will appear. And when he does, we must be prepared."

"I'm prepared." Kiki eased forward, but Sister Becky gripped her arm.

"A moment, Ms. Masterson, if you please! Some time yet remains to us, so let us use it well. Let us be patient. Let us wait."

Kiki glared at the hand on her arm. Sister Becky quickly removed it. Slowly, Kiki swiveled her eyes back to the scene below. "For what? The odds won't get any better."

"For guidance, Ms. Masterson - preferably Divine. We are hardly in condition to conduct a proper scrap, even were we capable of harming this damnable creature." Sister Becky lay down again, pondering, praying, wracking her brain. As she did, she felt a poke in her ribs. With sudden inspiration, she recalled the folded parchment she had taken from Fujika. Shifting awkwardly in the cramped confines, she drew out the rumpled, age-worn *Ashi Keiyaki*. A spark of hope kindled.

"Keep watch, my dear!" she whispered. "Careful watch. You must notify me the very instant there is any change. Now, let us see if we can find a miracle..."

Unfolding the parchment, she began to read. The light was poor, the script faded and written in archaic Japanese. Sister Becky's arm hurt, throbbing with pain.

She had read the contract twice by the time Kiki's sharp hiss came a few minutes later.

"Something's happening!"

Sister Becky knew, even before she looked, what it was. She could feel it, creeping slowly over her entire being, a prickle of vague unrest and discomfort, like the first indication of an illness. It was a sensation she had felt before. And one she would never get used to.

"What is that?" Kiki croaked. She rubbed fingertips gone suddenly numb, blinked against a wave of disorientation. "I feel... bad..."

"It is the demon, Ms. Masterson," Sister Becky replied softly. "The *Kuro Shikiten* is complete. Ashihitokage is coming." She started to pray.

Below, a small spot of darkness began to form, centered in the air between the three altars. Lamps flickered, though there was no breeze.

Red shadows danced and crawled grotesquely across the dais and the figures below - the Samurai, Fujika, the Warlord himself, kneeling face down on the floor.

A faint sense of nausea stirred in Sister Becky's stomach. Her skin prickled more insistently as below the smudge of black began to grow. She relaxed her thoughts, forgot words and sought comfort in her faith. Beside her, Kiki shuddered violently and moaned through gritted teeth, knuckles white on her shotgun.

"Steady, Ms. Masterson," Sister Becky breathed. "Steady. The presence of this cursed Infernal affects us most deeply on a spiritual front. Your discomfort will pass." Beside her, Kiki's noises subsided slightly. She felt her trembling.

After a minute, the sensations lessened. After another, they faded. But, they never left, just hovered, right at the edge of awareness. Becky opened her eyes and looked.

Ashihitokage had come.

Above the dais hovered a roiling dark cloud, a stain in space and time. No creature of flesh and blood hung suspended there, but something far worse, far more sinister. *Something* moved inside the cloud, something restless and wicked; it lacked definite form or substance but possessed instead a palpable sense of malice and dread, like an evil thought that just wouldn't go away.

Sister Becky studied the cloud earnestly, watching, waiting. If the demon sensed them now, all would be lost. The Warlord's hideous face was unreadable, but it did not turn from Ashihitokage. As for the demon... she waited another moment, then nodded to herself. They were still alive. That was proof enough.

"We are safe, my dear, at least for the moment. And blessed, as well - this is merely an Apparitional Visitation. A spiritual telephone call, if you will. Were Ashihitokage to fully manifest..." she shuddered. "I have seen grown men run their colors, if you take my meaning."

Kiki said nothing. Her eyes were screwed shut, her breathing shallow and rapid. Below, the Warlord knelt before Ashihitokage, arms spread wide in supplication. He began to speak, his own coarse voice mingling with the penetrating, whispering rush of sound that seemed to emanate from inside the cloud, raising the short hairs on the necks of the watching women.

Sister Becky's concentration was intense, her brow knit in deep furrows, lips moving silently as she struggled to make out words. "They are treating. The new contract... bargaining... for the new *Ashi*

Keiyaki. Strange..." she scrunched forward, pressing her face to the vent, straining to hear.

"What?" Kiki forced her eyes open and squinted through the grate, finger touching the King's trigger, then moving away, then touching again. The strain was almost too much. She looked as if she might snap at any moment and hurl herself through the screen. Sister Becky, absorbed with the scene, took no notice.

"The demon is displeased," Becky murmured. "With Fujika. His weakness, his... cowardice. Apparently, in spite of his recent atrocities, our Shogun is not bloodthirsty enough." She shook her head wryly. "Ashihitokage is angry enough to deal. They are arranging a new bargain. Wait..." she lifted a cautionary finger, listening hard. "The Warlord seeks, among other things... oh my... a return to life. An end to his shadow walk." She paused again. The Warlord's voice swelled with fierce passion, filling the room. "In return, he pledges himself to wreak such... carnage... chaos... as has never been seen before, in all the days of the Earth. He shall bring an end... an end to all the living..." her voice trailed off into a deep frown. "And other blasphemies which I will not speak."

The Warlord fell silent, head bowed, hands resting on his thighs.

"The Warlord has plead his case," Sister Becky's eyes narrowed shrewdly. "We shall see what Ashihitokage replies."

It was the demon's turn now. The whispering rush filled the room and crept into their minds, like a flurry of evil urges or the nagging remnants of a half-remembered nightmare. There were no words, no translations, just a dizzying sense of darkness and nausea. Again, the lanterns flickered. Shadows reeled.

Abruptly, it ceased. Something in the communication must have surprised the Warlord, for his head snapped up and looked back sharply at Fujika. The Shogun stood quietly nearby, his face turned from the awful, terrible presence on the dais. The Warlord stared at him for a moment, considering. Then, he turned to face the demon. He bowed, slowly, until his face touched wood.

Something seemed to click, darkly.

The deal was done.

Becky's eyes flew wide. "Heaven's gates!" She lifted her head, bumped it against the roof of the shaft. She clutched for the *Ashi Keiyaki* and scanned it rapidly. "Yes... yes, here! Of course!" Her voice was a tense whisper. She read a line of text again, then, satisfied, waved the parchment at Kiki. "The contract, Ms. Masterson! If this wretched Infernal holds true to its nature... then there is at least a chance, however slim! It is not the stone I would choose to skip, as they say, but it is the only one on the beach. There is no time to explain, my child..." Becky tucked the contract away quickly. "And, although I greatly regret it, I am afraid that I must reverse my earlier position concerning the Shogun. So dark is the hour that we have no other option." Her features clouded with distaste, and she drew a steadying breath. "He must die."

"I'm on it." Kiki wriggled to her back, put her feet on the grate.

"Ms. Masterson... I do not think that you fully..."

"Yeah. I do." Kiki was in position, boots pressed tight against the cover, ready to kick.

Sister Becky glanced down at her injured arm. She sighed. There was no time to argue. "You will find no pleasure in it, dear child."

"We'll see about that." As she readied herself, Kiki's hand strayed to the bandana on her arm.

"Very well. We have no choice in the matter, if we are to prevent the loss of many, many lives. Now, here is the most vital..."

Then the door to the hallway crashed open, and Dex was there, stumbling, staggering, bleeding, the broken end of a heavy floor lamp in one hand, the other clutching his side. He slammed the door, slumped against it, sucking deep lungfuls of air. All eyes locked on him, both living and dead, and, for a moment, no one moved.

Ever so slowly, Dex lifted his head and looked around. Realization dawned. His rumbling voice reached Kiki and Sister Becky even where they lay. "Oh, *&^%#!..."

Kiki took one look. Then she drew her knees to her chest.

"No, wait...! You must know...!"

Kiki kicked out hard, sent the panel flying and then followed it into space. Her legs took the shock of the fall, and she was up and running, straight for Fujika, her face a mask as grim and fierce as any *menpo.* She swept past the dais, the demon, the Warlord, without sparing so much as a sidelong glance, banging into the helmet stand in her single-minded zeal. The helmet wobbled and so did she, but neither one fell. She straightened and put on speed, lifting her voice:

"Dex! Weapon!"

Dex whirled. The King spun through the air toward him, flung with all the power of Kiki's lean shoulder. He caught it neatly, stepped away from the door and blew a hole in one of the samurai flanking Fujika, sending it flying. As the other drew steel and rushed him, the door burst wide and a horde of howling zombies broke loose. Dex went to work.

Kiki, meanwhile, had slowed her charge to a steady stride, controlling her breathing, pistol out and leveled. She marched directly at Fujika, who was now unguarded. It was an executioner's march, unblinking, unwavering, unflinching. She stopped within arm's reach.

Fujika met her gaze. He could read the intent in her expression but showed no fear. The gun hovered, poised, pointed straight at his face. Kiki stood like a lightning rod, body rigid, every muscle tensed. A faint, haughty grin teased Fujika's lips. He opened his mouth to speak...

Bang!

Fujika dropped like a stone.

Kiki lowered her smoking pistol. "There..." she stared down at the corpse, blue eyes like ice. "Now, we're finished."

Over the echoes of the gunshot, there arose a soulless, raging roar that filled the room with terror. It was the raw, unbridled wrath of the Warlord of Death, and it carried with it the full potence of his dark will, tossing zombies like leaves in a hurricane as his power, unleashed in full fury, tore blindly through them. Burning black eyes bored into Kiki from the shadows of the fearsome *kabuto*, once more in place on the gruesome head. Fujika's execution had not gone unnoticed. In a towering rage, the Warlord surged forward, yanked Kiki back by the hair and planted an open-handed blow that nearly snapped her neck.

Before her body touched down, the Warlord had drawn its katana and was springing forward, fluid and lethal, the blade sweeping high, poised to strike at her throat.

Boom!

A deafening blast tore through the air and most of the Warlord's arm, sending his sword spinning and skittering across the floor. The creature whirled, turning his nightmare grimace on Dex and his still-smoking shotgun. In one huge leap, the Warlord was on him, before the guard could pump and fire again. The Warlord snaked out an arm, too swift and straight to dodge, and laid a hand on Dex's chest.

Dex screamed.

The big man's knees buckled, and he went down, features sagging, the shotgun slipping from stiff fingers as his heavy frame shook and spasmed. The room was suddenly, deathly silent. Helpless on his knees before the monstrous figure, Dex reeled and shuddered. His head tilted slowly back, eyes screwed shut, face a study in agony, mouth jerked wide in suffering beyond screams. A gray, sulfurous smoke rose up from his sizzling chest.

The Warlord bent close... closer... his own horrible mouth was mere inches from the guard's. Cadaverous lips parted, opened wide on a yawing black pit rimmed with crumbling brown teeth. In its dark recesses, a wisp of black smoke began to form. The smoke swirled, took shape, grew, reaching out a single, sinister tendril toward Dex.

"Enough!"

The Black Breath puffed and was gone. Startled, the Warlord sprang back, slipped loose a short *wakizashi* blade with a lethal whisper. Dex's body crumpled to the floor and lay still. Sister Becky stepped forward and stood beside it.

Straight and stern, she favored the Warlord of Death with a cold, steely gaze. One arm hung limp and bloody at her side, while in her other gleamed the heavy crucifix. The metal seemed to glow with a bloody sheen in the red light. That same light reflected in Sister Becky's features, drawn, deathly pale, but full of iron determination. With slow deliberation, she made the sign of the cross.

The Warlord hesitated, wary and on guard. A serpent's hiss issued from clenched teeth as he sized up the new threat: a mere stick of a nun, battered, bleeding, swaying on her feet. With a fiendish chuckle, the Warlord straightened. The creature swelled with pride and menace, drawing in more shadows about itself and sending a fresh wave of chill into the room. Nearby, the sprawling zombies began to jerk and twitch. With a wave of the Warlord's hand, their eyes yanked open, and they clambered to their feet. Ominous moaning filled the room as they shambled closer, forming a loose ring around the nun.

Sister Becky shifted her eyes, gave the corpses a dangerous look. A cold half smile played on her lips. She lifted her cross. The zombies paused and moaned in discomfort.

"Do your worst, Sorcerer," Sister Becky's voice made the same sound as the Warlord's sword being drawn form its sheath. "Pharaoh once tested the Lord of Hosts, and it was his undoing. Come, if you dare... we shall see whose God is greater!"

The Warlord lunged. Sister Becky responded with a great shout, brandishing her cross. The Warlord crashed back as if struck, the zombies raising a chorus of agonized wails. With a snarl, the Warlord gathered himself and lunged again, throwing the full weight of his malice like a battering ram. Sister Becky took the blow and held. They stood locked, teetering, reeling back and forth. Sister Becky muttered a steady stream of prayer, while from the Warlord's lips came a low hiss, mixed with strange words and whispered utterings. Behind them on the dais, the sinister, roiling cloud of Ashihitokage seemed to swell, pulsing with hate and anticipation, fueling the Warlord's rage.

Slowly, the fearsome assault began to take its toll on Sister Becky. The tremendous strain showed in every rigid feature, her whole body wound unbearably tight, like a piano wire about to snap. She gasped desperately, eyes flaring open. They lit on Kiki, lying just outside the ring of zombies.

"Ms. Masterson!"

Kiki stirred, shook her head, rose to an elbow. Sister Becky faltered. The zombies, sensing her weakness, pressed in, their groans eager and hungry.

"Nnnnnn...!"

"Ms. Masterson!" Sister Becky cried out again, the cross like lead in her hand, arm shaking with the strain, dizziness sweeping through her. Kiki shook her head again, struggled to sit, cast about with agonizing slowness for the source of the voice. Sister Becky gasped, her knees buckling. With a wordless cry she rallied, pushed back against the Warlord's crushing will, and straightened.

There was a flutter of movement outside the circle, and she caught sight of Kiki again, now on her feet, weaving and weak. She blinked, eyes glazed. She seemed, somehow, almost like her old self once more. The light of madness that had lit her eyes was now gone, and in its place was a dazed uncertainty. Kiki's gaze strayed to the Warlord. She half-raised her pistol, struggled to point it.

"No...!" Sister Becky gasped. "It must...!"

But that was all she could manage. At long last, worn down by pain, injury and exertion far beyond the limits of both body and spirit, Sister Becky's indomitable will faltered. The black wall of hate and malice pressed on by the Warlord of Death rushed to envelope her, and the zombies came with it.

"Forgive me, Father..."

She swooned. Blackness took her.

Sister Becky awoke moments later on one knee, heaving, head spinning. The zombies were already clutching at her robes, drooling. Looming over her, the Warlord's face split in a contemptuous sneer of triumph.

Then, for the second time that night, the doorway to the inner sanctum banged open. From outside, a single, hungry moan arose.

"Nnnnnn....!"

A ragged, broken figured appeared in the doorway.

It was Carson.

Kiki stared at him. Her eyes seemed to clear, and confusion faded from her features, replaced by a sudden, deep sorrow. Her pistol dropped, clattering to the floor. She took a step toward him.

Carson's dead eyes lit on her. Moan turned to growl. He lurched into the room, arms out, reaching for her. Kiki made no attempt to flee. Sister Becky watched helplessly, too exhausted even for words... watched as Kiki slowly advanced... watched as she reached into her back pocket and drew out something small and black.

From the floor at Becky's feet there came a gasp.

Dex was awake, somehow, staring blearily at the object in Kiki's hands, his eyes like saucers, blinking against the pain. His voice was a hoarse rattle. "Det... onator...!"

Sister Becky's heart caught in her throat.

Carson was charging now, head down, mouth gaping. Kiki stood silently in his path, her face twisted in anguish, waiting, arms hanging limp at her sides. The Warlord looked on with its awful, deathly grin. Imperious. Dominant. Victorious.

Only Dex found his voice. "*Nooooo...!*"

A split second before Carson was on her, Kiki lifted the detonator to her chest and closed her eyes. Sister Becky could only stare in horror.

There was impact.

Like a bull plowing into a fencepost, the force of Carson's rush blasted Kiki backward, and they crashed to the floor, Carson on top, his full weight falling on the detonator trapped between them.

Even over the noise, Sister Becky could hear, clear as day, the *click* as the button went down.

A heartbeat passed.

Then, with a *whump!* that shook the lanterns and a poof of white smoke, the back of the Warlord's head exploded. The blast knocked its body forward and the gloating, hellish smile from its face. It swayed for a moment, teetered... then slowly pitched sideways and dropped with a clatter of armor. The grand *kabuto* rolled away across the floor, trailing smoke and showing a great black hole where a wad of explosives had detonated and destroyed its brain.

Then, the zombies were dropping too, falling where they stood like a band of evil marionettes that had suddenly had their strings cut. They lay still and did not rise.

The body of the Warlord of Death began to sizzle, smoke leaking through the seams and creases of its armor. Consumed by an unholy fire that none could see, the corpse crumbled into ashes, until all that was left was the blackened *o-yoroi* and a dark scorch in the floor.

In a moment, it was done.

All was silent.

Sister Becky knelt in the center of the room, a look of stun and shock stamped on her face. For a moment, no one moved. No one spoke. No one could.

At last, a tiny, sad smile broke over the nun's haggard face. "Well done, dear girl," she murmured. "Well done indeed."

With infinite weariness, Sister Becky dragged herself the few feet to where Dex lay, clutching at the pale, smoking ruin of his chest and wheezing softly. His flesh had cauterized around the hand-shaped wound, and his eyes were still glazed, but he was conscious.

"Saving your life has become quite wearisome, Mr. Jackson," Sister Becky scolded. "I should very much appreciate it if you would stay out of harm's way for the next few moments... at least until I may catch my wind."

Dex's brown eyes roved sluggishly back and forth between the pile of armor that had once been the Warlord of Death and Kiki's sprawled form. She had made no effort to rise or even to move. Carson lay near her where he had rolled after the impact, limbs twisted and contorted like a horrible, life-sized, nightmare Raggedy Andy.

"Wha..." Dex slurred. "H... how...?!"

"How indeed, Mr. Jackson." Agonizingly, Sister Becky hauled herself to her feet. She swayed a moment, straightening her robes. They were a tangled, torn and bedraggled mess, covered with blood and worse. She struggled with them for a moment, then gave up.

Limping to Kiki's side, she observed her quietly. Kiki lay still, eyes closed. Tears leaked quietly out, but she appeared unharmed. Sister Becky stepped past her and knelt at Carson's side. She sighed. His face, like the other zombies, remained ghastly green and veined.

And yet, somehow, finally at peace.

"The answer is here, Mr. Jackson," Sister Becky fluttered a rumpled parchment. "In the *Ashi Keiyaki*. Fujika claimed that the Warlord could not be slain. That assertion, as it turns out, was flawed. The *exact* wording, as recorded in the contract, is that the Warlord could not be slain *by mortal hand*. Our dear Mr. Dudley was deceased when he struck the death blow. And thus, it was no mortal hand that delivered it. It was a dead one." A wry smile touched her lips. "Demons are frightfully legalistic."

At her feet, Kiki whimpered. A shudder ran through her body. Her eyes flickered open, but only half-way. They focused blearily on Sister Becky's face. "He's still dead, isn't he?" Her voice was small. A child's.

"Yes, Ms. Masterson."

Kiki's shoulders began to shake softly. The tears resumed.

"Courage, dear. There is one final matter yet to attend to." With a grimace, Sister Becky summoned the last of her waning strength and rose once more to her feet. Picking her way slowly across, she limped to the center of the room. With effort, she hoisted herself onto the dais, staggered a few steps and stopped, directly before the dark cloud of Ashihitokage. It hung there still, in the air between the altars, roiling and black and brooding.

Inside, the *something* stirred.

Sister Becky drew herself up before it. She fixed the thing with a cold gaze. "The bargain has been struck, wretched spirit. Now, keep your end."

There was no reply.

Sister Becky screwed up her face, pursed her lips and spoke again, this time more firmly. "As twisted as your tongue may be, your word is your bond. That much you know as well as I. Even your Master, when his word is given, must keep it. The Father sees to that. You know that you are beaten. You know that I speak the truth. The contract is fulfilled! Now, keep your bargain, spawn of Hades!" Again, silence was her only answer. This time she lifted her cross. "In the name of our Lord Jesus Christ, I command you: *make good your vow!*"

The cloud roiled... dangerously. Waves of malice rolled out from it in sheets. Sister Becky stood her ground, implacable and immovable. Then, the roiling ceased.

Something seemed to click, darkly.

The deal was done.

As Sister Becky's stern expression dissolved into a satisfied smile, the cloud suddenly pulsed, the lights in the room dimming almost to darkness. Inside the black mass, a shape began to form, half-seen, half-imagined, at once beautiful and terrible. A piercing, sibilant whisper slunk into the room, worming its way through human consciousness and turning knees to water. There were words in the whisper, and, though all sensed them, only one understood. They were directed at Sister

Becky and her alone. And it was clear, they meant her ill.

Then, it was gone - the voice, the cloud, the presence, all of it. The air above the dais was clear.

"Well," Sister Becky dusted her hands, crossed herself and turned a pious smile to the others. "That, my friends... is that."

As she did, a voice rose from the floor near Kiki. It was weak, faint and slurred, but familiar. Very, very familiar.

"Okay... somethin' stinks..."

Kiki's head snapped around, her face in absolute shock. A second, she stared. Then, she surged forward, caught up Carson in her arms.

Still bloody, still beaten, still broken... but Carson.

"Sonofa...!" Dex exploded.

The sound of wailing sirens rose from the plaza below, but Kiki paid them no mind. Nor Dex, nor Sister Becky, nor anything else in the world.

Cradling Carson in her arms, she wept with joy.

 300

CHAPTER FIFTEEN

The Remains of the Day

Carson's eyes flickered open. For a moment, everything was blobs of color: white, yellow, red. Slowly, gradually, the fuzziness faded, and details began to emerge. The crisp, clean walls of a hospital room. Sunlight, streaming through an open window. A vase stuffed with happy flowers. He blinked. Framed by it all, a face hung before him. A familiar face. A face under a red stocking cap. Smiling.

Carson cleared his throat, tried for his voice. It was weak, but it worked. "Either you're the best looking zombie I've ever seen... or we made it." He flashed the medicated version of his lopsided smile.

Kiki sat by his bed, beaming. The sun, streaming through the window behind her, bathed her with the brightest yellow he had ever seen. It mingled with her hair so that it looked like she was glowing. He studied her face, letting the haze in his brain slowly fade. She *was* glowing. She had a nasty bruise on her cheek and a black eye to match, but if it hurt, she didn't show it. She looked, Carson thought, better than he'd ever seen her. Perfectly content, inside and out.

Happy.

"Welcome back." She gazed at him unashamedly, drinking him in, grinning from ear to ear like joy was her job. Carson let the warmth of the sun, the smile and the moment soak into him. He closed his eyes, breathed deeply.

When he opened them a few moments later, his voice was a bit stronger. "How long have I been out?"

"Two days, fourteen hours and seven minutes."

"You didn't even look at your watch."

"Didn't have to. Plus, it sort of got destroyed by the zombies. Or the ninjas. I forget which."

Carson struggled to sit up, but Kiki gently pressed him back.

"I gotcha..." she reached for the bed remote and raised him to a more comfortable position, fussing with his blankets.

Carson let her, enjoying the delicious, lingering lethargy of a long healing sleep. He glanced around lazily, letting his eyes wander the recovery room. They drifted across an overstuffed loveseat in one corner strewn with a rumpled blanket and several techie magazines. "You stayed here the whole time?"

"It's nicer than my place."

"I'm touched."

Kiki blushed. "Well, I didn't have a job to go to, thanks to you." She made a show of arranging his pillows. "And work study is on hold until Palm Hill hires a new IT director - also your fault. So, I didn't have a lot of options except to sit around and wait for the guy in the zombie-induced coma to snap out of it..."

"Hey..." Carson stopped her, held her eyes. "Thanks."

She smiled.

Although he still didn't know her very well, he felt like it was the closest he had ever come.

"Don't mention it."

Kiki fetched him a drink of water, and he lay back, feeling the warmth and softness of the bed around him. There was a faint itchiness and a slight tug on his right side, but not enough to cause discomfort. His heart monitor beeped slowly, steadily, reassuringly. Outside, far away, he could faintly hear the sound of children playing. A warm breeze ruffled the curtains and his hair, carrying the smells of the beach. He breathed deeply.

"But I can't take all the credit."

"Dex and Beck?!" Carson's eyes flew open. "They okay?!"

"The big guy carried you down in his own two arms... which is saying something, considering the shape he was in. Of course, he didn't have far to go. The paramedics were already in the tower."

"Tower..."

"And the Warlord of Death was gone by then."

"Warlord of...?"

"The demon, too."

"Demon?!" Carson struggled to sit up again. Again, Kiki gently pressed him back.

"You don't remember much, do you?"

"There might be a few gaps."

She hesitated. "So... what *do* you remember?"

Carson stared at a bright Impressionist painting of a beach scene that hung on the wall. Seagulls wheeled. A sailboat tacked the wind. "I remember when they bit me."

"What about... after..." Kiki's voice was small.

"Nothing. Zero. Like a long, empty dream." There was a girl in the painting, walking on the beach, toes in the sand. Carson studied the gauzy outline of her form. She looked happy, without a care in the world. "It's funny," his voice was lost in quiet reflection. "Speaking of dreams... it just hit me. In my, uh… vision, I guess... with Pete... I think he was trying to warn me about this. Or prepare me."

"What did he say?"

"He said, 'when it happens you'll know.' Boy was that was an understatement. And then he said... 'move toward the light.'"

"And was there?" Kiki's voice was still small. "Light?"

Carson let his mind drift back to the empty, shattered chasm of his memory. "Yeah," he nodded finally. "There was light. When I moved toward it, that's when I woke up. First thing I saw was you." He looked at her.

Kiki blushed again and turned away.

She was rescued at that precise moment by a grandfatherly doctor who chased her out to consult with his patient. Still, Kiki didn't go far. She was there again immediately when the doctor left, slipping through the door before it had even closed. She resumed her place by the bed, where Carson was just dozing off.

He awoke some time later, blinked a smile at her, then gave way to a mighty, irresistible, face-stretching yawn. When he was done, he followed it with a contented sigh. "So... Warlord of Death. Do I get the whole story?"

There was a knock at the door.

Kiki rose and headed for it. "Yeah. But, they tell it better." She opened it, and there, framed in the doorway, stood Sister Becky. The nun was swathed in her customary black, except for one arm that hung in a clean white sling. She stood silently, her eyes lit by a peaceful smile. But just for a moment. Then, Dex bulled past her, his face split by a grin as big as he was.

"Hell, Dud... 'bout time you woke up! I thought you were gonna sleep 'til Christmas!" The guard crushed him in a powerful hug.

"Umm... Dex..." Kiki hovered like a mother hen, watching Carson's pained expression. "Recently at the threshold of death..."

"I know, I know!" Dex relinquished his hold. "But, if killin' this fool didn't kill him, then a little man hug ain't gonna do it!" He chuckled and dragged up an overstuffed chair, dropped heavily into it. Dex looked at ease, but Carson noted traces of weariness and wear around the edges, as well as a host of bandages, cuts and bruises. A chest wrap peeped up from under his blue button down, and various additional scrapes could be seen on bare legs under khaki shorts. Dex's amazing fortitude, however, was already at work; his eyes were clear and his voice strong.

Sister Becky strode to the bedside at a more stately pace, firing off a passing look at Dex that almost withered the "Get Well" flowers. "So fine to have you back, Mr. Dudley!" she embraced him, pressed her cheek to his and gripped his hands fondly. "So very, very fine. Praise our Father in Heaven, but it does this old heart good to see..."

"Yeah, yeah, it's a regular Hallmark special," Dex waved off the nun's affections. "But, I bet you're more in the mood for some tales of *&^%$ zombie killin'! Whaddaya say, Dud..." he threw his hands behind his head and kicked back in the chair. It groaned dangerously. "Story time?"

"I'm all ears, big man," Carson winked at Sister Becky, gave her hands a squeeze. Her quick frown melted back into a smile. "Take it from the point of zombification and don't stop 'til I end up here. And tell it slow - I *do* love me some zombie killin'..."

Dex and Becky did most of the talking while Kiki listened quietly, offering a few words here and there. Mostly, she just stared at Carson and smiled. For his part, Carson focused intently as they recounted the escape from the Super Maxi-Pad, the trek to Fujikacorp HQ, their meeting and revelations with the Shogun, the first attack on the Warlord of Death and the running battle through the highrise offices.

They were interrupted at that point by Carson's lunch, delivered by a hapless nurse who entered the room during an animated retelling of the ninja battle. Sister Becky smoothed over the moment and assured the shaken girl that Dex had meant no harm. In no time, the tale had resumed and reached its dramatic climax: the showdown with the Warlord of Death.

Sister Becky had taken up the tale and was running with it, recounting the tense, final moments in the inner sanctum. Unfazed by her bandaged arm, she gestured and pointed like a strange old crow with an injured wing. "And so you see, Mr. Dudley... even though you were technically dead, you were in reality our greatest weapon! In fact, had you not been in that regrettable state, I doubt that any of us would have survived. In the end, it was *you* who defeated the enemy."

Carson nodded sagely. "That was actually my plan all along."

Sister Becky laughed, a schoolgirl's laugh, rocking back on square heels. "Ah, Mr. Dudley! It is indeed refreshing to have you on the mend!" She beamed at him, shining like the sun. Then, her crow's feet scrunched into a more sober expression, both wise and kindly. "The Lord's ways are truly a mystery. Through tragedy, He has brought triumph, yet again. How quick we are to assume that bad news is worst news, forgetting that He - and He alone - can turn it to best news."

"But this time," Dex rumbled, "He had a little help from Kiki." He shook his head, eyes wide with the memories. "Talk about your wrath of God. She made the Angel of Death look warm and fuzzy."

Kiki made no comment. She just sat, leaning forward over the back of a chair, smiling. There was no trace of her dark and dangerous persona, nor had their been since that night. Beneath her smile, though, there lurked the faintest hint of *something*... something that said, if she had to, she would do it all over again. And then some.

"Anyway," Dex broke into a smile. "If that was your booty-kickin' evil twin, girl, I'm glad she's gone. This group's only got room for one loose cannon, and I like it bein' me. But, one thing I got to know..." he eyed her shrewdly. "My detonator - how did you get your hands on it?"

Kiki shrugged. "I needed it. I took it."

"Uh-uh," Dex wagged a finger at her. "Cut the crap, girl. This ain't no slumber party truth or dare. You stole from the big man... you owe me! Spill it."

"There's not much to tell. I heard you two whispering before we headed up the elevator, and I just figured the detonator would be safer with me. So, I lifted it on the way up."

"And the C-4? What about that?"

"I took it off Carson when we ran into him, after you conked him with the urn. Then, I stuck it on the Warlord's helmet just before you busted in... when I was heading for Fujika. The way I saw it, that was the biggest weapon we had, and our best chance of doing damage. And at that point, I *really* wanted to do damage."

"Mission accomplished," Carson took a slurp of his broth. "You blew up the dude's head. A little more low tech than your usual solutions, but hey... it worked."

Dex shook his head in grudging admiration. "Alright, Five-Finger Sally - you got the best of me. *And* saved our bacon. But, when did you figure it out? That it had to be a dead dude that whacked the Warlord? I mean... damn! How did you know it was gonna work?"

Kiki looked at him. "I didn't."

"You... didn't?"

She shrugged. "It just made sense to let Carson be the one to do it. After all he'd been through."

Carson swallowed. "It just made... um... so you... guessed?"

"You could say that."

Carson opened his mouth, closed it. "Good guess."

"As it turns out. But Sister Becky here... she had the whole thing figured out from reading the *Ashi Keiyaki*. I was just a little too... preoccupied... to listen. She's the real genius..." Sister Becky had taken a seat by the window, gazing out into the warm sunshine as she listened. She inclined her head modestly. "...and it was also her who figured out how to bring you back to life."

"Yeah," Dex made an exasperated little motion. "That one *still* gives me a headache. One more time - for Carson."

"It is a simple matter, really, Mr. Jackson," Sister Becky smoothed her skirts. "Firstly, as a condition of the new *Ashi Keiyaki*, Ashihitokage demanded that the Warlord slay his Shogun, both to prove his loyalty and to punish the weakness of a leader the demon felt was unworthy. If we had allowed that to happen, all would have been lost and not just for Mr. Dudley. Thus, it became necessary to remove Fujika from the equation."

"Couldn't have happened to a nicer guy."

"Quite. I pity his immortal soul, but, in the end, a man brings his own fate upon himself. We must hearken to the words of Proverbs 22:8: 'He who sows wickedness reaps trouble.' And I daresay, Fujika reaped it aplenty." There was a hint of flint in her eyes. Then, her expression softened. "At any rate," she continued on cheerfully, "that was merely the first step in restoring Mr. Dudley and not the most pivotal. No, the hook on which that particular hat was hung was the phrasing of the new *Ashi Keiyaki*. And I quote: 'When the Servant of Death slays the Master, his curse shall be lifted and life restored.' Ashihitokage, of course, meant the Warlord and Fujika as servant and master. However, with Fujika dead, and given their close ancestral ties, I assumed the Warlord would become the next rightful Shogun. That in turn made you, Mr. Dudley, the 'Servant of Death', at least after a fashion. Thus, when you slew the Warlord, the demon was bound by his own word to lift the curse and restore life - yours, in this case. As I said before... demons are frightfully legalistic."

Sister Becky folded her hands in her lap and smiled benignly, as if she had just explained to a Sunday School class why Noah built the ark.

Carson whistled. "That's a fancy piece of thinkin', lady. Only one thing..." he stirred his broth thoughtfully. "How'd you know it would work?"

"I guessed."

Carson's spoon paused halfway to his mouth. "You... you guessed, too?"

"Given the circumstances, there were few other options, dear."

Carson set down his spoon. "I'm gonna need some more morphine."

"While we're on the subject of demons," Kiki interjected. "Ashihitokage said something, right there at the end, just before he left. I didn't quite catch it - or understand it, for that matter - but it sounded... bad. Really, really bad."

Sister Becky dismissed Kiki's concern with a wave of her hand. "It was nothing, child, just a bit of demonic backtalk. 'Beware, your days are marked, vengeance is coming,' or some such nonsense. Mere words. Do not trouble yourself with them."

"Yeah," Kiki looked uneasy. "But, he sounded pretty sure..."

"Tut tut, my child, no sour faces! This is not the first time I have been threatened by a demon, and I daresay it shall not be the last. Let us trouble ourselves no further with the forked tongue of this Infernal. If that blasphemer had truly held power over me, he would have showed his cards on the spot and not run the table with a hollow bluff."

Kiki settled back without further comment. She still looked unconvinced but kept her thoughts to herself.

"Alright, alright..." Dex butted in. "So, both the ladies got lucky. Good for them. I think it's time you recognized *my* little contribution."

"Which was?"

"I beat the crap out of you." Dex grinned, the world's biggest, blackest Cheshire Cat. "Told you I could. Plus, I *didn't* shoot you in the brain. I know I gave my word and all, but... hell, guess my ex is right. I'm a little choosy about when I keep it."

"Yeah," Carson grinned back. "You couldn't keep a promise to save your life. But, you'd break one to save mine." He fell silent a moment, and his face sobered. The mileage of the last few days made him seem, in spite of rest and recovery, older somehow. Wiser. It was a minute before he spoke again. "Thank you. Thank you all. If it wasn't for you guys, I'd still be wearing the 'Got Brains?' bib and toadying for the Warlord of Breath." He looked at them, each in turn, sitting or standing by his bedside. "A guy never had better, more loyal, more awesome friends. Ever."

No one said a word. They just smiled.

"So, that's about it then," Carson lay back on his pillows. "Wham bam thank you ma'am... er... *ma'ams* - and, to be fair, giant chainsaw-wielding angry black man - and ol' Carson is back in business. A little banged up, but still kickin'."

"Er... yeah," Kiki's face clouded. "So, did the Doc tell you...?"

"What... that I'd never play the piano again?"

"No, um..." Kiki looked uncomfortable. "About your..."

"Sheesh, I'm kidding! Yeah, he told me. I lost a kidney. Turns out, they don't like having an iron pipe rammed through 'em. Go figure."

"You're not...?"

"Hey... two days, eight hours and 56 minutes ago, I was the color of rancid bratwurst, smelled like roadkill and was trying to hollow out the brain pans of my three best friends. So, I lost one of the twins - I'll take it." Carson's smile was genuine. "Besides, the Doc tells me you can still live a normal, healthy life without one. I'm more worried about you guys. You're a mess," he gestured at Sister Becky's sling. "Speaking of playing the piano."

"What, this?" The nun raised an eyebrow, clucked dismissively. "A trifle, dear lad, nothing more. Sixteen stitches, which is barely worth mentioning and not even near my record."

"There's a record? You've got a record?! What's the record?!"

"Forty-seven. From multiple wounds, mind you, but all in the same vicinity and delivered by a single blow, so I count them as a whole."

"Forty-seven! Cats n' dogs! What are you waiting for?! They

 308

don't count unless you show us the scars... so show us the scars!"

Sister Becky smiled modestly. "Alas, I cannot."

"Aw, c'mon, Sister B., you show me yours, I'll show you mine."

"Mr. Dudley - I cannot."

Carson caught the faintest hint of rosy blush on her cheeks. "Er... right. Moving on..." he turned hastily to Dex. "How 'bout you? You're wearing hurt like a shirt. What's your total?"

"Nothin' like Attila here. Not like it's a contest or nothin', but I guess I clock in around twelve."

"Respectable, Mr. Jackson," Sister Becky inclined her head politely, but there was the undeniable hint of triumph lurking behind her green eyes.

"Unless," Dex drawled, "you count this one... and these here..." he indicated several bandages on his arms and legs. "Plus, the ones that should've been stitched that I just plain said 'no' to... and a couple I put the Super Glue to in the car cuz the blood was getting on my seats. Then it's..." he eyed the ceiling, calculating. "Something like forty."

Sister Becky gave him a critical stare. "Alas, Mr. Jackson, the wounds must be treated by medical personnel in order to qualify for the official tally. I believe sixteen still stands for the record of this encounter - not, as you have observed, that it is a contest."

"Alright, Darth, how many points for Touch of the Grave?!" Dex yanked open the front of his shirt, showing the white bandages across his chest. "I got the Touch of the Grave! Sixteen stitches..." he snorted. "You can keep your sixteen stitches! I got the *&^%$ Touch of the Grave!"

Sister Becky turned a tight smile toward the window but offered no reply.

"How about you, kiddo?" Carson nodded at Kiki. "Any new scars?"

"None that show."

"Well, if you ever want to..."

"No." Her tone was final. "Thanks."

"Fair enough. So, now that we're done with Who's Got the Biggest Boo-Boo, I guess I should ask about other possible pain points - the cops, for example. What are they making out of all this?"

"That's the beauty," Kiki's smile was mischievous. "They pinned it all on Fujikacorp. Not much of a stretch, really. And it wasn't *just* the cops: FBI, CDC, EPA, you name it. They're calling it biological warfare, illegal research and experimentation, that sort of thing.

According to the papers, they figure it was some sort of black ops science that got out of hand. City was in a panic for a few days, but things are settling down. Except at Fujikacorp. I think it's safe to say the grand opening of the Super Maxi-Pad has been postponed indefinitely."

"And us? What about the questionable involvement of a certain group of mini-mart aficionados?"

"Funny. Sometimes police reports and hospital records seem to go missing. Or get changed. Or both."

"Funny and convenient," Carson gave her an exaggerated wink. "Well, that's it then. End of story, roll credits, turn in your 3D glasses. The city is moving on, the bad guys are in the hurt locker, and, more importantly, we're off the hook. Pretty soon, the only thing we'll have to remember this by is hospital bills and an occasional bad dream."

"Er..." Kiki looked at her boots. "There is *one* little thing..."

"Little? How little?"

"Hm... how do I put this..."

Dex cleared his throat. "Josh."

"Josh?" Carson struggled, thinking back. "You mean Zombie Josh? Lessee, last we saw him was... on the scaffold. I gave him a whack and then..." Carson snapped his fingers. "Truck! He fell into the truck, right?"

"Affirmative. Only... well it ain't that simple. Kiki and I went back to the Super Maxi-Pad a few days later to check things out. Didn't want there to be any more surprises. Good news is the place was clean. Bad news is the truck was gone."

"Gone? As in...?"

"No longer there."

"Uh-huh. So. That's not a real issue, right? I mean, you said once the Warlord died, all the zombies just sort of collapsed. De-zombified. I'm sure the same thing happened to Josh. Right?"

"Not necessarily, Mr. Dudley. The negation of the *Ashi Keiyaki* might have only affected those creatures in the same room - or the same building. Or the same town. Or not at all. We have no way of knowing."

"Well. That's awkward. So, this truck... where'd it go?"

"I tracked it back to a private freight company," Dex rumbled. "Got in touch with dispatch, ran 'em some BS about security audits and had 'em pull the truck's transit logs."

"You?" Carson shot him a surprised look. "Investigation?

Subtlety? I'm impressed."

"Hey... my badge ain't just for show. Anyway, that's where the trail went cold. Shipping destination was confidential."

"Leet and I took it from there," Kiki joined in. "After I tracked him down, of course. *Never* tell a professional geek it's the Zompocalypse. They believe you. Anyway, we cracked the company's servers and found out where the truck was going."

"Which was...?"

Dex dug a rumpled slip of paper out of his breast pocket, squinted at it. "Pittsville."

"You're kidding."

"Nope. Middle of Arizona nowhere. Armpit of the West. Only claim to fame is a jumbo landfill, private type. No questions asked."

"Of course," Kiki added, "by the time we pieced this all together, the truck had already made its delivery. It was long gone."

"Made its... um... yikes. That can't be good."

"Yeah." Dex's expression was matter-of-fact. "We thought about callin', but... what are you gonna say?"

"Well." There was an awkward silence. "That is a bit of a loose end." They stared at the floor, the walls. Outside, a bird chirped. At last, Carson looked up. "Well," he said again to no one in particular. "Moving on."

"Quite right, Mr. Dudley," Sister Becky nodded primly. "That wash is still out to dry and no sense in bringing it in until it is, if you take my meaning. Best to turn our attention to mending and to picking up the threads of life. Your career advancement, for instance."

Carson blinked. "Career...?"

"Why yes, dear boy. Night manager! Certainly, you have not forgotten? I have the utmost confidence that you will win the day."

"Ouch," Dex winced. "It's gotta hurt to be *that* out of touch."

Carson's stomach gave a jolt. He was amazed that, even after returning from a state of undead half-life, mention of Kinkade and the promotion competition *still* gave him the heebies.

Sister Becky frowned at his expression. "Have I said something untoward, my boy?"

"No no, Old Goat," Dex waved off her concern. "But, that turd floating in the punch bowl is *yours.*"

"It's alright, Sister B.," Carson cut in. "There's some stuff you didn't know. Stuff that was said... done, actually. *Really* done. Stuff that can't be undone. Ever." He sighed. It was true, and there was no sense denying it. "You said it's time to pick up threads - well, it may be time to lay some down, too. I've been through a lot lately, and it's made me do some thinking - about life, purpose and what Freezies have to do with all of it... if anything. It's time to face facts. I'm just not the corporate type. Things have really changed since Jack left, and they've changed too much for me. I don't even know if I've got a job to go back to, but if I do... I think I'm gonna quit."

"Heaven's Gates, Mr. Dudley!"

"Stick it to the man, man!"

"Carson... are you sure?"

"Darn sure. In fact, I wish Kinkade would walk through that door right now, so I could tell him to his face."

There was a knock on the door. A cute blonde in pink scrubs poked her head in. "You have a visitor, Mr. Dudley." The nurse disappeared, and, with his customary miserable timing, Ross Kinkade stepped briskly into the room, a brand new tablet tucked importantly under one arm.

"Whoa..." Carson blinked. "That was weird."

"Dudley," Kinkade nodded curtly, then swept the small group of friends with his usual emotionless expression. He adjusted his box-frame spectacles. "I am sorry to interrupt, but, under the circumstances, I felt this was best to do in person. If you would like me to return later..."

Carson shook his head. "No sir, Mr. Kinkade. This is family."

"Very well. I will make this brief. I have made my decision concerning the night manager position - as well as other matters."

"Yeah," Carson cleared his throat. "About that. Like I was just telling these guys..."

"I have chosen you, Mr. Dudley."

The beeping of Carson's heart monitor stopped. It took a few seconds before it started again.

"It was not an easy decision," Kinkade clipped right along. "But in the end, I am confident it was the correct one. I am certain - given time - that you will be a fine addition to the Seven Corporation management family. Welcome aboard, Dudley." Kinkade shook Carson's limp and unresponsive hand. "That is..." he looked Carson in the eye, his magnified pupils looming. "If you accept."

Carson stared at Kinkade as if he were trying to place his face. His mouth hung slightly open. He nodded, once, in slow motion.

"Very good." Kinkade tapped his tablet, scrawled a brief note.

 312

"Now then, I have a new manual for you," he dropped a thick volume on the bedside table, "and there is a great deal of knowledge transfer ahead of us, but all that can wait until you're healed. Take as much time as you need. When you feel up to it, the 24/7 will be waiting. I'll cover for you until then. Once again, Dudley, congratulations." With that, Kinkade headed for the door.

Just as he reached it, Carson found his voice. "But..." he blurted. "Why?!"

Kinkade stopped, hand on the knob. When he looked back, there was something curious in his expression. "It is my job to observe, Dudley. To judge a person's character. A prospective leader must be evaluated on many levels, not just on the basis of his job performance. After all, some things are more important than work. Wouldn't you agree?" Kinkade's mouth twisted into a small, strange, completely out of character expression. It was a smile.

As he opened the door, he paused once more, turned and looked Carson straight in the eye. "*That's* the kind of person Seven Corporation is looking for, Carson," he said softly. "Someone with... vision."

Then, he was gone.

For several moments, no one spoke.

"Did... did I just get a promotion?" Carson was still staring at the door as if he expected it to explode.

"Yeah," Kiki rubbed her temples. "And I just got a headache."

"And I just got hungry," Dex heaved out of his chair and trolled Carson's half finished food tray. "You gonna eat that pudding?"

Carson shook his head slowly, still in shock. "What the... how did... I don't... I don't get it! I never even finished my disaster-preparedness plan!"

"Whatever was in there, it wouldn't have covered it."

Sister Becky was staring after Kinkade as well, wearing the same thoughtful expression she had worn when he had chased them out of the 24/7 weeks before. "A strange turn of events, Mr. Dudley," she murmured. "Strange indeed..."

Carson shook himself out of his stunned reverie. "What the hoo-ha-hey... why not?! As the man says, why sniff a gift fish... or a zombie, for that matter?!" He whooped and knuckle-bumped Dex, who was busily stuffing soup crackers into his mouth.

"Grats, Dud," the guard said thickly. "You da man! I'm gonna start a diet tomorrow... can I have the rest of this chicken?"

As Dex tucked into his meal, Carson threw himself back onto the bed, practically bursting. "Holy guacamole! Back from the dead *and* a promotion, all in the same day! There *is* no stopping the satisfactory flow!" He laced his hands behind his head. "Night manager... man, I can't wait to tell Jack! He's gonna bust his hula skirt! And I know *just* what I'm gonna do first."

"Read the manual?"

"Not even close. Name the bathroom. My first act as night manager of the Belfry 24/7 will be to officially dedicate the Josh Decker Memorial Restroom. I may even put up a plaque. A moment of silence, if you please..."

They obliged. Sister Becky murmured a prayer.

"And the second," Carson said a moment later and fixed a serious eye on Dex, "is to get you your job back, big guy. I have the feeling Fujikacorp's legal department is a little too preoccupied right now to push a lawsuit against a certain friendly neighborhood security guard. And now, I've got pull, baby!"

"Thanks, bro," Dex grinned. There was pudding in his teeth. "But even if you can't, don't sweat it. The way the wind is blowin', I got the feeling my days at the Gold Shield are numbered. I need a backup plan. So, I been thinkin'... I'm gonna be a cop."

Everyone stopped. The announcement was, if possible, even more stunning than Kinkade's.

"A cop?!" Carson laughed in surprise. "Whoa there, feller. Whatever happened to 'cops suck?'"

"They do. When they ain't me."

"Cops have rules, you know. How are you with rules?"

Dex shrugged. "Rules are fine. When they don't suck."

"Ladies and gentlemen... Las Calamas' finest."

"Officer Dexter Jackson," Kiki said. "For real. I always liked the way that sounded."

Dex puffed up his chest. "Or maybe even Detective Jackson. Hell, I dunno. Anyway, I always kinda liked the idea. It's one of the reasons I joined the Army, became an MP. My daughter used to ask me... 'Daddy are you a policeman?'" He smiled suddenly, not his usual big grin, but a tender, gentle expression that softened his face and made him look, just for a moment, like someone's dad. He had the necklace in his hand again.

"I daresay, Mr. Jackson," Sister Becky rested a hand on his shoulder, "that she would be very, very proud."

For a moment, they sat quietly.

"Well," Carson pushed on with a boisterous smile. "We're sure turning the world of work upside down! I get a promotion after destroying my store, Dex breaks most of the laws in Las Calamas and goes into police work... Sister B., I expect, now that you've killed your immediate supervisor, they're going to appoint you the first lady Pope."

"Only if they find the body, Mr. Dudley."

"Er... right. So, in the meantime, I guess it's back to the Little Angels' Clubhouse, eh?"

"Hardly, my lad. If it is one thing working with children has taught me, it is that I should not be working with children. After giving the matter much prayer and consideration, and taking the advice of a dear friend, I have tendered my resignation from St. Timothy's child care services. Commencing next week, I shall assume the responsibilities of my new appointment with the Cathedral."

"Which is?"

"Choir director."

Dex immediately brightened. He opened his mouth to speak, but sister Becky silenced him with a hawkish look. "Kindly refrain, Mr. Jackson, from referring to me as 'Whoopie'. I am well aware of the ironies."

"Whatever you say, Whoopie."

"Now then," Sister Becky pressed on briskly, "we have one final matter to discuss." She stepped to the center of the room, hands tucked in sleeves, face stern. She had shifted into a different gear, and it was one the others recognized well - one she used when she was ready to tackle the big issues. The room fell silent as the others exchanged curious looks, wondering what possibly could have remained unsaid. Outside, the sun was setting, casting long shadows through the window and adding to the sense of anticipation that was slowly building. They waited as Sister Becky gathered her thoughts.

"I have been holding back a question since the night of our encounter. A question which, on the surface, might seem of small significance, but which might, in the end, be perhaps the most momentous of all. It is now time we addressed it." She turned purposefully to Carson. "It concerns, Mr. Dudley, our showdown with the Warlord of Death - and it is one that only *you* can answer."

"Me? But... but I don't remember anything. I was the dead one, remember?"

"Nonetheless, this secret is one that only you can tell." Sister

Becky's eyes were shining. "I am curious, Mr. Dudley... how were you able to remove yourself from the closet?"

Carson's face went blank as he searched for memories that weren't there. "I... I don't know."

"But surely, Mr. Dudley, you must have some vague recollection? Some snippet, some fragment of memory that will aid us in piecing together this last bit of truth?"

Carson pondered hard, struggling to recall. He tugged at his beard, racked his brain. Eventually, he shook his head. "Sorry... I got nothing. Dumb luck?" He offered a half-hearted smile.

"Luck, Mr. Dudley?! Poppycock! You were sealed, alone and far from aid, behind a securely locked door! I saw to that myself. Your moldering companions did not have the presence of mind to release you, nor did you have the means to do so yourself. Yet somehow, you escaped - then managed to make your way to the ceremonial chamber, in the dark, a witless minion, arriving at the *precise*, *exact* instant that you were most needed to bring victory. 'Luck' is far too feeble a word, Mr. Dudley. No... there is only one possible explanation."

Dex rolled his eyes. "Here we go again with the miracles..."

"It was a miracle!" Sister Becky exulted. "An event engineered by the very hand of God Himself, inexplicable by any other means! And, I may add, a veritable duplicate of our triumph over the vampire trollop Vanessa!"

"Okay... it's weird, I'll give you that. Supernatural weird. Goose pimply. Downright off-the-charts-mother-flipping strange. I'd even be willing to concede that our survival in both events bordered on the miraculous. But, I gotta ask... what does it *mean?*"

"It means, Mr. Dudley," Becky's voice dropped. "That we are caught up in higher matters. Our involvement is no mere coincidence. It was *meant* to be."

A hot flush ran through Carson, and it wasn't, he knew, from the morphine drip. He couldn't argue with Sister Becky. Even worse... he didn't want to. "I agree." His voice sounded surprisingly strong in his own ears. It felt good to say the words. "So, what do we do about it?"

Sister Becky was on her feet now. She spoke with quiet intensity. "I think, Mr. Dudley... that *you* must answer that question."

Carson spoke without hesitation. The thought simply sprang into his mind, and the words followed. "We form a team."

Dex stroked his chin, intrigued. "A team? A team for what?"

"I have no idea. But, something's going on in Las Calamas,

something downright full-tilt head-on wicked strange, and it's bit us twice now. Like Sister B. said - that can't be coincidence. Trouble's been looking for us. Maybe it's time we went looking for it."

Dex tilted back, staring at Carson as if he couldn't figure out whether his friend was kidding or not. "Monster whackers?"

"I'm sure there's a name with better marketing appeal, but... yeah. That about sums it up."

"A team like that could use a cop."

"Only one that doesn't suck."

"Hell... I'm in."

"I shall join you as well, Mr. Dudley," Sister Becky struggled to keep her voice neutral. She was practically floating. "You may also require some spiritual guidance."

Carson glanced at Kiki, who was looking on with an unreadable expression. "How 'bout you, woman? We could also use a... how do I say this..."

"Criminal?" Kiki offered. "Lawbreaker? Thief? Con?"

"I was thinking 'Legally Challenged Problem Solver'. Or maybe 'Felony Engineer'. But, whatever you call it, we could use it. Think about it - we may even get our own reality TV show."

"I've had about as much reality as I can handle, thanks," Kiki shook her head. But, there was a twinkle in her eye. "Still - TV, hunh?"

"Local Access Channel 19, at the very least."

She paused, considering. "Well... I guess I can see how the first season turns out."

"Fat catfish! It's done, then. We're monster whackers!" Carson thumped his pillow excitedly. "Until we find a name with better marketing appeal. So, what's our first step? Danger room? Pimp out a van? *Get* a van? Make up call signs?"

"Herron."

"Yeah... no offense, but I was thinking something with a little more punch, like maybe 'Vigilante'. Or 'Madman.' Or 'Ogre'..."

"Not a call sign, you ninny. It's our first step." Kiki pulled a folded slip of yellow paper from her pocket. "You remember the girl from your dream? The one who showed up at your door... Tic-Tac? Well, I did a little digging. Pulled the credit card records from the 24/7 from around the time we scrapped with Vanessa and cross referenced them against a zoological database. And wouldn't you know it? I found a match. Turns out you were right - she *did* have a bird name. Only, it wasn't Hawk or Crow. It was Herron." She handed him the paper.

"Family reported her missing, but the cops never found a body. As much as it creeps me out, I can't deny the facts: *some* of your dream *seems* to have come true. Makes sense to check out the rest of it. Who knows? Could be nothing."

"Or it could be something." Sister Becky stood quietly in the center of the room, the lines of her face hard in the rays of the fading sun. "I concur with Ms. Masterson. This lead is most definitely worthy of pursuing. And there was something else in your vision, Mr. Dudley, that bears investigation. Something that has long intrigued me and which I now believe to be connected with *both* of our recent encounters."

"The Curio Shop." A chill trickled through Carson. "You're talking about the Curio Shop."

"Precisely."

Carson thought. "Leet did say something about Fujika making a purchase there. One of his little demon-bait trinkets. Never had time to check it out, but it was on the list."

Sister Becky gave a slight nod. "And let us not forget the unwarranted revival of the Warlord of Death. The Shogun himself told us that he had possessed the remains of Hironagi Tomoru for years; they only reanimated once he arrived in Las Calamas."

"Could it... the Curio Shop..." Carson squinted at her. "Could it really have done that?"

"A source of great evil will sometimes spark others to life," Becky tapped her chin, brooding. "Or even attract them. It was only after the Curio Shop arrived that Vanessa appeared."

Carson's head spun. Fresh recollections from his dream washed over him, dragged him back to the little Curio Shop.

Pete. The girl. The cryptic warnings.

Shadows and memory swirled and tugged at him, and he felt once again the sense of overwhelming malice that he had when he had entered the shop in his dream. A brooding, timeless evil.

Watching.

Waiting.

When he came back, his thoughts were clear and sharp. His mind was already made up. "Right. Okay, here's the plan," Carson gave them all a steely look. "First, I'm gonna sleep. A lot. And then..." he paused. "The Curio Shop."

"You mean...?"

"We're going in."

 318

About the Author

Chris Weedin was born in 1970 and grew up with a healthy dislike for horror. But somewhere along the line, his life was forever changed by a strange supernatural event... and now he absolutely loves the stuff! He has worked as a furniture deliveryman, security guard, professional tutor, youth minister and computer system administrator and holds both a Bachelor's Degree in History and a black belt in Tae Kwon Do. He is the creator and developer of *Horror Rules, the Simply Horrible Roleplaying Game* and spends his time speaking, writing, running marathons, going to church and creating and playing crazy boardgames. He lives in Selah, WA with his lovely wife and two lovely and obedient children, all three of whom are almost never scary.

Another Rotten Night is finally over, but don't fret!
Carson and the Gang will soon return in Book 3:

PARTS

Science gone bad, a Ghost from the past, Granny's secret, the Curio Shop and (gasp) someone DIES!

Want MORE Zombie Action?!

Find out what happens when the HORDE hits Pittsville...

Pick up right where the book left off. In trouble.

A Brand New Zompocalyptic Card Game From Crucifiction Games

Get the Game That Started It All...
Before It Gets YOU!

Horror Rules™

The Simply Horrible Role-Playing Game

A Complete (and Completely Different)
Horror-Comedy RPG

by Chris Weedin

A fun, quirky little horror-comedy RPG based on your favorite horror movies, like *Zombieland, Slither and Shaun of the Dead!* Perfect for beginners and hard-core gamers alike... and still guaranteed to make you ☠️⚰️ laughing!

"⭐⭐⭐⭐⭐"
-- *Gaming Report*

*Gaming Genius
Nominee:
Best Game*

*RPGNow
Electrum Pick*

Hey, You! More Stuff!!

Games, Expansions, Supplements, Adventure Scripts, Bits, Novels and More

Available now at game stores, bookstores, Amazon.com and other retailers that ain't too chicken.

And Check Us Out Online at
www.crucifictiongames.com

- *Free Horror Rules Adventures*
- *Online Character Creator*
- *Bonus Content and Downloads*
- *The Random Obituary Generator of Doom*
- *and More!*

Just when you thought it was safe to go back on the Web...

CPSIA information can be obtained at www.ICGtesting.com
Printed in the USA
BVOW041716250512

291112BV00001B/2/P